Raves for the Award-Winning Novels of
RICK RIORDAN

"In Rick Riordan's case, believe the hype. He really is that good." —Dennis Lehane

"Riordan writes so well about the people and topography of his Texas hometown that he quickly marks the territory as his own." —*Chicago Tribune*

"Rick Riordan has a Texas-size talent for spinning a great story." —Tami Hoag

"There's a reason why this guy keeps winning awards. . . . Rick Riordan is a master stylist. I can't wait for his next." —Harlan Coben

"If not the king of Texas crime writing, Rick Riordan is certainly among the princes!" —*Denver Post*

REBEL ISLAND

Named One of the Best Books of the Year by the
San Antonio Express-News

"Red herrings abound (perhaps courtesy of the storm-tossed sea), the dialogue is smart and incisive, the characters superbly drawn. For longtime Riordan fans and newcomers alike, *Rebel Island* is a guaranteed-to-please page-turner of the first order." —*BookPage*

"Taut, humorous, and fun. Tres is one of the funniest and most rip-roaring detectives out there. . . . A top-shelf mystery. *Rebel Island* offers a potent concoction of humor and suspense that is as refreshing as a Sunday-afternoon Bloody Mary. . . . The Navarre novels aren't cozies, police procedurals, thrillers or even traditional P.I. fare; rather, they're smoothly written novels about wonderfully engaging characters who happen to have a Texas-size penchant for trouble." —*San Antonio Express-News*

"Navarre is a shrewd sleuth. . . . An amusing book."
—*Dallas Morning News*

"Satisfying and complex."
—*Mystery Lovers Bookshop News*

"A highly readable tale that retains surprises right up to the end. [Riordan] has a deft touch with pacing, and his prose is smooth with just a hint of the hard-boiled. . . . A worthy continuation of the series, a series that, in my judgment, supplies the best crime fiction so far produced by a Texas writer."
—*Houston Chronicle*

"Among the many great qualities of Rick Riordan's mysteries is his ability to use comfortingly familiar plot devices while adding a modern edge. . . . Riordan always gives us something to like about Tres and Maia, and he just keeps piling on the tension and the dangers." —*San Jose Mercury News*

"A slick, well-written military thriller that will keep readers guessing almost until the very end . . . Highly recommended for the murder mystery fan who doesn't mind a little action."
—*Wichita Falls Times Record News*

MISSION ROAD

"A satisfying exploration of passion's dark powers . . . moves along at a cracking pace. . . . [Riordan delivers] several nifty twists. What had seemed to be merely an entertaining crime novel reveals itself as a clever mystery, too." —*Booklist*

"As usual, Riordan does not disappoint. Tres Navarre is one of the best PI series being written today. The streets of San Antonio make the perfect backdrop and Riordan's knowledge of the city is better than a travel guide. . . . One of the best books of 2005." —*Crimespree*

"*Mission Road* is well worth the price of admission just for its array of bad cops, good crooks, and swell characters. Throw in Riordan's clever twist at the end, and you're getting top value for your entertainment dollar." —*Texas Monthly*

"Riordan pens a swift and often funny plot with plenty of action . . . and Riordan comes up with some wonderful characters, including Sam, a retired FBI special agent who carries a fully loaded water pistol and isn't afraid to use it."
—*Rocky Mountain News*

"Engrossing." —*Washington Post*

"Riordan's Tres Navarre thrillers are the best thing to come out of Texas since the Dallas Cowboys hired cheerleaders. His stories are fast, hard-hitting and infused with atmosphere. They remind me of James Lee Burke's Louisiana stories. Good stuff."
—*Rocky Mountain News*

"If you're a fan of fast-paced crime novels and haven't discovered mystery author Rick Riordan yet, you're in for a real treat." —*Lansing State Journal*

SOUTHTOWN

"Just when you think the shamus subgenre might have been milked to death, along comes talented Riordan to demonstrate what brisk pacing, smart plotting, and an immensely likable protagonist can do to revive it." —*Kirkus Reviews*

"Superb . . . Navarre walks a thin, highly believable and surprisingly suspenseful line that should delight old Riordan fans and win new ones."
—*Publishers Weekly* (starred review)

"The cast Riordan has assembled around Tres has a satisfying roundness, and the story has a cagey, tight-lipped warmth that Navarre fans will enjoy."
—*Washington Post*

THE DEVIL WENT DOWN TO AUSTIN

Shamus and Anthony Awards Nominee

"A heady nightcap of sass and suspense with a twist of mayhem . . . A blast . . . A thrilling and intelligent detective novel—and a giant leap forward for the Tres Navarre series." —*Austin Chronicle*

"Pure heaven for mystery fans . . . Riordan combines all the elements of award-winning fiction: unforgettable characters, intriguing plots, and delicious suspense. . . . Navarre just may have become the most appealing mystery hero in Texas." —*Booklist*

"Rick Riordan is on a roll. . . . If you like the writing of Dennis Lehane . . . you'll enjoy getting acquainted with Rick Riordan." —*BookPage*

"Funny and tough . . . Riordan kneads plots like lovingly baked bread, and they are almost as tasty." —*New York Daily News*

"Powerful . . . A fast-paced tale, expertly told." —*Denver Post*

"Terrific . . . just about everything you could want from an action adventure." —*Houston Chronicle*

"Sarcastic humor, memorable characters, and spectacular acting scenes round out a spellbinding adventure." —*Library Journal*

THE LAST KING OF TEXAS

Winner of the Edgar, Shamus, and Anthony Awards

"Tres's taste for excess is as ferocious as his addiction to fiery food, and the fearless joy he takes in his roughneck adventures gives a real kick to this colorful series." —*New York Times Book Review*

"A winner . . . perfect pacing, expert switching between subplots and an unusually strong cast of supporting players." —*Washington Post*

"Rick Riordan has a Texas-size talent for spinning a great story, and *The Last King of Texas* is exactly that!" —Tami Hoag

"Riordan's writing sparkles."
—*Kirkus Reviews* (starred review)

"Starts off with a literal bang and then gathers speed from there." —*Entertainment Weekly*

"Raise your margarita to Rick Riordan. . . . This tale of revenge and remorse sizzles and skids like drops of water on a hot skillet." —*Texas Monthly*

"Reads like a fast train, roaring on and taking enthralled readers for a great ride. And it has depth. . . . It's a delight to see what [Riordan] can do when he breaks away with a stand-alone."
—*San Jose Mercury News*

"It's Mallory's struggle for survival that captures us, providing the fierce finale that tests her mettle. We're rooting for her because Riordan never lets us forget the terrified and innocent child she once was." —*Boston Globe*

"Strong characters, tense situations, and vivid action sequences make this book hard to put down."
—*Library Journal*

"Riordan packs an incredibly complicated scenario into this book. . . . As he does so often and so well, he builds this story around a cast of dysfunctional, painfully believable people, all trying to work out their anger and pain in some way that makes sense. . . . The real gripper is what will happen to the shattered lives of the characters."
—*Houston Chronicle*

"A first-rate thriller." —*San Antonio Express-News*

"Riordan has written a crime thriller that ranks with the works of Patricia Cornwell, Dennis Lehane and Thomas Harris. . . . This is a must-read for anyone who wants to read an unforgettable thriller."
—*Midwest Book Review*

"An emotionally powerful and gripping story of one man's struggle to survive in the present while righting the wrongs of the past." —*Tampa Tribune*

"A complex chiller of a novel, touching and terrifying by turns." —*Flint Journal*

"A winner . . . More than a finely tuned murder mystery; it is also a story of family strife, estrangement, loss and personal growth. . . . This author's rich style is a pleasure to read."
—*Winston-Salem Journal*

Also by Rick Riordan

BIG RED TEQUILA

THE WIDOWER'S TWO-STEP

THE LAST KING OF TEXAS

THE DEVIL WENT DOWN TO AUSTIN

COLD SPRINGS

SOUTHTOWN

MISSION ROAD

AND THE

PERCY JACKSON AND THE OLYMPIANS SERIES

THE LIGHTNING THIEF

THE SEA OF MONSTERS

THE TITAN'S CURSE

REBEL ISLAND

RICK RIORDAN

BANTAM BOOKS

REBEL ISLAND
A Bantam Book

PUBLISHING HISTORY
Bantam hardcover edition published September 2007
Bantam mass market edition / October 2008

Published by Bantam Dell
A Division of Random House, Inc.
New York, New York

Library of Congress Catalog Card Number: 2007014510

ISBN 978-0-553-58784-5

Printed in the United States of America
Published simultaneously in Canada

www.bantamdell.com

OPM 10 9 8 7 6 5 4 3 2

REBEL ISLAND

1

We got married in a thunderstorm. That should've been my first warning.

The Southwest Craft Center courtyard was festooned with white crepe paper. The tables were laden with fresh tamales, chips and salsa. Cases of Shiner Bock sweated on ice in tin buckets. The margarita machine was humming. The San Antonio River flowed past the old limestone walls.

Maia looked beautiful in her cream bridal dress. Her black hair was curled in ringlets and her coppery skin glowed with health.

The guests had arrived: my mother, fresh from a tour of Guatemala; my brother, Garrett, not-so-fresh from our long bachelor party in Austin; and a hundred other relatives, cops, thugs, ex-cons, lawyers—

all the people who had made my life so interesting the past few decades.

Then the clouds came. Lightning sparked off a mesquite tree. The sky opened up, and our outdoor wedding became a footrace to the chapel with the retired Baptist minister and the Buddhist monk leading the pack.

Larry Cho, the monk, had a commanding early lead, but Reverend Buckner Fanning held steady around the tamale table while Larry the Buddhist had to swerve to avoid a beer keg and got blocked out by a couple of bail bondsmen. Buckner was long retired, but he sure stayed fit. He won the race to the chapel and held the door for the others as we came pouring in.

I was last, helping Maia, since she couldn't move very quickly. Partly that was because of the wedding dress. Mostly it was because she was eight and a half months pregnant. I held a plastic bag over our heads as we plodded through the rain.

"This was *not* in the forecast," she protested.

"No," I agreed. "I'm thinking God owes us a refund."

Inside, the chapel was dark and smelled of musty limestone. The cedar floorboards creaked under our feet. The crowd milled around, watching out the windows as our party decorations were barraged into mush. Rain drummed off the grass so hard it made a layer of haze three feet high. The crepe paper melted and watery salsa overflowed off the edge of the tables.

"Well," Buckner said, beaming as if God had

made this glorious moment just for us. "We still have a holy matrimony to perform."

Actually, I was raised Catholic, which is why the wedding was half-Buddhist, half-Baptist. Maia had not been a practicing Buddhist since she was a little girl in China, but she liked Larry the Buddhist, and the incense and beads made her feel nostalgic.

Buckner Fanning was the most respected Baptist minister in San Antonio. He also knew my mom from way back. When the Catholic priest had been reluctant to perform the ceremony (something about Maia being pregnant out of wedlock; go figure), my mom had recruited Buckner.

For his part, Buckner had talked to me in advance about doing the right thing by getting married, how he hoped we would raise our child to know God. I told him we hadn't actually talked to God about the matter yet, but we were playing phone tag. Buckner, fortunately, had a sense of humor. He agreed to marry us.

We were a pretty bedraggled crew when we reassembled in the old chapel. Rain poured down the stained-glass windows and hammered on the roof. I glanced over at Ana DeLeon, our homicide detective friend, who was toweling off her daughter Lucia's hair. Ana smiled at me. I gave her a wink, but it was painful to hold her eyes too long.

It was hard not to think about her husband, who should have been standing at her side.

Larry the Buddhist rang his gong and lit some incense. He chanted a sutra. Then Buckner began talking about the marriage covenant.

My eyes met Maia's. She was studying me quizzically. Maybe she was wondering why she'd agreed to hook up with a guy like me. Then she smiled, and I remembered how we'd met in a bar in Berkeley fifteen years ago. Every time she smiled like that, she sent an electric charge straight down my back.

I'm afraid I missed most of what Buckner had to say. But I heard the "I do" part. I said the vow without hesitation.

Afterward, we waded through the well-wishers: my old girlfriend, Lillian Cambridge; Madeleine White, the mafia princess; Larry Drapiewski, the retired deputy; Milo Chavez, the music agent from Nashville; Messieurs Terrence and Goldman, Maia's old bosses from the law firm in San Francisco; my mom and her newest boyfriend, a millionaire named Jack Mariner. All sorts of dangerous rain-soaked people.

We ate soggy wedding cake and drank champagne and waited for the storm to pass. As Maia talked with some of her former colleagues, Garrett cornered me at the bar.

My brother was wearing what passed for wedding garb: a worn tuxedo jacket over his tie-dyed

T-shirt. His scraggly beard and poorly combed hair looked like a wheat field after a hailstorm. His tuxedo pants were pinned up (since he didn't have legs) and he'd woven carnations through the spokes of his wheelchair.

"Grats, little bro." He lifted his plate of tamales in salute. "Good eats."

"You congratulating me on the tamales or the marriage?"

"Depends." He belched into his fist, which was for him pretty darned discreet. "What you got planned for the honeymoon?"

Right then, my internal alarms should've been ringing. I should've backed away, told him to get another plate of tamales and saved myself a lot of trouble.

Instead, I said, "Nothing, really. Maia's pregnant, you may have noticed."

Garrett waved his hand dismissively. "Doing nothing for your honeymoon don't cut it, little bro. Listen, I got a proposition."

Maybe it was the joyous occasion, or the fact that I was surrounded by friends. Maybe it was just the fact that it was raining too hard to leave. But I was in the mood to think well of my brother.

I would have plenty of time to regret that later. But that afternoon, with the rain coming down, I listened as Garrett told me his idea.

2

He got to the cemetery at sunset, drove around it twice to make sure there was no surveillance. He doubted there would be, but he'd learned to be paranoid.

The sky was blood red. Corpus Christi Bay glowed like metal on the forge. The old cemetery had iron gates and limestone markers, the oldest worn smooth by storms and Gulf winds.

He found the graves with no effort: one large, two small, lined up cozily on a knoll, enjoying the million-dollar view. Like they come to watch fireworks, he thought.

He knelt and ran his hands along the names, as if that would erase them.

The top of the smallest tombstone was lined

with seashells: a cockle, an Easter oyster, a blood ark. He'd spent years collecting shells like these along the Texas coast. He'd dug them out of the sand, let the ocean wash them clean, held them up to the sunlight and admired the pattern of their veins.

Had the child liked seashells? He didn't know.

He'd never even met them.

The mother's obituary picture had run in the newspaper. Her smile had seemed so familiar, the dates of her birth and death. Cold had gripped him as he realized what he'd done.

He'd caused this. And now there was no way to bring them back.

The only thing he could do was make amends. *If* he had the courage.

He took something from his pocket: a tiny sugar skull, grinning and blind. He crushed the skull and dropped it on the mother's grave.

Never again.

A flash from the bay caught his eye—a rich man's yacht coming in for the night. The afternoon had been beautiful, as unexpected as yesterday's storm. Forecasters were optimistic about a nice weekend. The bad weather was supposed to skirt around them. But he knew better. A bigger storm was on the way.

He watched the yacht disappear behind the fishing piers. The Texas coast had always protected him. However far he roamed, he always came back here, putting his feet in the water, hoping it would wash away his travels and his mistakes the way it washed sand off shells.

But maybe not this time.

Sunset. He had to catch the evening ferry.

He took one last look at the tombstones, lined up so peacefully, long evening shadows pointed toward the sea. Then he turned to leave. The island was waiting.

3

For a guy who was rumored to have killed six men in cold blood, Jesse Longoria looked downright pleasant.

He stood on the dock of Rebel Island as if he'd been expecting us. A jovially plump Latino in his mid-fifties. Smile lines crinkled around his eyes. He wore a gold A&M college ring, a navy blue summerweight suit with his U.S. Marshal's badge pinned to the lapel and a satisfied expression as if he'd just enjoyed a stroll with a beautiful woman.

"Tres Navarre," he said. "If I were you, I'd get back on that boat. Now."

Wind buffeted the dock. Maia was supervising the hotel manager taking our bags off the ferry. Garrett was setting up his wheelchair. We'd just endured a twenty-minute ride from Aransas Pass through choppy seas and I was tempted to throw up on the marshal's shoes.

"What brings you here, Longoria?" I asked. "Collecting seashells?"

"I don't need your interference, son. Not this time."

Thunder crackled over the Gulf. Storm clouds were piling up, turning the air to a wet stew of salt and electricity.

The hotel manager lumbered over with our bags. He stopped when he saw Longoria's hand resting on his sidearm. "Uh, problem, gentlemen?"

"There was," I said. "Two years ago. Never found the body, did they, Longoria?"

The marshal's eyes glinted. "I heard you quit detective work."

"Sure. Didn't you get an invitation to the retirement party?"

He stepped so close I could smell the lemon starch sweating out of his clothes. "Who hired you?"

"I don't know what you're talking about, Longoria. I'm here on my honeymoon."

I pointed behind me. Maia and Garrett were just coming up the dock—Maia eight and a half months pregnant, Garrett a bilateral amputee.

Funny, Longoria didn't look too convinced by my honeymoon story.

"Hey, Marshal," the hotel manager said. I tried to remember his name. Chris Something-or-other. He was a former pro surfer, tan and well-built, but I doubted he'd dealt with many conflicts worse than deciding what kind of beer to buy on the mainland. "Mr. Navarre isn't—I mean, they have a reservation, sir. They're friends with the owner."

Longoria seemed to weigh his options. The ferry was already pulling out for Aransas Pass. The next boat wouldn't come until tomorrow afternoon. That meant he could shoot me, throw me off the dock or leave me alone. I'm sure the first two options had their appeal.

"Bad storm coming," he told me. "I'd make it a one-night honeymoon and get off this island."

Then he turned and headed toward the hotel, the first few splatters of rain making buckshot patterns on the boards at his feet.

"Old friend?" Maia asked.

"Something like that." I looked at Garrett accusingly.

"Hey, little bro, you can't blame me for *that*. Is there any place in Texas where you *don't* stumble across some cop you've pissed off?"

He had a point. Besides, there were plenty of other things I *could* blame my brother for.

We followed the hotel manager up the clamshell path toward a place I had sworn never to revisit.

Rebel Island was a mile long. Most of that was a thin strip of beach and cordgrass that stretched north like a comet's tail. The southern end was half a mile wide—just big enough for the lighthouse and the rambling old hotel that had once been home to the island's most infamous owner.

My father used to relish the island's history. Every summer when we came here, he'd tell me the stories. To my horror, as I got older, I actually found myself interested in them.

Inconveniently placed near the mouth of Aransas Bay, the island had needled its way into local history like a sticker burr. In the early 1800s, Jean Laffitte had used its treacherous sandbars to lure Spanish ships into the shallows, where they floundered and became easy prey. Laffitte had supposedly buried a treasure here, too, in a grove of live oaks, but if there had ever been live oaks on the island, hurricanes had scoured them away long ago. The only trees now were a dozen palmettos, which according to legend had been planted by Colonel Duncan Bray.

Bray had fought at the final land battle of the Civil War—Palmito Ranch, two hundred miles south. The last irony in a war filled with ironies, Palmito Ranch had been a Confederate victory. Bray considered it the definitive word on the war's outcome. He planted palmetto saplings from the battlefield on his family's island, refused to speak of Lee's surrender or Juneteenth or any of the other new realities. He shot at federal troops who attempted to talk to him about repairing his lighthouse, and he lived the rest of his life in voluntary exile on what he considered the last patch of Confederate soil. The island got its name from him. He wasn't the last crazy rebel to own the place.

Bray's house, now the Rebel Island Hotel, was a three-story French Second Empire. It had a mansard roof like reptile skin and cedar-slatted walls painted an odd color that mirrored the sea— sometimes blue, sometimes green or gray. The oldest wooden structure in Aransas County, it had weathered half a dozen hurricanes.

Good karma, our friend Alex had told me, right before he bought the place. At the time, I'd felt like I was watching somebody buy my childhood— nightmares and all.

The lobby smelled of sandalwood and straw mats. Seashells in nets decorated the walls. In one corner, a Latina maid was trying to calm down a guest—a middle-aged blond woman whose eyes were red from crying. Chris the manager excused himself to go help. The blonde was saying something about a gun and her ex-husband. I really didn't want to know.

A college-aged guy in a UT football jersey came stomping down the staircase with a bottle of José Cuervo and a fistful of limes. He asked an older gentleman reading a newspaper on the sofa if the ferry had already left. The old man said he thought it had. The kid cursed and bounded back upstairs.

Outside, thunder rumbled. The whole building rattled.

"Remind me again," I told Garrett. "A quiet honeymoon? Way too early for hurricane season?"

"What, little bro, now global warming is my fault?"

"I think the building is charming," Maia said.

"See?" Garrett said. "Alex! Yo!"

Alex Huff grinned crookedly as he came around the front desk. The hotel owner gave Garrett a bear hug, lifting him out of his wheelchair before setting him back down again. The whole sight was pretty disturbing.

"Damn, Garrett!" Alex said. "Have you gotten taller?"

"Eat me, Huff. You remember Tres. And this is Maia, his better half."

Alex and I shook hands. He had a grip like a pecan cracker. He hadn't gotten any prettier in the past few years. His face was scarred from acne. His wiry blond hair and the wild light in his eyes always made me wonder if he slept with his finger in a light socket.

"Yeah, Tres," he said, pulling me closer. "Need to ask you a favor later, all right?"

That immediately made me wary, but before I could say anything—like *hell*, *no*, for instance—Alex's attention moved on. He gave Maia a hug, admired her third-trimester belly. "Honeymoon, huh? Not a moment too soon."

"They weren't gonna take a honeymoon at all." Garrett wagged a finger at me. "I told Tres, 'That's no way to treat a lady. I'll set the whole thing up for you.'"

"Yeah," I grumbled. "And then he said, 'By the way, I'm coming along.'"

Alex and Garrett both laughed like this was a good joke. I wished it was.

Maia squeezed my hand.

"Well, I guess you lovebirds want to see your room." Alex winked at me. "Garrett's right next door. I hope that's okay."

He ran up the stairs before I could hit him. Garrett cackled and slid out of his chair, then followed Alex, climbing on his hands.

Maia and I got the Colonel's Suite, a second-floor corner bedroom with a parlor and a bay window looking out at the lighthouse.

The octagonal brick tower was seventy feet tall, so no matter what floor of the hotel you were on, the lighthouse loomed overhead. It dated from the 1850s. It hadn't worked in fifty years. As a kid, looking up at the glassed-in top, I'd imagined that the beacon light would mysteriously flicker on. It never happened. But I never got tired of watching for it.

"Ow." Maia dropped the shirt she was unpacking. She sat down on the canopied bed.

I was at her side in about a millisecond. "What is it?"

"Just my back." She managed a smile. "Relax."

"Relax," I said. "I remember that word...like, eight months ago."

I put my hand on her belly. The baby wasn't kicking.

"He's fine," she said. "Don't obsess."

"Coming here was a bad idea."

"Will you stop? We needed to get away."

Thunder boomed.

Get away . . . Right. A sunny vacation. One last holiday before the baby arrived.

Maia scooted up on the bed and tried to get comfortable. Even eight and a half months pregnant, she'd never been more beautiful. Her black hair was thick and glossy. Her eyes seemed to trap the light like amber. "So are you going to tell me about the marshal?"

"Jesse Longoria. Just somebody I've run across a few times."

"And?"

"And nothing to worry about."

"Nothing you want to talk about, you mean."

Outside, rain was coming down in sheets instead of sprinkles. It probably wasn't sundown yet, but it looked like midnight. On the bedstand, the cranberry glass lamp flickered.

"You know," Maia said, "if you wanted to revisit your retirement decision—"

"Okay, now who's obsessing?"

"It's been what—six months?"

"Six and a half."

"But who's counting?"

"That's entrapment, counselor."

She smiled. "Unpack for me? Then I could *really* use a foot massage."

• • •

We didn't see Garrett, but we heard him next door. As the storm got louder, he cranked up Jimmy Buffett on his boom box. *Songs You Know by Heart* vibrated so hard against the wall it might've been *Songs You Know by Braille*. There was another sound, too—a blender, I think. Leave it to my brother to pack his own tropical drink factory.

Maia couldn't take a shower because of the storm, but she spent a long time in the bathroom freshening up. Warm water always made her feel better. Being pregnant, she missed her daily steamy hot bubble baths. She said she would take up that grievance with our kid once he was an adult.

As the storm got louder, so did our neighbors. Some college kids were right above us, stomping and whooping. One of them yelled, "Hurricane party!" Down the hall, a hammer was banging. Maybe Alex and his staff had decided to board up the windows.

I wondered what Alex wanted to ask me. Probably an investigative favor. An employee problem. A cheating girlfriend. Private investigators got everything, which was why I'd quit being one. Well . . . that was one reason, anyway.

I tried to convince myself Jesse Longoria's presence on the island was a total coincidence. Nothing to worry about, just like the storm.

If I closed my eyes and concentrated on the music coming through the walls, I could almost ignore the hammering and the rain.

• • •

The last time I'd seen Jesse Longoria had been the week of my best friend's funeral.

January in San Antonio. The grass was crunchy with ice. Frozen cactuses turned to mush in the tiny gravel lawns of the South Side. At San Fernando Cemetery, the sky was the same color as the tombstones.

I'd come to lay fresh flowers on Ralph's grave. I found Jesse Longoria standing on it, reading the headstone. He wore a black wool overcoat and his customary pleasant smile, as if he could imagine no place he'd rather be on a bitter cold day.

"I missed the funeral," he told me. "I wanted to make sure he was dead."

"Get off."

I expected a fight. I probably wanted one.

Longoria chose not to humor me. He stepped off the grave. "I never got to hunt Ralph Arguello. Shame. I would've enjoyed that."

"You need to leave."

"Going to blame yourself for his death, too, Navarre? You never had any sense about criminals."

I was crushing the stems of the marigolds I'd brought. "I don't murder fugitives in my custody. That what you mean?"

Longoria's laugh turned to mist in the cold air. "You're not honest with yourself, son. You knew exactly what would happen to that client of yours, sooner or later. He was no different from your friend here." He gestured at Ralph's headstone.

"Where'd you dump the body, Longoria?"

His smile didn't waver. "If you can't stop feeling guilty, son, maybe you should find a different line of work. Nobody's ever stopped me from doing what was necessary. Nobody ever will."

He strolled away down the line of tombstones. As he passed a child's grave, he flicked a multicolored pinwheel and set it spinning.

I turned on the nightstand radio. All I could get was a garbled AM news station from Corpus Christi. Tropical Storm Aidan, which forecasters had dismissed as dying, was regaining hurricane strength. Despite Garrett's assurances that it would veer north—that no hurricane had ever hit the Texas coast so early in the season—Aidan was bearing down on top of us. Ferry service to most locations had been suspended. Power was down in several communities. Evacuation routes were jammed.

"What's the news?" Maia came out of the bathroom, toweling her hair.

I turned off the radio. "Nothing much."

Thunder shook the windows. The power blinked out then came back on. Somebody upstairs yelled, "*Yeah*, baby!"

I stared at the clock flashing 12:01. I was just thinking how useless that would be if I were trying to time the occurrence of a crime, when I heard the shot.

Maia and I locked eyes.

"A board cracking," I said. "Something slammed into the building."

"Tres, that was a gun."

I looked at the bay window, which I'd closed with the storm shutters. I tried to believe the noise had come from somewhere out there, but I knew better. The shot had come from inside the hotel.

Garrett's music was still playing next door. The college kids were still stomping around upstairs. I'd heard enough gunshots in my life. Maybe if I just let this one go, let a few more bars of "Cheeseburger in Paradise" play through...

"Tres," Maia said, "we need to check it out."

"We're on vacation. They have a staff here. Alex can handle it."

"Fine," Maia said. "I'll go."

"No, you won't."

"Hand me my dress."

"All right," I relented. "I'll go. Just ... stay put."

There was a knock on our door. Garrett yelled, "Y'all arguing in there? Thought I heard a gunshot."

Maia did not stay put. Neither did Garrett.

They followed me down the hall as if I knew where I was going. Garrett was in a wheelchair I'd never seen before. Apparently he kept a spare on the second floor, which told me he'd been visiting the hotel a lot more than I'd known.

On the stairs we ran into the older gentleman I'd

seen in the lobby. He was taller than I'd realized, almost seven feet. With his shock-white hair and his black linen undertaker's suit he was a bit disconcerting to meet in a dark stairwell. That, and the fact he was armed with a .45 Colt Defender.

"I heard a shot," he explained.

I wasn't sure what bothered me more—the gun, or the way his hand shook as he held it. He must've seen the way I was looking at him, because he slipped the gun into his pocket. "I thought the sound came from upstairs."

"I was thinking downstairs," I said.

"I'll follow you, then."

Great, I thought.

We trooped into the lobby and I got plowed into by the blond woman I'd seen crying earlier.

"Whoa," I said. "Where are you going?"

She pushed past me and raced up the stairs.

Chris the manager came out of the office in hot pursuit. He stopped short when he saw us. "Hi, uh . . ."

His ears were red. He was breathing heavy.

"We heard something," I told him. "Sounded like a shot."

"A shot? No, couldn't have been a shot."

"Did you hear it?"

"No. I mean . . . no. Who would have a gun?"

I thought about that. The old gentleman had one. So did Maia. She never left home without her Lamaze pillow and her .357. Who else?

"The marshal," Maia said, following my thoughts. "What room is he in?"

Chris paled. "Oh...uh..."

"Come on, man!" Garrett growled. "I got margaritas melting upstairs!"

You don't argue with a no-legged man who wants a margarita.

"Room 112," Chris said. "End of the hall on the left. Now if you'll excuse me, I, uh—" He ran after the blond lady.

"Busy place," Maia said.

She started to lead the way down the hall, but I put my arm out to stop her. "Pregnant women do not take point."

"Pooh," she said.

We found room 112. The door was ajar. I knocked anyway. "Longoria?"

No answer.

Maia and I exchanged looks.

"Go ahead, point man," she told me.

Trespassing in Longoria's room didn't sound like the safest idea. On the other hand, I had Maia, Garrett and an old guy with a .45 for backup.

I opened the door.

The first thing I noticed was the broken window. Glass was strewn all over the room. Rain blew in, soaking the carpet, the dresser and the open suitcase.

Jesse Longoria was sprawled at the foot of the bed, half wrapped in the blanket he'd clawed off as he fell. He was staring at the ceiling, a pained expression on his face, as if embarrassed that he had not managed to cover the bullet hole in his chest.

4

Chris ran down the hall. The wind shook the walls. The storm had taken him by surprise. After surfing the Gulf Coast waters so long, he thought he knew the weather. But he'd anticipated nothing like this. It wasn't natural the way the hurricane had turned toward them, bearing down on Rebel Island with a malicious will.

If he'd known, he never would've arranged things the way he had.

When he caught up with Lane, she was in his bedroom, looking through his dresser.

"Stop it!" he said.

She looked up, her eyes still red. Her blond hair was stringy and wet from the shower.

"What have you done?" she demanded.

Chris balled his fists. He stared at the picture on his dresser mirror: a photo of the beach at Waikiki. Thinking of Hawaii usually calmed him down, but now his dream of moving there seemed childish. Had he really believed he'd be able to get away from here?

"I didn't do anything wrong."

"Chris, I know you better than that."

"I would never . . . I'd never hurt you, Lane."

She looked down at the drawers she'd pillaged and sobbed in frustration.

Chris wanted to hold her. He wanted to apologize for bringing her here, but he'd needed to see her so badly. And she needed protection. He knew that better than anyone.

"I'll make it all right," he promised.

She shook her head miserably. The bruises on her face had faded weeks ago, but he could still imagine their shadows around her eyes.

"How many more people are going to die, Chris? You've been saying it's all right. You're going to fix it, but—"

"I will. Right now."

He held Lane's gaze, trying to make her believe him. Whenever he had trouble sleeping—and that was often—he would imagine her eyes, the way they shone when she was happy. He would remember the times he'd made her laugh when they were younger, in high school, before everything went wrong. Since then, he had messed up over and over. His plans had failed. But tonight it had to end.

"Stay here," he told Lane. "I'll be back."

Without waiting for her answer, he headed down the hallway. He knew where he needed to go. How many more needed to die?

One, he thought. *Only one.*

5

At least Jesse Longoria was having a worse vacation than I was.

He'd been shot once at close range. There was no visible murder weapon in the room. Longoria's holster was empty.

"I need to get out of here," Maia murmured.

I nodded. Pregnancy had made her queasy about things that had never bothered her before—strawberries, hamburger meat, corpses.

"Garrett," I said, "take her back to the room, please."

"Jesus," he said. "That's like a dead cop."

"Very much like one." I looked at the old gentleman in the black suit. "Sir, would you go find the owner, please? Alex Huff. Tell him to call the police."

After they were gone, I debated the wisdom of walking farther into the room. Glass shards were everywhere. Blood and rain spattered the bed and the carpet. Whatever crime scene integrity there had been, the storm was rapidly blowing it to hell.

I stepped inside. Two beds. There was an outside door. It was closed. I couldn't tell if it was locked. As I recalled, few rooms in the hotel had private exits. On the second bed were an open suitcase and something else—a small curl of red like a ribbon. I stepped closer. It was a set of plastic handcuffs. They'd been cut.

A cold feeling started in the pit of my stomach.

Alex Huff ran into me from behind. "I heard... Oh, crap."

He looked only slightly better than the corpse. He had a bruise under his left eye, and superficial cuts on his arms, like he'd been sprayed with glass. His clothes were soaking wet.

"What happened to you?" I asked.

He tore his eyes away from the dead marshal. "The—the windows in the dining room blew out. I was boarding them up, but... *Jesus*. What happened to him?"

"You mean aside from getting shot dead? I'm not sure. Any idea what he was doing on the island?"

"No, I mean..." He faltered, apparently considering something he didn't like. "Chris checked him in."

"When?"

"Yesterday? It's been so crazy with the storm and..."

"And what?"

"Nothing. Just... *Damn* it. Why did he have to go and die in *my* hotel?"

I studied Alex's battered face and wondered what he wasn't telling me. "Call the police. Who's got jurisdiction here? Aransas Sheriff's Department?"

"I—I can't call the police."

"Why not?"

"The phone lines are down."

"Cell phone?"

"We've never had mobile service out here."

"Email? Smoke signals? Message in a bottle? What do you use for emergencies?"

Alex's eyes got unfocused, like he was going into shock. I wanted to slap him. He needed to take charge. This was his problem, not mine.

"I don't... Wait. The radio. It's in the lighthouse. I was just out there checking the backup generator. I didn't even think about it—"

"We're on backup generator?" I interrupted.

"Yeah. Regular power is down. But it's cool. We got enough juice to get through the night, assuming the house stays in one piece."

As if on cue, a piece of driftwood flew in the window and slammed against the wall.

"We need to get out of here," I told Alex. "Radio first. Then we'll try to seal that window."

He nodded hazily. I steered him out of the room and made sure he locked the door behind us.

In the hallway, the older gentleman was talking to three college guys, trying to convince them to go away.

"Dude!" one of them said to me. "Is it true?"

He had a mop of red hair, yellow shorts and a white T-shirt, so he was the same colors as a candy corn. His shirt said OU SUCKS, a little diplomatic statement from the University of Texas football department.

Thunder rattled the building.

"You all need to get to the center of the hotel," I said. "Alex, safest place for storm shelter?"

"Parlor," he said. "Right in the middle of the building, no windows."

I looked at the old man, who seemed pretty calm. "You are—"

"Benjamin Lindy," he told me. "From Kingsville."

"All right, Mr. Lindy from Kingsville. Would you mind rounding everyone up, getting them into the parlor? We need to make sure everyone is safe. Then we need to have a group talk."

He nodded.

"Dude!" the redheaded kid said. "A guy got shot? That is freaking awesome!"

Mr. Lindy turned on him and the college guys all took a step back. The old man's expression was hard and cold as a blue norther.

"I hope," Lindy said calmly, "that you are using the word 'awesome' in some fashion I do not understand. I would hate to think you were treating a man's murder as entertainment. Now, why don't you all help me notify the other guests?"

He held out his arms and, without touching the college guys, swept them toward the parlor.

I watched Lindy walk away and wondered what he would've been like forty years ago, before his hair turned white and his hands began to shake. I imagined he rarely needed his Colt .45 to make his point.

"Lighthouse," I told Alex. "Let's go."

In the lobby, the tearful blond lady was standing by the sofa, looking lost. As soon as she saw us, she slipped out of the room.

"Who's *La Llorona*?" I asked Alex.

He stared at me blankly.

"That lady," I said. "She looks like the weeping ghost in the legend...the one who drowned her kids."

Alex looked like he was about to cry himself. "She drowned her kids? I got a guest who drowned her kids?"

"Never mind."

We got to the front door and I made the mistake of opening it. That's when I realized we were going to die before we ever reached the radio.

The lighthouse door was only fifty feet from the hotel entrance, but it might as well have been a mile. The air was a blender of sand and rain and swirling flotsam—oyster shells and chunks of wood that looked suspiciously like planks from the island's boat dock.

I swung back to Alex and yelled "Forget it!" but he must've thought I said something else because he forged ahead into the storm. Like a fool, I decided I'd better follow.

We skittered around like a silent movie comedy, my feet slipping on the wet path. I should've fallen several times, but the wind kept pushing me upright and propelling me forward, like I was being shoved through a mob of linebackers. Sand needled my exposed skin, but by some miracle I didn't get smashed by anything larger.

Alex shouldered open the lighthouse door. We collapsed inside, soaking wet, and Alex forced the door shut.

"Christ," he gasped. "Feel like I just ran a marathon."

He rummaged through his coat pockets, found a flashlight and clicked it on.

His face, already cut up and bruised, was now plastered with wet cordgrass. He had twigs sticking out of his curly hair. He looked like a scarecrow that had just gotten mugged. I doubted I looked much better.

Alex swept his flashlight around the room. We were at the bottom of a hexagonal well of unpainted limestone. Just as I remembered, metal stairs spiraled around the walls toward the lantern gallery far above. I'd only been inside the tower once before. My memories of the place were not good.

Here, the roar of the storm was muted, but there was another sound—a grinding in the walls, as if the limestone blocks were moving.

I reminded myself that the tower had stood for over a century. No way would it pick this moment to collapse. The chances were better of getting struck by lightning.

Thunder boomed outside.

Okay. Bad comparison.

"Where's the radio?" I asked Alex.

He pointed to the platform seven stories above us.

Great.

I knew the beacon hadn't worked in decades. I wasn't sure why Alex would keep the radio up there, but I didn't ask.

We began to climb.

The first time I'd ventured inside this light-house, I'd been trespassing.

I was twelve years old and running from my dad.

I thought I'd escape to the northern end of the island. That's where I usually went to be alone. But as I passed the lighthouse, I remembered my dad's stern warning that the place was much too danger-ous. I should never go in there.

What angry twelve-year-old boy could resist a challenge like that?

I ran to the door and was surprised that it creaked open easily. Inside, the air was cool and damp. I shut the door and put my back against it.

I tried to steady my breathing. I wanted to for-get the scene I'd just witnessed in our hotel room. I probably would've started sobbing, but a faint noise from above made me freeze.

Scrape. Scrape. Scrape, like an animal clawing at wood—a *large* animal.

At the top of the stairs, in a crescent of daylight, a shadow rippled, as if someone or something was up there.

My instincts told me to leave, but then I heard my father's voice outside.

"Tres!" he yelled. "Come on, now. I'm sorry, goddamn it! Where are you?"

He sounded as if he was coming toward the door. I decided to take my chances with the giant animal upstairs.

I took the metal steps as quietly as I could, but my own heartbeat sounded like a bass drum. The limestone blocks were carved with graffiti. One said, *W. Dawes, 1898.*

I smelled sweet, acrid smoke and the scent of fresh-cut wood. I didn't realize the scratching sounds had stopped until I reached the top of the stairs and found a knife pointed at my nose.

A seventeen-year-old Alex Huff glared at me. "What the hell are you doing here, runt?"

I was too scared to speak. I was already terrified of Alex, a delinquent who hung out with Garrett every time we came to Rebel Island. I knew that Alex lived on the island. He made amazing fireworks displays every Fourth of July. I was vaguely aware that his dad worked for the owner, though I'd rarely seen his dad. I knew Alex hated me for some inexplicable reason, and Garrett treated me worse whenever Alex was around.

Behind him, the floor of the lantern gallery was

covered in wood shavings. There was a two-foot-tall figurine standing on a stool, a half-carved woman. A hand-rolled cigarette was smoldering in an ashtray on the windowsill.

"You're smoking pot," I said stupidly.

Alex sneered. "Yeah, and if you tell anyone, I'll gut you. Now what are you—" He tensed as if he'd heard something.

Somewhere below us, outside the tower, my father's voice, heavy with anger and remorse, rang out: "Tres! Tres, goddamn it!"

Alex and I waited, still as death. My father called again, but this time he sounded farther away.

Alex locked eyes with me. "You're hiding from him?"

I nodded. I was determined not to let Alex see me cry.

Alex didn't speak for a full minute. He studied me, as if deciding how to kill me.

"You can't hide on this island, runt." He said it bitterly. "Come on. The boathouse is out back."

"Where are we going?" The last time Alex and Garrett had taken me out on a boat, Alex had threatened to pour cement in my shoes and drop me overboard.

But for once, Alex's expression didn't look mean. His eyes were filled with something else—pity, perhaps?

"We're going fishing," he said, as if fishing were something grim, possibly fatal. "Trust me."

• • •

Now, twenty-five years later, Alex and I climbed back up those steps together. The tower groaned in the storm. In the yellow beam of Alex's flashlight, the limestone walls glistened with moisture.

At last we reached the lantern room—a circular platform surrounding the huge golden chrysalis that was the Fresnel lens. There were no wood shavings on the floor this time, nothing but a couple of crushed beer cans. The gallery's outer walls were storm-proof glass, but I could see nothing through them. With the rain slamming against them, they looked more like marble.

The radio sat on the table in front of us.

I knew almost nothing about shortwave radios, but I did know how to tell when one had been smashed to pieces. This one had been.

I started to say, "Don't touch—"

But Alex picked up the ball-peen hammer. "How...what the hell—"

"Who else knew about this radio, Alex?"

"Nobody! I mean, just me and the staff."

I thought about that. I thought about finger-prints. Whoever had shattered the radio had left the hammer behind, which meant he was either sloppy and rushed or unconcerned about being identified. Either way, I didn't like it.

"Alex, when Longoria arrived on the island, did he come alone?"

"I—I don't know. I told you, Chris checked him in."

"It's your hotel. A small hotel. But you don't know?"

Alex stared at the window. Outside the storm was a blur of gray and black, like ink coming to a boil. "Look . . . Longoria wanted a first-floor room, away from the other guests. He wanted a private exit. That's what Chris said."

"There were handcuffs on the bed."

"Tres—"

"Longoria was a U.S. Marshal. Was he, by chance, transporting a fugitive?"

Alex stared miserably at the radio. It was hard to believe he was the same person I used to be afraid of as a kid—the same Alex Huff who had pointed a knife at my face.

"Longoria came in late last night," he said. "A charter boat brought him in from Rockport. Chris arranged it. I had nothing to do with it."

"And?"

"And I didn't see him come in. I don't know if he was alone, Tres. I didn't want to know."

Lightning gilded the windows silver. The whole tower seemed to sway beneath me.

"We need to find Chris," I said. "We'll talk in the parlor."

"You're not going to tell the other guests?" Alex looked horrified.

"That we might be stuck on this island with a fugitive who just murdered a U.S. Marshal? Yeah, Alex, I kind of think they need to know that."

6

To get away from the old man, Chase pulled his friends into an unused bedroom.

"Well?" he said. "What the hell do we do now?"

Markie rubbed his chin. He was a big guy, usually good in bad situations, but even he looked shaken. "That was a cop. Did you know he was a cop?"

"How was I supposed to know?"

"We've got to get out of here." Ty's face was pasty. He seemed to be having trouble swallowing.

"Nobody's going anywhere," Chase told him.

"Listen to the storm, man," Ty insisted. "There's no way we can do this."

"We will," Chase said. "We've got no choice."

Markie and Ty said nothing. They knew damn well he was right.

Chase had done his best to pretend the murder didn't bother him. It was critical that the other guests believe the three of them were just stupid college guys. But he couldn't shake the image of the bullet hole in the marshal's chest. He couldn't help thinking it was a warning. If this weekend didn't go right, he could end up just like that.

He studied Markie's face, trying to gauge his loyalty. They'd been friends, if you could call it that, for almost three years now. But what they would have to do this weekend...things like that could strain loyalties, make business relationships unravel. Chase would have to watch his back. And Ty—shit, the guy was a basket case. Chase shouldn't have brought him along, but he didn't trust Ty to stay quiet otherwise. He wanted the bastard where he could keep an eye on him.

Chase had worked his way up from nothing. He'd gotten himself into college. He supported his whole fucking family back home. He'd learned how to make a lot of money and deal with hard people. He wasn't going to let anyone mess up his plans.

"All right, look," he said, trying to sound calm. "It's got to happen tonight. I don't give a crap about the storm. We've got no choice."

Markie looked like he wanted to say something, but then changed his mind. He nodded.

"Come on, Chase," Ty pleaded. "You know I can't—I can't stand this much longer. You know how I get."

"You're *gonna* stand it." Chase pointed a finger

at Ty's face like the barrel of a gun. "You're gonna help us. Or you're gonna end up like the cop in there."

Ty shuddered. "All right, I'm just saying—"

The old man, Benjamin Lindy, appeared at the end of the corridor. "You gentlemen coming or not?"

The old man gave Chase the creeps, but he tried for a light tone. "Yeah...uh, sir. We're on the way."

Mr. Lindy scowled, but he started down the hall.

"We've got to play along," Chase said. "And for Christ's sake, Ty, stop looking like you're going to throw up."

"I feel like that."

"Well, don't. Nobody else here knows shit about what's going on. I want to keep it that way."

"What about the dead cop?" Markie asked. "And Chris Stowall?"

"We'll figure it out," Chase said. "Believe me. Stowall is *not* going to fuck with me again."

He led his friends to the parlor. Anger made red spots dance in front of his eyes. He'd been played for a fool. This whole setup sucked. But he was going to make the best of it. He would come out of this weekend in one piece, even if he was the only one who did.

7

Even when I was a child, the hotel's parlor was decorated in dead fish. A five-foot-long marlin curved over the fireplace. Redfish and bass lined the walls. Their frozen eyes and gasping mouths used to scare the hell out of me—almost as much as the hotel's owner.

Every time we arrived at the hotel, my parents would make me sit with them in the parlor while they "caught up" with Mr. Eli. Garrett was excused from this ritual, theoretically because he was helping Alex Huff with the luggage, which I resented to no end.

Mr. Eli had bought the hotel at public auction after federal agents seized it from its previous owner, a Thirties bootlegger who had been South Texas's answer to Al Capone.

Eli was eccentric in a different way. He was an old bachelor who never wore anything but pajamas and a Turkish bathrobe and slippers. He smelled faintly of lilacs. His skin was milky, his hair as black as an oil slick, and he had a strange mustache shaped like a seagull's wings on his upper lip. Years later, I realized that he must've been gay—one of those men who choose, for whatever reason, to live in a climate as hospitable to them as the Arctic is to a tropical plant. That wasn't what scared me. It was the fact that he seemed able to read minds. He would look at me with his watery green eyes and say "I believe young Tres is thirsty for lemonade," or "I see you had a hard year at school," or "Don't worry about Alex. He means well." Whatever happened to be troubling me at the moment.

In all, Mr. Eli seemed like the sort of man my father would detest, but my father always showed him the greatest deference.

On our last visit to Rebel Island as a family, Mr. Eli greeted my father in his usual manner. "Sheriff Navarre, shot anyone lately?"

"Not lately, sir," my father replied. Whether it was true or not, I didn't know.

We sat in the parlor with all the glassy-eyed fish staring down at us. My mother told Mr. Eli he was looking well. In truth the old man looked paler and thinner every summer, but he accepted the compliment with a nod. My father and Mr. Eli talked about the weather and fishing conditions. Mr. Eli seemed to know everything about the sea, though as far as I could tell he never set foot outside the hotel.

After a while, Mr. Eli asked what we would like to drink, and my father requested whiskey.

"Jack," my mother chided. "Remember?"

I didn't know what she was talking about, but apparently my father did. His face flushed. He could be a scary man, my father. His huge girth was intimidating enough, and when he got angry his eyes were as bright as a hawk's.

"I'll have a drink with our host," he told my mother.

"Jack, you promised."

My father rose from his chair. The air in the room was as sharp as broken glass. He turned to Mr. Eli and said, "If you'll excuse me, sir."

Once he left, my mother muttered a quick apology to Mr. Eli. "I'd better go, ah, talk to him. Tres, stay here, will you?"

That was the last thing I wanted—but my mother left me alone with Mr. Eli.

The old man smiled so his seagull mustache seemed to spread its wings. "Let's get you a soda."

He called for the maid, an elderly African American woman named Delilah. She brought me a Coke over ice with a maraschino cherry. Delilah had scars on the inside of her wrists, crisscrossed swollen pink lines like Chinese words. I'd asked my father about those scars once, and he'd told me that Mr. Eli had saved Delilah's life. He wouldn't explain how.

I sat on the sofa, drinking my soda and trying not to look at Mr. Eli. I wanted to leave, but my mother had ordered me to stay here. For once, I hoped Mr. Eli would read my mind: take pity on me and tell me to go away.

"Alex fixed the fishing boat," he said. "Perhaps he can take you out."

"Maybe," I said halfheartedly.

"You don't like Alex," Mr. Eli said. "But you must be patient with him."

"Why?"

Mr. Eli nodded. "Fair question. Alex and his father have had a hard life, Tres. A lot of tragedy. But they're good people. Loyal and compassionate."

I couldn't believe Mr. Eli was talking about the same kid who stuck bottle rockets in my shorts.

Mr. Eli smoothed a fold in his bathrobe. "Tres, I take in all kinds—all sorts of wounded souls. Enough time on this island can heal most scars eventually. Alex, as far as I know, is the only person who's ever been born here. That makes him special, in my opinion. I have a feeling someday Alex is going to pay me back many times over."

"Pay you back for what?" I asked.

Mr. Eli smiled benignly. "I think it's safe to go to your room now, Tres. 102, as usual, but I'd knock first."

And so I left Mr. Eli in the parlor. Years afterward, I wondered if he'd been including the Navarre

family among the wounded souls he'd invited to
Rebel Island. I decided he probably had.

Now, so many years later, the same marlin hung
over the mantel. The trophies were a little dustier,
but they had the same glassy eyes and surprised expressions, not too different from the half-dozen
guests who were milling around the room.

I looked at Alex. "Where's Chris?"

He chewed his thumbnail. "I'm not sure. Jose,
the cook, said he was helping move the body—"

"They *moved* the body?"

Alex blinked. "Hey, I didn't—they just—"

"Whose brilliant idea was that?"

Next to me, Garrett tugged on my sleeve. "Yo,
little bro. Come here a sec. Alex, man, go get yourself a drink or something."

Garrett wheeled himself into the hallway and
waited for me to follow. "Back off Alex, okay? He's
having a tough time."

"He's being evasive," I said. "And he's being stupid. His staff just ruined a crime scene."

"You never liked him, did you?"

"Garrett, that is *not* the point."

He wheeled his chair back and forth, digging
tracks in the carpet. "Little bro, Alex is having
some trouble. I mean, even before tonight. I didn't
ask you down here just for the honeymoon."

"My brother had a selfish ulterior motive? What
a surprise."

"Yeah, well. The truth is—"

Maia came up behind him and placed her hands on Garrett's shoulders. She looked better after lying down. The color had returned to her face.

"I hate to interrupt," she said, glancing inside the parlor, "but it looks like your audience is ready."

If they were my audience, I needed a warm-up act.

The upset blond lady sat in an armchair. She was wearing pink silk pajamas and hugging a pillow like she was afraid I'd hit her. The three college kids stood at the wet bar, browsing the labels on liquor bottles. There was the redheaded guy, a big bald dude and a skinny Latino kid with nervous eyes and shaggy black hair. Two staff members— the cook and the maid—were casting me worried glances from the steps by the pool table. The only person who seemed at ease was the old man, Benjamin Lindy, immaculate in his charcoal suit, sitting cross-legged on the sofa next to Alex, and even Lindy was looking at me warily, as if I might try to sell him something.

Then there was the storm, which was an audience member as much as any of the people. It resonated in the timbers of the house, making the walls creak and the floor vibrate. There were no outside windows in the room, but I could feel the storm grinding, like a surgeon's saw cutting into bone.

"So," I said. "My name is Tres Navarre. I, uh—"

"You a cop?" the redheaded college kid asked.

"No."

"Then why the hell are you in charge?"

"Nobody said I was in charge."

"Because he's a private investigator," Alex offered.

"*Was* a private investigator," I corrected.

"And he knows a lot more than any of us about what to do when there's a murder."

The storm kept sawing into the timbers.

The cook raised his hand. "Señor, it was for sure, then, *homicidio*?"

His accent was borderland Spanish—Laredo, maybe, or Juárez.

"You're Jose?" I asked. "The one who moved the body?"

He glanced at the maid, then nodded. Something about the way the two of them sat together, leaning toward each other as if for protection, told me they were married. As mad as I was about Jose moving the body, I decided I'd better not berate him too badly in front of his wife.

"All right, Jose," I said. "You noticed the gunshot wound in Mr. Longoria's chest?"

"*Claro*, señor."

"Did you happen to find a gun when you were in the room?"

"No, señor."

"Then we can be pretty sure it was murder. A person who commits suicide doesn't normally hide the weapon after he shoots himself. Besides, Longoria was a U.S. Marshal. He'd rented a room with two beds. There was a pair of cut handcuffs on one bed."

"A prisoner?" the blond lady asked. "You think he was escorting a prisoner?"

Her tone surprised me. I expected hysterics, but she sounded calm and alert.

"That's possible," I admitted.

"But..." She looked around, like she was afraid to say more. "That can't be it."

"The young lady is right," Mr. Lindy said. "It doesn't make sense. Why would a marshal escort a prisoner here? Rebel Island isn't on the way to anywhere."

"I'd like to understand that, too," I said. "Did any of you see the marshal when he arrived? Was he with anyone?"

No one answered.

Jose and the maid shook their heads.

The redheaded college kid cleared his throat. "So let me get this straight. You're telling us there's, like, an escaped fugitive on the island."

Alex was silently pleading with me to tone it down, to avoid further panic in his hotel.

"That," I said, "is a distinct possibility. At any rate, whoever shot Longoria is stuck on this island until the storm passes, and we have no way to contact the mainland."

"That's whacked," declared the college kid, which I thought covered the situation pretty well.

"Has anyone seen Chris?" I asked. "Chris— What's his last name?"

"Stowall," Alex answered miserably. "Chris Stowall."

"The manager?" Mr. Lindy asked.

"Yeah," the college guy said. "That freak who told us to turn down our music."

"We need to find him," I said. "He checked Longoria in. He may have some answers. Who saw him last?"

The blond lady developed a sudden interest in her pillowcase.

"We'll find him," the college guy said. "Beats sitting here."

"Don't go anywhere alone," I said. "And don't try to go outside."

"Yes, mother." The guy nodded to his friends and they headed off. The shaggy-haired Latino kid looked a little nervous about it, but the big bald dude put a hand on his back and kept him moving.

Mr. Lindy spread his arms across the couch. "So, Mr. Navarre. What do you suggest we do now?"

"Stay in here, together, as much as possible. If anyone has to go somewhere, go with someone else."

"Hell, little bro, we don't need bathroom buddies," Garrett grumbled. "We're grown-ups."

It was the first time I'd ever heard my brother claim to be a grown-up, which in itself was pretty disturbing.

"The killer has no place to go," I told him. "At

least not until the storm passes. Cornered people tend to be desperate."

The maid raised her hand. "Señor, where could this man hide? It is a big house, but—"

"We could search it," Alex suggested, a glimmer of new hope in his eyes. "Me and the staff. I bet we won't find anybody. Then we can all rest easier."

I thought about that. I didn't like the idea of more people roaming around the hotel. Then again, I didn't like the idea of spending the night in the parlor, either.

"All right," I told Alex. "Why don't you and your staff, Jose and—"

"Imelda," the maid provided.

"Imelda," I said. "Why don't the three of you search. Alex, you have any kind of weapon?"

"Here," Lindy said, and offered his .45.

Alex didn't look too happy about it, but he took the gun.

"You know how to use that, son?" Lindy asked.

Alex nodded. "I was in the army, but..."

Whatever he was thinking, he didn't say it. He nodded at Jose and Imelda, who followed him out.

"Well, ain't this cozy?" Garrett winked at the blond lady. "You mind being my bathroom buddy, darling?"

The blond lady squeezed her eyes shut, like she was hoping we'd all disappear. When we didn't, she grabbed her pillow and ran out of the room.

Garrett's smile dissolved. "Aw, hell, I didn't mean—"

"I'll go after her," Maia said.

"No," I said. "I'll do it."

Maia raised her eyebrows.

"Please," I said. "Just...I'd rather you and Garrett stay where it's safe."

Maia muttered something in Chinese, probably a curse on her overprotective husband. "Fine. If I start labor, I'll just have Garrett help me out."

"Now wait a minute, sister," Garrett protested.

I was about to go search for the blond lady when Mr. Lindy said, "Mr. Navarre?"

"Sir?" The *sir* came automatically—South Texas breeding. Something about the old man brought it out in me.

"You failed to mention the most obvious place for this murderer to hide," he said. His eyes were frosty blue. "Right here. As one of the guests. How do we know it's not one of us?"

The blond lady was sitting in the empty dining room.

A row of five tables with white linen cloths ran down the middle of the room. In the dark, they reminded me of gurneys in a morgue. Damaged windows were covered with tarps and hastily hammered boards, but rain leaked in the edges, soaking the carpet. The floor was strewn with silverware and overturned flower vases.

I sat down across from the lady.

"Tough night," I said.

She brushed a carnation off the table. "Tough year."

"What's your name?"

"Lane."

"That your first or last name?"

"First. Lane S—" She pursed her lips. "Lane Sanford."

She was younger than I'd first thought: in her late twenties, pretty the way a sun-bleached cotton dress is pretty—comfortably worn, slightly faded. The roots of her hair were ginger brown.

"Okay, Lane. The thing is, we should be sticking together. I'm a little worried about you."

She hugged her arms. "A little worried..."

"You're staying alone at the hotel?"

"I *thought* I was alone."

"I heard you talking to Chris and the maid this afternoon. Something about your ex?"

"I tried to warn them. Bobby will do anything. He's been tracking me and..." She started breathing shallowly. "And that marshal who was shot—"

"Lane, I want you to take a deep breath and hold it."

She gave me a desperate watery look, but she tried to hold her breath.

"Good," I said. "Now let it out slowly, and tell me about your ex."

She exhaled. "You don't understand. You don't know him."

"Do you have any evidence your ex is here? Have you seen him?"

"I...No, but—"

"Was there some reason he would've targeted Longoria?"

"Longoria?"

"The marshal who got shot."

"I don't...I don't know. I *told* Chris I shouldn't have come."

"So the hotel manager, Chris...you know him personally?"

She stared at the boarded-up windows. "I told him I couldn't run anymore. I'm so tired of hiding from what happened."

"What do you mean?"

Before she could answer, the college guys came tromping into the room. "Yo, Navarro," the red-headed guy said.

"Navarre," I corrected.

"Whatever," he said, but he wasn't pulling off his angry-young-man routine very well. His face was ashen. His two friends looked queasy. "We, um, found something maybe you should see."

In the back of the kitchen was a triple-wide stainless-steel refrigerator. The college kids—who strangely enough possessed names: Chase, Markie and Ty—had decided to raid it looking for snacks. They'd lost their appetites when they saw what was on the floor.

"You were all together?" I asked.

Chase, the redhead, glanced at his friends. "Well, we were kind of...not." He nodded at the sickly-looking Latino kid. "Ty was throwing up."

"Too much information," I said. "And you two?"

"Markie was getting glasses from the cabinet

over there," Chase said. "I was gonna get the food. Then I saw *that*."

"It's blood, isn't it?" Lane Sanford's voice trembled.

"Chase," I said, "you and your friends take Miss Sanford back to the parlor, please. Tell my wife..." My voice faltered.

I was used to relying on Maia's opinion, but she already felt queasy. I couldn't ask Maia to look at this. "On second thought, ask Mr. Lindy to come in here."

I finally convinced Lane to go with the college guys, which left me alone, staring at the skid mark of red on the white tiles.

I didn't hear Mr. Lindy come up behind me until he spoke. "Blood, all right," he said. "Someone slipped in it. Partial shoeprint, there."

I looked at the old man. "Are you retired law enforcement, Mr. Lindy?"

"Criminal lawyer. Thirty-seven years. I've seen my share of blood."

His voice was as dry as a South Texas creek bed.

"Maybe this is from when they were moving Longoria's body," I said hopefully.

Lindy shook his head. "I stumbled across Chris Stowall and the cook, Jose, while they were doing that. I tried to convince them it, ah, wasn't a good idea...but Mr. Stowall was not entirely rational. He insisted he couldn't let the guests see the body. At any rate, the cellar where they took the body is around the corner there. They didn't come through this way, and no one tracked blood as far as I could see. They used a plastic tarp."

I crouched next to the red smear. Sure enough, the edge of a shoeprint was visible—a man's shoe, I thought. Smooth sole, about a size 11. There were no other red prints on the floor, though, as if the man had slipped in blood, then taken his shoe off to avoid leaving a trail. But if that was the case, why had he left this stain?

"I don't want to think this is someone else's blood," I said. "I mean, besides Longoria's."

Lindy's eyes glinted. "Mr. Huff said you'd retired from private investigations. I take it you've dealt with murders before?"

Had I dealt with murders? Under different circumstances, I might've laughed. "Yes, sir. A few."

"And you knew Marshal Longoria?"

I wondered if Lindy was grilling me. I suspected he was the kind of lawyer who could set his victims at ease, then work out a confession before they realized what had happened.

"I knew him," I admitted. "And I don't want anything to do with solving his murder. You've got more experience than I do."

The old man shook his head. "Until the police can be called, you do what you think is best, son. I'll back you up. The others looked to you naturally, you know. There was no doubt that you would be in charge."

"Thanks a lot," I said. "And now we have a bloodstain along with a dead body. How am I doing so far?"

Lindy patted my shoulder. "You go find that wife of yours, try to relax a little. Lock your bedroom door. I'll call you if anything else happens."

"We should all stay together."

Lindy smiled. "Too late for that, son. These people are not the types that stay together well. Now, go salvage what you can of the first night of your honeymoon. I'll get my gun back from Alex Huff. I'm increasingly beginning to wonder if I will need it."

8

Imelda watched nervously as Señor Huff ransacked the building. He muttered to himself, throwing open doors and clutching his borrowed gun. She had seen him in many moods, but never like this before.

"Where is he?" Señor Huff growled. He pulled sheets out of the linen closet and dumped them at Jose's feet, then moved to the next guest room and kicked open the door. "Where is the bastard?"

"Señor—"

"No." Huff stuck his finger in her face. "You don't talk to me. Neither of you."

Jose cleared his throat. "But, Señor Huff—"

"Get back downstairs," he ordered. "Make the

guests some food. I don't want to see you. I don't want to hear you."

He stormed down the hallway and left them alone.

Imelda looked at her husband. "What do we do?"

She was used to Jose having answers. Usually, no matter how bad the situation, he would give her a reassuring smile. She loved the way the edges of his eyes crinkled, his gaze warm and brown. He was a handsome man when he smiled.

Now his expression was grim. He knelt and gathered up the fallen linens. "We make the guests food."

"Jose . . . please. It's killing him."

He folded up the sheets clumsily and stuffed them back into the closet. He was never good with linens. That was her job, folding the corners perfectly, smoothing out wrinkles.

"Señor Huff will survive this," he promised. "We all will."

"We owe him—"

"I know what we owe him," Jose said. She heard the steel edge in his voice and knew better than to argue.

"We'll go downstairs," Jose insisted. "And do our jobs."

He trudged off, not waiting to see if she would follow.

Imelda hesitated, staring into the empty guest room. It was room 207. It hadn't been used in weeks. Every day, Imelda would go in anyway to dust and fluff the pillows. She would open the window to let in fresh sea air. She loved empty rooms. They were clean and full of promise. They had no past. Unlike their own room. Terrible memories could not be smoothed out. They couldn't be neatly folded and tucked away.

It had all started to go wrong last fall, when the visitor arrived from the mainland. That day, she had known their lives would be shattered yet again. Their hopes of finding peace would be dashed.

She gathered her strength. She could not give up now. The young man, Señor Navarre, might be a new opportunity. She would know, soon enough.

She closed the door of room 207 and followed after her husband.

9

I should've followed Lindy's advice and gone straight to my honeymoon, but I couldn't stop thinking about Jesse Longoria's body in the cellar.

In the hall, I ran into Garrett, who was hand-walking down to check on me.

"Got worried," he told me. "Lane said something about a bloodstain."

"Is Maia all right?"

Garrett shrugged. "She's calming Lane down. Rather have that job than looking for you, little bro. Lane's a lot hotter."

"Don't even think about it."

He gave me the innocent eyes—a look Garrett doesn't do very well. "Can't a guy want to comfort a young lady without people getting ideas?"

"No. Now come on."

"Where we going?"

"To visit a dead man."

It was rare for a house on the Texas coast to have a basement, but the first owner, Colonel Bray, had insisted on it. The walls were original 1880s shellcrete—a cementlike mixture of sand and ground oyster shells. The floor was damp. The air smelled of mildew and fish.

When I was a kid, Garrett and Alex used to spend a lot of time in that cellar. Some of their time, no doubt, was spent doing drugs, talking about girls, planning great teenage adventures. I wasn't included in any of that. But most important, Alex made his fireworks there.

As July fourth got near, he would spend every spare moment with his beloved project. He got so preoccupied he forgot to pick on me. He didn't care if I sneaked downstairs to watch, as long as I touched nothing. He even ignored Garrett, which pleased me more than anything.

The cellar would fill up with plastic tubes, coils of fuse, rolls of aluminum foil and boxes of caps, plugs and Mexican fireworks. Alex would save money all year, then clean out the local roadside stands and cannibalize their chemicals to make his huge mortar displays.

Our last summer, a few weeks before my fateful trip to the lighthouse, I crept down the cellar stairs and watched as Alex rigged up his row of plastic tubes. Garrett sat on a folding chair nearby, drinking tequila from a Coke can and looking bored.

It's hard for me to remember the way Garrett used to look before he had a wheelchair, but this was long before the accident that took his legs. He was getting ready to graduate from high school. He was just starting to grow his beard. He'd been accepted to MIT (my mother's idea) but turned them down because he said he would never be a "damn sellout." He had plans to drive around the country, maybe go to Europe. He was trying to convince Alex that this was an excellent idea.

Normally, Alex would've been encouraging. No matter how crazy Garrett's schemes got, Alex was always his number one cheerleader, almost as if Alex wanted to see how far he could push Garrett to go. That was the main reason Garrett liked Alex so much. But today, on a fireworks day, Alex was a tougher sell.

"Come on, man," Garrett said. "You want to stay on this island your whole life?"

Alex looked up briefly from twisting his fuses. "I don't know."

"You got no ambition, man. Whole world's out there. You want to turn into Mr. Eli, sitting up there in a bathrobe all day?"

"Mr. Eli's not so bad. He helped my folks out."

"Whatever, man. You ask me, it wasn't much help."

Alex didn't answer. He covered a mortar with aluminum foil and began unwrapping a case of Roman candles.

"Sorry," Garrett muttered. "I didn't mean anything."

Alex took out a box cutter and sliced a Roman candle, splitting it open like a bean pod. "You think it'll be easier meeting the right girl, if you go on this trip?"

Garrett's face flushed. He'd broken up with a girl named Tracy a few weeks before. I guess he had told Alex about it. She'd hung around our house for maybe a month, and when she finally broke up with Garrett, his moods turned even blacker than usual. At night, he listened to Led Zeppelin and ripped pages out of his yearbook. During the day, he'd take his air gun into the backyard and shoot at soda cans for hours.

"What's that supposed to mean?" Garrett demanded. "You think I won't meet someone?"

Alex uncoiled a length of wire, measured it against a yardstick. Even at seventeen, his hands were scarred from knife cuts, fishing hooks, rope burns. He was always busy, always creating something.

"Thing about fireworks," he said, "it's all in the timing. You got to measure the fuse just right or the ignition is no good. You burn everything up too fast, or it doesn't go off at all."

"I don't get you, man," Garrett said. "You're gonna sit on this island your whole life, waiting like your dad? You think love is gonna come to you?"

The cellar was silent except for water dripping from a busted pipe in the corner. A moth batted at the single bare lightbulb above, casting enormous shadows across the shellcrete walls.

"Get out," Alex said finally. "I'm working."

Garrett looked like he wanted to argue, but then he thought better of it. He cursed and got up to leave. He glowered at me as he passed me on the stairs.

I didn't move. Alex glanced at me without emotion. I might've been another fuse or plastic tube—not something he needed right now, but not something he was going to bother throwing away, either. He went back to work, and I watched in silence as he fused together a row of pipes like a church organ, loading it with chemicals and measuring his fuses to just the right length.

There were no fireworks in the cellar now. Jesse Longoria's body had been laid out on a butcher-block table.

A single bare lightbulb flickered dimly above us, but we relied mostly on a flashlight, which cast long shadows across Longoria's face. He didn't look like a man at peace, even if one ignored the bullet hole in his chest. He looked like a man who needed to use the restroom.

"I hate dead bodies," Garrett mumbled.

I couldn't tell if my brother was really pale and sweaty, or if it was just the light. His color wasn't much better than Longoria's. Of course, Garrett was at a height disadvantage. He'd had to hand-walk his way down into the cellar. Now, sitting in a metal chair, he was eye level with the gunshot wound.

"Hold up the flashlight," I told him.

The body was wrapped in a plastic tarp. The inside of the tarp was spattered with blood, but there was none that I could see on the outside, or on the floor, or on the steps into the cellar. Jose and Chris may have ruined a crime scene, but they seemed to have done it without making a mess. It seemed unlikely that the blood smeared in the kitchen had come from this corpse.

I checked through Longoria's pockets. I came up with a wallet, car keys, an Aransas Pass ferry schedule and thirty-six cents. In Longoria's wallet were his badge, sixty-five dollars in cash and the usual credit cards.

"So you knew this guy?" Garrett asked.

"He killed a client of mine."

"Before or after the client paid you?"

"You're just Mr. Sensitive, aren't you?" I put Longoria's wallet back in his coat pocket. "Longoria had a reputation in the South Texas Marshal's Office. He apprehended something like fifty fugitives in twelve years. Once in a while, as he was bringing them back, the fugitives would, ah, try to escape."

"And this dude would use force."

"Deadly force. Every time, Longoria was cleared of wrongdoing, but—"

"I gotcha," he grumbled. "Fucking cops."

"Dad was a cop."

"What's your point?"

He had me there.

I scanned the room. Chris or Jose or somebody had set the dead man's suitcase in the corner. I hauled the brown Tourister to the table and opened it at the dead man's feet.

Garrett shifted uncomfortably in his chair. "So this client of yours ... he was a fugitive?"

"Charged with arson. He had a felony record. He panicked and skipped town before his trial. The wife paid me to find him and convince him to turn himself in. I didn't have time. Longoria found him first and killed him."

"You know that for sure?"

"The body was never found. My guy's officially still listed as a fugitive. But I asked around. The guy had had a run-in with one of Longoria's SAPD buddies the year before. Longoria took matters into his own hands. Settled the score."

Garrett looked down at the dead man's face. "See, asshole? This is what we call karma. Now can we get out of here, little bro?"

I rummaged through the marshal's suitcase. I found two changes of clothes. No paperwork, no files from the Marshal's Office. Nothing interesting, until I checked one of those easy-to-miss side pockets that I'd trained myself not to miss. Stuck inside were a crumbling candy skull wrapped in plastic and a business card that read:

Chris Stowall
Manager

Rebel Island Hotel
510-822-9901

Handwritten on the back was a date.

"June fifth," I read.

"That's today," Garrett said.

"Yeah."

"So what's important about it?"

"Good question." I slipped the card in my pocket and examined the candy skull. There was nothing special about it. Any Mexican candy store would sell them.

"That's one of those Day of the Dead candies," Garrett said. "Your friend here have a sweet tooth?"

"Maybe," I said.

But something about the skull bothered me. It reminded me of something I'd read, or heard on the news...

Above us, the lightbulb flickered and went out completely, leaving us with nothing but the flashlight beam shining on the dead marshal's face.

Garrett took a shaky breath. "Okay. *Now* can we get out of here?"

Maia had lit candles in the Colonel's Suite.

Against my better judgment, Garrett took charge of Lane Sanford and led her away. He said they'd go find Alex, maybe drop in on the college guys, who'd resumed their hurricane party above us. Garrett would teach them how to make a good margarita. They could listen to Jimmy Buffett until the batteries in Garrett's boom box wore out. It would cheer Lane right up.

Once they were gone, I lay down on the bed next to Maia and listened to the rain pounding the walls. There was a leak in the corner of the roof. Maia had put a silver cup under it. The drops sounded like tiny bells.

"Are we having a romantic getaway yet?" I asked.

Maia nudged my foot. "With a homicide magnet like you? A girl can't help but have a good time."

She snuggled next to me, wincing as she changed positions.

"What is it?" I asked.

"Just my back."

"You sure?"

"Of course. Stop worrying. Tell me what you found."

I got the feeling she was just trying to change the subject, but I told her about the bloodstain in the kitchen, and the business card and candy skull in Longoria's briefcase.

"Bad," she said.

"That was my expert opinion, too." I nodded toward the AM radio on the dresser. "Any news come through before the generator went out?"

"Couple of garbled alerts. Power's been knocked out in Corpus Christi. Some smaller coastal towns are underwater. The rainfall is setting records."

"So the earliest we could expect the ferry—"

"Twenty-four hours at least. We'll have to hope

the phone lines get reconnected sooner than that. Or maybe a Coast Guard patrol will come by."

"Damn, I would love that."

She touched the space between my eyebrows—her way of telling me I was scowling too much. "You did the right thing, taking charge."

"I didn't take charge."

"They need you to, Tres. I know you want to switch off that ability—"

"What ability?"

Instead of answering, Maia rested her head on my chest.

The wind outside battered the hotel. I could almost feel the storm pushing us toward the mainland, carving new channels out of the coastline.

"Who do you think killed the marshal?" Maia asked.

"I don't want to think about it."

"But you can't help it."

I hated that she was right.

"Chris Stowall's business card was in Longoria's suitcase," I said. "And now Chris has disappeared."

Maia picked at a button on my shirt. "Chris Stowall doesn't strike me as much of a killer."

"And yet he's missing."

"Whoever the killer is, he's still in the hotel."

"Are you sure it's a he?"

"Unless you think Lane or Imelda did it. Or me."

"Hmm. Probably not Lane or Imelda."

She elbowed me. "Lane was telling me some disturbing things about her ex-husband. She made him sound abusive. And relentless."

"Homicidal?"

"Possibly."

"I doubt there's a connection," I said. "Lane admitted she hasn't seen her ex here. With this storm, he couldn't be outside. He'd have been blown all the way to Kingsville by now. And why would he target Longoria?"

"One of the other guests, then? Or the staff? Your friend Alex?"

My friend Alex.

I thought about the time Alex pushed me against a window on the third floor when I was around ten years old. I think I'd asked him what his parents did—some stupid, innocent question like that. He held me so far out my shoulders cleared the windowsill, his fingers digging into my forearms. *None of your goddamn business, mama's boy,* he'd told me. *Nobody asked you to come here! You got that?*

Still, it was difficult to imagine Alex Huff shooting a law enforcement officer at point-blank range. As far as I knew, his only flirtation with guns had been his time in the military, which from his own account had been undistinguished—something about serving breakfast in Kuwaiti mess halls. Since then, his most dangerous hobbies had been his amateur fireworks, buying questionable real estate and hanging out with my brother.

"I don't know about Alex," I said halfheartedly. "He got scuffed up pretty bad somehow, and he's acting nervous. I don't trust him."

"Because he's capable of murder, or because he's Garrett's friend?"

"Whose side are you on, anyway?"

She kissed me. She was pretty convincing. "What about the old lawyer, Mr. Lindy? He had a gun. He was in the hallway."

"Yeah," I said. "I don't understand what he's doing here. On the other hand, he's a lawyer. He's got to be close to eighty. He could barely hold that .45. Did that look like a .45 wound in Longoria's chest?"

Maia shook her head. She looked a little green.

"Sorry," I said. "Forgot you were feeling squeamish."

"It's okay. But that doesn't leave many people. At least . . . people we know of."

"If the killer wants to get off the island, there aren't many options."

"None," Maia agreed. "It doesn't make sense that Longoria would bring a fugitive here. This island's a dead end."

I closed my eyes and listened to the storm.

The sound was familiar. Then I realized the storm sounded just like a freight train—the way the Kansas-Texas used to roar past the Arguello family house, back in high school. I wished it didn't sound like that.

"I don't want to solve this problem," I said. "I'm an English teacher."

"You're thinking about Ralph."

The image never went away—Ralph lying on the shoulder of Mission Road, staring into the sky. He'd taken a gunshot to protect Maia. He'd died and left a wife and kid behind. No matter how many times I replayed it, trying to convince myself there was nothing I could've done...PI work had brought me nothing but pain. It had never been just a job. It had seeped into every part of my life, endangered everyone I was close to.

"Ralph wouldn't want you to quit," Maia told me. "That wouldn't make him feel better."

"Nothing can happen to you or the baby."

"Tres, you can't control everything. You can't stop things from happening."

The storm roared. There was a draft somewhere. The candles flickered and guttered.

Maia propped herself up on one elbow. "Did you hear that?"

"What, the wind?"

She listened, looking around the room until her eyes fixed on the door. "Someone's outside."

I didn't ask how she knew. I got out of bed.

"Tres." Maia pointed to her luggage.

I retrieved the .357 from her suitcase and I went to the door.

I threw it open, but there was no one there. The hallway was dark and silent. I realized I was making a great silhouette if anybody wanted to take aim at me. The candlelight behind me was the only illumination.

As I stepped back inside, paper crumpled under my foot.

"What is it?" Maia asked.

I picked up the envelope. Hotel stationery, cream with brown lettering: REBEL ISLAND HOTEL. It was unsealed with the flap folded in, the contents too thick for a single letter.

I should've been more careful. It might've been a letter bomb for all I knew.

But I opened it and looked inside. Newspaper clippings. I unfolded them—articles from the *Corpus Christi Caller-Times* and the *San Antonio Express-News*, a few pieces printed from the national wire services. I scanned the headlines. Among the articles was a white card with a note handwritten in pencil, carefully anonymous block letters.

"Well?" Maia asked.

I showed her the note. Two simple words:

FIND HIM

"A warning," I said. "About our killer."

10

Alex crouched in the attic. He hammered the last support beam in place, but he had no illusions that it would help. The ribs of the building were trembling. Leaks were sprouting in so many places he felt like he was in the hull of the *Titanic*.

The attic was crammed with Mr. Eli's old leather suitcases. They smelled of lilacs. The old man had once been a traveler. He'd crossed Europe on trains and sailed a steamer to China. He'd visited Istanbul and Cairo. And then for reasons he never explained, Mr. Eli settled on Rebel Island, stowed his luggage, his clothes and his mementos in the attic. He threw away all his shoes except his slippers and vowed never to leave.

Above Alex's head, there was a ripping sound,

more of the mansard roof getting scoured away. Soon Mr. Eli's things would be exposed to the wind, swept off to Refugio County.

Let them get ruined, the old man would've said. *A man's better off without his baggage.*

Alex climbed down the ladder and closed the trapdoor. He stood in the hallway, his wet clothes dripping on the carpet. He should've run away from this place months ago. What the hell was he still doing here, pretending he could make things right?

He stared at the doorway of Jose and Imelda's room. It had always been the servants' room, probably as far back as Colonel Bray's time. Once, Alex's parents had lived there. His mother had been bedridden during her final years. Alex would leave the window open so she could hear the sea. The room would be filled with light, the sounds of gulls and the smell of salt. On days when his father took out the fishing boat, she would close her eyes and listen to the sound of his engine as it receded into the Gulf.

Years later, when Alex had finally gotten up the courage to leave the island, his father hadn't understood. Why join the army? Why leave the coast? Even Mr. Eli had told him it was a mistake.

There's nothing out there for you, Alex.

But they'd let him go, and it didn't take him long to realize they were right. Eventually he had come straggling home. He'd reconnected with his old friends. He'd tried to help them, the way Mr. Eli would've wanted him to.

And in exchange, he'd been deceived, betrayed, used. His fists tightened.

Alex *had* to stop trusting people. He'd thought Tres could help, but who was he kidding? He should have left this island when he first suspected the truth. Yet here he was, paralyzed. All he could do was go on fixing leaks, hoping the hotel didn't collapse around him.

He wanted to tell the Navarres the truth, at least. He owed them that much. Yet whenever he tried, the words stuck in his throat.

From the attic came an ominous creaking— wood being strained to the breaking point. But instead of going up again, Alex went downstairs.

There was one thing left he could do: one more leak he needed to fix.

11

I'd heard of Calavera and his big mistake.

No single article told the whole story. Journalistic etiquette, such as it was, prevented reporters from telling the most grisly details. But I pieced them together, inferring some things, remembering others that I'd heard from various cops.

Six months ago, Corpus Christi District Attor-ney Peter Brazos had been in the middle of a career-making case. He was prosecuting five members of a South Texas drug cartel for trafficking, kidnapping, accessory to murder. He had everything he needed for a conviction. If things went his way, Brazos would gain national attention. He could write his own ticket—a job with the state attorney's office. Maybe even a federal appointment.

On New Year's Eve, two weeks before the trial, Brazos sequestered himself at his weekend house in Port Aransas to prepare his case and collect his thoughts. This was his habit. He was well known for going on such retreats. The fact that it was New Year's Eve meant nothing to Brazos. He did not celebrate such things. He had no time for anything except his work and—as time allowed—his family.

Brazos's weekend house was in a bayside community of million-dollar homes with a boating channel between every block. There was no security. No gate, no surveillance. Island mentality. Most of the residents didn't even lock their front doors. Brazos left his retreat only twice that day, once for a jog on the beach, once for groceries in the afternoon. During one of those times, the assassin must have set his trap.

Around sunset, Peter Brazos was cooking a quiet supper for himself when he was surprised by his wife, Rachel, and their two daughters, ages nine and seven. A spur-of-the-moment decision. Daddy should not spend New Year's Eve alone. Brazos was irritated at first. Rachel knew better than to interrupt him while he was on retreat. But he couldn't stay mad at her or the girls, so he set aside work. Plans were changed. They shared a dinner of shrimp and filet mignon, chicken strips and sparkling cider for the girls. The clock ticked toward midnight. The girls tried to stay up for the television broadcast from Times Square, but they fell asleep in the master bedroom, curled between their parents. Peter Brazos kissed his wife and asked her if it would be all right if he snuck away to study his case notes one more time.

Rachel Brazos smiled. She knew her husband too well to argue. She wished him a happy New Year, and Brazos took his laptop out to the back deck.

The winter air was cool and pleasant. Across the channel, a few of the neighbors' houses were lit up for parties. That didn't bother Peter Brazos. He read through his notes and thought about how much better South Texas would be when the men he was prosecuting were finally put behind bars.

He was proud that he hadn't bowed to the pressure from nervous politicians, reluctant police, death threats from the mob. So what if these drug barons were well connected? Brazos knew the cartel had several rural sheriff's departments on their payroll, possibly a few Corpus Christi cops and city council members, too. That didn't matter. Brazos was doing the right thing.

He was relishing the idea of a conviction when the fireworks started down at the beach.

In the flickering of red and blue starbursts, something caught Peter Brazos's eye. At the edge of his dock was a small white lump that looked like an ice cube.

He wasn't sure why, but he set down his computer and went to see what the thing was. A tiny skull made from rock candy—a *calavera*, like children got for treats on the Day of the Dead. Brazos picked it up and stared at it, baffled by what it was doing on his dock.

Then something began nagging at the back of his mind—stories he'd heard. A hired killer. A calling card at the scene of a crime. But those kinds of hits happened to Mafia informants, people on the other side of the law . . .

Later, he would blame himself for those precious seconds he wasted, paralyzed by disbelief, before he ran toward his house and shouted his wife's name.

As his house erupted in flames.

By the next afternoon the overwhelmed Port Aransas Police Department had turned the arson investigation over to the FBI.

Lab techs found evidence of six incendiary devices in the house. The wiring was consistent with the type of device used by the most notorious hired assassin in South Texas—a man known only as Calavera. High-grade materials, completely untraceable, timed to explode precisely at midnight. The work of a craftsman. Only this time, the craftsman had missed his mark.

The agent in charge's comments to the press were cryptic, but she couldn't help revealing some of her rage. The explosion was needlessly elaborate. The assassin was an incompetent show-off. Now a mother and two children were dead.

But Peter Brazos didn't believe this assassin was incompetent. The explosion should've worked. The assassin had studied Brazos, knew exactly where he would be. The only thing Calavera hadn't counted on was Rachel and the girls' spur-of-the-moment visit, an act of love.

The murder method had been superbly chosen. It had been meant to send a message to other prosecutors in a way that a simple bullet through the eyes wouldn't do: *Try to touch us, and we will burn you to the ground.*

Brazos did not quit his drug cartel case. His grief enraged him. His rage made him determined. He prosecuted the South Texas Mafia leaders with redoubled vigor because he knew they would blame the assassin for not doing his job. They hadn't gotten what they paid for.

Calavera, who had acted with impunity for years and carried out dozens of hits, had finally screwed up.

I passed the articles to Maia.

While she read them, I looked again at the handwritten note:

FIND HIM.

I wanted to open our door and yell down the hallway, *Find him your own damn self!*

But I doubted that strategy would work.

Maia looked up. "You've heard of this Calavera?"

"Some. Just stories."

"Two little girls. Nine and seven."

"Yeah." I suddenly wished I hadn't shown Maia the articles. Her eyes had that steely glint they got whenever she wanted to beat up someone—like me, for instance.

"Tres, if this is the guy Marshal Longoria was after, and if he's in the hotel—"

"What the hell would he be doing here? And who slipped me this note?"

Maia was about to say something when there was a knock on our door.

I picked up Maia's .357 again and moved to the side of the door. "Yeah?"

"Mr. Navarro?" One of the college kids. Chase, the leader.

I opened the door. Chase didn't look good. His skin was blanched and his eyes were so bloodshot they were the same color as his hair. He had that consternated expression that comes from trying to solve problems while drunk.

"What's up?" I asked him.

"I just wanted..." He saw Maia. "Oh, hi."

"Hello," Maia said.

"Damn," Chase said, "you *are* pregnant."

"Chase," I said, "is there something we can do for you?"

He scratched his ear. "Um, yeah. It's my friend Ty."

"Latino kid?" I said. "Shaggy hair, looks like he's going to throw up most of the time?"

"That's him. He's not doing so well. With the

killing and the blood and all...there's something I thought you should—"

The building groaned like a sailing vessel listing in a storm. There was a crashing sound. The floor shuddered.

"What the hell was that?" Chase asked.

"I don't know," I said, "but we'd better go see. This night just keeps getting better."

As it turned out, there was nothing to worry about. Part of the second story had caved in, collapsing onto a ground-floor bedroom on the west side of the house, but no one had been staying there. Maia, Chase and I found Alex Huff busily sealing the door to the destroyed room with extra lumber and plastic tarp.

"Hated that room anyway," Alex grumbled.

"Damn," Chase said. "A whole room collapsed? Damn!"

"We're gonna have dinner," Alex said, wiping the grime off his forehead. "In the dining room. You know...everybody. A nice, late dinner. Jose figured out the food."

The wild look in his eyes bothered me.

"Chase," I said, "why don't you go get your buddies and we'll meet you in the dining room."

"But, um—"

"It's all right," Maia assured him. She gave him her I'm-practicing-to-be-a-mother smile. "We'll talk later. Go get your friends."

Chase nodded with reluctance. "All right. But

that guy Garrett's up there teaching Markie to slam tequila. Not sure I can tear them away."

"We need to talk," I told Alex.

"I don't have time, Tres. I've got this demolished room, no electricity, and the guests—"

"Alex." Maia used her best calm, lawyerly voice. "We have a problem."

"A problem?" He laughed in a brittle way. "You don't say."

Maia showed him the envelope with the newspaper clippings. I explained to him about the attempt on Peter Brazos's life, the murder of his wife and children.

Alex looked at us like we were explaining a technical diagram in Japanese. "What does that have to do—"

"The assassin is called Calavera," I said. "He leaves a candy skull at the scene of every hit."

"An assassin. Candy. Did Garrett put you up to this?"

"Look, Alex, Calavera is real. He's done dozens of hits. All of them explosions. Mostly he works for the drug lords, silencing informants. Knocking off the competition. He took down the leader of a Juárez cartel about a year ago. Then he tried to kill Peter Brazos. You sure you haven't heard about this?"

Alex shook his head, but I could tell his mind was going a million miles an hour.

"The explosion was in Port Aransas," Maia said.

"It must've been big local news. Surely you heard about it."

"Maybe—maybe I've heard the name Brazos or something. But an assassin? Why would someone give those articles to you? What does it have to do with anything?"

"Someone apparently thinks Calavera is here," Maia said.

"That's nuts."

"Jesse Longoria came here for a reason," I said. "We found Chris's business card and a candy skull in Longoria's suitcase. I think Chris tipped him off that Calavera would be here. Today. June fifth."

"Look, Tres. I can't..." Alex ran his hands through his hair. His fingers were trembling. "I can't handle this right now, okay? The hotel is falling apart around my ears."

"You haven't found Chris?"

"Not a sign. The guy's disappeared."

"Then I'm glad you arranged a dinner," I said. "We need to warn the others. They need to know."

"You're going to scare the hell out of everyone because someone slipped an envelope under your door?"

"Alex, if this guy Calavera *is* trapped on the island, he's got no way off until the ferry tomorrow night."

"Well, I guess, unless—"

"He can't afford to have anybody get in the way of his escape."

"What are you saying? He's going to kill us all?"

"That's what I would do," Maia said.

Alex and I both stared at her.

"If I were a cornered assassin," she amended.

Alex shook his head miserably. "A nice dinner. All I wanted was a nice dinner to take everyone's mind off things."

He ripped off another piece of duct tape, slapped it across the doorway like a bandage, then trudged off down the hall.

"He's hiding something," I told Maia.

"Maybe you just don't like him."

"Yeah, I don't like him. But he's also hiding something. He used to make fireworks when he was a teenager. Fuses. Timers."

"Tres, a hit man using explosives and a kid playing with fireworks are two very different things. Something *is* a little fractured about Alex. I'll give you that. But he doesn't seem dangerous."

"I don't believe he's never heard of Calavera."

"What if he's the one who gave you the articles?"

"That doesn't make sense either," I said. "I don't think Alex reads."

Maia rolled her eyes. "You really *don't* like him."

The plastic and boards and duct tape billowed and creaked against the ruined door, like some kind of artificial lung. I wondered if it was my imagination, or if the wind sounded like it was lessening a bit.

"If Calavera is here," Maia said, "he'll need to leave. And if he knows that we know he's here—"

"Somebody knows." I tapped the envelope in her hand. "And Longoria was shot. We have to assume Calavera is already desperate."

"He can't have us raising the alarm. He can't risk getting quarantined on this island."

"Yeah."

"We're in serious danger. All of us."

"Pretty much."

She took my hand. "Want to go to dinner?"

"Yeah," I said. "Dinner sounds good."

12

Benjamin Lindy pointed his gun at the mirror.

How had he gotten so old? He recognized his eyes, sharp as ever, but his hair was thin and ghostly white. His face looked like the moon's surface, all scars and craters. The year he'd met his wife, 1963, seemed like yesterday. So did his daughter's birth. How had he allowed so many years to pass? To get this old and have nothing to show for it...Nothing but desolation, the loneliness of having outlived everyone he'd ever cared about.

The gun shook in his hand. He swung it to the left, then the right. He found that if he did this, he could swing the barrel back to center and find his mark. He'd practiced on the ranch, just to be sure.

Thunder shook the mirror and his reflection rippled. He lowered his hand. He hadn't realized how tight his finger had been on the trigger.

The photo album lay open in front of him. All the happy moments were there. He tried to concentrate on them, but what he saw were other scenes: faces from photographs he'd burned. He saw his wife the day she left. The sun caught her hair and turned it from brown to gold. She wore a white cotton dress that showed off the freckles on her shoulders.

The baby was crying in the house, but Benjamin ran out the front door, after his wife. She didn't turn when he called to her, but he caught her in the driveway and tried to grab the suitcase—the same brown leather case she'd taken to Italy on their honeymoon. It spilled open and her few possessions tumbled out—a few extra dresses, some lingerie he'd never seen. The only thing he recognized: a photograph taken of her on vacation, standing in front of the Bray Mansion on Rebel Island.

"Goodbye, Ben," she said.

He was too stunned to stop her as she got in the car, leaving her things behind on the front lawn. Afterward, what stuck in his mind were her earrings: silver seashells. She never wore the jewelry he gave her. But she was wearing those, a gift from another man.

I told you not to trust her, Jesse Longoria's voice spoke in his head.

Longoria thirty years ago, sitting in his San

Antonio office, cigarette smoke swirling through the hot light slanting through the window. He looked smug and confident in his caramel suit, his eyes black as a crocodile's. Longoria had counseled revenge.

You let her walk out on you . . . You're going to live with the fact that she's laughing at you every day, sharing another man's bed, raising his children instead of yours?

Benjamin had refused, but the words irritated him for years, like a grain of sand at the core of a pearl. And this spring, he had called Longoria again.

This time, Longoria said, *we do it my way.*

Benjamin remembered the hotel staff dragging Longoria's body through the kitchen on a plastic tarp. Longoria's eyes had still glittered darkly, as if being alive or dead made absolutely no difference to him. The gunshot wound was right where a tie clip should have been.

So much for doing it Longoria's way.

Benjamin heard footsteps in the hallway outside his room. "Mr. Lindy?"

It was one of the college boys: the burly one, Markie. The boy seemed like the calmest of the three, the most polite, but there was a cruel light in his eyes that Benjamin didn't trust. Markie reminded him strongly of a young Jesse Longoria.

"You lose your way, son? The liquor cabinet is in the parlor."

Markie's eyes registered the gun. "Dinnertime, sir. You want me to say you're not coming?"

"I'm coming," Benjamin said.

He set down the gun. He closed the photo album, still seeing the picture that he'd burned long ago: his wife smiling in front of the Rebel Island Hotel, smiling for another man.

13

I had to give Jose and Imelda credit. It's difficult to set an elegant dinner with the dining room
windows boarded up and the floor littered with
broken glass, but they'd done their best.

Most of the furniture had been scooted aside,
leaving one large table with clean white linen and
settings for ten. Apparently Jose and Imelda would
not be sitting with us, which I thought a bit formal
for a natural disaster. On the other hand, two more
chairs would've brought our number to twelve, like
the disciples, and I wasn't anxious for this meal to
resemble the Last Supper.

No electricity, so the food was nothing fancy—
bean tacos, Vienna sausage and crackers, apples
and cheese, still-cold beer, wine, bottled water.

As Maia and I took our places, Mr. Lindy was in deep conversation with one of the college guys—the big bald one, Markie, who looked like a bodyguard version of Humpty Dumpty. Lindy was drawing on a napkin, showing him something like a football diagram. Garrett was telling Lane Sanford a joke, and Lane was actually trying to smile. Alex Huff was pouring Chase a glass of wine, explaining the difference between merlot and pinot noir, and Chase was looking very confused. Imelda and Jose bustled around setting out plates and trying to keep candles lit, since the flames kept sputtering and dipping. There was no dinner music, but the storm against the plywood provided a rhythm track of pops and thuds and atonal moans.

There were two empty seats. One for our missing manager Chris Stowall, I guessed, and the other . . . Ty, the third college guy, was also not here. Maybe I shouldn't have put off Chase when he wanted to talk about his friend.

Once everyone was served sausage and fruit and wine, Alex got to his feet and tapped his glass with a fork.

He'd taken a few minutes to wash up. He'd bandaged his cuts, so his face now looked like it had been properly barricaded for the storm. "Well, here's to . . . making the best of it."

"And the body in the basement," Markie added. Alex winced.

"Hey, c'mon," Garrett said. "Everybody relax. Listen outside. The storm's lightening up."

"That is the eye coming ashore, señor," Jose said as he refilled Garrett's glass.

Everybody looked at him.

"I have been in hurricanes before," Jose explained uncomfortably. "That is the eye."

"Well, whatever it is," Alex said, "we can use the break. We need a little time to just relax and forget about . . . you know."

He glanced at me, silently pleading. Being the heartless guy I am, I said, "We shouldn't relax."

Now everybody looked over at me. I had a general idea how a cancer doctor must feel coming into a waiting room. Nobody wanted to hear what I had to say.

"Somebody slipped this under my door." I set the envelope on the table. "It would be helpful to know who."

Facial expressions are important. In those first few seconds, I tried to register everyone's. Alex I'd already tested, and unless I had completely misread him, the envelope was a total mystery to him.

Chase looked confused and uneasy, but he'd looked that way before. His friend Markie glared at me, holding his fork like a dagger. Benjamin Lindy narrowed his eyes. He barely glanced at the envelope, and seemed much more interested in what I might be thinking. Lane Sanford looked terrified, as if her ex-husband might leap out of the envelope at any moment. And Jose and Imelda . . . they stood in the background, trying to be inconspicuous, but I saw them glance at each other. I wasn't sure what they were communicating.

"A death threat?" Garrett asked me. "The killer wrote to you?"

"This isn't from the killer," I said. "This is *about* the killer, a man called Calavera."

Again I checked everyone's reaction. I couldn't tell much.

Jose cleared his throat. "Señor, this is the... *hit man* they talk about?"

"Who's they?"

"Everyone, señor. The newspapers, sometimes."

"I know who you're talking about," Mr. Lindy told me. "Calavera the assassin. He kills with explosives."

"Did you ever work on a case that involved him, sir?"

Lindy shook his head. "I retired long before he started. But I know the name. I know he's murdered many innocent people. You believe he's here?"

I felt the weight of everyone's eyes on me. I knew how badly they wanted me to say no.

"I'm not sure," I admitted. "But someone... probably someone at this table, gave me this information for a reason."

I told them about the newspaper articles and showed them the message: *FIND HIM*.

"That's *my* hotel stationery." Alex looked offended.

"Wait a second," Garrett said. "So now we're looking for two people. We got a killer. And we got somebody who wants to find the killer."

I nodded. As reluctant as I was to admit my

brother was capable of logical thinking, he'd pretty much nailed it.

"So we got two empty chairs," Garrett said. "Where's the Mexican kid? What's his name?"

"Hey, Ty ain't no killer," Markie growled. "That's bullshit."

"Well, what about that Chris guy?" As soon as Garrett said that, Lane stiffened next to him. "He ran the hell away as soon as the marshal was shot. Hasn't been back yet. How much you know about this guy, anyway, Alex?"

"He's a local," Alex said. "I've known him since he was like six. There's no way he could kill anybody."

Garrett scratched his beard. "Well, then, where the hell is he? And where's the other dude? Ty?"

Chase shifted uncomfortably. "I tried to say something *privately* to Navarre. That didn't work."

"It's all right, Chase," Maia said. "What did you want to say?" She did a better job sounding soothing than I would have.

Chase scowled. "Ty's claustrophobic."

Garrett snorted.

"This ain't a joke, man," Markie piped up. "We brought him here thinking he could get over it, you know? It's been a nightmare. He's been drinking for two days just to keep from flipping out. Being on a damn island was bad enough, but now with the boarded-up windows, the storm, being trapped inside...he's really starting to crack."

"Where is he?" Alex asked. He sounded stunned

that anybody could be unhappy staying on his island.

"He ran out of the room about half an hour ago," Chase said. "I thought maybe he just needed to walk the halls or something, get some air. I didn't want to embarrass him by making a big deal about it, but..."

"But?" I prompted.

"He wants off this island bad," Chase said. "Bad enough to do something crazy."

"There's no way off," Maia said.

Jose and Alex exchanged jittery looks.

"What?" I asked.

"There is the fishing boat," Jose said. "In the boathouse behind the hotel."

I stared at Alex. "That's still there? Why didn't you mention this before?"

"Ah, hell, Tres. It's just a little charter fishing boat. It ain't no good in choppy surf. It hasn't even got a full tank of gas."

"But, señor," Jose said, "if a man were desperate—"

I cursed, then asked Jose to cover my sausage and bean tacos for later.

"Come on," I told Chase and Markie. "We've got some hiking to do."

Outside, the wind and rain had died to almost nothing. The air smelled so clean and charged with electricity it hurt to breathe. The night was unnaturally black—no city glow, no stars. But I could feel the presence of storm all around us, like the walls of a well.

Chase, Markie and I all had flashlights. We wore attractive black plastic garbage bags as rain ponchos. As we trudged around the side of the hotel, the beams of our flashlight snagged weird images— dead shrimp sprinkled in the sea grass, a child's orange life vest half buried in the sand, an uprooted palmetto, an outboard motor wedged upside down in the dunes, its propeller spinning lazily.

And footprints—fresh footprints sunk deep in the wet sand. They led toward the west shore of the island, where a covered boathouse extended on pylons over the water.

A faint light flickered in the window.

"Does Ty know how to drive a boat?" I asked.

Chase shook his head. "But that wouldn't stop him. I mean, the poor guy was freaking."

"We gotta yell before we go in," Markie warned, "so he doesn't shoot us."

"Whoa," I said. "He has a gun?"

Chase nodded. "A marksman's pistol. He's a shooter on the college team. Didn't I mention that?"

Ty wasn't making much progress with the boat.

He'd partially wrestled off the tarp, which now hung from the prow like a deflated hot air balloon. He stood in the boat, trying to start the engine, despite the fact that it still sat on rails, five feet above the water.

"Yo, Ty," Chase said. "Come on down, dude."

Ty's expression wasn't much different from the many bail jumpers I'd nabbed over the years—cornered, desperate, more than a little dangerous.

"Help me with this," he pleaded. "I gotta get out of here."

"Ty," I said. "You can't. You'll die out there."

"The storm's calming down! I can make it easy. I *have* to get out of this place."

Markie belched, which I guess was meant to be a gesture of sympathy. "Dude. Ty, c'mon. The eye's passing over us, is all. You'll never make it. Look at the fricking water under you."

Sure enough, in the launching slip, green water was sloshing around, splashing everywhere. The boathouse floor was slick. The supplies strewn about the boathouse were soaked. On a nearby worktable was a red canvas duffel bag.

"I tell you what, Ty," I said, "come back into the house for fifteen minutes. Just fifteen minutes. We can sit and talk. If the storm is still dying down when we're finished, you can come back down here and I'll help you launch the boat. If the storm gets worse, you'll stay until the morning. And then we'll see."

Ty's left eye twitched. I tried to picture him on a firing range, shooting in a competition. It was a troubling image.

"I can't breathe in there," he said. "I can't go back in that house."

"Just fifteen minutes," Markie said. "Come on, dude. That's fair. I'll get you a drink."

"I'll need a bottle," Ty said. His face was beaded with sweat.

"Sure," Chase agreed. "You can't start that boat by yourself, anyway. You're a screwup with engines."

Ty took a shaky breath. He started climbing down.

"You can take him inside?" I asked Markie. "I want to look around for a second."

"No problem." Absolute confidence. I started wondering if maybe there was more to Markie than the ability to belch.

Ty got out of the boat. "Only fifteen minutes," he reminded me. "Start counting."

"I will," I promised. "And, Ty, if you've got your gun..."

He blinked. "My gun? Not with me. It's...back in my room?"

I didn't like the way he made it into a question. I looked at Markie. "Find it."

"Yeah, sure."

"And don't touch it. Put it in a bag or something. Bring it to me for safekeeping."

Markie raised an eyebrow, but then he nodded and led Ty away.

"Hold up," I told Chase.

I walked him over to the worktable and showed him the canvas bag. "Is this Ty's?"

"Never seen it before. Why?"

A new red duffel bag in the middle of grimy bait

buckets and tackle boxes and mildewed coils of rope. It was packed full, and what bothered me most were the shapes pressed against the canvas, like the bag was filled with bricks.

I unzipped the top. Cash—twenties and fifties, all neatly bundled.

"Whoa," Chase breathed. "How much—"

"Quick estimate? About twenty thousand."

"Dude. What's it doing sitting out here?"

"Good question." I fingered the old airline tag on the shoulder strap. It was an address different from Rebel Island, someplace in Corpus Christi. But I recognized the name. "Christopher Stowall," I said.

Chase swore. "That little turd. Stowall stashed this cash here? How the hell—"

"I don't know," I said. "But twenty thousand... It's time I searched his room. I should've done that before."

"Yeah," Chase said. "If there's more money in there we can, like, split it fifty-fifty."

I stared at him.

"What?" he said defensively.

I turned and studied the fishing boat—the only way off the island. In the choppy water, the reflection from my flashlight beam looked like a fire. Like flames in the window of a burning house.

"Chase," I said, already regretting what I was about to do. "I need your help with one more thing."

14

Lane could still feel the impression of her wedding band, a month after she had thrown it into the sea. She massaged her fingers, trying to get rid of the cold and tightness.

Garrett placed his hand on hers. "Hey, it's gonna be all right."

She studied his face. He was unlike any man she'd ever known, and not just because he was an amputee. She'd gotten over that, because he seemed so completely comfortable without legs. He sat in his wheelchair like it was a throne—a source of power. He wasn't attractive in any conventional way. His teeth were crooked and his gray-brown hair was a rat's nest. He had a potbelly and didn't seem to care much whether or not his Jimmy Buffett T-shirt had margarita stains on it. But he had nice eyes—surf green, full of humor and warmth. He smelled like patchouli and wood smoke. She liked the roughness of his hands and his gravelly voice.

"Things haven't been all right for me for a long time," she said.

"Hell, you don't know my brother," Garrett told her. "He's gotten me out of worse shit than this. I'm telling you, if there's a killer here, Tres'll find him."

If there's a killer here.

A wave of guilt surged through her. She kept thinking the burden would get easier, but every day, month after month, it just got worse. She couldn't close her eyes without seeing the dead man's face. He had smiled as she served him lunch. She remembered the knife, freshly sharpened for cutting apples...

"You know what you need?" Garrett asked.

Lane forced herself back to the present. "What?"

"A tropical vacation in my room."

In spite of herself, she smiled. "I'm not sure I know you that well."

"Trust me," Garrett said. "You'll find out plenty."

His room was strangely personal for a hotel room. The walls were decorated with posters of the Caribbean and the Florida Keys. They reminded Lane of Chris and how much he loved beaches, but she kept that to herself. On the dresser, Garrett had set up a full bar—rum, tequila and triple sec, glasses, a blender, a bucket of ice. He'd hung different-colored Hawaiian shirts on the shuttered windows. Music played from a little battery-operated stereo: Jamaican steel drums and guitar. A dozen votive candles flickered on Fiestaware saucers.

"It looks like you live here," she noticed.

"My favorite room. I come here a few times a year. Alex lets me keep it the way I like."

He mixed tequila and lime juice and triple sec over ice in a carafe, stirred it and poured. "Margarita of the gods. No salt. Cuervo white. Mexican triple sec. My brother disagrees with me about every ingredient. Thinks I'm a damn cretin."

"You sound proud."

"Of pissing off my brother? Hell, yes. *Salud!*"

The warmth of the alcohol knit into Lane's limbs. She sat in a wicker chair, facing Garrett. She listened to the Caribbean music and the rain outside.

"Earlier you were talking like you admire your brother," she said.

Garrett sipped his drink. A droplet of margarita gleamed in his beard. "Sure, I admire him. I still like to irritate him. You got siblings?"

Lane shook her head.

"Then you wouldn't understand, but that's cool. I want you to take a vacation."

"Garrett—"

He held up a finger. "No problems. No hangups. Imagine those windows are open. You're looking out at clear blue sky and a calm sea. Listen to the music. Drink your drink and relax."

Lane tried. She liked the feeling of Garrett

sitting near her, confident and calm. Then she remembered the night in the woods, her right eye
swollen shut where Bobby had hit her. Her whole
body ached. They dragged their burden into the
woods wrapped in stained blue sheets.

"You're crying," Garrett said.

"I'm sorry."

Garrett's eyebrows furrowed. "What did that
bastard husband do to you?"

Before she could answer, she heard voices in the
hall.

"—can't believe you did that," Markie was com-
plaining.

"I didn't have a choice," Chase protested. "I'm
telling you, Navarre forced me. He's a damn—"

"Shut up," Markie hissed as they passed the
room, probably noticing that the door was open.
The sound of their footsteps faded down the hall.

Garrett drained his margarita. "My brother
must be back. I'd better check on him."

"Why?" Suddenly Lane didn't want to leave the
room. She didn't want to go out there and face the
others.

"Tres is always where the trouble is," Garrett
said. "And I want to find out what's happening."

He put down his glass and held out his hand.

Tentatively, she took it. He gave her fingers a
squeeze.

"We'll continue the vacation later," he promised. "For now, let's go see what crap my little
brother has gotten himself into."

15

I was standing at Chris Stowall's dresser, going through his underwear drawer, when Garrett and Lane Sanford came in. I was about halfway through searching. So far I'd come up with nothing except underwear, and I was kind of wishing I'd worn latex gloves.

When I told Garrett what had happened at the boathouse, he arched his eyebrows. "You did *what*?"

"I scuttled the boat."

"Hold up, hold up." Garrett looked at Lane for moral support, then back at me. "You sank Alex's fishing boat. Forty thousand dollars' worth of fishing boat. And you just—"

"Opened the bilge valve and sank it," I agreed. "Now, are you going to help me search or not?"

Garrett shoved the underwear drawer closed so fast I almost lost my fingers. "ARE YOU NUTS?"

I counted to ten, trying to contain the impulse to tip him out of his wheelchair.

To my surprise, Lane interceded. "Garrett, Tres is right."

Garrett scowled at her. "Say what?"

She put her hand on his shoulder. "We can't let the killer off the island. He'll hurt more people. Right now he's trapped here. We have to keep it that way until we can contact the police." She glanced up at me. "That is why you did it . . . yes?"

"Yes," I said. I decided it was time to revise my estimation of Lane Sanford.

"Whatever, little bro," Garrett grumbled. "You're gonna be in deep crap with Alex." He nodded grudgingly toward the dresser. "What the hell are you looking for, anyway?"

"I don't know," I admitted. "Something to explain the cash in the duffel bag."

"What cash?"

I told him about the twenty grand, which was now locked in the hotel's office, thanks to Jose and Imelda. I couldn't tell whether the news surprised Lane or not.

"Damn," Garrett said. "Find one more bag like that, and you can pay Alex back for his boat."

I decided to ignore him. Being his brother, I'd had lots of practice.

"Lane," I said, "is there anything you can tell me about Chris? Anything that would help?"

"I've known Chris since high school. He's a good person. He's not a killer."

"But?"

She twisted the silver ring on her finger. "It isn't like him to disappear like this. He wouldn't do that. Something is wrong."

"He invited you here for the weekend, to get away from—"

"Yes." Her tone was clear: now was not the time to bring up her ex-husband.

"Chris didn't mention Marshal Longoria?" I asked. "Didn't make any comment to you about why he was here?"

She shook her head, but she was holding back. I could feel it as clearly as the storm outside. I glanced at Garrett, hoping he would help me out.

He took her hand protectively. "Come on, Lane. It's getting late. And, little bro, if you find anything else valuable—like more money or the keys to a Porsche or something—you might want to give me dibs on it before you destroy it, okay?"

I turned Chris's room inside out. I didn't learn much. His stuff smelled of salt water and suntan lotion. He wore size 32 jeans. He liked extra-large cotton T-shirts. He had a picture of Waikiki Beach taped on his dresser mirror. There was a surfboard behind his closet door. Next to his bed was a guitar case—nothing inside but a Yamaha acoustic and the lyrics to an old Nirvana song on a piece of crumpled notebook paper.

No weapons. No duffel bags full of money. I found no evidence that he'd been packing. The closet was full of clothes. His toiletries were all there.

In all, it seemed to be the room of a fairly simple guy who liked to surf and had taken a job that allowed him the time to do it.

Too simple. Almost always, there was something interesting to be found in anyone's personal space... I called it the jalapeño factor. You had to have that little slice of spice on the nacho.

I sat on Chris's bed and pondered that. Outside, the storm intensified. Wind battered the walls. The plywood on the window bowed in and out with a hollow popping noise.

Had I checked the bed?

I knelt down and I slipped my hand between the mattress and the box springs. My fingers brushed against a book, and I brought out Chris Stowall's diary.

I was about midway through reading it—far enough to realize I had trouble on my hands— when the college guys burst into the bedroom, Ty followed by Chase and Markie.

The good news was that Ty had found his gun. The bad news was he was pointing it at me.

"You bastard," he said. "You wrecked the boat?"

"Ty, put the gun down."

Now that his friends had caught up with him, they didn't seem to know what to do. They had their hands out, crouching like they were about to catch a ball.

"Dude," Chase said, "I tried to explain—"

"Shut up!" Ty said. "You *helped* him. You told me I could leave in fifteen minutes!"

"Ty, listen to the storm," I said. "You couldn't have gone anywhere. The wind's already too strong."

I didn't try to stand. I didn't look at the gun. I kept my eyes on Ty's, because I knew that was the best way to keep him from firing at me. Not a great way, mind you, but the best.

"You sank the boat." Ty's voice trembled. "You trapped me in this place with...with a goddamn killer. I'm gonna—"

That's when Markie hit him on the back of the head. Ty crumpled and Chase tried to catch him without much luck. Ty landed facedown on the carpet between the dresser and the bed. Markie pounced on the pistol. I checked Ty's head. He'd been hit in just the right spot to knock him out—directly behind the ear.

I looked up at Markie. "Sap your friends often?"

He opened his fist and showed it to me. "Sorry, dude. No choice."

"You always carry a roll of quarters?"

"Pretty much," he said. "You never know."

Ty moaned.

"Find him a place to lie down," I told them. "Not in here. And get him some ice."

"Guess I messed up," Chase murmured, "telling him about the boat."

Markie snorted. "You guys are whacked, wrecking the only way off the island."

"The killer may have been planning to use the boat," I said. "I don't want him to have options."

Markie studied me. "Dude, you ever hear about cornering wild animals?"

Once the guys had dragged Ty away, I finished reading Chris Stowall's journal. He wasn't a prolific diarist. The entries were sometimes six months apart. Then he would write daily for a week. Then he'd lose interest again. He wrote about wave conditions. He made plans to move to Hawaii, where he'd apparently been once before on spring break. He had dreams of taking some girl named Amy there. They'd start a surf shop. At the bottom of the entry, he wrote: *I wish it was Lane.*

No explanation.

He made some vague references to a brother, whom he affectionately called "the psycho." He drew pictures of seagulls and guitars. He wrote lines that might've been song lyrics. They were pretty bad.

He also talked a lot about Alex Huff, and how much they hated each other. According to Chris, Alex went on drinking binges about once a month. If there were guests on the island, Chris would have to scramble to keep Alex out of sight. Sometimes Alex left the island for days at a time and wouldn't tell anyone where he was going. When he was drunk, he'd get paranoid. He'd accuse Chris of snooping around his room, embezzling the hotel's money.

I'd quit, Chris wrote, *except I owe the bastard. I'm scared what he might do if I left. Maybe one more time, and I'll have enough to get out of here.*

I read that last line several times. I didn't like it.

The final entry seemed to contradict the earlier one. It was dated last April. It read: *He wants to sell the hotel. He thinks he can just walk away. He can't do this to me.*

In the middle of the diary, stuck between two pages, was a folded printout of an email. The date was May 5, exactly one month ago. The sender was a U.S. Marshal named Berry. I knew him vaguely. He was a higher-up in the West Texas District, based in San Antonio. Roughly speaking, he was Jesse Longoria's boss. The only time I'd met Berry, we'd discussed a deal to get a client of mine into the witness protection program.

The printout read:

```
We can talk, but it has to be
in person. Specify a time and
place.
```

Below that, apparently clipped from the email to which Berry was responding:

```
At least twelve names. Pay-
ments. Instructions. Enough to
```

put my employers in jail for a
long time. But I need ABSOLUTE
assurance. Any leak, broken
promise or hint of betrayal,
and I vanish.

I was still sitting on Chris's bed, staring at his picture of Waikiki Beach, when Alex came in and yelled, "You did WHAT to my boat?"

I didn't so much placate him as wear him down. He was too drunk and tired to do much more than yell and complain and throw Chris's clothing around.

"Damn it," he muttered at last. He sank on the bed and buried his head in his hands. "That's it. That's just about everything gone now."

I felt no satisfaction at his misery. As much as I'd begrudged him buying Rebel Island, I knew he'd be facing hundreds of thousands in repairs, assuming we weathered the storm at all. He had his life savings tied up in this hotel.

I thought about Chris Stowall's diary, his descriptions of Alex's drunken paranoia. *I'm afraid what he might do if I left.*

"Alex, when we first got here you wanted to ask a favor. What was it?"

He laughed—a broken, unhappy sound. "Doesn't matter now. I was going to ask you to help me convince Garrett."

"Of what?"

"I'm selling the island. Or I *was,* before this storm."

"Selling the island? You've wanted to own this island since—"

"I know." He stared at the boarded-up window. "I used to believe in this place. Now…I don't know, Tres. It's falling apart. This was my last weekend for guests. I have a couple of potential buyers. Thing is…I'd rather you and Garrett have it."

"What? The island?"

He nodded. "I thought Eli would've liked that. The idea of you guys keeping it running. You could do better than I did."

It seemed unnecessary to point out just how crazy that idea was. How could Alex think we'd have the money? How could he think I'd want Rebel Island? Still, I couldn't help feeling a little honored.

I remembered all the summers I'd come here before my parents got a divorce, in that small window of years when my childhood had seemed somewhat normal, before the day Alex took me out in that boat.

"Neither of us has the money," I told him. "Even if I did…there's too much history here for me. This is a goodbye visit."

I hadn't thought about it until I said it, but it was true. I'd come here to bury a lot of things—my memories of Dad, my PI work, my years as a bachelor. The whole idea of possessing this island made me feel kind of like Ty—like the walls were closing in.

A cracking noise echoed through the house. Alex closed his eyes, as if he were trying to sense where the damage was. "I'd better go check that."

"Tell me about Chris," I said. "Were you two getting along?"

He hesitated. "I told you, we've known each other forever."

I waited, but Alex didn't add anything.

"Did Chris have a personal computer?"

"He used the office computer," Alex said. "That's it, I think."

"Do you have one?"

"A computer? Hell, no. I hate the things. Chris did most of my spreadsheets and stuff."

"I need to check the office."

"The power's out. Computer won't work."

"I still want to look around. Maybe sift through paperwork, any printouts Chris might have made."

"You're not thinking Chris murdered that marshal."

"I don't know." I held his eyes. I didn't mention the cash in the duffel bag. If Alex had heard about it, he didn't mention it either.

"All right," he said. "I'll get Jose to show you. He helped Chris sometimes. Knows more about computer stuff than I do, anyway."

He took a deep breath, like he was preparing for another round of battle. "Now I gotta get upstairs. I think the damn roof just blew away."

16

Maia hated the staircase. It seemed to get steeper every time she climbed it. She wasn't sure why Imelda decided to escort her, but she welcomed the help. Imelda held her arm, steadying her, encouraging her when she was out of breath.

"I feel like an invalid," Maia said.

"You are doing well, señora. Someday you will tell your child about this weekend."

"He's never going to hear the end of it."

"It is a boy?"

Maia stopped for a breath. "Imelda, I don't know. I just started calling him 'him.' I think so."

"My *abuela* used to dream the gender of babies before they were born. She told me—" Imelda stopped herself. "She was never wrong."

"About your own children?" Maia asked.

Imelda nodded reluctantly. "We are almost to the top, señora. A few more steps."

They took the rest of the climb in silence. Maia imagined she was back at the house in Southtown, just going upstairs to the bedroom. No storm. No killers.

Her doctor had thought she was crazy for agreeing to this trip. Tres didn't understand either.

"It's just Garrett," Tres had told her. "We can say no. Hell, we *should* say no."

But Maia had convinced him to accept. The last few months she'd felt stifled. Not by the house or by her marriage or even by her decision to put her legal career on hold. She felt claustrophobic within her own skin. Just her and the baby, stuck in here for so many months, waiting.

The idea of going somewhere new, seeing a place that was part of Tres's past, had intrigued her. Especially since it was a place Tres had never mentioned before. Not even once.

"You spent every summer here?" she'd asked.

He nodded reluctantly.

"And...did what?"

"You know. The usual stuff kids do at the beach."

Maia imagined things from movies and books, or things she'd witnessed at the beach when she was an adult. Her childhood had had no beaches. No family vacations. Her only escape as a child had been climbing the mulberry tree to get away from the misery in her family's one-room shack, her father's depression and her brother's illness.

"I want to see Rebel Island," she'd decided.

"No," Tres said. "You really don't."

But the more he tried to dissuade her, the more curious and determined she'd become. With Tres, she always felt as if she were fighting to keep hold, always competing with his roots here in Texas, a place she had never understood. She was determined to weave herself into his territory, to be part of his landscape.

Even after all that had happened this weekend, Maia did not regret her choice. She just wished she understood why Tres disliked this old hotel and Alex Huff so much.

Imelda helped her into the suite. She turned down the bed, but Maia didn't feel like lying down. She walked a slow circuit around the room, steadying her breathing. Water dripped from the ceiling, falling into the cup she'd placed on the dresser. The candle sputtered on the nightstand.

"Señora, do you need anything?"

"Probably many things," Maia admitted. "Can you tell me how you came here?"

Imelda blinked. "To the hotel, señora? We used to live in Nuevo Laredo. It became too dangerous. We came north to Corpus Christi because I had a cousin there. We were very lucky to find Señor Huff."

Maia didn't ask if Imelda and Jose were in the country illegally. In South Texas, she'd learned, that was like asking someone what denomination of Christian they were. It hardly mattered.

"And how did you find Alex Huff?"

Imelda smoothed out the comforter, trying to make the corners perfect. "By chance. Jose had been working construction, but work was slow. We went to the fireworks, for the Fourth of July, to cheer him up. They have fireworks at the beach in Corpus Christi. Señor Huff was there, next to us, and he began telling Jose how the fireworks were made. Jose...he liked Señor Huff immediately. They both liked the fireworks. By the end of the night, Señor Huff had offered us jobs at the hotel."

From the little Maia had seen of Alex, she could believe he'd do something impulsive like that. Chris Stowall, the manager, had struck her as a similar hardship case Alex had taken in. Still, something about Imelda's story seemed incomplete.

"Imelda," Maia said. "Your grandmother—your *abuela*. What did she dream about your children?"

The maid's face darkened. "Señora, I should go. The other guests..."

She closed the door behind her so carefully the latch didn't even click.

Maia stood at the dresser. She looked at the old photo hanging on the wall. It was black-and-white, in a frame made from pieces of driftwood. Tres hadn't said a word about the photograph, and so at first Maia had paid it no attention. She assumed it was just another rustic decoration, no different from the stuffed fish or the nets with seashells. But when she studied it, she realized the photo was much more.

It showed three men standing at the docks, the mansion looming behind them on a gray morning. The man in the middle had white hair and milky skin. He wore a dark robe over what looked like pajamas, as if he'd just been dragged out of bed. He squinted in the light and his posture was stiff. The man on the left was a little younger, mid-forties perhaps, with a weathered face and sad eyes. He wore a Greek fisherman's cap and a plaid shirt and faded jeans, and he held a boat line in his hand. He had Alex Huff's crooked smile and beak nose. Alex's father, Maia guessed. The third man dominated the picture. He was a large man in a crisp white shirt and dark slacks, eyes as black as gun barrels. He smiled, but there was no kindness in it. His face was flushed from drinking. A lawman—Maia could see that just from his posture, the expression of power. He was used to people getting out of his way. He had Tres's face—but so different. It was Tres without his sense of humor, his self-doubt or his kindness. Maia had known Tres for years, and this was only the second or third time she'd ever seen a picture of his dead father, Sheriff Jackson Navarre.

Maia wondered why Tres hadn't even commented on the photo, or tried to remove it from the wall. She doubted it was an accident the picture was hanging here. Perhaps Alex had put it here as a reminder: *Our families are tied together.* Or maybe something less charitable. Maybe the message was more: *You owe me.*

17

Before heading to the hotel office, I reread Chris Stowall's journal. One entry caught my attention, because it was one of the few written in detail. It described how Lane Sanford had convinced Chris to take the job as Rebel Island hotel manager.

Lane Sanford had just gotten engaged. Chris was cryptic about the details, but he clearly wasn't happy.

They were walking together at the seawall in Corpus Christi. Chris didn't record the time or the weather, but he wrote very specifically about what Lane was wearing. Her sleeveless dress was pastel blue. Her sandals were decorated with cowry shells. Her hair hadn't been dyed blond yet. It was ginger brown, braided down her back.

Chris was trying to convince her that marrying Bobby was a terrible idea.

"You don't believe people can change?" Lane asked him.

"No. Look at me. I can't."

It must have been chilly, because Lane hugged her arms. Her fingernails were pink, which Chris found disturbing. She never painted her nails. She must've done it for Bobby.

"Chris, you've got to stop," Lane told him. "You can't keep doing what you're doing."

"I gave it up," he told her. But he could tell she didn't believe him.

"I know where you could get a job," Lane said. "Alex would take you in. He bought the hotel, you know."

Chris protested. Alex was an old friend, but they hadn't seen each other in years. Not since Alex had joined the army. Besides, Alex had gotten a little weird ever since his old man died. How the hell could he afford to buy Rebel Island, anyway?

"His father had some money," Lane said. "He never spent anything. And I think Mr. Eli wanted him to have the place. He sold it really cheap."

Chris didn't think much of Mr. Eli. The man had been creepy. Alex living on that island so long with just his dad and that old guy in the bathrobe—it seemed pretty damn strange.

"I've got no experience," Chris said. "Nobody would hire me."

"Alex would," Lane insisted. "He believes in

giving people a chance. He's got big plans for the hotel."

She took out a business card and pressed it into Chris's hands. He paid a lot more attention to the warmth of her fingers than he did to the card.

"Just call him for me?" she asked.

Chris gazed at the waves, thinking about surfing, how he would like to be out there riding the crests. Things were simpler in the water. The waves came to you. You just needed patience and balance. You didn't need to think too much, or prove anything. You didn't get in trouble just because you wanted to make some money.

"I'll call him," Chris promised.

A week later, Chris wrote: *I took the job. It'll only be for a while. Besides, I've got an idea. I could have enough money for Hawaii in a few months.*

The hotel office looked like a hurricane had blown through, though it was one of the few rooms where the hurricane hadn't.

Paperwork was strewn everywhere. Notes and old photographs overflowed the bulletin board. There were a wall calendar and two desk calendars, and as far as I could tell none of them was for this year.

"Here, señor." Jose handed me the phone bill from last month.

"Please," I said, "just call me Tres."

Jose had a quick, natural smile that would've gotten him labeled impertinent in school or the military. He probably didn't find anything particularly funny. His mouth was just shaped that way. He was built like a wrestler, low and thick and solid, with hands that could've crushed rocks. But his smile and the gleam in his eyes made him look nonthreatening. Almost cuddly.

I decided not to share that observation with him.

I scanned the list of calls from the hotel's land line. Most were to Port Aransas or Aransas Pass. Some to Corpus, Kingsville, San Antonio, Brownsville. All the closest metropolitan areas. The places you might expect.

"Can you tell which room dialed which number?" I asked.

Jose looked at the phone bill. "No, señor."

"How about cell phones? Does Chris have one?"

"I think, yes. But mobile phones do not work on the island."

"Don't suppose you have any idea where his might be?"

Jose shook his head. "*Lo siento*, señor."

I stared at the dark computer screen. No way to access the thing. I found some printed-out emails, but nothing interesting. Confirmed bookings. Catering invoices. Responses to creditors and guests. It looked like Chris had written most of the hotel's correspondence. There was nothing that matched the printout from U.S. Marshal Berry.

"Jose, how long have you worked here?"

"Two years, señor, in July."

"You like it?"

"The work is good. I enjoy preparing the brunches on Sunday. Usually, I make better than Vienna sausages."

I went back to the phone numbers. Something about them nagged me but I couldn't pinpoint what.

"Did Chris hire you?" I asked.

"No, señor." A hint of distaste in his voice. "Mr. Huff hired me. Mr. Stowall came later."

It seemed weird for Jose to be calling a young twerp like Chris "Mr. Stowall."

"They treat you okay?" I asked. "Chris and Alex?"

"Yes, señor. They have been most kind to me and Imelda."

Something in his voice—as if it were difficult to say Imelda's name. "You *are* married, aren't you?"

"Yes, sir."

I noted the shift from *señor* to *sir*. His tone had become guarded, maybe a little obstinate.

I decided not to press him further. For one thing, I wasn't sure it would do any good. Also, I wasn't sure it would be wise. Despite the smile, there was an undercurrent to Jose that I didn't quite understand.

I looked back at the phone numbers. Corpus Christi, Kingsville, San Antonio.

"Jose, do you have the registration cards for this weekend's guests?"

"At the front desk, sir." He looked relieved to have an excuse to go. "I will get them."

• • • •

While I waited, I stared at one of the photos on the bulletin board: Alex Huff as a teen, squatting at the dock with a rope curled in his hands. The boat in the photo wasn't anything like the forty-thousand-dollar one I'd just scuttled. It was a simple twenty-footer—the same boat Alex had once taken me fishing in. Despite all the time that had passed, the sight of it still unsettled me.

That afternoon, twenty-five years ago, the sky had been clear and bright. We took the boat out so far Rebel Island seemed to sink into the sea. The water was green as chlorophyll, hot with the smell of salt and fish. In the distance, a shrimp boat trailed its nets, a mob of seagulls circling above the wake.

"Bait your hook," Alex told me.

He'd brought a bucket of live shrimp—translucent gray things that snapped and jumped in the lukewarm water.

I hated the way they felt—like slimy fingernails. My twelve-year-old mind couldn't comprehend why adults would ever want to eat these things. I pinched one between my fingers and proceeded, grimly, to impale it on the hook, its crescent body just the right shape.

Put the point through the brain, my father would've advised me. *That little black dot. Don't worry. It can't feel anything.*

I had trained myself to bait a hook without flinching. But whenever I did so, I felt like I was deadening my own brain—forcing myself not to feel. It was just a stupid shrimp. Its entire nervous system consisted of a gray line and a black dot in a colorless body. Why should I care?

Alex cast his line. "Old man giving you a hard time?"

He sounded almost sympathetic, but I didn't trust him. I was pretty sure this was some kind of setup, a prank that Alex and Garrett would laugh about later. Yet I didn't want to go back to the island. I didn't want to see my parents.

"Didn't they tell you?" Alex asked.

"Tell me what?"

He studied me. "Not my place. Ask Garrett."

He might as well have told me to ask God. I figured I'd be more likely to get an answer.

We fished until the sun began to slant into my eyes. Alex hadn't brought any bobbers, so I couldn't tell if I got any bites. He said he didn't believe in bobbers. He could feel a tug on the line just fine. Couldn't I?

The ocean toyed with me, plucking my line like a guitar string. Every swell was a false alarm. I reeled in and found my shrimp still impaled on the hook.

I had just recast when something scraped against the hull. At first I thought we'd run into a sandbar. Then I looked off the port side and saw the beige tip of a fin going underwater.

"Shark," Alex told me calmly.

I dropped my fishing pole as if it had become an electrical line. I scrambled away from it, trying to get to the dead center of the boat.

"What are you doing?" Alex demanded.

"Shark," I repeated.

"Jesus." Alex leaned over and saved my fishing rod from getting dragged into the water. "We're in a fishing channel. Lots of blood and guts from the big boats. Of course there are sharks. Take your rod."

I just stared at the water. It was calm and green, no sign of anything stirring underneath. "I want to go back."

"Suit yourself." Alex reeled in my line. My shrimp had been nibbled into a fluffy gray mass. "Your parents are getting a divorce."

"What?"

"Your parents. They're getting a divorce."

"No, they're not."

Alex didn't argue. He could probably see the impact his words were having on me. For months, I'd known something was wrong: my dad's angry outbursts, my mom's evasiveness and tears. Then there'd been the scene in the hotel room.

"He's been screwing around," Alex said. "Nothing new. Garrett's known about it for years. Your dad's a drunk. A dirty old man."

"That's not true." Which was a stupid thing to say.

Alex laughed. "Whatever, Tres."

Anger built up in my throat. I'd heard Alex brush me off too many times before, whenever he and Garrett played a cruel joke on me because they were bored.

"My dad's better than *you*," I said, my voice cracking.

"Yeah?"

"I saw in the lighthouse."

I should've known from the steely light in Alex's eyes that I was entering dangerous territory. I needed to stop. "You get high and carve girls out of wood," I said. "Who were you making up there, anyway? Your girlfriend?"

Alex grabbed me by the shirt collar and pitched me headfirst into the water.

I came up spluttering. Salt water burned in my nose and my eyes stung. I dog-paddled frantically, clawing for the side of the boat. My shoes weighed a thousand pounds. I knew the shark must be close, already crazed from the smell of fish blood.

Alex looked down at me. His face was cold and harsh. "Don't ever, *ever* mention that again. You can swim home. Do you want to swim home?"

I couldn't answer. I couldn't even beg. I tried to grab the side of the boat but my hands wouldn't work.

Alex swore in disgust. He grabbed my shirt and hauled me soaked and trembling into the boat. When we got back to Rebel Island, Garrett was waiting for us on the dock, scowling as I trudged ashore dripping wet.

"What the hell happened?" he asked.

I was too ashamed to speak. When Alex explained, I expected Garrett to bust out laughing, like he'd done many times before, but this time Alex seemed to have gone too far even for Garrett.

"You fed my little brother to the sharks?" he demanded. "What the hell for?"

He and Alex began to argue. Under different circumstances, this would've pleased me. Garrett was actually standing up for me. At least he didn't think I quite deserved to be shark bait. But watching him and Alex yell at each other, all I could think of was my parents—the way they'd been at each other's throats the past few weeks, the idea that their marriage was over.

"Stop!" I yelled. "It was my fault."

I didn't wait for a reply. I ran, and I didn't stop until I reached the northern tip of the island.

Alex and Garrett stayed mad at each other the rest of the weekend. I refused to speak to either of them. I never explained to Garrett why Alex had pushed me overboard.

Neither Garrett nor Alex ever mentioned the incident again. As for me, I did not develop a lifelong fear of sharks or deep water. But I never forgot the shock of asking the wrong question of the wrong person and getting pitched headfirst into the warm sea with the blood and the sharks. For my last ten years as a private investigator, every time I interviewed someone or prodded for information, part of me was that twelve-year-old boy, and I imagined myself holding tight to the edge of the boat so I could not get surprised again.

"Señor?"

Jose was back, smiling blandly, holding the registration cards I'd asked him for. "You are fine, señor?"

"Yeah," I managed. "Great."

I took the cards and began flipping through them.

The first was in my handwriting: *Mr. & Mrs. Navarre*. I stared at it, marveling at the weirdness of there being a Mrs. Navarre.

I flipped through the other cards, went back to one of them, checked it against the phone records.

"Here," I said.

"Señor?"

"Three calls to this number from the hotel. All in the last two weeks."

"Is that bad, sir?"

"I don't know." I held up the registration card with a name, a Kingsville address and a phone number, all written in neat block letters. "But I think I should ask Benjamin Lindy."

18

Garrett found Alex in the parlor, staring at the marlin above the fireplace.

"Yo, Huff."

Alex's shirt had a tear in the back, like it had snagged on a nail. Plaster and dust speckled his curly hair. "You sure you don't want to buy this place?" he muttered. "Price is getting cheaper by the minute."

His tone reminded Garrett of another friend—a fellow programmer who'd climbed out onto the tenth-story ledge of his Bee Cave Road office in Austin after the high-tech bubble burst. The guy's voice had sounded just like that—fragile as glass— right before he jumped.

"You're gonna get through this, man," Garrett promised.

Alex turned. He was holding his old whittling knife—the knife his dad had given him for his thirteenth birthday. The blade was folded against the handle, but it still made Garrett uneasy.

"I was wrong to bring you all down here," Alex said.

"You said you needed help. I'm telling you, man. Tres can help."

"It's too late. I've screwed up too much."

Garrett remembered the body in the basement. A shiver ran up his back. Even so many years after he'd lost his legs, there were times he missed being able to run away. Down in the basement had been one of those moments. The way Tres had calmly shone a light over the dead man's face, gone through his pockets and completely ignored the dried blood and the gunshot wound in the chest—how did little Tres, the annoying kid who used to complain to Mom whenever Garrett so much as touched him, grow up being able to examine dead bodies?

"Alex, if there's something you ain't told me—"

"Shit, Garrett. You couldn't even start to guess."

"That stuff about Calavera. If you had anything to do with that—I mean, you would tell me, right?"

Alex's expression was hard to read—fear, maybe even shame. "You remember Mr. Eli's funeral?"

Garrett nodded. It wasn't one of the days he liked to remember. He'd come down to Corpus for the memorial, mostly to console Alex. There hadn't

been many people there, which had surprised
Garrett. After all the people old Mr. Eli had helped,
all the good things people said about him, Garrett
figured there would be a mob scene. But it was just
Garrett, Alex and a couple of ladies from the local
Presbyterian church who seemed to have nothing
better to do.

Afterward, Alex and he had gotten blind drunk
at the Water Street Oyster Bar.

"You promised you'd be there at my funeral,"
Alex reminded him.

"I was drunk, man. And you're really starting to
freak me out."

Alex put the knife back in his pocket. "I'm going
to get a drink."

"Don't think you need one, man."

"This coming from you? Sorry, Garrett. I need a
drink."

"Alex," Garrett called after him. "You didn't kill
anybody. You couldn't do that, right?"

Alex's eyes were as dead as the fish on the walls.
"I'm sorry I got you here, Garrett. It's gonna be just
like Mr. Eli's funeral. Nobody's even gonna remember I did anything right."

After he was gone, Garrett picked up a pillow
and threw it at the wall. That didn't make him feel
better.

He thought about how long Alex and he had
been friends. Seemed like forever. They'd gone to
concerts together, howled at the moon from the
roof of this old hotel. When Garrett had lost his
legs, Alex was the first one to come find him in the

hospital—one of the few friends that stuck with him and never made him feel like a freak. Garrett didn't like what he was seeing tonight. He wanted Alex back the way he used to be—a pain in the ass sometimes, but fun. Admirable, even. Alex was the guy who always knew the right thing to do. Hearing him talking now about screwing up—no. That was Garrett's job. Alex was supposed to be the smart one.

Suddenly Garrett wondered where Lane had gone.

They'd been apart like five minutes, and already he missed her. Alex, in the old days, would've had something to say about that. He would've warned Garrett against falling too hard. Garrett probably needed somebody to remind him of that. He had trouble thinking straight when it came to Lane.

"Hell with it," he muttered. Maybe he didn't know Alex as well as he thought. And if you couldn't know somebody after thirty damn years, who's to say you couldn't get to know somebody just as well in one day?

He wheeled himself out of the parlor and went to find Lane.

19

I finally located Mr. Lindy in a room I never knew existed—a small library on the third floor. Judging from the limestone fireplace, the place was directly above the parlor. The shelves were lined with tattered hardcover bestsellers from twenty or thirty years ago. Ludlum. Trevanian. Guy books.

Lindy sat in a leather recliner facing the door— a good defensive position. He still wore his dark suit, though he'd loosened his tie. His demeanor was so formal that even this small concession to comfort seemed like a shocking breach of decorum. He was flipping through a copy of *Field & Stream*, but I got the feeling he wasn't paying it much attention. His cologne filled the air with a faint amber scent.

"Mr. Navarre," he said.

"Mr. Lindy. We need to talk."

"Then you might as well sit down."

I sat across from him on the arm of the sofa. It was the only way I could have a height advantage.

Lindy set aside his magazine. That's when I noticed his .45 in his lap.

"If the gun bothers you," he said, "I can put it away."

He sounded courteous, but I wondered if there was a veiled warning in the offer. As if: *The gun is the least of your problems.*

"What's your interest in Calavera?" I asked.

"Aside from the fact that he may be a direct threat to our lives?"

"Aside from that."

Lindy glanced at the ceiling. Even here, in the middle of the house, I could hear the storm blowing strong. Footsteps creaked above us. I wondered if Alex was up in the attic again, blocking off some section of the roof that had been torn away.

"I'm curious," Lindy said. "What makes you believe I have a personal interest in this killer?"

"There it is again."

"What?"

"The way you said *personal.* I didn't say your interest was personal. Earlier, you said you'd retired before Calavera started murdering innocent people. *Innocent people.* Most of Calavera's hits were Mafia men. Only his last hit, his big mistake, killed innocent people. You've got some personal stake in the Peter Brazos case, the murder of Brazos's wife and daughters. You slipped that envelope under my door."

Lindy studied me, his eyes as bright as broken glass. "If you were right, would it matter?"

"What do you mean?"

"We have a murderer in this hotel. If he's allowed to leave the island, he will disappear. Now that you know who he is, you must agree he has to be caught. Given our circumstances, you may be the only one who can do that. Does it matter who gave you the information?"

His tone was calm and reasonable, but he said the word *murderer* with an intimate loathing, the way a preacher might say *Satan*.

"Why are you here?" I asked. "Why did someone at the hotel call you three times over the last week?"

"I came to fish." Lindy pointed to the *Field & Stream*.

"For Calavera?"

"I'm an old man, Mr. Navarre. I'm in no shape to track down a murderer."

Which, I noticed, was not exactly a denial. "Did you know Marshal Longoria?"

"Not well."

"Which means you did."

Lindy's gaze wobbled, as if he were looking back through decades. "I once asked his advice on a personal matter. He counseled me as best he could. That was many years ago. I wouldn't say we were friends."

"What was the personal matter?"

"I don't see that it is relevant."

"Your family?"

The muscles in his jaw tightened. "My wife."

I waited, but Lindy was not about to draw water from that well.

"You knew Longoria would be here this weekend," I said. "He had reason to think Calavera would be on the island."

"How can you be sure?"

"Chris Stowall's business card and a candy skull were in Longoria's suitcase. There was a note written on the back: *June 5.*"

"That seems slim evidence."

"I also found an email stuck in Chris Stowall's diary. Part of a correspondence between Calavera and a U.S. Marshal named Berry, Longoria's boss."

I couldn't tell if that surprised Lindy or not, but he seemed to be composing his thoughts before he spoke again. "What was the nature of this correspondence?"

"I think Calavera was negotiating surrender. He wanted to offer testimony against his employers, probably in exchange for a new identity and federal protection."

"And why would he make such a deal?"

"The Brazos hit at New Year's might've shaken him up, made him remorseful."

Lindy shook his head. "Mr. Navarre, an assassin like Calavera has no remorse. More likely his cartel employers were unhappy with his failure to kill Peter. Calavera was bargaining information to save his own worthless—"

"Peter," I noticed. "First name."

Lindy stared at me. Slowly he nodded with grudging appreciation. "You missed your calling, sir. You should have been a trial lawyer."

"I married one," I said. "That's good enough."

"If you think Calavera could be shaken up, if you think he had any conscience at all, you clearly haven't read enough." He picked up a yellowing newspaper from the table and handed it to me. It was a copy of the *Kingsville Record,* Lindy's hometown newspaper, dated almost three years ago.

Before I could ask Lindy what this happened to be doing here, there was a tentative knock on the door: the maid, Imelda, stepped into the library, looking frazzled. "Excuse me, Señor Navarre. It's your wife. I think you should come."

Maia was lying on her side, a pillow between her legs, two under her head, one hugged against her chest. She looked uncomfortable and a little pale.

"Too much excitement," she said. "That's all."

"She is having mild contractions," Imelda said. "Pre-labor."

I tried to keep my panic from showing. "Are you sure, Imelda?"

"I've had children, señor," she said, like it was a subject she preferred not to talk about. "The señora needs to rest and be very still."

"Or?"

"She might deliver."

Be calm, I told myself. *Keep it upbeat.*

"You can't deliver on Rebel Island," I told Maia. "I want our child to have U.S. citizenship."

Imelda looked confused. "But, señor, this is—"

"He's teasing, Imelda," Maia said. "Tres, the baby is fine. I'll be fine."

"We're all fine," I agreed. "Sure."

Maia sighed. "Imelda, could you find some more pillows for my husband? I think he's going into labor."

Imelda looked more confused. "But—"

"She's teasing," I said.

"*Ay,* too much teasing," Imelda scolded. "You should rest, señora. Perhaps some red-raspberry-leaf tea?"

"That sounds wonderful. Can you do that?"

"We have some in the kitchen, señora. And a portable heater for the water." She fussed with Maia's pillows a little more, then trudged off to get the tea.

"Don't go anywhere," I told Maia.

I followed Imelda and stopped her in the hallway.

"Hey," I said, keeping my voice down, "if it came down to . . . you know—"

"Delivering the child, señor?"

"Yeah. Could you help?"

She tugged nervously on her wedding ring, which I didn't figure was a good sign. "I would try, señor. But this is the señora's first child. She is older. There could be complications."

"How many children do you have?"

"I . . . two."

"Grown?"

"...No."

"Oh."

Imelda twisted the cords of her apron. She had brown hair streaked with gold and white, like marbled fudge. If her husband's face was fashioned for smiling, Imelda's was made for stoic suffering. She had the pinched expression and weathered skin of someone who might have spent her life toiling in the fields, squinting against a hot sun.

"I will help if I can," she told me. "I have done it before back in...back in Mexico. I think I could. I remember."

"Thank you."

"I will get the tea." And she shuffled off like the hot fields were waiting, just at the bottom of the stairs.

I sat on the bed and massaged Maia's feet. Her ankles looked swollen. I tried to remember what that meant. A normal thing? A danger sign? Maia and I had agreed on one thing about the childbirth process: the standard "how-to" advice and facts about what happened when stayed with us about as well as Japanese VCR instructions.

Early on, Maia had decided to listen to her body and just go with that. What the doctors had to say was too scary, anyway. She'd refused amniocentesis. Too risky. There was nothing it would tell her that she really wanted to hear.

The baby was at high risk for muscular dystrophy.

We both knew that. Maia carried the genes. Fifty-fifty chance our child would have it. The possibility of MD was like the loaded gun Maia kept in her underwear drawer, or the blackmail file she kept on her enemies. We both knew it was there. We knew it might come into play someday. But there was no use talking or worrying about it, so we didn't.

At least that was the theory.

"Take my mind off the cramps," Maia said. "Tell me what's happening."

A murderer running loose in the hotel was the last thing I wanted to talk to Maia about, but I could tell she needed distraction. Her conversational tone was forced. I'd never seen her look quite so worried, or rather try so hard not to look worried.

I kept massaging her feet as I told her about my trip to the boathouse, the bag of money, then finding Chris's diary and the email to the U.S. Marshals Service. I told her about my conversations with Jose and Benjamin Lindy.

Maia focused on my words the way she did in Lamaze class, as if this were another breathing exercise. "You really think Chris is the killer?"

"I don't know what to think. You met Chris. Does he strike you as a bomber?"

"*Bombed*, perhaps. Not a bomber."

"Exactly."

Maia pressed her toes against my hand. "But it certainly looks like Chris was talking with the marshals. And the money makes it look like he was planning an escape if things went wrong."

"If Chris brought Longoria here, why would he kill him?"

"Perhaps Longoria reneged on the deal."

"Doesn't make sense," I said. "I know this other marshal, Berry. If I were him, trying to negotiate a delicate surrender, Longoria is the last person I would send. Longoria would never let this guy Calavera skate. He'd kill him first. Berry certainly wouldn't send him alone."

"And yet Longoria came here. Alone."

I nodded. It made about as much sense to me as childbirth manuals. Or maybe I was just too tired to think. As I sat on a comfortable bed with Maia, my body was reminding me just how long it had been since I slept. I had no idea what time it was. Close to midnight, probably.

"What's in the newspaper?" Maia asked.

I looked at the copy of the *Kingsville Record* that I'd set at the foot of the bed. I'd completely forgotten about it.

"Old news from Mr. Lindy," I said. "We don't want to know."

"Sure we do," she said. "Go on."

And so reluctantly I picked up the paper. The story Mr. Lindy had wanted me to read was easy enough to find. It had been front-page news in Kingsville, three years ago.

The meeting was held in a closed club called Gatsby's on the north side of Kingsville. Someone, perhaps to prove they'd actually read the

Fitzgerald book in high school, had duplicated the eyes of Dr. T. J. Eckleburg on a billboard outside. The parking lot was marbled with weeds. The front doors were elegant mahogany with beveled glass, which did not at all fit the plain white building that might have been anything—a warehouse, a beer barn, a pawnshop.

Three cars arrived within fifteen minutes of each other. Two new Mercedes sedans, each with Coahuila license plates, and a red Ford F-350 that belonged to Papa Stoner, one of South Texas's most notorious middlemen in the heroin trade.

Stoner was sixty-two. Thirty-three of those years had been spent in prison. He was called Papa Stoner because he had a son, Eduardo, "Stoner, Jr.," who had gone on to an illustrious career as a gang leader on the South Side of San Antonio. Eduardo had been murdered by rivals shortly before his twenty-fifth birthday, but Papa was still proud of him. He'd avenged himself ruthlessly on his son's killers, and still wore Eduardo's name tattooed on his arm, encircled in snakes and flames.

Papa Stoner came to the meeting alone, unlike his guests. Mr. Orosco and Mr. Valenzuela each brought two guards. Traveling with any less would have been suicide for such important men.

They met in the restaurant's bar, which still smelled of stale beer and cigarettes and lemon furniture polish. Papa Stoner had personally inspected the place that morning. He'd found no traps, no wires. He'd taken care of bribing the right cops to make sure their meeting would not be disturbed. When you're entertaining guests from across the border, after all, you want to show them hospitality.

Orosco was the nervous one. His operation was still small. This was a bold play for him, going behind the backs of the major cartels. He dressed too well for the meeting—an Armani suit, leather shoes, a new Patek Philippe watch. His hair was parted in the middle, well oiled, so he looked a bit too much like a maître d'.

Valenzuela was older, more confident. He wore beige slacks and a white guayabera as he did every day. He was a large, messy man with unkempt hair. Everything about him suggested disorganization, but he ran one of the tightest drug operations in Central America. Not a kilo escaped his notice, and he never forgot a name or an insult.

The men talked for almost an hour. They agreed that the border war between the cartels was a major opportunity for smaller players. They could form a new pipeline, quadruple their profits within the year. With the cartels at each other's throats, the border could become a free trade area, a NAFTA for drugs.

Stoner just about had Orosco and Valenzuela convinced. Everything would be fine. They didn't need to fear reprisals. Orosco started to relax.

Lunch arrived, specially catered from Stoner's favorite Kingsville deli. The four guards took the meal boxes from the delivery boy at the door. Valenzuela and Stoner were breaking out the cold beer when Orosco's phone rang.

No one knew where he was. Only a select group of people had his mobile number. He answered the phone.

A man's voice said, "Go to the bathroom."

The line went dead.

Orosco hesitated only briefly. He'd been in the drug trade most of his life. He knew that some things went beyond logic. Most people would ignore something like a random phone call, but Orosco's gut instincts had saved him dozens of times. He excused himself from his colleagues and went to the restroom.

He was standing at the urinal when the restaurant exploded. The restroom door blew off its hinges and smoke billowed into the room. Orosco dropped to the tiles and curled into a ball. He was shivering like a child when he stood up.

He looked into the dining room, which was now in flames. Papa Stoner, Valenzuela, the bodyguards—all sprawled motionless on the floor, their clothes smoldering and peppered with holes. The walls bubbled with fire.

Orosco ran for the exit, tripping over bodies. His eyes stung with acrid smoke. He made it outside and ripped off his smoldering jacket. Thank god he had his own car keys.

He opened the door of his Mercedes and found a note on his seat, next to a sugar-candy skull.

The note said, *They are watching. Never again.*

Orosco was whimpering. His hands couldn't work the keys. He heard sirens getting closer. He had to get away. He got in the car and slammed the door. He didn't know why he'd been spared. Perhaps he was too insignificant to the cartels. Perhaps they wanted him on their side, so they had let him keep his life.

He turned the ignition, and the steering wheel blasted apart.

He was still alive when the paramedics found him. The police could identify him from his license plates and the ID in his wallet, which was fortunate. His face was hardly human.

Later, the police described with grudging admiration how the bomber had rigged the airbag system, turning it into a bomb that delivered high-speed metal filament shrapnel rather than air.

Orosco lived for three days, long enough to tell the police what had happened. He served the purpose the assassin required. He spread a warning to anyone else contemplating a break with his cartel employers.

The assassin left no trace, aside from several other candy skulls strewn around the perimeter of the restaurant. The police were never able to find the man who delivered lunch. Orosco could not give a description. Orosco's mobile phone gave no information about where the call had been placed.

It was this incident that led the media to give the assassin a name: Calavera, the skull. Some were horrified by the assassin's efficiency. Some decided that criminals killing criminals was none of their concern. But everyone agreed: Calavera had earned his pay. He had as much capacity for mercy as the candy skulls he left in the Gatsby's parking lot, grinning up at the eyes of Dr. T. J. Eckleburg like some kind of challenge.

When I was done relaying the story to Maia, we were both quiet, listening to the storm outside. There wasn't much to say about Calavera. The story spoke for itself.

"You scuttled the boat," Maia said. "Why?"

"I don't want Calavera to get away."

"Why not?"

I didn't answer.

She was right. It would've been easier to leave the killer an out, let him brave the storm, hopefully sink to hell if he tried. Why would I want to cross a man like Calavera?

"You want to control the situation," Maia said. "It's not so much about the killer, is it? It's about Ralph again."

"It's always Ralph with you, isn't it?"

Maia dug her toes into my ribs. "I've got guilt, too. But I handle it differently. I wouldn't try to stop my career. If I wasn't pregnant, I mean."

"Convenient excuse."

"Oh, yeah." She winced as she rearranged her legs. "So convenient. The point is, Ralph's death made you feel powerless. You don't want anything else to get out of your control. You tried leaving investigation completely, but now that you've got a killer on your hands, you can't stand the idea of him getting away from you. You're maybe not so different from Jesse Longoria."

"All right, that was low."

"I'm wrong, then?"

"Completely. Well . . . mostly."

"Ralph, I think, would have something to say about now."

"Yeah?"

Maia nodded. "'You're full of shit, *vato.*'"

Her imitation was so good it made my heart sore. "That's irreverent."

"Ralph was irreverent. He was also right about a lot of things."

I pulled myself up next to Maia as best I could without jostling her. I kissed her forehead. If I didn't look down, I could almost imagine that she wasn't pregnant. Like old times—before everything changed.

Ralph's death and my decision to marry Maia were not as simple as cause and effect. But they were connected emotionally. We both knew that. They resonated from the same terrible winter week.

"I miss him," I said.

Maia's breath was sweet and warm. Our forearms touched. The storm outside wailed steadily. I felt my eyes closing.

"Try to sleep," Maia told me. "You need the rest."

"Wake me up in an hour?"

"I will."

I drifted off, imagining Ralph Arguello grinning above me, telling me I was a pretty sorry piece of work.

• • •

In my dream, I was sitting on the back deck of Peter Brazos's house in Port Aransas. It was night-time, New Year's Eve. Lights from the houses across the channel reflected like oil fire on the black water. On the edge of Brazos's dock, a little candy skull glittered.

Peter had his computer in his lap, a vodka Collins in his hand. He was talking to me casually, telling me about his case against the drug cartel.

I wanted to warn him. I knew his house would explode any minute, but my dream self felt it would be rude to interrupt.

"It's all about emotional leverage," he told me. "What do they fear worse than their bosses? What makes them crumble inside? Find that, and they'll tell you what you want. They'll testify to anything."

Peter had dark glittering eyes like the little skull on his dock. His skin was pale in the moonlight.

When he lifted his glass to his lips, I said, "Shouldn't you get your family out of the house?"

He glanced behind him. "Too late," he said sadly. "You can't control everything."

Then I noticed the building behind us wasn't Brazos's house. It was the Rebel Island Hotel. And as the windows flared red, I realized that it wasn't Brazos's family in there. It was Garrett and Maia.

"Here's to leverage." Peter Brazos lifted his glass to the flames. "Happy New Year, Tres."

• • •

"Tres." Maia was shaking my shoulder. **"Tres, I** can't get up. You need to get it."

Someone was banging on the door. "Navarro!"

I had no idea how long I'd been out. My eyes still burned from the fire in my dream. I stumbled out of bed and opened the door.

Chase was standing there, looking like the ghost of keg parties past. "We went for ice."

I blinked. "Chase, as direly important as that information is, why did you wake me up?"

"We found him." His voice cracked with emotion. "I think you'd better come see."

20

Jose heard yelling from the floor below.

"It's in the kitchen," Imelda said.

"Yes," he said. "We will stay here."

She bolted for the door, but he caught her arm. "It can wait, Imelda. We have enough trouble."

She slumped down miserably on a stack of folded sheets. The linen closet was almost the size of a guest room. In the illumination of his flashlight, the shelves of folded sheets and towels reminded Jose of mummies—small bodies wrapped in white. He'd seen things like that in Mayan villages, long ago, in the Mexican army. He didn't like the memory coming back now.

"Señora Navarre asked for tea," Imelda murmured. "I told her I would bring her some."

"Will she give birth here?"

"I don't know." Imelda shivered. The twenty years they had been married, they had lived in only hot places, but Imelda was always cold. Jose told her it was because her heart was so warm. Back home in Nuevo Laredo, she once cared for a dove with a broken leg for a month before it finally died. She would cup moths in her hand and release them outdoors rather than kill them. And the children...the last day they had gone to school, she had buttoned their shirts and fussed with their hair and slipped iced oatmeal cookies into their lunch bags.

"Jose," she said quietly. "We can't—"

"Don't say it," he warned. "It's your own fault."

A tear traced her cheek. He didn't like being harsh with her, but the truth was the truth. Imelda had brought them so much trouble. Her warm heart again. She would never understand that some broken birds would not heal. They would die whether you cared for them or not. It was no mercy to prolong the pain.

He knelt beside her and took her hands. "We will survive this, *mi amor*. The storm will pass over."

She met his eyes, but he couldn't tell if she believed him. It seemed cruel to him, that she had suffered with a husband like him. He was not worthy of her. He had known that since the day they first met, at the dance at Señor Guerrero's ranch. They had talked under the orange trees and watched the stars. She had been beautiful in her white dress.

She had seemed to him like an empty cup, waiting to be filled with his stories. She found him fascinating, rough, perhaps a bit scary. She thought she could change him, make him into a good man. She had never given up on that idea. And he had married her anyway, knowing he would only bring her pain.

But he just kept promising things would be better. And she kept believing.

More noises came from the kitchen—distressed voices, the sounds of an argument.

"We should go down," she said.

"No," he told her. "Let them do what they will. They are like the storm, *mi amor*. Their sounds mean nothing."

And they stayed in the linen room, holding hands, Jose kneeling before her as he had under the orange trees, telling her stories she chose to believe.

21

Never underestimate the resourcefulness of a college guy searching for booze.

After ransacking the refrigerator looking for ice for Ty's head (and, more important, beer), Chase and Markie found a storage room in the back of the kitchen with an industrial freezer. They decided to open the freezer on the theory that any self-respecting hotel would have vodka on ice.

They were right. The vodka was wedged right between the corpse's feet.

Chris Stowall lay curled in the fetal position, frost on his eyebrows. His skin was the same color as the ice-crusted sides of the freezer.

Next to me, Benjamin Lindy muttered a curse that was probably shocking back in the 1940s.

Apparently the old lawyer had gotten some sleep since I last saw him. His shirt was wrinkled and his gray hair was mussed, but he still managed to look like the most dignified person present.

He turned to Chase. "Son, did you touch the body?"

"N-no, sir." But when Chase looked at me, I got the distinct impression he wanted to say something more. The bad boy attitude had drained out of his eyes. He looked like a kid who'd just been chased by the neighborhood pit bull. I noticed for the first time how he and Markie were dressed. The cutoffs and T-shirts and flip-flops were gone. Now they both wore jeans, hiking boots, dark long-sleeve shirts. Markie had a flashlight clipped to his belt. At Chase's feet, as if it had dropped there in a moment of panic, was a little hand shovel like a gardening trowel.

"Where were you two going?" I asked him.

Markie stepped between us. "You've got a freaking dead man in the cooler, and you're asking stupid questions? Ty's already going nuts upstairs. If he hears about this—"

"I'm not upstairs." Ty was leaning against the cutting board, his hand a little too close to the butcher knives for comfort. His face was seasick green.

"Happy now, Navarre?" he demanded. His words were slurred. "We're stuck here and this... this Calavera guy's gonna kill us all."

"C'mon, man," Markie said. "That ain't gonna—"

"Shut up! Try to knock me out with those... those pills."

"Sedatives," Chase said defensively.

Ty snorted. "Told you we shouldn't have come. Told you something would go wrong. Couldn't get out, could you?"

"You gotta rest the head, dude." Markie's voice was cold. "Let me get you upstairs."

"Screw that." Ty grabbed a knife, but he was too messed up to be dangerous to anyone but himself. Chase and Markie wrestled the cleaver away from him. They dragged him out of the kitchen, Ty still yelling that we were all going to die.

I looked at Benjamin Lindy, who sighed.

"I believe those boys had one good idea." Mr. Lindy pulled the chilled vodka out from between Chris Stowall's feet. "May I buy you a drink?"

Lindy leaned into the freezer, putting his face nearer to Chris Stowall's than I would've done. The old man's breath turned to mist.

"Contusion on the back of the head," he decided. "That slick of blood you found earlier on the kitchen floor."

"I didn't find it." This seemed a trivial point to argue, but I was running out of ways to distance myself.

Lindy straightened. "What would you say happened here?"

"He was killed in the kitchen, not long after Longoria was shot. Hit from behind. No struggle.

Either someone sneaked up on him, or the killer was someone Chris knew. Someone he didn't fear turning his back to."

"Someone reasonably strong," Lindy added. "Strong enough to drag a grown man into this freezer."

"Why go to the trouble of hiding the body and not clean the blood splatter on the kitchen floor?"

"No time. Perhaps the killer was interrupted. Or perhaps he simply overlooked the blood."

I thought about that. A bloodstain in the middle of a white floor seemed impossible to overlook, but I'd heard of crazier things. Convicted murderers will tell you that killing someone puts you in a daze. You might cover your tracks perfectly except for something obvious . . . your wallet on the kitchen counter, your coat across the arm of the victim's couch.

"The kitchen is a staff area," I said. "The only people in here would be Chris, Alex, Jose and Imelda."

"And thirsty college students, apparently."

I nodded. I didn't like the way Chase and Markie had been dressed, or the fact that they'd tried to drug their friend. "The service entrance is right down the hall," I said. "They were planning on sneaking out the back door."

"That would be insane," Lindy said, "unless they had a very compelling reason. Like moving a dead body."

I shook my head. "If that was the plan, why would Chase run up and get me?"

"I don't know," Lindy admitted. "But if they

were sneaking out for some other reason, what would make them check the freezer?"

I didn't have a good answer. Nothing logical. But, somehow, that was the part of Chase's story I had no trouble believing. They really *were* looking for vodka, possibly to steel their nerves before... whatever they were going to do.

I looked down at Chris's cold face. I thought about the little seagulls he'd drawn in his diary, the picture of Waikiki Beach hanging on his dresser mirror.

"Chris wasn't the guy you're looking for," I said. "But he got tangled up with the killer somehow."

"I'll find him." Lindy's hand trembled as he held his glass of vodka.

"Your plan was to kill Calavera," I guessed. "You were helping Longoria set some sort of trap for him."

Mr. Lindy raised his eyebrows. "You understand that I'll have to deny that."

"Chris Stowall and Longoria are both dead. Do you even care?"

"Of course I care. I don't want any more death. Not for anyone innocent, at least."

I wanted to ask who, if anyone, Benjamin Lindy considered innocent, but I was interrupted by the sound of a woman's scream.

"He's in there!" Lane shouted.

She was on the floor behind Garrett's over-turned wheelchair, pointing at her closet. Garrett was sprawled next to her, rubbing his head and looking disgruntled. In her panic, Lane had apparently tripped over him and toppled him out of his chair.

Mr. Lindy and I shone our flashlights on the closet. The door was ajar, but there was no sign of movement. No noise.

"*Who's* in there?" I asked Lane.

Her eyes were frantic and unfocused. "Bobby. My ex. I saw him. We came in and he was *right there* in my closet!"

I looked at Garrett.

"I don't know, little bro," he grumbled. "I didn't see much. Lane backed into me. Next thing I knew we were both on the floor. But there was movement in the room. Somebody was in here."

Mr. Lindy produced his .45 Colt Defender.

Footsteps came tromping down the hall, and Alex Huff appeared in the doorway. "What is it now?"

I shushed him then followed Lindy toward the closet. The old man threw open the door.

"There's no one in here," he said.

"There was!" Lane looked at us like we were about to give her medication. "I saw him!"

"Okay," I said. "I believe you."

"Son..." Lindy said uneasily.

"Check the bathroom," I suggested.

Lindy did. He shook his head. No prowler in the room.

"All right," I said. "Whoever he was, he's gone now."

"Who?" Alex demanded.

I looked at Mr. Lindy and gestured toward the door, hoping he'd get the hint. I figured the fewer men around Lane Sanford, the better.

"Come on, Mr. Huff," Lindy said. "There's something you need to see in the kitchen."

"Oh, that doesn't sound good," Alex said miserably, but he allowed Mr. Lindy to lead him down the hall.

I turned to Lane Sanford. "Why don't you sit down? I mean...on the bed."

Garrett helped her up. He righted his wheelchair and climbed back into it, still looking disgruntled. For him, getting tipped out of his chair was about as bad as getting mugged—a complete violation of his dignity, such as it was.

"Lane." I tried to sound soothing. "Tell me exactly what you saw."

"My husband."

"Back up. You and Garrett were coming down the hall..."

She nodded.

"Were you making much noise?" I asked.

"Just talking," Garrett said, catching my meaning. "Nothing somebody inside the room could've heard over the storm."

"Was the room locked?"

"Yes," Lane said. "I used my key."

I thought about that. A key didn't make much noise compared to a hurricane. If there had been someone in the room, he wouldn't necessarily have heard anything until Lane turned the handle.

"Okay," I said. "So you opened the door and—"

"He was looking through my closet," Lane said. "The closet door was open."

"It was dark in the room?"

"Yes. I just had a flashlight. I shone it on him—"

"You saw his face?"

"Well . . . no."

"What *did* you see of him?"

"A shape. But it was a man."

"Clothing? Skin color?"

She shook her head hesitantly. "Dark shirt? Maybe that was just the shadows. I—I backed up into Garrett and dropped the flashlight . . ."

"Little bro, there was somebody in here," Garrett insisted.

"Is there any way he could've gotten past you, out the door?"

"I don't see how," Garrett said.

I checked the closet. A garment bag hung on the rod. A pair of ladies' slip-on shoes. Empty coat hangers. An ironing board on metal hooks. An extra pillow on the upper shelf. I checked the bathroom. Nobody was hiding behind the shower curtain. No one had dug an escape tunnel through the floor tiles. Back in the bedroom: nobody was hiding under the bed. The window was boarded over with plywood.

"Well, he vanished," I said. "He went up in smoke."

"Secret passage?" Garrett asked.

I stared at him.

"I'm serious, little bro! This was a damn bootlegger's mansion during Prohibition. Ask Alex. They used to bring up cases of tequila from Mexico."

"You want to check for secret passages, be my guest."

Garrett huffed indignantly, rolled over to the closet and started banging on the walls.

I sat down next to Lane. "From what you tell me, you didn't actually see your ex-husband."

She took a shaky breath. "No one believes me."

"I believe your ex is a dangerous guy. But you couldn't tell if this person...whoever it was... was him."

"I—I suppose it could've been someone else. Another man. But..."

"Let's get you out of this room," I said. "For peace of mind."

Garrett wheeled himself over, having unsuccessfully banged inside the closet looking for a way to China. "For once, my little bro has a good idea. Come on, Lane. I'll take you—"

"Downstairs," I interrupted. "We should try to get everyone together. I'll call the boys."

Garrett glared at me. "Why? What else is wrong?"

"The kitchen," Lane remembered. "Mr. Lindy was taking Alex to the kitchen."

Even in the dim illumination of my flashlight, I could tell her face had gone paler. "It's Chris, isn't it?" she said. "You found him."

I didn't know any easy way to break the news, so I simply told her.

Lane twisted the sheets in her hands. "I want to see him."

"Not a good idea."

"No," Garrett agreed. "Lane, you don't need that."

"Chris didn't do anything," she said. "*I* got him killed. He tried to help me and—"

"Hey, stop that," Garrett said. "Come here."

She slipped off the bed and into his lap, pressing her head against his. She let out a sob, and I lowered the flashlight. In the dark, they made a strange silhouette—like one large, misshapen person.

"You didn't do anything wrong," Garrett told her. "What happened to Chris isn't your fault. Neither is your bastard ex-husband. You did the right thing. You saw an out and you took it."

"I thought . . . I thought it was an out."

The shadows closed around us. The wind battered the window. I didn't believe in ghosts, but this was a good room for them. If I'd been the first one through the door, I wondered what personal boogeyman I might've seen vanishing into the closet.

"Come on," I told Garrett and Lane. "Let's get out of here."

22

Ty missed his gun. Markie pushed him onto the bed and said, "Stay," like he was a dog. Ty wanted to shoot him.

Chase glared down at him. "You're worthless, man. Fucking worthless."

Ty's head still ached from where Markie had sapped him. His vision was blurry and he wasn't sure exactly what drugs they'd given him. His claustrophobia was still smothering him—hot and heavy like an extra skin—but it was muted now. His nerves felt deadened.

"I'm sorry," he lied, trying to save himself another beating.

Markie cursed. "You belong in the freezer with Chris, dude."

"Don't say that. I panicked, is all."

"Enough," Chase said. "This isn't helping."

Chase was still dressed in his dark clothes—his *night run* clothes. He paced at the foot of the bed, rubbing his knuckles.

Ty wished he had his target pistol, and not just because he wanted to shoot them. The gun calmed him down. He only felt truly at peace at the firing range, standing behind the cinder-block partition on a cold winter morning, pistol in his hands. When he fired at targets, he had no anxiety. His hands didn't shake and his skin didn't feel too heavy. He didn't need pills. His fear and anger were compressed into the barrel of the gun and fired right out of him, at least for a while.

If he could just live on the firing range, life would be okay. But he always had to return to the narrow hallways and the cramped dorm rooms of Jester Hall. The crowds pressed in on him. Even the auditorium classes were too small. He couldn't concentrate on lessons. He watched the ceiling, sure it was going to cave in and bury him alive. He would long for home—the ranch back in Del Rio, where he'd never had any problem with small places and crowds. But he couldn't go back home. His father would never allow it. And so he'd found other ways to cope. And that had led him to Chase and Markie.

"What do we do now?" Markie asked.

Chase picked up an empty tequila bottle from the dresser. "We try again."

"Gonna be hard," Markie said.

"We've got no choice. Unless you want to end up like Chris."

Markie's face paled. "Bastard deserved it, after the shit he tried to pull."

On that, at least, Ty agreed. Chris was better off dead. It was his fault they might not make it off the island alive. God, Ty wished he had taken the boat. He should've been faster. He shouldn't have listened to Navarre.

"We'll stay low for a while," Chase decided. "But be ready. We see an opportunity, we go."

Ty's stomach churned. He resented Navarre for keeping him here. He wanted to kill the guy. But at the same time...he seemed smart. He wasn't afraid of Markie or Chase. If there was a way to stop them, or make it so Ty didn't have to share their fate, Navarre might know how.

"I'm gonna be sick," Ty muttered.

Chase looked at him with disgust. "Not in *my* room, you're not."

"I got my medicine next door," Ty said meekly. "I'll go throw up there."

"Not now," Chase insisted. "We're going downstairs. The fucking detective wants another group meeting. And *you* are gonna behave yourself."

Ty nodded miserably. He slid off the bed and hobbled toward the door. He would have to wait. He would be looking for an opportunity, but not the kind Chase meant.

Out in the hallway, he took a deep breath, trying to gather his courage. The walls closed in on him, but he concentrated. He could make it down the hall. It was just like the barrel of a gun. He was aiming at his target. And his target was to get free of Chase and Markie, to get off this island in one piece. If other people died, that wasn't his problem.

He took a tentative step, then another. Chase and Markie walked on either side of him, but Ty promised himself he'd be rid of them by tomorrow, one way or another.

23

On my way downstairs, I thought about Alex. I wondered how he would react to Chris Stowall's death. The booming and groaning of the storm outside made me think of the last fireworks display I'd ever seen Alex do.

It had not exactly been a celebration.

That July fourth, my mother had asked Garrett to watch me, which was never a good sign. She wasn't feeling well. She couldn't handle the company of others that night. At sunset, Garrett took me down to the beach, where Alex was setting up his display.

His tubes and wires looked like a miniature power plant. He'd set everything up on a length of wooden flats and was busy running around, checking his fuses one more time.

The other hotel guests—there were never that many—brought picnic blankets and barbecue prepared by Alex's dad. Even Delilah, the old maid, had come down to watch the show. Alex's fireworks displays were some of the only times I ever saw her smile.

My brother was in an unusually good mood that night. New guests had arrived the day before, and they had a teenage daughter. Garrett had big plans to get to know her tonight. He'd combed his unruly hair, which made him look even geekier than usual, and put on fresh jeans and his Pat McGee's Surf Shop T-shirt.

"You help Alex out, okay?" Garrett told me. "I'm just gonna, you know, get a soda or something."

He went off in search of the new girl. I suppose I should've been relieved that he was preoccupied and happy, but I knew it just meant he'd be in a foul mood tomorrow or the next day—whenever his romantic prospects fell apart, as they inevitably would.

Alex was too busy working to pay attention to me. The sky was turning purple and the guests were starting to cheer and call for the show. Behind us, the hotel at sunset looked like a perfect haunted house.

I didn't hear Mr. Eli come up behind us until he spoke. "Are you ready, Alex?"

It was the first time I'd ever seen Mr. Eli outside. He wore his maroon bathrobe as always. The cuffs of his pajama pants were neatly folded up to keep them out of the sand. His feet were bare, so pale they were almost luminous in the dusk. I wondered if the old man was a vampire, coming out only after dark, but I suspected that a real vampire wouldn't look so sickly and weak.

Alex brushed his hands on his pants and stood up. "Ready, sir. About ten minutes until full dark."

"Wonderful." Mr. Eli smiled. "Your mother would be proud, you know. She loved fireworks."

Alex looked down at the mortars. The aluminum foil had been peeled away. Shreds of it blew across the sand, glinting in the last light like pieces of metallic eggshell.

"You all better get clear, okay?" Alex said. "Show's gonna start."

I watched from the sand dunes. I suppose, compared to professional shows, Alex's display was pretty paltry, but I thought it was fabulous. Maybe that's because I'd watched him put the whole thing together. Maybe I was just amazed that something so loud, bright and colorful could come from a dour kid like Alex Huff. The fact that I didn't like Alex, that I feared him, in fact, made the show all the more fascinating.

The wind was warm blowing through the sea grass. Sand fleas started a seven-course meal on my legs, but I didn't want to move. The smoke was almost as interesting as the starbursts and fireballs. It made ghostly faces in the night sky, swiftly stretched by the breeze and blown to shreds.

"He gets better every year," a voice said at my shoulder.

I jumped in surprise. It was Mr. Eli, but he wasn't talking to me. He stood in the dunes with another man. Both of them were only shadowy silhouettes, the tops of their heads illuminated by bursts of fireworks.

"Know what he told me today?" the other man asked. It was Alex's father. His voice sounded deep and sad. "He said he wants to join the army."

Mr. Eli was silent as a triple burst of silver lit up the water over the boat dock.

"He wants to get away from here," Mr. Huff said. "I can't blame him. Nothing but bad memories."

"Do you really believe that?" Mr. Eli asked.

Alex's father sniffed. I couldn't see his face, but I could almost feel the grieving radiating from him, like the heat of a sun lamp.

"I don't know, sir. I don't mean to sound ungrateful."

"It's all right," Mr. Eli said. "Let him go, if he wants to. He's got his mother's spirit. Hard to tie that down."

"Yes." Mr. Huff's voice sounded ragged. "Suppose it is."

Down at the beach, I caught a glimpse of Garrett and his new potential girlfriend. Garrett's crooked smile lit up blue in a burst of copper chloride light. The girl was too pretty for him. I could tell just by looking, the way she held herself apart from him. She would never fall for him.

"Alex will come back," Mr. Eli said. "Mark my words; he appreciates this place more than he lets on. If I had a son . . . well, I wish I had someone as good as Alex to inherit this place. He has a good heart."

I wanted to tell Mr. Eli that he was wrong. People with good hearts didn't treat younger kids the way Alex treated me. But I bit my lip and said nothing.

"Suppose he got that from his mother, too," Mr. Huff said gruffly. "Sure didn't get a sense of forgiveness from me."

A series of fireballs shot in the air—yellow, green, red. They began to die and fall, only to explode into interlocking spheres, like the Venn diagrams we did in class. My English teacher's lessons, forcing me to think inside the curves: How are these things alike? Where do they overlap?

"Are you sure..." Mr. Eli began to say. "Do you think you ever will tell him?"

"No," Mr. Huff said. His tone was absolutely firm.

"He's bound to find out someday. South Texas is just too small a place. Everyone is connected somehow."

"They never found us," Mr. Huff said.

"No," Mr. Eli said. "That's true. This place is separate. But if he leaves—"

The old man never finished his sentence. The fireworks finale filled the sky, so bright that I could suddenly see the men's faces, and they looked down and saw me.

Perhaps I should've played it cool. But in that moment I felt too much like a trespasser. I ran down the sand dune and along the beach into the dark until the fireworks were far behind me, echoing against the side of the hotel like cannon fire.

• • •

The others were gathering in the parlor.

Benjamin Lindy stood by the fireplace. Maia had come downstairs, ignoring my objections. She looked a little better. She sat on the sofa now, comforting Imelda, who was crying into her apron. Chase and Markie were arguing with Ty, who seemed to have calmed down a little, or perhaps Markie had simply threatened to sap him over the head again.

Lane took a deep breath and walked into the room. I started to follow, but Garrett pulled me aside. "Now would be a good time, little bro, if you got something to say."

It took me a moment to realize what he was asking. "About Lane."

"Yeah, of course about Lane."

I shook my head. "Not really. Maybe there are some things I shouldn't *have* to say. But it wouldn't make much difference, would it?"

"You think I'm taking advantage of her."

"I think she's fragile. I think you're both emotionally strung out."

"You have any idea what she's been through? You realize who her husband is?"

"That's not the point."

"I like her, Tres."

He rarely called me Tres. He tended to save my name for times when he was seriously pissed off or needed money.

"Garrett, the circumstances are extraordinarily bad for starting to like somebody."

He grunted. "How is that different than every other day of my life?"

• • •

"It is true?" Imelda asked.

I looked around the parlor. Alex sat on the steps with his head in his hands. Ty had crashed on the couch with an ice pack on his head. I couldn't tell if he was conscious or not. I was hoping not. Chase and Markie leaned against the pool table behind him, each with a pool cue in his hands. Benjamin Lindy stood by the kitchen door as if he were guarding the exit. Garrett, Lane and Maia shared the other couch. Nobody looked happy to be here.

"Chris Stowall is dead," I said. "That's true."

Imelda crossed herself and murmured a Spanish prayer.

"Ty was right," Chase said. "This Calavera guy is gonna kill us all."

"He hasn't yet," I reminded him.

"Dude," Markie said, "he can't let anybody raise the alarm. He needs to get off the island."

"It won't help us to panic."

Garrett snorted. "A body in the cellar and one in the freezer, and we shouldn't panic. Thanks for the advice, little bro."

Always nice to know your brother is on your side.

"Whoever the killer is," I said, "I don't think we're looking for a stranger. Chris brought Longoria to the island because he knew Calavera would be here this weekend. Calavera is probably in this room."

Chase and Markie exchanged wary looks. Imelda's hands clenched on her apron.

"So why hasn't he killed the rest of us?" Garrett asked. "If this guy's such a cold-blooded murderer, it would be easy to do."

"I don't think he wants to," I said. "I don't think he enjoys killing."

"Yo, little bro. Tell that to Chris Stowall."

"Calavera was cornered," I said. "First by Longoria, then Chris Stowall. But I don't think he relishes the idea of murdering everyone in this room."

"If he has to," Lindy said, "he will."

"We don't know that."

"I'm sorry, son. I *do*. If you have any idea who the killer is, you need to tell us now."

Alex stood suddenly, as if Benjamin Lindy had just slipped ice down his back. "And what will you do about it, old man? Start killing the suspects?"

"Alex," I said. "You want to say something?"

He looked around at all of us, like our presence horrified him. Then he took a shaky breath. "Garrett?"

"Yeah, man?"

"Here." Alex handed him an envelope—beige hotel stationery, like the one that had been slipped under my door. "In case something happens—"

"Nothing's gonna happen, man. It's okay."

"In case it does, keep charge of that, okay? Don't read it unless..."

"Whoa, man. I told you—"

But Alex raised his hands to block Garrett's words and stormed out of the room.

I stood in uncomfortable silence, everyone's eyes

on me. I felt like I was back in front of my English class at UTSA. I'd just assigned an unpopular essay on Chaucer's use of dirty jokes and the class was about to rebel. The only difference was that in most of my classes the students weren't armed.

"We should stay in here for what's left of the night," I suggested. "Safety in numbers."

"All right," Lane said.

Garrett looked unhappy. I had a feeling he'd had other plans about where to spend the night, and they did not involve anyone but Lane.

"What about Mr. Huff?" Lindy asked.

I looked at the doorway. I wasn't sure how to explain Alex's sudden exit.

"I'll talk to him." I turned to Imelda. "*¿Y dónde está Jose?*"

It was the first time I'd spoken Spanish to her. I could see her doing a quick mental rewind, trying to figure out if she'd said anything embarrassing around me in español.

"Upstairs, señor. The news about Señor Stowall—"

"I'll find him, too. Garrett, you and Mr. Lindy try to keep everybody else together."

"I don't have a gun," Garrett complained. "He's got a gun."

I handed him Maia's .357. "Now you have a gun."

It must've been a Texan thing. Two pistols in the room made me feel easier than just one. I turned and headed out the way Alex had gone.

• • •

At the end of the third-floor hallway, light leaked through an open doorway. I peeked inside and found Jose sitting on a bed. It was raining inside the room. The ceiling drizzled and sagged. It looked more like a washcloth than sheet rock.

The room smelled of marigolds and limes. In one corner was a little altar covered with a turquoise shawl. It held a statue of the Virgin of Guadalupe and a few framed photographs, probably Jose and Imelda's dead relatives. A row of candles sputtered and flickered.

The bedspread was soaked. Everything was soaked. But Jose just sat there, holding his flashlight, watching the candles die one after the other.

"Jose."

It took him a second to focus on me. "The attic. I think the roof above us is gone."

"Do you know where Alex is?"

His eye twitched. "No, señor."

"Your things are getting ruined. You want help covering them?"

Jose's flashlight beam traced a figure eight on the soggy carpet. "There is not enough tarp in the whole house, señor. God's will, what He keeps or destroys."

I approached the altar. Among the photos of the honored dead, one showed Jose and Imelda, ten or fifteen years younger, each of them holding a baby.

"Your children," I guessed. "Twins?"

He nodded.

"How did they die?"

He looked up, anger flaring in his eyes. We were

suddenly man to man. No subservience, no careful deference. "I don't talk about that."

Translation: *None of your damn business, señor.*

A trickle of rain spattered on my back. The drops against the damp carpet sounded like kisses.

"Chris Stowall was in the freezer for hours," I said. "You didn't have any reason to go in there when you prepared dinner?"

"No, señor."

"Who else goes into the kitchen, usually?"

"I didn't kill him, señor." There was an odd tone in his voice...almost like regret.

"You said you'd heard of Calavera before. Was it only from the news?"

Jose's nails bit into the palm of his hand. "That man, Señor Brazos. When he came here—"

"Wait a minute. Peter Brazos came here?"

"In November. He...talked to Señor Huff."

"Why didn't you mention this before?"

"It was not my place, señor. The man stayed for only a few hours. He asked questions and left. At the time, I did not think—"

"He talked to you?"

"*Un poco*. He asked how long we knew Señor Huff. He mentioned names I did not know, showed me photographs of some men and asked if I had seen them."

"The drug bosses he was prosecuting?"

"*No sé*, señor. Perhaps."

On the altar, a raindrop hit a candle and it fizzled out. In the old photograph, the faces of Jose, Imelda and their children flickered. I didn't like

Jose's story about Peter Brazos. I especially didn't like that Alex never mentioned the visit. He'd pretended to know nothing about Brazos or the murder of his family.

"Señor, I'm sorry you came here," Jose said. "You and your wife."

I tried for a reassuring smile. I'm not sure I pulled it off very well. "By tomorrow, the storm should pass. With any luck, a boat will come. We'll all be able to leave."

"Yes."

"Alex wants to sell the hotel. What will you and Imelda do?"

He stared at me, as if the future tense meant nothing to him. "What can we do, señor? Mr. Huff gave us a home here. This is all we have."

The contents of a room. A few photos and candles. A turquoise shawl and some Mexican blankets. All ruined by the rain.

"Six months ago, Calavera killed a woman and her two young daughters," I said. "I don't think he planned to do that. I think killing them shook him up so much that he started to think about retiring. Possibly even making amends."

"Anyone who kills children, his soul is lost," Jose said. "There are no amends."

"We need to stay together," I told him. "We'll all sleep in the parlor."

"I have to check the basement first. Mr. Huff..." He hesitated. "Mr. Huff said it was flooding."

"Doesn't it bother you that there's a body down there?"

Jose gave me a look I couldn't quite read. I thought he might be about to tell me something. Then he rose and left the room, leaving me alone with the rain and the scent of extinguished candles.

I had no luck finding Alex. Maybe because I was sidetracked.

Somehow I got turned around on the first floor, running into a dead end where Alex had closed off the collapsed room, then heading back.

Yes, it's true. Despite being a former sleuth, my sense of direction is sadly lacking. Maia has a great deal of fun reminding me of this whenever we're lost on the highway.

I found a bedroom door ajar and figured it would do no harm to knock.

No answer. Natural curiosity, I looked inside.

After getting used to wreckage and chaos, I was a little shocked to find a completely neat room. The bedspread was folded down. An old-fashioned brown leather suitcase sat on the chair. One navy blue suit and a dress shirt hung in the closet. On the dresser lay a leather notebook, a ballpoint pen and a box of .45 ammunition.

Benjamin Lindy's room. Either that, or I had seriously misjudged the college guys.

Under normal circumstances, I would've backed out.

Well, okay. Perhaps not. But at least I would have hesitated, pondering whether or not I should

invade Mr. Lindy's privacy. As it was, I went right in
and opened the notebook.

He was a lawyer, all right. Everything was
documented—neatly organized, dated and labeled, even though it appeared to be a personal
scrapbook. The first thing inside was a studio portrait of a woman in her early forties, a little older
than me, maybe my brother's age. She had short
blond hair and green eyes. Her sharp nose and the
determined angle of her jaw reminded me very
much of Benjamin Lindy. She had his wry smile,
too, though on a beautiful woman, the effect was
quite different than on an old gentleman. Her
name was printed at the bottom of the photo:
Rachel Brazos. The date: *Last Christmas*.

The next page: a letter Rachel had written to her
father. She asked whether the family ranch had gotten any rain. She invited her father to visit in Corpus
Christi. She wrote about the tiles she had chosen for
her kitchen remodeling, a play her two little girls
had performed in school. She signed the note *XOX,
Rae*. Nothing consequential. The letter was dated
about a month before the photo was taken.

Some pictures of the two Brazos girls followed.
Halloween. School picture day. I flipped through
them quickly. They were painful to look at.

There were some news clippings about Rachel's
career at a local law firm. Following in her father's
footsteps. One article recounted a criminal case
she'd worked in conjunction with the district attorney's office. Apparently that's how she'd met her future husband, Peter Brazos. Rachel's successful

legal career had been put on hold. Relatively late, she'd decided to become a wife and mother.

Like Maia. A little too much like Maia.

I kept turning pages. A few years farther back in time, one picture was labeled: *Rachel Lindy, graduation, Texas A&M.* Her hair was longer, swept over one shoulder. Her eyes gleamed with humor and confidence.

Next page: a poem by Rachel Lindy, clipped from a college anthology. The poem wasn't very good. It described a storm. I didn't want to read about storms.

Another letter from Rachel to her father. Judging from the date, Rachel would've been about twenty-two. She promised to visit over Thanksgiving. She gently chastised her dad for asking about who she might be dating. *Nothing serious, Dad! He would have to be as good as you, right? Guys like that are scarce!!!*

The oldest clipping was about Rachel's swim team in high school. Nothing earlier than that. Nothing from her childhood. No pictures of Rachel with her parents.

I flipped back to the most recent photograph of Rachel. Even without knowing her background, I would've guessed she was married with kids. The humor in her eyes was tinged with a kind of weary satisfaction—the look of a new mother who had a family counting on her.

"Finding what you want?"

Benjamin Lindy was standing in the doorway.

• • • •

"Your daughter," I said.

Lindy walked to the bed. He sat down stiffly, then folded his hands. "Yes."

"Rachel and your two granddaughters were killed in that explosion. I'm sorry."

In the dim glow of my flashlight, Lindy's eyes glittered. "I'm done with sympathy, son."

"You were friends with Jesse Longoria."

"I told you, I asked his advice once. After that, we saw each other professionally a few times. I wouldn't call him a friend. Then his supervisor Berry started communicating with that evil man."

"Calavera wanted to make a deal."

"He wanted to trade information for a new identity. Berry was helping negotiate his surrender. When Marshal Longoria found out, he did not approve."

"Longoria tipped you off to what was happening."

"On the contrary. I notified *him* what his boss was up to."

"How did *you* find out?"

"Chris Stowall."

"You knew Stowall?"

"No. I had never heard of Mr. Stowall until he called. He told me he knew who killed my daughter. He told me the killer was trying to make a deal with the Marshals Service to escape justice. I was incredulous. I contacted Longoria, and he was able to confirm the negotiations. Between us, we decided we could not let that happen."

"How did Chris know to contact you? Why

wouldn't he just tell the police if he knew something?"

"Greed, sir," Lindy answered. "Mr. Stowall wanted money for his information."

"And he knew you wouldn't go to the police? How?"

Lindy hesitated. "This whole area is a close-knit community, Mr. Navarre. Most people have heard of me. Rachel's death was in all the media. I made no secret of my desire for revenge when she and her girls were murdered. I was quite vocal about the police's failure to apprehend Calavera. I assume Chris Stowall knew all this."

"How much did he want?"

"Fifty thousand dollars. Nothing, really."

"You'd already paid him twenty thousand?"

"You mean the money you found in the duffel bag." Lindy shook his head. "I don't know where Stowall got that money. I had not paid him a dime. I did not intend to until we had found Calavera."

I thought about the entries in Chris Stowall's journal—the cryptic references to how much he needed money, and the suggestion that Lane had been encouraging him to leave behind his past shady dealings. Apparently, Stowall had other money-making schemes besides providing revenge opportunities to bitter old men.

"Chris promised Calavera would be here this weekend," I said. "He sent Longoria a business card with the date, June fifth."

"Yes," Lindy said.

"Somehow he found an email from Calavera to

the Marshals Service. Did Chris tell you anything else? Anything that hinted who Calavera was? Hotel employee? Guest?"

"Very little, Mr. Navarre. He brought us here. He promised irrefutable proof. He said..."

"Yes?"

Lindy tapped a finger thoughtfully on the top of his ammunition box. "He assumed I knew Rebel Island. He said I should have reason to hate this place."

"Do you?"

He hesitated a little too long. "No. Perhaps he simply meant this is where I would find my daughter's killer. That's why I should hate the place."

I looked down at the scrapbook, the picture of Rachel Brazos. She looked happy with her family and her life. She'd had every reason to expect many more years with her husband, watching their two daughters grow up.

"Mr. Lindy, once you find Calavera, what do you intend to do?"

The old man looked gaunt and hungry. Despite his formal clothes, his clipped gray hair, his grandfatherly manner, he reminded me suddenly of heroin addicts I'd known—polite, friendly, until you withheld what they wanted.

"Son, I know what happens in the legal system. You do too. My daughter's death will go unpunished, because that's a lesser evil when weighed against catching Calavera's employers. I can't allow that."

"You can't just kill him."

"How many has Calavera killed?"

"Give me your gun," I told him.

He shook his head.

"Give it to me," I repeated. "Or I'll take it away."

His face flushed, but I held his eyes. I could take the gun. I had no doubt. And I let him see that.

Lindy opted for the dignified solution. He took out his .45 and gave it to me. I ejected the clip, slipped it and the gun into my pockets. I took his box of ammunition.

"Son, you're making a mistake."

Suddenly the electric lights flickered on.

Somewhere in the distance, my brother's muffled voice yelled, "Yes!"

Music cranked into gear. The steel drums of "Margaritaville" wafted down a hallway.

"No!" Garrett shouted. "Not *that* song. Kill it!"

I sighed. The way Garrett hated that song, I figured I'd better get back there before we had another homicidal maniac on our hands.

I left Mr. Lindy sitting on his bed, staring at the scrapbook of his dead daughter's life.

24

The day Alex got out of the army, he found himself on the streets of San Antonio with no plans, no home and not much money. He drove out of the gates of Fort Sam Houston, bought a six-pack of beer at the nearest convenience store and meandered down Broadway to the Witte Museum. He sat on the banks of San Pedro Creek, watching the geese glide by in the green water. Huge live oaks cast mottled shadows on the grass. Alex's eyes still hadn't adjusted from the harsh sunlight of Kuwait. He felt like he had sand in his boots, and not the good kind of sand from the Texas beaches. Desert sand—fine, dry and all-pervasive—from a world of unrelenting heat.

He took out his father's knife and ran his finger

down the blade. He imagined himself walking on the edge. Today he had to decide. After four years of letting the army tell him what to do, where to go, when to eat, how to dress, he had to make choices again, and that scared him.

Finally he pulled out his address book. He hadn't used it in months. Most of the numbers belonged to friends who had died or girlfriends who'd left him. He walked to a pay phone at the corner of Broadway and called Garrett. He got an answer immediately.

Garrett was in town, it turned out, visiting his brother, Tres. "I'll meet you at Liberty Bar," he said. "Gimme thirty minutes."

"You bringing Tres?"

Garrett laughed. "You think I should?"

Alex hung up.

Thirty-three minutes later, Alex arrived at the Liberty Bar. The two-story whitewashed building hadn't changed in decades. It was famously slanted like a carnival funhouse, with a balcony around the second floor. Inside, the hardwood floor creaked under the waiters' feet, and the leaning walls made Alex feel like he was in the belly of a ship. Liquor bottles gleamed against the bar mirror. Locals crowded the tables, tucking away pot roast sandwiches or chiles rellenos.

Garrett sat near the back exit. He was already on his second Shiner Bock. Alex hadn't seen him in over three years, but when he sat down Garrett started right into it, as if Alex had simply come back from the bathroom.

"So I was talking to Tres today, and he's gonna get a state license. Become a legitimate PI. Can you believe that?"

Alex shook his head. He'd seen Tres a few times over the years, but it was still hard to think of him as a grown-up, much less an investigator. "I need advice," he said.

Garrett nodded like this was the most natural request in the world, despite the fact that Alex had never once taken Garrett's advice on anything. In fact, Alex had pretty much defined himself as a teenager by doing the opposite of whatever Garrett suggested.

Alex talked about his different ideas: starting a fireworks business and traveling the country, or moving to California. Or . . . there was always Rebel Island.

The name hung in the air between them. Glasses clinked at the bar. Trucks rumbled by on Josephine Street.

Garrett drained his beer. His eyes glinted as dangerous as sparks on kerosene. "I could go for dinner on the island."

They left after lunch. By sunset they were on the beach, toasting the Gulf of Mexico and reminiscing. Within a week, Alex had decided to buy the hotel.

Now, sitting in the dark, Alex unfolded his father's knife. Once more, he felt like he was teetering on the blade. He thought about the letter he'd given to Garrett. He hoped Garrett would understand. It wasn't much to make amends, but it was all he could do. Hopefully some of the others would be spared.

Alex didn't care about himself anymore. He felt just like his hotel: battered, torn by the wind, coming apart at the joints.

He stared at the candy skull on the table. He had tried to fix things. He had tried to put aside his anger. But it hadn't worked. With the edge of his knife, he flicked the skull off the table.

"Calavera," he said.

And like magic, the door to the room creaked open. Alex stood. He knew he was going to fall off the wrong side of the blade this time. Nothing would save him—not Mr. Eli, not Garrett's advice, not even the hope that people sometimes change. They didn't. And Calavera would win.

25

I shared a sofa with Maia and Garrett while I told them about my conversations with Jose and Mr. Lindy. Lindy and most of the others were also in the parlor, but between the storm and the Jimmy Buffett music, it wasn't hard to talk without being overheard.

"Brazos visited the island," Maia said. "Two months later, his family was murdered."

"Yeah," I said.

"Why didn't Brazos come back here afterward? Did he ever follow up?"

"I don't know. If I could find Alex—"

"There's gotta be a reason," Garrett insisted. "So this Brazos guy asked some questions. So what? That doesn't mean Alex—"

"Garrett, Alex should've said something. He didn't."

"What about this Lindy guy? How do you know he isn't Calavera?"

"It was Lindy's daughter who died," I said. "He isn't an assassin. I mean...he wants to kill somebody in cold blood, but he's not *that* assassin."

"Great," Garrett grumbled. "That clears it right up."

"The poor man." Maia sipped her red-raspberry-leaf tea. She looked over at Lindy, who sat in conversation with Jose. Jose looked uneasy to have the old lawyer's attention.

"The poor man?" I asked Maia.

"He lost his daughter and granddaughters. How would you feel?"

"Like tracking down Calavera and butchering him. But I wouldn't do it."

She raised her eyebrows.

"Okay," I said. "I'd think about doing it, but you'd kick my butt if I tried."

"Lindy has nothing left to lose," Maia said. "No family. His career is behind him. He's too old to care about jail time."

"You think I should give him his gun back?"

"On the contrary. I think he may be more dangerous than this assassin. More unpredictable. But I also don't want to see him killed. If Calavera finds out why he's here—"

"I still think Lindy is nuts," Garrett said. "You sure he doesn't have another gun?"

"I'm not sure," I admitted. "And speaking of that, give me back the .357."

Garrett looked offended. "I'm your brother."

"A good reason for extreme caution. Gun, please."

Garrett muttered a few curses, but he gave me Maia's gun.

Jimmy Buffett kept singing about Key West. The time must've been well past one in the morning, and everybody looked even more tired than I felt. Ty was out cold from whatever medication his friends had given him. I kind of envied him. Chase and Markie were teaching Imelda to play Spit in the Ocean, which probably had some sort of cosmic significance when played in a hurricane. Lane had made herself a nest of blankets next to the wall. She was curled into a fetal position, but her eyes were wide open. Mr. Lindy was still talking to Jose, who was looking frazzled and soaked. Ceiling plaster flecked his black hair.

There was no sign of Alex.

"He'll be back," Garrett said, apparently reading my mind. "He won't do anything crazy."

"I hope you're right. What was in the envelope he gave you?"

Garrett's face darkened. "Just personal stuff."

"Nothing about Calavera."

"No."

"You'd tell me if it was."

"Hey, little bro. It's cool. Alex will be back. The power came back on. Alex must've done that."

I wasn't so sure. The generator seemed about as

predictable as the storm tonight. I also noticed that Garrett had not answered my question.

"When you told me Alex was having some problems even before this weekend, what did you mean?"

Garrett folded the bottom of his Hawaiian shirt like he was rolling a joint. "Money problems. The hotel wasn't keeping afloat too well. Maybe there was more. I don't know. He said he and Chris..."

"Were arguing?" I supplied.

"Yeah. But don't get ideas, little bro. It doesn't mean anything. You know Alex couldn't hurt a soul."

I remembered Alex's steely look the afternoon he pushed me out of the boat, into the water with the blood and the sharks. I wasn't sure Garrett was being completely honest. I wanted to know what Alex had given him in that envelope. But I also knew my brother well enough to know I couldn't force the issue. He'd tell me only when he was ready.

"You guys get some sleep," I told them. "I'll keep watch."

Maia closed her eyes without protest. "Wake me if somebody else dies."

Garrett looked over at Lane.

"Go ahead," I said. "She could use some comfort."

He studied me, like he was trying to detect sarcasm. But he didn't look too hard, or maybe he just didn't care.

"Good night, then," he said. "And you watch. Alex is gonna prove you wrong."

I'm not sure when I fell asleep. I must have been too exhausted to even notice I was fading.

I dreamed I was teaching a class at UTSA. We were discussing *The Pearl*, talking about grief and the death of children. It was raining in the classroom. The students were trying to take notes but their laptops and legal pads were getting soaked. Lindy's daughter, Rachel, was one of the students. Ty, Markie and Chase were there. So was Imelda, holding a baby in either arm. Ralph Arguello sat in the back of the room, a beach umbrella over his desk. He kept grinning at me like he found my lecture amusing.

I talked about the Black Plague and medieval parenthood. I discussed the sociological theory that parents in the Middle Ages, who were so accustomed to loss, did not have the same emotional attachment to children as modern parents. Personally, I didn't buy that.

"Why not, *vato*?" Ralph asked.

"Just because death was more commonplace," I said, "doesn't mean life was cheaper."

Ralph smiled. "I love this guy. He thinks he's a professor."

The students shifted uncomfortably in their seats. Rachel Brazos and Imelda and Ty were all watching me intently. Rain pattered against their papers.

I looked down at the podium. My lecture notes had disappeared. "The, uh, intense emotion in *The Pearl*—"

"People don't change," Ralph interrupted. "They let grief tear them up. That's what you're saying, huh?"

"Well, yes."

"And you had to look in a book for that, *vato*?" Ralph laughed. "Why don't you look around?"

"Tres." Maia was shaking my arm. "The water."

I sat up groggily. "Your water broke?"

"No. Look."

I might've still been dreaming. The carpet was spongy with salt water. Garrett was rowing around in his chair, waking people up. His wheels made strange squishy sounds.

"Hey, get up." He shook Mr. Lindy, who was slumped in the armchair. "Your shoes are wet."

Lane paced nervously, a blanket wrapped around her like a queen's robe. Chase and Markie were stirring on the floor. Their clothes were drenched.

"What the hell?" Chase said.

Water flowed down the steps into the parlor. The hall looked like a wood-paneled storm drain. The storm was still roaring outside, but louder now, like the waves were right against the building.

I got up and helped Maia to her feet.

Imelda ran in from the kitchen. "The basement is flooding. The señor's body—"

"We can't worry about that," Maia said, trying to sound calm. "We need to get out of this room."

"Imelda," I said. "Help me with Mrs. Navarre."

The maid seemed glad to have something to do. She took Maia's other arm and together we walked toward the stairs.

"Look how fast the water's coming in." Lane's face was ashen. "Where are we supposed to go?"

"Up," I told her. "The second floor."

"And if that floods?"

Garrett and I exchanged looks.

"Come on, darlin'," he told Lane. "We've made it this far. Everything's gonna be fine."

He wheeled himself to the steps. Several inches of water were swirling in the foyer, racing down the hallway. "I don't swim too well, little bro."

"You won't have to," I promised. "Leave the chair and let's go."

He nodded uneasily, then slipped out of his wheelchair and hand-walked up the steps. As he navigated the hall, his torso in the water, he looked like a man wading up a deep, unfriendly river.

Getting Maia upstairs wasn't easy. The stairs creaked and groaned. Below us, the first floor sounded like a public swimming pool, water sloshing everywhere.

It was possible the whole hotel would get washed away. I knew that. But I didn't see any alternative other than getting into the middle of the building and hoping it didn't happen.

We settled everyone into a row of guest rooms on the second floor. Imelda bustled around making sure we all had enough sheets and flashlights. I figured the generator would go out again any moment, but strangely the power stayed on.

Maia got comfortable on one twin bed while Garrett and Lane collapsed on the other.

I fiddled with the nightstand radio and to my surprise found a garbled AM station. Three-twenty A.M. and the tail end of the storm was coming ashore. Winds of one hundred thirty miles an hour. Massive flooding from Port Lavaca to Port Isabel. Fifteen-foot waves. On the bright side, the rainfall should lessen by midday. The Spurs were playing tonight in game seven of the playoffs. Anyone who was still alive would have something to look forward to.

There was shouting in the room next to us. It sounded like Ty, Markie and Chase had gotten a second wind and Mr. Lindy was trying to referee. I decided not to interfere. They probably needed the exercise.

Head count: Maia seemed all right for the moment. Garrett and Lane were fine. The three college guys and Benjamin Lindy were next door.

"Alex," I said. "Did he ever come back?"

"Haven't seen him," Garrett admitted. "I thought for sure..."

He didn't finish. Even *he* looked worried.

I thought about Ralph Arguello, grinning in the raining classroom. *Maybe you should just look around,* vato.

"Imelda," I called.

She came to the doorway, her arms full of towels.

"Have you seen Alex Huff?" I asked.

"No, señor."

"Where is his bedroom?"

She looked down, hugging the towels to her chest. "Mr. Huff is very private about his room, señor. I don't—"

"I need you to show me."

Jose appeared next to her, breathing hard. His pants were wet from the knees down.

"*¿Que pasa?*" he asked his wife.

"He . . . he wants to see Señor Huff's room."

Jose frowned. "We will show him, then."

"I'll go, too," Garrett said.

"No," I said. "Stay here. Take care of Lane and Maia."

Garrett didn't look pleased, but the fact that I'd included Lane made it difficult for him to say no. Lane was curled on the bed, staring forlornly at the wall as if it would blow apart any moment.

"All right," Garrett said. "But, little bro, nothing crazy, okay?"

"On a night like tonight? Of course not. Nothing crazy at all."

Alex's room was just down the hall on the left. The door was locked, which was a first. I'd started to think nobody at the hotel ever locked doors.

"Alex!" I yelled.

No answer.

The noise of the storm was louder on this end of the hall. It almost sounded like it was inside his room.

I pounded on the door. Still nothing.

Imelda stood next to me, twisting her apron. Jose's body was turned away from me, like he was trying to evade me, though I wasn't sure why. It seemed odd that just a few hours ago, I'd thought of him as a man with a perpetual smile. That smile was long gone.

"You have the key?" I asked them.

Imelda's eyes widened. "Señor Huff is the owner. He told us never to enter without permission."

"You don't clean his room?"

"Never."

"But you have to have a master key."

"I...Back downstairs," Imelda said.

"Downstairs."

She nodded halfheartedly.

I looked at Jose. "You?"

"No, señor. I'm just the cook. I have no master key."

"Fine," I said. "I'll break down the door."

Jose tensed. Imelda started to say, "Señor—"

I put my shoulder to the door and smashed it open.

Inside, the room was a wreck. The window had been demolished, but the wood splinters and glass shards pointed toward the storm, as if something had been hurled out. A strip of torn red cloth fluttered from one jagged tooth of glass. The curtain was sprinkled with pink spots, like diluted blood.

I tried to come up with some other explanation, but I kept coming back to the same conclusion. Someone had been pushed out the second-story window. And whoever it was had been wearing a shirt the same color as Alex Huff's.

26

Maia couldn't sleep. The pangs had passed, but they'd scared her worse than she'd let on. She lay on her side, trying to keep still. Lane Sanford was also awake. She was curled in the other bed with Garrett sitting at her feet.

"We used to have storms at the ranch," Lane said. "Once lightning hit a tree and it burned almost an acre. But I've never seen anything like this."

"Your family ranch?" Maia asked.

"No . . . Bobby rented the place."

Lane spoke his name like a cuss word she'd trained herself to say, a word proper ladies weren't supposed to know.

"You should get a restraining order," Maia said. "I'd be happy to help."

"I can't," Lane said. "Thank you."

Her tone was final. There was a secret there she wasn't ready to share yet. Abuse, probably. Something else, too—something Lane thought she couldn't bring to the police. The problem with working criminal cases so long: Maia could come up with a whole array of depressing possibilities, all equally plausible and horrible. And yet she could still be surprised. The worst violence, the most awful forms of depravity, always happened in a so-called loving relationship.

At least that made it easier for her to count her blessings. Whatever faults Tres had—however much he tortured himself with guilt or wrestled with his own demons—he was kind. He was a good man. He'd make a good father, Maia had no doubt, whatever happened with the baby. She depended on that. She counted on him so much it scared her. And she tried to tell herself Tres would be safe. They would make it through this weekend.

The storm rumbled overhead like an endless train. Noises from the other rooms eventually died down. Lane closed her eyes and began breathing deeply. Garrett stayed at his post at the foot of her bed, his hand protectively on her ankle.

Maia studied Garrett's face, looking for similarities to Tres. The hawkish nose and green eyes were the same. Garrett hid his chin behind a scraggly beard, but she imagined it was the same as Tres's— a strong jawline, hinting at stubbornness. Time had not been as kind to Garrett, though. He was the same age as Maia. She remembered they had talked about that when they first met, how both of them were just turning forty. His complexion had turned sallow from too many years of hard drinking. His eyes were constantly bloodshot. His hair was frosted with gray. But he was still handsome in an unkempt way. He looked at her and smiled, and Maia couldn't help feeling a little better.

"You doing all right, darlin'?" he asked.

"Worried about Tres."

"Ah, hell. He'll be fine. That bastard will drive you crazy if you keep worrying about him."

"You have a point."

"I've known him longer, darlin'. I just hope that baby gets some of *your* good looks."

"He'll be beautiful, I'm sure."

"He?"

"The last few days, I've started to think of the baby as a *he*."

"A nephew to corrupt. I could handle that. *Uncle* Garrett..."

Maia pictured Garrett with a baby in his lap, the two of them taking joy rides in the wheelchair. The baby would be wearing a tie-dyed jumper, a miniature Jimmy Buffett hat. "Did you ever think about getting married?"

He glanced down at Lane. "I'm not exactly an attractive package, in case you hadn't noticed. Kind of an extreme fixer-upper."

"Don't sell yourself short."

"You're telling this to a man without legs?"

"You know I didn't mean it that way."

Footsteps in the hall. Maia hoped it was Tres

coming back, but it was only Mr. Lindy and the college boy Ty. Ty was clutching his stomach as if he were sick, and Mr. Lindy was helping him walk. They didn't look inside the room as they passed.

"Maia, you're lucky," Garrett told her at last. "You and Tres. You stuck with it."

"It wasn't easy," Maia promised.

"I used to think there was a perfect match out there for everybody, you know? Alex told me that. Older I get, I realize there's just matches you make work, and matches you give up on. Ain't nothing perfect about it."

"You'll find the right person, Garrett."

He scratched his beard. "That's not what worries me. Question is, will the right person stick around?"

In the dim light, the lines on his face seemed deeply etched. His hair looked even more gray than usual. He gazed down at Lane Sanford as she slept, as if trying to memorize her face.

Maia felt the baby kick. She put her hand against her belly.

A boy, she thought. And though she had never been religious, she prayed: *Please, let him be healthy*.

"Why don't you get some sleep, darlin'?" Garrett told her. "I'll wake you if anything happens."

She wanted to stay up. She wanted to wait for Tres to return safely. But her eyelids were as heavy as lead. She closed them and drifted off, imagining Tres holding the hand of the baby as he took his first step away from her.

27

"Tell me," I said.

Jose took his eyes from the broken window. "Señor?"

"You didn't want me to come in here. What happened to Alex?"

He shook his head, no longer evasive. Just bewildered. "I don't know."

A shard of glass shook loose from the window frame. It flew past us, embedding itself in the wall.

"Señor, we must leave," Imelda said. "Señor—"

I pushed toward the window, screening my face with my hands. The dark shape of the lighthouse loomed through the horizontal rain. The ocean churned below, waves surging against the side of the house. If Alex had fallen into that maelstrom, there was no chance of finding him.

I yanked the piece of red fabric off the window. A piece of Alex's shirt. No doubt about it.

"Señor!" Imelda shouted over the storm. *"Please!"*

Wind buffeted me back into the room.

I didn't want to leave, but the glass and debris were too dangerous to contend with.

I stepped back and tripped over something hard.

I looked down. It was a wooden statue of a woman, about two feet tall, carved from cedar. The details, especially the face, were amazingly intricate. She had her arms crossed, one hand raised palm up, as if she were asking a question.

My mouth tasted like metal.

I was sure of two things about the statue—two things that were impossible to reconcile. First, this was the same statue I'd seen Alex Huff carving when I was a child, the day I'd surprised him in the lighthouse. Second, the woman's face looked a lot like a young mother I'd recently seen in a photograph.

She looked like Rachel Lindy Brazos.

Garrett crumpled the piece of red fabric. "You're telling me Alex jumped?"

"I doubt it was suicide. If he went out that window, he was pushed."

"No way, little bro. So his window was broken.

So what? Half the windows in the place are broken."

"It was busted from the inside."

"He's not dead," Garrett insisted. "We gotta search the house."

I didn't answer. I didn't mention the wooden statue I'd left in the bedroom. I still couldn't process what I'd seen—the adult face of Rachel Brazos, carved in cedar by Alex Huff when Rachel and he would've both been teenagers.

"Fine," Garrett said. He glanced over at the beds, where Maia and Lanc were both asleep. "I'll search outside. Little bro, you stay here for a change."

"Garrett, you can't. It's too dangerous."

His stare was a little on the crazy side. "I'm not gonna sit here if something's happened to Alex."

"We'll find him," I promised, but I was thinking about the ocean pounding the walls of the house, washing over the entire island.

There was a loud knock behind me. "Tres."

Benjamin Lindy stood in the doorway, looking weary and rumpled from his time with the college guys. He'd lost his tie. A strand of gray hair curled over his forehead, geriatric Superman–style. "I need to talk to you."

"What a coincidence," I said. I turned to Garrett. "Give me two minutes. We'll figure it out."

Garrett glared at me like I'd just suggested torching a Jimmy Buffett album, but he nodded grudgingly. "Two minutes."

At the end of the hall, Lindy looked around to

make sure we were alone. "That young man, Ty. I took him to the bathroom just now."

"That's terrific news."

"You don't understand. He asked me to take him to the bathroom in his own room to get some Tylenol. He orchestrated that so he could talk to me away from his friends."

"And?"

Lindy's eyes were as cold as steel. "He has something to tell you privately. He says it has to do with Chris Stowall's murder."

Ty sat at the bottom of the stairwell, watching the water lap against the steps. In the dim light of the hallway fixture, he looked like a wax figure, his face soft and sallow.

"Chase and Markie?" he asked nervously.

"Mr. Lindy is keeping them occupied."

"This was a bad idea," he said. "Forget it."

"Ty, you got me down here. What did you want to tell me?"

He chewed at his thumb. "You should've let me leave last night. You don't understand what they're into. What they're doing to me."

The fear in his voice was beyond claustrophobia.

I thought about the way Markie had sapped Ty with a roll of quarters. No emotion in his face. Just cold efficiency. Few things would make a kid that age develop that kind of ruthless edge.

"Those drugs they sedated you with," I said. "Where did they get them?"

Ty laughed weakly. "Starting to catch on, huh?"

"You're trying to tell me Chase and Markie are dealers?"

"Dealers...Man, that sounds so *small*. For the UT campus, those two are the freaking *Wal-Mart* of drugs."

"Chase and Markie can barely open a tequila bottle. Are you sure we're talking about the same people?"

Ty spit into the water. "That's what they want you to think. 'Oh, they're just stupid kids. It isn't possible.' Bullshit. Those two haven't been kids since elementary school."

The hall light flickered. I sat next to Ty. Together, we watched foam and dark water course down the hallway.

"Why are you telling me this?" I asked. "They're your friends."

"They're my *bosses*. They got hooks in me like you wouldn't believe. I agreed to do this one last trip to clear my debts. I didn't agree to murder."

"You think they killed Chris?"

"Chris was part of the system. That money you found? That came from Chase and Markie. They paid him off every time they came down."

"But why would they kill him?"

Ty shook his head miserably. "This was supposed to be the last run, before the hotel shut down. Chris was pretty bummed about that. Maybe he leaned on Chase and Markie for more money."

Again, I thought about Chris's journal, the comments he'd made about escaping to Hawaii, his anger at Alex for closing the hotel. "So you've been smuggling in drugs from Mexico. What are we talking about? Heroin? Marijuana?"

"Oh, man, that is *old school*. We brought in Mexican pharmaceuticals. Ritalin. OxyContin. Codeine. You name it. That's what the people in the dorms want. Prescribe your own high."

"You could get pharmaceuticals here."

"In cheap bulk shipments? Easier to arrange that from Mexico. Warehouse security down there is a joke. Plus the cartels and *federales* don't bother you. They're all focused on the 'illegal' stuff."

"How were the drugs brought in?"

"Fishing boat. See, that's the thing. You said there was no way off the island until the ferry. Maybe that's not exactly true. Chase and Markie have this plan—"

Steps in the hallway above. Chase called down, "Yo, Ty. You all right, man?"

Ty closed his eyes and swallowed. "Yeah. I feel like shit. But I'm . . . I'm better, I guess."

Chase and Markie came down the steps. They checked us out, trying to read what was going on.

"He's not making much sense," I told them. "You gave him too much sedative."

"He'll be okay," Chase said. "Come on, buddy."

Ty gave me one last look, like a convict going back inside the pen. Then he let his buddies lead him up the stairwell.

• • •

I went back to our refugee room, wanting to talk to Maia, but she was still asleep. For once, she looked comfortable. I didn't want to disturb her. Lane slept more fitfully. She was mumbling something that sounded like a protest. Garrett lay next to her, his arm around her waist.

He glanced up as I came in. We had a brief, silent conversation that went something like this:

Me: *No sign of Alex.*

Garrett: *If I could get up without waking Lane, I'd beat you with a large stick. Search again!*

I checked the next room and found Benjamin Lindy asleep on the couch. Chase and Markie sat on the bed having a quiet, earnest conversation with Ty. I decided to move on.

The next bedroom's door was also open, but Jose and Imelda were nowhere to be seen.

What now?

There was too much to think about, too much trouble besides the storm blowing through this hotel.

I stood at the end of the hall, looking down the stairwell into the shadows. I thought about the story Ty had told me. Given my past luck, I shouldn't have been surprised to find myself cooped up with a trio of drug dealers, as well as a paid assassin.

I had no trouble believing that Chris Stowall had been making money by helping drug runners. In South Texas, that was a well-established part of the economy, right up there with ranching, drilling for oil and making acrylic-rattlesnake toilet seats for the tourists.

Still, I doubted Chris had died because of a drug deal. Certainly Jesse Longoria wouldn't have come down here for anything as petty as a crate of Mexican Valium. Both of them had been playing a much more dangerous game.

I rubbed my eyes. I kept seeing Rachel Brazos's face carved in wood.

Two bodies downstairs, and the death that haunted me most was a lady I'd never known.

I imagined Ralph Arguello laughing. *You hang out with the dead too much,* vato.

No contest, I pleaded. Then I turned and headed toward Alex Huff's bedroom.

Inside, the storm had sprayed everything with broken glass and sand like sugar coating on a pan dulce. Somebody, probably Jose, had nailed a quilt over the smashed window. The wind and rain had already ripped it to shreds.

I wondered if it was just wishful thinking, or if the storm sounded a little less intense now. It wasn't much louder than your average booster rocket.

I picked up the wooden statue and set it on the dresser. She still looked like Rachel, her hand out, asking some question I couldn't answer.

I went through Alex's dresser drawers, then his closet. After ten minutes of turning his room upside down, I'd found nothing remarkable. Nothing except the statue.

And that bothered me.

I knew Alex well enough to know that I

should've found some memorabilia: the photos he'd once shown me from his fishing expeditions, his dad's army knife, maybe the signed Jimmy Buffett poster Garrett had given him for his twentieth birthday.

Despite his temper, Alex Huff was a sentimentalist. He kept old things. He remembered people he'd known as a child. He'd spent his life savings to buy this hotel because it had been dear to his father.

And yet this room looked like any other room in the hotel. Except for the wooden statue of the dead woman.

I got up and went to the window. The wind was definitely slacking now. Its howl was less insistent. Woven Guatemalan pictures rippled across the tattered quilt—men with machine guns, helicopters over a rain forest.

On an impulse, I ripped it down.

I was standing there, staring into the angry edge of the dying hurricane, when the hotel's power went out again.

As my eyes adjusted to the deeper darkness, I noticed something out in the storm—a flicker of light, and then it was gone.

I might've imagined it. Storms can play a lot of tricks with the light. But I was pretty sure I'd just seen a candle extinguished in the top window of the old lighthouse.

28

Calavera squatted in the dark stairwell, listening to the noises of the house. Four in the morning was a good time for murder. He would not normally choose to work in a house that was occupied. This had already caused him problems, almost given him away. But under the circumstances, he had no choice.

He set his hand on the unpainted timbers. The walls here were so close together his shoulders touched on either side.

He remembered his first job, so much like this one.

A police commander, a judge and a lawyer walked into the brothel. It sounded like the beginning of a joke, but the three men would never come out alive. Calavera had spent weeks studying their habits. He knew they would stay overnight on Sunday, as they always did, and so Calavera had visited on Saturday as a client. In the early morning, when everyone was asleep, he had laid the trap.

Monday at 4 A.M., he watched from the building across the street. He lay on the roof with a rifle, just to be sure. The brothel's back doors were barricaded. He had seen to that. If anyone came out the front, or made it through a window, he would take care of them. He did not like loose ends.

He needn't have worried. The explosion was beautiful: flame blossoming simultaneously in the windows. The screams were short-lived. And no one came out of the building.

The display was better than fireworks. Blood rushed through his veins. He felt more alive than he had in years.

Soon, setting bombs had become his addiction. The money was good, necessary for his survival, but he would have done the work without pay. He had finally found something he was good at.

Now, he wished he could recapture that thrill. But this time was different. Necessary, yes, but he would take no pleasure from it.

He connected the last wire to a simple timer. So much could be accomplished with a single electrical pulse.

He sat for a few moments listening to the sounds of sleepers on the other side of the wall— gentle snoring, restless turning in bed. Tomorrow, he would be away from here. He would start again, and this would be his last display. A work of necessity, hastily done. He didn't like that. But the beauty of fire wiped out one's imperfections. Fire was very forgiving.

He set the candy skull on the timer, knowing no one would ever see it. But he would know it was there, small sugary eyes watching as the seconds ticked down in the dark.

29

I meant to venture out into the storm to inves-tigate the lighthouse. Instead, I went to check on Maia, lay down next to her thinking it would only be for a few minutes and ended up falling asleep.

So much for the intrepid hero of the tempest.

Most of my dreams were surreal, kind of like my life. Unfortunately, this time I dreamed about the day I quit private investigations, and that dream was always exactly true-to-life.

I was in my office—the converted dining room of our Victorian on South Alamo. It was winter in San Antonio. The wall furnace hissed. Outside, the sky was heavy gray and the bare pecan trees looked like charred bones.

I'd just returned from San Fernando Cemetery, from my encounter with U.S. Marshal Longoria at Ralph's graveside. Longoria's words kept coming back to me: *If you can't stop feeling guilty, son, maybe you should find a different line of work.*

I had a pile of paperwork on my desk. A few skip traces. A divorce case. An undercover job I needed to set up with a local jewelry store. I also had a stack of essays to grade from my part-time teaching gig at UTSA. I was trying to decide whether I wanted to write a report about my client's cheating husband or grade sophomore papers on Chaucer's use of alliteration. The fun factor seemed about the same, either way.

Maia was in the living room, talking on the phone with her doctor. She'd been on the phone since I got home. I tried not to think about that. She was constantly telling me not to worry. The doctor was probably trying again to convince her to do amniocentesis. She was politely but firmly saying no.

She wasn't showing too much yet. She had white paint flecked on her fingers. She'd spent the morning painting the baby's room upstairs, even though I'd told her she should take it easy.

I checked my email. I had a lot of messages. My boss at UTSA, asking again if I wouldn't reconsider taking another course. They were shorthanded as usual. He could easily move me to a full-time position. He mentioned the magic words: *health care.*

There was a message from a client, thanking me

for finding her runaway daughter. There was an email from Ana DeLeon, Ralph's widow, with a photo attachment of their baby girl, Lucia. Lucia had her father's crazy grin as she dumped the candy out of her Christmas stocking.

Worst of all, there was a Happy New Year e-card from Rosa Gomez, the lady who had hired me to find her fugitive husband. I didn't know why Rosa kept me on her holiday list. She claimed I was the only one who listened to her, the only one who even tried to help her husband. I'm not sure I would've been so generous in her position. I had failed her miserably.

I shouldn't have tortured myself, but I found the file on Julio Gomez and looked through it again. Like homicide detectives, PIs get certain cases that just won't let you go. They are never resolved. They haunt you.

I'd never even met Julio Gomez, but I knew him well.

His photo showed a thin Latino in his late twenties. A good smile. Intelligent eyes. He didn't look like a criminal. You wouldn't latch your door if you saw Julio Gomez walking down your street. When he was seventeen, he'd been messing around on a highway overpass with some friends, throwing rocks down at cars. One rock went through a Ford pickup's windshield with the force of a cannonball and killed a passenger. Julio had been tried as an adult, but he managed a plea deal—involuntary manslaughter. Light sentence. That had been his first strike. When he was twenty-one, he'd gotten in a fight at a bar. Unfortunately, the man had been an off-duty cop. This got Julio an assault conviction and a bad reputation among the city's police.

When he got out of jail again, Julio married his longtime sweetheart, Rosa. Julio tried to go straight, despite the fact that the cops often harassed him, knowing he had a short temper. Julio was doing all right—holding down a job, thinking about community college. Then the gas station where Julio worked was burned to the ground a few days after Julio had argued with his boss. Julio was brought up on arson charges. He made bail, panicked and ran. He told Rosa he couldn't take another felony count. More jail time would kill him.

Rosa was our down-the-street neighbor. She passed my business sign every day on her way to work. She came to me, begging me to find her husband. Julio was innocent of arson. Julio had to come back and stand trial.

I never found him. Within a few days, rumors started surfacing about Jesse Longoria. The marshal had been asking questions about Julio, following the same trail I had. Except Longoria had been more efficient and more ruthless.

What bothered me most was that I never found the body. I couldn't prove what had happened. I couldn't give Rosa any closure. All I had were suspicions. But that morning at the cemetery, Longoria's smile had given me all the proof I needed. I thought about his pleasant eyes, his black wool coat, his gold college ring. He was a hunter with no remorse. He had found Julio Gomez, probably put a bullet through his head, dumped the body and gone out afterward for dinner and a show. He would've done the same for Ralph Arguello, or me for that matter, if we'd happened to cross him.

Why did I want people like that in my life?

I slipped Julio Gomez's file back into my cabinet. I stared at the picture of my dead best friend's daughter Lucia on my computer screen. Ana DeLeon's brief note: *Love from both of us.*

I closed the email program.

In the living room, Maia hung up the phone. She sat with her fingers laced, staring at the coffee table. I knew she was gathering her composure before she came to talk to me. Especially during the first trimester, pregnancy had played hell with her hormones. She got emotional much more easily than usual, and she hated it. She spent a lot of time alone at the coffee table.

In six months, give or take, I would be a father. When I thought about the legacy I had from my own dad, what did I come up with? His old service revolver, a warped view of law enforcement and some painful memories from a childhood spent on Rebel Island.

I stared at the telephone. Then I picked it up and dialed my boss at UTSA. I told him I was thinking of going full-time. He said he'd start the paperwork immediately.

30

Benjamin Lindy watched the sunrise through a hole in the wall.

He'd always been an early riser. When he was a child, his job had been to tend the chickens on the ranch. He'd get up before first light and check for eggs, remove snakes from the hutch when necessary and let the chickens out to feed.

Early rising had been bred into him. It was a physical need. Around four in the morning, his feet would start to tingle and the sheets would begin to feel itchy. He *had* to get out of bed. On the rare occasion when he overslept and woke up to daylight, he felt sluggish and out of sorts, cheated of his best time.

This morning, he'd had several hours to think

before the sun came up. He'd decided he would have to kill someone today.

The room he was standing in had been a parlor suite. Sometime during the night, a telephone pole had pierced the wall—crossbeams, wires and all. It stuck about five feet into the room, hanging crookedly in the ragged hole it had made, the top of the pole pushing against the ceiling. Lord knew where the telephone pole had come from. There were none on the island, as far as Benjamin could recall. When he came into the room, his first impression was that a sailing ship had rammed the building with its bowsprit.

He slipped his hand into his pocket. The gun was still there. It was his spare sidearm, too small for his hand, but now he was glad he'd brought it. Years ago, he'd bought the gun for his wife, but she'd never touched it—one of the many things she'd left behind. He supposed there was some sort of justice in him using that gun today.

He watched the sky turn from black to steel. He still burned from the indignity of having his .45 taken from him, as if he were a child. A year earlier, the state had tried to take away his driver's license, simply because he was old. Then a murderer had taken away his daughter, as if old age did not rob a man of enough. Navarre had no right to rule over him. Benjamin had been wrong to trust Navarre. He would do no more than the law.

He remembered his last conversation with Peter Brazos, who of all people should've been his ally. Peter had turned all his attention to prosecuting the drug lords. He poured his rage into his work. But Calavera...Peter saw the assassin as a tool, not the real target. When Benjamin had tried to warn him what the Marshals Service was doing, tried to suggest they take action before the assassin could cut a deal, Peter had shut him down.

"Not another word," Peter snapped. "Ben, this conversation never happened. If they can bring the bastard in, I'm all for it. I want his bosses' names. All of them. But you will do nothing outside the law. Do you hear me? *Nothing.*"

Benjamin backed down. He pretended compliance. And they had not spoken since.

Outside, the rain still fell, but the storm was dying. Today Calavera would try to escape. Benjamin wasn't sure how, but he could not allow anyone to leave the island, not until the assassin was dead.

He would have to watch.

He replayed last night in his mind. His brief conversation with Ty had bothered him. Those boys were up to no good. Ty knew something about Stowall's murder, but he'd wanted to talk to Navarre. He wouldn't tell Benjamin anything.

Then there was Alex Huff, the way he'd left abruptly last night. And now where was he? Every time Benjamin looked at Huff, he had to constrain his anger. It could not be a coincidence that the trail to his daughter's murderer had led here, to this vile hotel. The very existence of the place was an insult to him. And Alex Huff...he would have to be found.

Benjamin rested his hand on the telephone

pole. He would have to be patient a little while
longer. He would have to control his anger. But
when the time came, he could not hesitate.

Blood for blood today. No one would take that
away from him.

31

As dawn broke, I stood at one of the many shattered windows on the second floor and surveyed the aftermath of Hurricane Aidan.

It was still raining hard, like white noise rather than water. The northern stretch of the island had disappeared under the waves. As far as I could see—which was only about two hundred yards—the Gulf churned in a foamy gray soup that blurred into the sky.

The main bulk of the island had been reduced to a few acres around the hotel. The path was scoured away. The remaining palmetto trees were stripped of fronds. The boat dock had vanished, but as the waves swept back, the tips of the old pilings peeked above the water.

In front of me, the lighthouse rose dark and un-damaged. Even the glass of the lantern house seemed to have survived the storm, which seemed impossible—insulting, really. But no light flickered in the windows. No sign of movement. I still needed to check out the light I'd seen the night before, but I wasn't anxious to brave the rain again. I was steeling my nerves to go downstairs when I heard a cough behind me.

"Is it over?" Lane Sanford asked.

She was standing bleary-eyed in the doorway. Her hair was flat on one side. She had pillow-wrinkles on her cheek.

"Looks that way," I said. "What brings you here?"

"This is my room."

I might've blushed. I hadn't even noticed the dresses hanging up in the closet, the makeup kit on the bathroom sink. The door had been open, the room soaked with rain like all the others. I'd just walked right in. The past night in the hotel had eroded my sense of private property.

"Sorry," I murmured.

"It's okay." She came to the window and looked out.

The sky was getting incrementally brighter. I still couldn't see the sun, but there was a yellow quality to the gray, like butter in oatmeal.

Lane looked healthier in the light. The wrinkles around her eyes might've been from smiling rather than weariness. Her blond hair had a silky sheen.

"When will the ferry come?" she asked.

"It's more likely the Coast Guard will get here first. They'll have some fast boats riding out the storm."

She strained her eyes toward the horizon, as if trying to imagine such a boat. I could relate. After last night, the idea of rescue—the notion that anything could exist beyond Rebel Island—seemed as fantastic as pink elephants.

"My ex-husband was never here," she said softly. "I owe you an apology."

Out in the ocean, something surfaced—a gleaming white arc of fiberglass, the bottom of a capsized boat—and sank again instantly beneath the waves.

"Why did you run from him?" I asked.

"He murdered a man."

"Who?"

Lane hugged her arms. "I don't even know his name. Isn't that terrible? He was...a migrant worker. Bobby and I lived near the train tracks outside Uvalde. One afternoon in March, while Bobby was at work, this man knocked on the kitchen door. He asked me for a drink of water. I shouldn't have let him in."

"You let a stranger into your home?"

"He was thirsty and hungry. He was about to collapse. I didn't see why not."

I could think of a lot of reasons. A young woman alone in the country, letting a strange man into her house. But the way she said it made it sound like the most reasonable thing in the world.

"I was alone most days," she told me. "It was hot. I had the kitchen window open and I was slicing apples. The whole house smelled like wheat from the fields. The man who came to the door... he had dark skin. He wore an old denim shirt, beige pants. His tennis shoes were worn through. He spoke good English. He said he'd hitched a train all the way from Piedras Negras. He had a wife and four children. He wanted to find work so he could send them money."

I pictured the scene—Lane at one end of the kitchen table, listening to the immigrant's story. It wasn't hard to see why the man had opened up to her. When she wasn't terrified, her face was kind and open.

"He ate a turkey sandwich and some apple slices and a glass of milk," she remembered. "Then Bobby got home."

She fell into a kind of trance as she told the rest of her story. It was as if she'd practiced it in front of the mirror many times, trying to make herself understand.

Bobby never came home before dark, she said. But that day he did. He'd had an argument with his foreman and walked off the job. He stopped at a store in Uvalde, bought a six-pack of beer and downed three of them in the truck on the way home.

When he found the Mexican sitting at his kitchen table, he turned on Lane. He struck her across the face, called her a whore. The Mexican man rose and told Bobby to stop.

Bobby grabbed a kitchen knife, the same one Lane had been using to slice apples, and the

Mexican man lifted his hands as if that would stop the blade.

Hours later, after dark and a lot more alcohol, Bobby buried the Mexican. He forced Lane to help. They dragged the body to a creek bed behind their rented property and spent hours digging a hole in the wet black earth. Afterward, he told Lane he had only been protecting her. He drove the point home with a good beating. He'd only done what he had to do, killing that Mexican. If she told anyone, he would kill her. Lane had no doubt he meant it.

Three months later, she finally got up the nerve to run.

"I knew he'd never let me go," she told me. "He's still looking for me."

"Go to the police."

She shook her head. "They'd put me in prison, too. I've stayed silent for months. I helped him hide the body. If I just hadn't let that poor man inside, or if I'd told him to leave a little sooner—"

"What Bobby did wasn't your fault."

She brushed the rain off her face. "I told Garrett all this. I told him he shouldn't get involved with me."

I didn't answer.

"I like him," Lane admitted. "I don't know what to do. He's the kindest man I've ever met."

"You need to get out more."

She pursed her lips. "I understand you don't approve. You don't want him to get hurt."

That stunned me. I'd been so worried about Garrett taking advantage of Lane, I'd never thought about Garrett getting hurt. But as Lane said it, I realized she was right. I didn't want my brother falling for anyone. I'd seen him do that before. His depression when he was dumped—and he was always dumped—was terrible and dangerous.

And yet, looking at Lane, I felt like some chances might be worth taking, even if they were dangerous. Maybe it was the right thing to unlatch your screen door for a stranger once in a while, let them inside for apple slices and milk.

"I know some good lawyers," I said. "I'm married to one. We can help you work a deal with the police."

"You barely know me. You would do that for me?"

"Yeah, I would."

She rested her hand on my arm. "Garrett was right about you."

"What did he say?"

"That you could solve any problem. Or you'd die trying."

"I'd like to avoid the 'die trying' part."

She smiled. "I should go check on Garrett, leave you in peace."

"It's your room."

"I just came to salvage my things." She looked around helplessly, as if she'd already decided that mission was no good.

"Lane," I said. "Did you know Chris Stowall was in love with you?"

Her eyes became unfocused. She stared into the storm. "Let me know if you spot the Coast Guard."

Then she turned and left me alone with a window full of rain.

I stood in front of Lane's closet and looked at her drenched clothes. A dozen cotton dresses, all pastels, all the same utilitarian style. Four pairs of simple flat-soled shoes. Two small brown suitcases. I had a feeling Lane had brought everything she owned.

At the back of the closet, next to Lane's shoes, a black electrical cord curled like a snake, frayed copper wires sticking up at the end. I knelt to pick it up, but it seemed to be attached, crimped between the wall and the floor. It took me a minute to process why this didn't seem right. Then my skin turned cold.

I remembered last night—Lane screaming, swearing she'd seen a man in her room. A man who had vanished into the closet.

I pushed aside Lane's dresses. I stepped into the closet and ran my fingers along the sides of the back wall. The latch was in the top left corner—a simple mechanism. I pulled it: the wall swung away from me.

A secret door, just like Garrett had suggested. The latch was much too high for him to have found it last night.

I backed out and found my flashlight. When I shone it into the closet, I saw that the secret area was narrow, no more than a few feet deep—a landing on a steep stairwell, crude wooden steps leading up and down, sandwiched between the walls of the guest rooms.

At my feet was the loose piece of electrical cord that had caught my attention. I picked it up. I wondered if it had been caught under the door last night when the man had fled in haste.

I swept the flashlight beam around the rest of the closet and into the stairwell, but I didn't see anything else suspicious. Just the frayed cord.

I stepped into the secret doorway. Down below I could see the flash of water. The flooding had not discriminated. Along with everything else on the first floor, it had found this hidden stairwell. I decided to go up and began to climb.

The steps were so steep they were almost a ladder, and they dead-ended at another door-size sheet of wood. I found the latch and opened it.

Voices. I was in someone else's closet. And judging from the smell of the clothes, I guessed it was a college guy's room.

"It's gotta be now," Chase was saying.

"Have you looked outside, man?" Markie's voice.

"I don't give a damn. It has to be now or it'll be too late."

"All right," Markie growled. "Christ, point that someplace else!"

"You're both crazy," Ty said. "Please, Chase, just let it go."

"Shut your mouth," Chase snapped. "You've screwed things up enough already."

Something went crunch. Unfortunately that

something was right under my foot. Conversation in the room stopped. I had two choices: back down the stairs or jump out and say "Ta-da!"

Given that Markie had just accused Chase of pointing something at him, I decided on discretion. I backed out and in the darkness relatched the wall panel.

I could hear the closet door opening on the other side. I was sure Chase and Markie were going to kick in the back wall and find me, but there was silence.

"It was nothing," Chase said. "Damn storm making noises again."

"Huh," Markie said. He didn't sound convinced, but the closet door closed, and I climbed down the stairs as quietly as I could.

Apparently, it was not my day for visiting clos-ets. When I came back out of Lane's, I found Benjamin Lindy standing by the window.

He turned as I emerged from the rack of dresses. He didn't look particularly surprised.

"Miss Sanford told me you were here, Mr. Navarre. I didn't realize she meant in the closet."

I couldn't think of another explanation, so I told him the truth.

He stepped past me and checked the passage for himself. He peered up into the gloom. When he came out again, he looked troubled. "The boys' room, you say?"

"I could hear them arguing. I couldn't tell what about."

He fixed me with that courtroom gaze. "They're drug dealers, Mr. Navarre. Surely you've figured that out. Now I'm wondering if they are murderers as well."

"They've got nothing to do with Calavera."

"Mr. Navarre." Lindy's voice held a touch of desperation. "We are entering the most dangerous hours of the weekend. The storm is passing. Sooner or later, a boat will come. Calavera will be getting restless to leave this island. He cannot let us leave as well. He cannot afford to have the authorities alerted."

"You don't want the authorities alerted, either," I said. "You want to resolve this yourself."

Lindy didn't answer.

I looked down and realized I was still holding the frayed piece of electrical cord. I felt it was important, but I didn't know why. It bothered me almost as much as the statue up in Alex's room.

"How did Chris know to contact you?" I asked Lindy.

"We've been through this."

"He didn't know you personally?"

Lindy hesitated. "I assume he saw the news about Rachel's murder."

"You hadn't been to Rebel Island before? You didn't know Alex Huff?"

"No."

"Alex wasn't friends with your daughter? They didn't go to school together or anything like that?"

"No," he said coldly. "Why are you asking this?"

I thought about Rachel Brazos's face, carved in wood. The face of a grown woman carved while Rachel was still a child. *A new mother.*

"What about your wife?" I asked.

Lindy's expression hardened. "What about her?"

"There were no pictures in the scrapbook. Who was she? Did Rachel look like her?"

There was a sudden electricity in the room that had nothing to do with the storm. I knew I had crossed a line Mr. Lindy would never forgive.

"That has no bearing," Lindy said.

"You said you asked Longoria's advice about your wife. She ran away, didn't she?"

Lindy stared at the suitcases on Lane Sanford's bed. The rain in the window made a frame of static behind him.

"My wife was a troubled woman," he said. "Rachel's birth left her deeply depressed. Unbalanced. She disappeared and left me to raise our daughter alone."

"You never found her?"

"I stopped looking. That was Marshal Longoria's advice. She was better gone. He was right."

The bitterness in his voice was so fresh his wife might've left yesterday.

"Longoria understood vengeance," I said. "He wasn't so good with love. It sounds like he steered you wrong more than once."

"My daughter was murdered, Mr. Navarre. Her killer is here. I intend to find him."

I nodded. "Maia was wondering who's more dangerous. You or Calavera?"

"Do not compare us."

"Don't try to kill him."

A knock on the door. Jose came in, looking worried.

"Señores," he said. "I'm sorry, but I thought... I happened to see. The three young gentlemen."

"What about them?" I asked.

"They went downstairs," Jose told us. "They just left the hotel."

32

Maia and Imelda returned to the Colonel's
Suite and found it hardly damaged at all. Rain still
dripped from the ceiling into the overflowing silver
cup. The air smelled of extinguished candles. The
picture of Tres's father and the other two men hung
crookedly on the wall.

Maia sat on the edge of the bed to catch her
breath. The bedspread was dry and warm.

"I will pack your things, señora," Imelda said.

"That isn't necessary. I can get them."

Imelda didn't seem to hear. She found the suitcase in the closet and set it at the foot of the bed.
"You should be ready to leave."

It didn't take long. Maia and Tres had always
been light travelers. Within a few minutes, Imelda

had folded their clothes and tucked them away. She found Maia's .357 wrapped in a nightgown and held it cupped in her hands as if unsure whether to pack it.

"What's bothering you?" Maia asked.

Imelda set the gun down. "I—I should help Jose get breakfast ready."

But Maia could sense her indecision—wanting to say something, afraid to do so.

Usually, silence helped. In her practice, Maia would sit quietly for a long time, creating a space for the client's statement. Let them fill the gap with words. But Imelda didn't.

"I decided," Maia told her, "the baby will be a boy." And without knowing why, Maia explained her fears.

Imelda stared at her, as if she'd just noticed Maia for the first time. "This...disease runs in your family, señora?"

Maia nodded. "My brother died when he was very young. We watched him get weaker and weaker. Grief destroyed my father."

"And the chances are good that your son will have this?"

"Yes."

"But you risk it anyway."

"I've thought about it. I've decided I am supposed to have this child."

Imelda pursed her lips. "I thought the same thing with my own children..."

Maia waited, but once again, Imelda backed off.

Whatever she was afraid of saying, the fear won out.

"Imelda," she said. "If there's a way I can help you—"

"You should get out of this old house, señora. Fresh air would do you good."

"It's still pouring," Maia said.

Imelda folded the .357 back in the nightgown and packed it in the suitcase. "You are ready, señora. I have to help with breakfast."

Alone, Maia reclined on the bed and listened to the rain plinking into the silver cup. She decided she should go down to the dining room, just to see what was happening. But she lay still and stared at the ceiling. She thought about her old home in China, how the rain would drum against the corrugated tin roof, and how she would fall asleep listening to her brother's labored breathing—until the day he died. Ever since then, she could never fall asleep in a silent room.

33

I got to the bottom of the stairs and found that the water was receding from the first floor, leaving a spongy marsh of carpet, seaweed and salt foam.

The front door had been blown off its hinges. Outside, rain made a steady downpour, but the wind was almost tolerable. Waves lapped a few feet from the base of the lighthouse. Mounds of sand stuck up here and there above the churning water—scattered bumps that emerged and disappeared with every surge, so what was left of Rebel Island reminded me of a smudged charcoal rubbing.

From the outside, the hotel didn't look as bad as I'd feared. The roof had been scoured away in places, leaving a skeletal frame of beams. The windows looked more like craters. Otherwise the building seemed intact, but something bothered me about its appearance. I couldn't decide what.

I asked Benjamin Lindy to stay behind. I wasn't sure how his legs would hold up in the floodwater, and, more important, I didn't like the angry look in his eyes. But of course he didn't listen. He followed as I trudged into the tide looking for our college friends.

It wasn't hard to spot them. They were about a quarter mile north, standing ankle-deep in the stormy water like disciples. One of the guys—red-headed Chase—was squatting down like he was looking for something. The other two stood and watched.

I did a quick scan of the horizon. Nothing in any direction except storm and ocean. On a clear day, the coastline would've been visible from Rebel Island. Not today. If I hadn't known better, I would've sworn we were a thousand miles from the mainland.

I wanted to stop at the lighthouse and check on the strange flicker I'd seen the night before, but Benjamin Lindy was already ahead of me, wading purposefully toward Chase, Markie and Ty. I didn't intend to let the old man confront them without me. We had quite enough dead bodies as it was.

Chase was on his knees in the surf, clawing at the wet sand that sucked back into place as soon as he tried to scoop it out.

"Dude," Markie told him. "We got company."

Chase looked up at us, a vacant stare in his eyes. "It should be here. Two crates. They can't just disappear."

"He's confused." Markie slipped his hand into his pocket. "Been cooped up too long. Doesn't know what he's saying."

I glanced at Ty. "Maybe he needs a Valium," I suggested. "Or codeine."

Markie's expression darkened. He turned to Ty. "You *told* him?"

"I—I didn't—"

"You sorry little—"

I saw the gun coming. I punched Markie in the gut as it came out of his pocket. The gun tumbled and was lost in a cloud of wet sand. Markie sat down hard in the water.

"Don't hurt him!" Ty yelped.

It took me a second to realize he was talking to me. He was terrified I might beat up the guy who'd been about to shoot him.

Markie rubbed his sore stomach. He eyed me with contempt. "Pretty fast for an old man."

He started to get up, but Benjamin Lindy stepped forward. "Stay down, son. Or this much *older* man will make you sorry. Now tell me about Calavera."

Coming from most eighty-year-olds, such a threat might've been amusing. No one laughed.

Markie looked at Chase and Ty. He shook his head cautiously. "We don't know anything about that."

"Calavera was connected to this island," Lindy

said. "He did most of his work for the drug cartels. You were moving drugs through the island—"

"Totally different thing, man!"

"When the police start asking why a U.S. Marshal and your friend Chris Stowall are both dead," Lindy said, "you will look very bad."

I had to give him credit. The old lawyer really knew how to sweat a witness. Markie squirmed like the ocean was boiling suddenly around him. "We don't know anything about murder, okay?"

"How often did you come to the island?" I asked. "How did you make the exchanges?"

"You think I'm going to tell you that?"

"Every two months," Chase cut in.

"Dude, shut up!"

"We'd stay for a weekend," Chase said. "The Mexicans would bring a boat on Friday night when it was dark. We'd never see them face to face. They'd bury the drugs . . . here."

He lifted his hands. Clumps of sand dripped through his fingers. "Later that night, we'd come down and put the stuff in bait buckets, like we were fishing, right? We'd bury the payment and leave. The Mexicans would pick it up . . . today. Saturday morning."

"They'd leave the drugs first?" I said. "They trusted you to pay?"

Chase was slumped over, his spirit broken. Hard to believe he was the same smart-mouthed kid I'd picked out as the leader of the gang last night.

"Trust had nothing to do with it," he said. "You

don't cross these people. Chris Stowall was the go-between, keeping an eye on the whole thing. If we'd tried to leave before the Sunday ferry, he would've radioed the Mexicans. We would've been dead before we got back to the mainland."

"Dude, why are you telling them this?" Markie demanded.

"What does it matter?" Chase said. "We're dead. We're completely dead."

"Explain the 'completely dead' part," I said.

Chase stared at the hole he'd made in the sand—no more than a dent now. Markie said nothing.

Finally Ty took a shaky breath. "We should've picked up the drugs last night. We couldn't because of the storm."

"That's why Chase and Markie were trying to leave the hotel last night," I guessed.

Ty nodded glumly. "Now it's too late. The drugs are gone. The thing is...the Mexicans won't believe us."

"You didn't make up the hurricane," I pointed out.

"Doesn't matter. They'll expect payment."

"You brought money to pay them?"

"Thirty-two grand." Ty glanced at Markie. "But it's gone, too. It disappeared from the room last night."

Suddenly their distress made more sense to me. No drugs. No money. Storm or not, their Mexican friends were not going to be happy.

"We've got to get them to come ashore," Markie said.

"They won't listen," Chase objected.

"Maybe not. But we take the boat."

Benjamin Lindy was studying the young men. It seemed to me his anger turned to disappointment as he did so. Once again, his vengeance was without a likely target. "What about Stowall? Did you kill him?"

"Hell, no," Markie said.

"That's not true!" Ty said. "Chris was blackmailing you—"

"Ty, shut up!" Markie warned.

"He wanted more money," Ty persisted. "They had a big argument. Chris said he needed to get away fast. He wanted an extra cut. He said he could make life really bad for us. He asked if we'd ever heard of Calavera."

Markie cursed. "That doesn't mean I killed him, dude."

"When was this argument?" I asked Ty, ignoring Markie.

"Friday afternoon. Not long before you got here."

"We didn't kill him," Markie said. "We don't kill people, okay? It's just drugs. It pays tuition, for Christ's sake."

I exchanged looks with Lindy. I hoped he was coming to the same conclusion as me—that whatever crap these guys had gotten themselves into, they weren't murderers. They knew as little about Calavera as we did.

Then I heard the sound of a speedboat engine.

A sleek black twenty-two-foot Howard Bow Rider rounded the southern tip of the island, cutting its way through the chop. Nobody except the Coast Guard or drug runners would've been insane enough to be out in seas like this. And I had a feeling this boat was not part of the Coast Guard.

Chase scrambled to his feet. He and Ty and Markie watched silently as the boat approached. Two men stood at the helm. Both wore black rain gear, their hoods pulled down over their faces.

One man steered. The other held an assault rifle.

We had no place to run. No cover. If they decided to shoot us, we were dead. So I just stood there with the college kids, waiting to see what they would do.

The boat slowed, passing a hundred yards off to our right. The driver seemed to know this area well. He navigated cautiously, keeping to the main channel, away from the submerged parts of the island.

The boat slowed to an idle. Chase held up his sand-caked hands in a gesture of surrender.

The two men studied us. What they saw: five gringos standing in ankle-deep water where their stash of money should have been.

Without a word or gesture, the driver sped up. The boat veered away. It headed out to sea, leaving a silver wake like a scythe.

Ty exhaled. "Close."

Chase stared at his empty hands. Markie's face was pale.

"What?" Ty asked. "They're gone, aren't they?"

I didn't have the heart to tell him. But their message was clear: the Mexicans wouldn't waste their time shooting Ty and his friends now. They would have it done properly, in a much more public place.

I knelt down and sifted through the water until I found the gun Markie had dropped. It was a .22, Ty's marksman pistol. It occurred to me that a .22 could've been the same caliber that had killed Jesse Longoria.

"Start planning your statement for the police," I told Markie.

"The drugs are gone," he said miserably. "What's the point of talking to the police?"

"Because it might be your only chance at staying alive."

I sloshed back toward the ruined hotel, leaving the college kids standing in the water where the source of their next year's tuition had washed away.

"What *kind* of wire?" Garrett asked.

We were sitting in the destroyed dining room. I was briefing Maia and Garrett on my fun-filled excursion into the surf. Garrett's question took me by surprise.

I dug around in my pocket, found the frayed copper wire and handed it to him.

He scowled. "You found this in Lane's closet?"

"Yeah."

"Ain't for computers."

I didn't argue. Garrett was the computer programmer in the family.

He twirled the wire between his fingers. "So what's it for?"

That's when it hit me—why the wire had bothered me, something that should've been obvious. "It's part of an IED."

"A what?"

"Improvised explosive device," Maia said, keeping her voice down. "A bomb."

"*A bomb?*" Garrett definitely did not keep his voice down.

Jose and Imelda looked over from the kitchen doorway. They'd been scavenging breakfast for the guests and were now dividing up their loot—a bag of saltines, five green apples.

"A little discretion," I told Garrett.

"Discretion," he said. "Somebody tries to blow up Lane and you want discretion?"

"We don't know that anyone was targeting Lane." Maia put her hand on Garrett's arm. As usual, she was able to calm him down a lot more than I could, but he still looked pretty damn angry.

He leaned toward me. "The guy we saw in Lane's closet—he was *real*."

"I think so."

"We scared him out of there before he could plant a bomb. He dropped this wire."

"One possibility," I agreed. "But why target Lane?"

Garrett stared outside. In a burst of optimism, Jose and Imelda had removed the plywood from the last intact dining room window. Slate gray sky and sea spread toward the horizon like unwashed sheets.

"It couldn't have been about her," Garrett decided. "Besides, we'll be outta here soon. Whatever this guy was trying to do—"

"Garrett," I said, as gently as I could. "Do you want to ask her about it, or should I?"

He twisted his linen napkin. In the stormy light, his three-day whiskers looked grayer than usual. "Yeah," he said wearily. "I'll talk to her."

Jose and Imelda went off to distribute their high-cuisine breakfast, which left Maia and me alone in the dining area, munching stale saltines and watching the rain make claw marks on the window.

"Drugs," Maia said. "Someday maybe I'll hear about a case that doesn't involve drugs."

We both knew the odds of that were long. It didn't matter if you worked with runaways, prostitutes, politicians, murderers or socialites. Drugs were as omnipresent as sex and greed.

"Chris Stowall used his manager's job to make some extra money on the side," I told her. "He was mad at Alex for closing the hotel because his revenue stream was about to dry up. The twenty thousand from the boathouse—that was Chris's life savings. He was getting ready to make a break for the mainland and disappear, as soon as he delivered Calavera to Longoria and Lindy. Chris stood to make an extra fifty grand from that. He figured he'd try to milk Chase and his friends, too. Get a little more money that way."

"You don't think he fabricated the Calavera story?"

"No. The email was real. Chris found it, somehow he realized what it meant. But I think he found something else, too. Something that really startled him."

I told Maia about the statue in Alex's room—the lady who looked like Rachel Brazos. I told her about my conversations with Lindy, who apparently had never visited the island before.

"Lindy's wife," Maia said. "You think that was a statue of her."

I nodded. "She ran away. Now that I'm getting to know Benjamin Lindy a little better, I can't blame her. I think she came here. The man who ran the hotel back in those days, Mr. Eli, he would've taken her in without question. She fell in love with Mr. Huff. She had another child, Alex. She died when Alex was young. I don't know how. But I think that statue is of Alex's mother."

Maia shook her head. "Hell of a coincidence."

"Not really," I said. "Welcome to South Texas."

I remembered what Lindy had said about the whole area being a close-knit community. Mr. Eli had said something similar, back when I was a kid: *South Texas is just too small a place. Everyone is connected somehow.*

Running into someone you knew, someone you were related to without realizing it—that was commonplace. The bloodlines in South Texas were as twisted as the barbed wire.

"Chris would've assumed the statue was Rachel Brazos," I said. "He'd probably seen her picture in the media many times."

"And that would've convinced him Alex Huff was Calavera," Maia said. "He may have been right for the wrong reasons."

I thought about that. Rachel Brazos and her two young daughters had died by mistake. I still had trouble believing Alex was a cold-blooded killer, but if he'd seen Rachel's picture in the paper after the explosion, and realized who she was... That might be enough to cause remorse even in a man like Calavera.

"Perhaps Alex is gone," Maia said. "Maybe he found a way off the island. When he left last night and gave Garrett that envelope... it sounded like he knew he wasn't coming back."

I wanted to believe her. If Calavera was gone, we were safe. Maybe.

"You really think that?"

"No," Maia sighed. Her facial color seemed better this morning. She'd managed the stairs all right, over my protests, but still, the idea of her packing bags or moving around at all made me nervous.

"Imelda helped me pack," she said. "She seemed distracted. I mean... even considering."

"You need to rest," I said. "We'll get you back upstairs. Safer up there."

She stared at the rain as it practiced pointillism on the window. "I'm tired of lying down. Tres, I think you should talk to her."

"Imelda?"

"She wanted to tell me something, but she wouldn't. Or couldn't. You should talk to her."

"I'm not leaving you by yourself."

"Please. I'm a big girl."

I looked at her belly.

"That's *not* what I meant, Tres. Find Imelda. See if she'll talk to you."

"Maia—"

"I'm perfectly fine. Besides, I'm not sure upstairs is any safer."

"Meaning?"

She gave me a reproachful look: the same look she always gives me whenever I try to protect her.

"Tres, we both know that wire is a timing mechanism. What if Calavera wasn't interested specifically in Lane? What if there are *other* bombs?"

By the time I caught up with Imelda, she was in the kitchen, salvaging linen from the floodwater. It seemed a hopeless task. She'd made a mountain of soggy napkins in the sink. Now she stood with her back to me, spreading out a tablecloth that looked like the Shroud of Turin.

My eyes drifted to the freezer room, then to the cellar door. I didn't know if Chris Stowall and Jesse

Longoria's bodies were still in their respective places. I couldn't see...or smell any change. That was fine by me.

"Imelda," I said.

She turned toward me with a soft gasp. Her apron was sprinkled with brown stains. Her hair was tied back in a bun, but strands of it were coming unraveled, like a yarn ball a cat had been playing with.

"Señor, I didn't hear you."

I pulled myself up on the butcher block counter. "Maia thought I should talk to you."

Imelda folded the tablecloth over her arm. "Is Señora Navarre well?"

"She's worried about you. She thought you might have something to tell me."

"Please, señor, if you wouldn't sit on the counter. Jose is very fussy—"

"How did you lose your children, Imelda?"

Silence. She picked up a knife and set it in the sink. "It was five years ago. In Nuevo Laredo."

"You lived in Nuevo Laredo?"

I tried not to sound surprised. These days, living in Nuevo Laredo was like sailing on the *Titanic*. For the past decade, the border town had been tearing itself apart as rival drug lords fought for control. Police, journalists, judges—all were gunned down on a regular basis.

"It was a *repriso*," Imelda murmured. "Jose did nothing wrong. He was a simple cook. But... someone believed he told the police something... It isn't important now. So many killed for no reason. A wrong look. A wrong word." Her voice was heavy with old grief. "They killed my children. When we came here, we had nothing. Mr. Huff took us in. We owe him everything."

"Which would make it hard to speak against him."

She held my eyes. She seemed to be struggling with something even heavier than the death of her children, some burden she was not sure she could carry.

"I understand you found a staircase," she said at last.

"You knew about it?"

She set down her tablecloth. She smoothed the flood-stained linen. "You can live here for many years, and still the walls surprise you. Now you must excuse me, señor."

After she'd gone I stared at the pile of wet napkins in the sink for several minutes before I realized what was bothering me.

The walls surprise you. I got up and headed for the collapsed bedroom that Alex Huff had cordoned off on the first floor—the bedroom that would be catty-corner below Lane's, at the bottom of the secret stairwell.

34

Garrett found Lane in Chris Stowall's bedroom, which didn't make him too happy. She was sitting on the bed, looking through a journal. She'd changed clothes: jeans, a white T-shirt, slip-on shoes. A lot more practical for a hurricane, but Garrett didn't remember anything but dresses in her closet upstairs. Then it occurred to him she'd borrowed the shirt and jeans from Chris Stowall's wardrobe. She was wearing a dead man's clothes.

"His diary?" Garrett asked.

Lane seemed to have trouble focusing on him. "Yes. It was just lying here."

He wheeled himself over, feeling like an intruder. He'd hardly known Chris Stowall at all, but he was jealous of the way Lane ran her hands over his diary pages. Chris and she had a long history together. Garrett had known her only one day. That was the hardest part, whenever he met a woman—getting past the ghosts.

"I was thinking about taking the journal," she said. "I don't know what I'd do with it, but . . . it's all that's left of him."

"Give it to his folks?" Garrett suggested.

Lane winced. "His mother would shut the door in my face. Or worse."

"Then leave it. Somebody found my diary after I was dead, I hope they'd burn it."

"That incriminating?"

"I don't keep a diary, darlin'."

She looked down at the last page of writing, traced her finger over a drawing of a wave. "Chris wanted to do so many things. None of them ever happened."

"Did he choose the room you'd stay in?"

"I suppose. It was just an open room. Why?"

Garrett shifted in his chair. "That guy you saw in your closet? Tres thinks he was there for a reason. He found a wire, see. It might've been part of a bomb."

"A bomb."

"Yeah." Garrett felt guilty, heaping this on Lane after all the other crap she'd been through. "My little bro, you know, he was just wondering—"

"Why a bomber would target my room."

"Something like that."

She closed the journal. She'd pulled her hair back in a ponytail, and Garrett liked the way it looked. He could see more of her face, her silver sand dollar earrings. She had a beautiful neck, smooth and white.

"Garrett, I've got skeletons in the closet. But Calavera isn't one of them. I don't know why he would bother with me."

"I figured it was crazy."

"But you had to ask."

"So these skeletons in your closet . . . it's not just your ex-husband, huh?"

"I don't keep a diary, either."

"Fair enough." He stared at the pocket of her T-shirt—*Chris's* T-shirt. It was decorated with a green crab and the words *Mike's Bar, Matamoros.* He and Alex had been there once. They'd borrowed the Navarre family sedan, told Garrett's parents they were going into Corpus Christi for the day to search for a used car for Alex. Instead, they'd driven to the border for a few drinks. The memory weighed on Garrett like a lead apron.

"I need your advice," he told Lane.

"My advice? You hardly know me."

But Garrett felt like he knew her as well as he needed. He didn't know why, but he had no trouble talking to her, and he figured Lane must feel the same way. After all, she'd told him all about the murder her ex-husband had committed, that awful night they'd dragged the immigrant's body into the woods. Maybe with a person like Lane, you didn't need to keep a diary. She was a better place to record your thoughts.

"I want to know what to do," he admitted. He brought out the letter Alex had left for him, and told her what it said.

35

Black plastic tarp and boards still blocked the end of the hall. I ripped them away as best I could. The door itself didn't look particularly damaged. The knob turned, but it wouldn't open. I kicked it, gave it shoulder treatment. Nothing. As if it was barricaded from the inside.

I tried to convince myself it didn't matter. One blocked-off room. One more damaged area in a hotel that was falling apart. So what?

Then I noticed the number on the door: *102*. I was standing in front of the same room my parents and I had always stayed in—the last room they'd ever shared as a married couple.

I remembered at age twelve limping down this hallway, the sole of my right foot burning from a jellyfish sting. I'd been exploring the northern tip of the island, imagining I was hiding from Jean Laffitte's pirates, when I bravely charged the surf and stepped straight into a blue and red bubble of pain.

My parents weren't anticipating me back until lunch. They expected me to take care of myself during the mornings. But I hobbled back to room 102, determined not to cry. Halfway down the corridor, I ran into Alex's father.

I'd only seen him around the island a few times before—cutting planks for a new dock or hammering tiles on the roof. He was a burly man. He had unruly blond hair like his son's, a scraggly beard, skin the color of saddle leather. His sun-faded clothes and unraveling straw cowboy hat always made me think of Robinson Crusoe. Up close, he smelled like whiskey, not so different from my father's smell, but Mr. Huff had a more kindly smile. There was an odd light in his eyes—the kind of look a sailor gets from staring too long at a watery horizon, as if the glare of the sun had burned permanently into his corneas.

He took one look at the way I was walking and said, "Jellyfish, eh?"

"Yes, sir."

A muffled shout came from down the hall— from behind my parents' door.

Mr. Huff pursed his lips. "Why don't you come to the kitchen, son? I'll put some baking soda on that sting."

"I want to see my parents." My voice quivered. My foot felt as if it were melting.

"Son, it's better you didn't. Sometimes things have to get worse for a long time before they can get better."

I didn't know what he was talking about. He put his hand on my shoulder, but I jerked away and continued down the hall.

I heard the yelling. I should've known better, but I opened the door.

Little details: the shattered glass on the floor, liquor soaking into the carpet. The cut above my mother's eye, a streak of blood trickling down her cheekbone. My father's clenched fist, his gold college ring biting into the white flesh of his fingers.

"Get out!" my mother screamed. And in that heartbeat, I thought she was talking to me.

I turned and ran, the pain in my foot forgotten.

"Tres!" my father yelled.

I knew he was coming after me, but I kept running. I caught a glimpse of Mr. Huff's face—pain and sympathy in his eyes. But he didn't try to stop me. He didn't intervene.

Sometimes things have to get worse for a long time.

Later, after my ill-fated fishing expedition with Alex, my mother found me and brought me back to the hotel room. The broken glass had been cleaned up. The cut on her eye was covered by a butterfly bandage. She treated my foot and tried not to cry as she explained that my father was gone. He'd taken the ferry back to the mainland without us.

My mother and he were taking a little vacation from their marriage.

I didn't understand. In my mind, vacation meant Rebel Island. My dad was already *on* vacation. Where would he go?

Now, thinking back on that day, my foot began to ache again. I pressed my hand against the battered door of room 102 and imagined pushing it open, seeing my parents inside.

Why would Alex block off this room?

Only one way to find out. I turned and headed back toward the stairs.

Lane Sanford was packing, but she closed her suitcase and latched it when I came in.

"Here to see me or my closet?" she asked.

"Your closet," I said. "Most popular one in the hotel."

"Naturally." She turned her back to me and bundled some clothes, then hesitated. Apparently she realized she needed to put them in the suitcase, but she'd closed it too quickly, and she didn't want to open it in my presence.

"Did Garrett talk to you?" I asked.

She folded a pink dress. "About the bomb. Yes."

"You sound pretty calm about it."

"I don't believe it," she said. "That's why."

"I can show you the door."

"Tres, I don't believe anyone besides my husband would want to kill me. That's what I mean. And frankly, a bomb isn't Bobby's style."

There was tightness in her voice, like a guitar string tuned an octave too high.

"Were you and Chris Stowall involved?"

She shook her head. "Not the way you mean."

"In what way, then?"

"I told you. I'd known him since high school. Chris was no angel, but he came from a hard family. He knew how I felt. He would never hurt anyone..."

"Unless?"

She sat on her bed and looked up at me. "It doesn't matter now."

"Is that what you told Garrett?"

Her cheeks colored. "I told Garrett I was sorry we'd met like this. I told him Chris was a friend, trying to protect me. Chris offered me shelter. He offered me more help, too. But I refused."

"What kind of help?"

"To get my husband out of the way."

"To kill him."

"I don't think he could have done it. Not really. But he was angry. He said he knew someone who could."

"Calavera."

"I don't know."

"Chris used the same threat on Ty and Markie. He was helping them run drugs, pressuring them for more money. He seemed to like having Calavera as an ace up his sleeve."

"Chris tried to help me, Tres. He didn't deserve to die for that."

The tone of her voice made me wonder if I'd

completely misread Stowall's feelings for her. "You talk about him as if he was a relative."

She got up and took her suitcase. "The closet is all yours. I'll take my things to Garrett's room."

She said it defiantly, daring me to protest her moving in with Garrett.

"Lane, was Chris your brother?"

The look in her eyes was close to pity, as if she felt sorry for how little I understood the world. "Tres, my married name was Stowall. Chris was my *husband's* brother. That's why he knew how much danger I was in."

The secret stairway was still there. I was kind of hoping it wouldn't be, but I was used to not getting what I hoped for.

I thought about Lane Sanford, and how she'd ended up with such an inconvenient room. I wondered if Chris had given her this room for some reason. I was no longer sure what to make of it.

If Chris had made plans to help Lane against his homicidal brother, it made sense that he'd want an escape plan, including a lot of money. I remembered the little pictures Chris had drawn in his journal, the photo of Waikiki Beach on his mirror. Perhaps he still believed he could convince Lane to go with him. In time, he could get her to love him. A surfer's happily-ever-after. Pretty simplistic. But I couldn't blame him for holding out hopes for Lane. As near as I could tell, she and Alex Huff were the only ones who'd ever given Chris a chance at a clean slate. Chris had messed things up pretty bad.

I took a deep breath and headed into the stairwell. This time I went down instead of up.

I almost fell through on the third step. It cracked as I put my weight on it and I flailed out, catching something with my hand that turned out to be a large nail. The metal bit into my palm. I could feel it bleeding, but I didn't want to look. One more souvenir I'd have from my honeymoon—a tetanus shot. I examined the remaining steps with my flashlight and found that they were in pretty bad shape.

I tested each one. Five steps down, two of them broke with a light kick. Finally, I managed to half walk, half wall-climb my way to the bottom, which was still covered in an inch or so of salt water. Unfortunately, there was another secret door. It opened into a closet, which opened into room 102. I didn't have to look around very long to see the place had been converted for use by a valued member of the hotel family. The assassin Calavera.

"Come in here," I told Garrett.

He didn't look too happy about it. I'd ripped down the plastic and boards, and removed the blockade of furniture inside the door, but the floor was still tough to navigate with a wheelchair. Besides, Garrett knew I wouldn't have asked him to come down here unless I wanted him to see something important and unwelcome.

"Look around," I told him. "What do you notice?"

I tried not to sound harsh. At least I think I kept my tone pretty cool. But Garrett winced like I was beating him up.

"Some of Alex's old stuff," he said. "His board. His fishing gear. That's the poster I got him in Frisco."

I resisted the urge to correct him. Nobody who'd ever lived in San Francisco called it *Frisco* any more than natives called San Antonio *San Antone*. There was something improper about it, like calling your mother *Toots*.

"What else?" I asked him.

"A refrigerator."

"The power is off," I said. "You can open it."

He looked confused by this statement, but he wheeled over and did as I suggested. Inside was no food. Only chemicals. Bricks of plastic explosives. Coils of copper wire. A selection of pipes and timing devices.

"A bomb maker's supply cabinet," I told him. "Notice the security system?"

"What?" Garrett looked dazed.

"The light," I said. "Look at the refrigerator light."

He stared at the green metal orb where the light should've been. "That looks like a grenade."

"It is," I said. "Old drug dealer's trick. You put a lightbulb cap on the grenade, stick the filaments inside. When the door opens, the electric current hits the explosives. Anyone who comes snooping and doesn't know to unplug the refrigerator first—"

"Jesus."

"I almost didn't unplug it. It occurred to me when my hand was on the handle."

He looked at me like I was a ghost. "Tres, there's no way Alex . . . This can't be his stuff."

I didn't bother to argue. The room spoke for itself.

Garrett picked up something from the workbench. A red plastic guitar pick. It sat there amid timing fuses and pliers and a pile of firing caps. "Alex couldn't kill people."

"He was in the army."

"He was a cook."

"Not where he started." I handed him some papers I'd found in the file cabinet—army transcripts. "He had demolition training, but he was transferred out."

Garrett looked up blankly. "Transferred . . . why?"

"I don't know. But he had the skills to make bombs."

"He made fricking *fireworks*!"

"A good cover for getting some of the supplies he needed."

Garrett shook his head. "No way. I can't buy it."

I'd expected denial. I didn't push him. There was nothing I could say that was more convincing than just being here, in the place where Alex had fashioned his IEDs.

"Look, little bro." Garrett's voice was ragged.

"Alex is a victim here. He's missing, remember? He's—he's probably been murdered."

"Or he made it look that way."

"Come on! Can you see Alex blowing people up? Or shooting a lawman in the chest? Or hitting his own manager on the back of the head?"

He waved the guitar pick as if it were weightier evidence than all the bomb-making equipment.

"Garrett, Alex went out of his way to barricade this room. He lied about the ceiling collapsing. He knew what was in here. He *had* to. He was making bombs."

"What do you want me to say? You want me to turn on my last goddamn friend?"

In the daylight from the unboarded windows, Garrett's beard looked grayer than usual. His shirt was pale blue with a fading parrot on it, a remembrance of Buffett concerts past. He looked exhausted and defeated, but he'd still taken the time this morning to comb his hair, the same way he'd done on the Fourth of July, so many years ago, hoping to impress a girl.

"We need to find Alex," I said. "He was ready to surrender before this weekend. He started negotiating with the marshals, anyway. We need to convince him to give up."

"You're enjoying this, aren't you, little bro?"

"Yeah, Garrett. It's been a hell of an enjoyable weekend. Exactly the honeymoon I had in mind."

He wheeled himself over to the refrigerator and stared at the equipment inside.

In the silence, I heard something in the hall—a

wet floorboard creaking. I tensed, looking around for something to use as a weapon, but there was nothing except my flashlight and several pounds of high-grade explosives. I opted for the flashlight.

I peeked outside. There was no one in the hall, yet I caught a scent that wasn't salt water or mildew or even death. It was the faint amber scent that might have been Benjamin Lindy's cologne.

When I came back into the workroom, Garrett had unscrewed the grenade and was holding it in his lap.

"Where is he?" Garrett asked.

"Who?"

"Alex. If he's hiding, we have to find him. Where is he?"

I thought about Benjamin Lindy, and what he might have overheard if he'd been eavesdropping. I thought about where a man could go on an island this size in the middle of a hurricane.

"I think," I said, "it's high time we visited the lighthouse."

36

Calavera checked his watch. Only minutes left now.

His things were safely stashed away. He would retrieve the money later, after the storm had passed. Then he would disappear for good.

What would the police think? They would have little to go on. They would scratch their heads about Alex Huff's fate, but eventually they would drop the case. They would accept the easy answer, because it meant less work.

No one would escape to contradict his story. He would make sure of that.

He looked at the last candy skull in his hand.

He had never meant it to be a calling card. The skull was a tribute, left at his early kills to remind himself of a dying child—a lone eleven-year-old girl.

It had been only one of many atrocities he'd seen in the army. Why this one stuck with him, he didn't know. He came into the hut just as his comrades had finished their business. They slashed the girl's throat to silence her. The killer turned to face him, his eyes glazed. The blade of his knife glistened red. Calavera watched the girl die. He saw the light go out of her eyes. Her family was already dead. No one would grieve for her or even know what had happened.

And Calavera said nothing. He walked out of the hut and carried on, checking for weapon caches.

But he memorized the faces of the attackers. Within a week, all three of them had died. Freak accidents: the first blown apart by a land mine where no land mine should've been; another burned alive by an incendiary bomb; the third the victim of a defective grenade. Afterward, before his division left the area, Calavera went back to the location of that hut—now a smoking pile of ruins—and placed an offering to the girl: a few cookies, a wilted flower, a candy skull.

Her death kept things in proportion for him. If an innocent like her could die senselessly, why should he feel guilt? Why not take the money of the wicked to kill the wicked?

Even so, he had tried to stop. He had thought the days of Calavera were behind him, until New Year's Eve.

Now it was different. He had to kill indiscriminately to protect the only thing he cared about.

It isn't too late, he thought. *I could stop it now. I could warn them.*

He threw the candy skull into the corner. There would be no tributes today. This was about survival.

He made sure his gun was loaded. Then he went out to complete his plans.

37

On our way out we passed the dining room, which is why I saw Jose with the bodies.

"Wait for me," I told Garrett.

"Why?" Then he saw what I saw, and he didn't look too anxious to follow.

In the dining room, Jose had laid out the two dead bodies on tables, each wrapped in white linen. I could tell which corpse was Chris Stowall. He was frozen in the fetal position. The other, Longoria, I would've been able to recognize from the smell. A day of death had mingled unpleasantly with his regular Old Spice.

Jose stared at the two men the way he might study a dinner setting, wondering whether he'd put the salad forks on the correct side.

"You moved them," I said. I have a talent for stating the obvious.

"Everyone was packing, señor. It seemed to me if we leave..."

He didn't finish the thought, but I got it. *The dead have to leave, too.*

When the police finally got here, they were going to have a forensics hissy fit. The bodies had been moved so many times. Yet Jose's feelings seemed sensible, somehow. He was tidying up. Looking out for the guests. Even Longoria deserved some measure of final respect. Or maybe I'd just been spending too much time in this damn hotel.

There was a jangling sound from the kitchen, and Imelda appeared in the doorway, flipping through a big ring of keys. "Jose, I can't—"

She stopped when she saw me. Her eyes were pink from crying. The keys in her hand looked like the same set Jose had used the night before, to let me look through the office.

"It's all right, *mi amor*," Jose assured her. "I'm almost ready."

Imelda met my eyes briefly, set the keys on the nearest table and backed out of the room. Not for the first time, I had the sense she wanted to tell me something, but I'd begun to wonder if that was just the way Imelda was—perpetually frustrated by her inability to express all the strange horrors she'd seen in her life.

When she was gone, Jose pocketed the keys. He picked up two tins of marigolds from the floor—

the same marigolds that had been on his altar upstairs—and set them at the feet of each corpse. I wondered if he'd packed up his old pictures, too, and the *ofrendas* for his ancestors.

"You'll leave the bodies here?" I asked.

"I'm not sure, señor." Then he focused on me, as if realizing that this was an odd place for me to be. "Where are you going?"

"To look for your boss."

Jose kept the same stoic look he'd had folding linen over the corpses. "Do not, señor. Please. It isn't worth it."

"You're trying to protect him?"

Jose said nothing. He picked up a bottle of tequila from the wet bar.

"You've suspected Alex for a while, haven't you?" I asked.

"Help will come soon, señor. Let the police handle things. You should take your wife outside. Wait there."

His tone was about as convincing as the cologne on the dead marshal.

"I'm going to the lighthouse," I said. "Come with me, in case it's locked."

"Only Mr. Huff kept a key to the lighthouse. No one will be there. Now forgive me, señor, but I need to finish setting things in order."

Putting the house in dying order. That's what my mother used to call it whenever she made me clean my room before our summer trips to Rebel Island. She never laid out corpses on the dining table, though.

I left Jose making his *ofrendas*—pouring shots of tequila for two dead men.

Outside, the rain had waned to a drizzle. I could almost tell where the sun was behind the blanket of clouds. There was still nothing on the sea but wreckage—no sign of a boat, a fish, a bird. The water was receding around the island. The northern stretch was still gone, but the main beach was almost back to where I remembered. The pilings of the boat dock jutted above the waterline. A Volkswagen-sized metal drum, like a septic tank, had washed ashore nearby.

The lighthouse was locked. It had a solid door, weathered oak with a deadbolt. I stared at it resentfully. That didn't convince it to open.

"He ain't in there," Garrett said. "Probably locked it when you two left last night."

"No," I said. "He didn't lock it."

"Well, it doesn't matter, 'cause we can't get in."

"Back up," I said. "Way back."

"No way you're gonna try busting that down."

I hefted Maia's .357. Hastily, Garrett wheeled himself way back. I put my face next to the door and yelled, "Alex, if you're in there, move away from the door."

I stepped back about fifteen feet.

In a lot of movies, I've seen people stand next to the door and shoot down at the lock, which always struck me as particularly stupid. The lock is metal.

What you're likely to get is killed by ricochet or peppered with splinters.

I shot three times down the center line of the door—top, middle, bottom. The .357 made three decent-size holes. I kicked the middle. The door split in half like a piece of perforated paper.

Inside, morning light filtered from the windows high above. Canvas sacks were stacked in one corner. Against the opposite wall were a table and chair and a bedraggled man slumped over with his head cradled in his arms.

"Alex," Garrett said.

Alex Huff's red shirt was ripped across the back. He wasn't wearing any shoes and his feet were bleeding. He seemed to be asleep.

He reminded me of a murderer I'd seen once in a police station—a guy who'd been caught after torturing three women. He'd been hauled into the station, put in an interrogation room to sweat. Far from getting agitated, the man had fallen asleep instantly, like he was relieved to be caught.

"Yo, Alex." Garrett wheeled himself over and shook his friend's shoulder. I stayed at the broken door. One of my bullets had chipped off a section of the limestone wall just above Alex's head. If Alex had stood up, he would've died.

He didn't wake when Garrett shook him, but he sighed deeply. An empty tequila bottle rolled off the table and clunked on the gravel floor.

I stepped closer, my finger still on the trigger, though I was pretty sure Alex wasn't faking. He smelled of tequila. His bare arms were crisscrossed with glass cuts.

I pulled him upright by his hair and he grunted, his mouth slack. His eyes opened and rolled back in his head and he coughed on his own spit.

"Alex," I said. "Wake up."

"Waaa."

"Get up, man," Garrett said. "What the hell are you doing out here?"

Alex blinked. He struggled to focus on everything around him, scowling, as if Garrett's question were an exceptionally good one. Then something seemed to occur to him. His expression turned miserable, and he put his head back down in his arms. "No," he groaned. "No, no..."

"Alex," I said. "We found the room with the bomb materials."

He mumbled something I couldn't make out.

"Come on, Alex!" Garrett pleaded. "Explain this to me, man. Please."

"Hotel," he muttered. "My hotel."

"What about it?" I asked.

He raised his head. The pain in his eyes told of a man who'd lost everything in the world.

"Is it over?" he asked me. "Has it blown up yet?"

I ran into Markie in the lobby. Ran him over, actually.

"Get out," I told him.

"What?"

"Now! Where's Ty and Chase?"

"In the parlor with Lane and the old dude. But—"

"Get them all and get out of the building."

I think he asked me what was going on, but I'd given him as much time as I planned to. I sprinted up the steps to find Maia. My vision was tunneling. My mouth tasted like salt. Nothing mattered except getting her and getting out.

She was in our bedroom, curled up asleep, but her eyelids fluttered as soon as I touched her shoulder.

"Mmm?" she said.

"Fresh air time."

"What?"

"Come outside."

She studied my face, her sleepiness quickly dissolving. "What's wrong?"

"We need to get outside."

"Right now?"

"Right now."

I was tempted to pick her up and carry her, but I knew she'd never allow it, and I wasn't sure I could do it safely. As it was, I let her lean against me as we took the stairs. Every step I imagined as a trip wire, a second ticking off a clock. I said nothing. I didn't want to make Maia upset. But the house was now a minefield.

Maia didn't ask. She knew it was that serious.

We got to the bottom of the steps and saw Ty, Markie and Chase lugging suitcases out the front door.

"A boat's here?" Chase's eyes were desperate, like a death row inmate waiting for a pardon.

"No, no boat."

Just get out of our way! I wanted to scream.

Finally we were outside. I guided Maia across the dunes, as far from the house as I could get her. Garrett's wheelchair was stuck in the wet sand and he'd given up on it. He was sitting on an intact section of boardwalk next to the ruins of the pier. The wind swept his hair to one side. Lane sat with him, hugging him tight. Chase, Ty and Markie plopped their suitcases down and sat on them, watching me. Benjamin Lindy was there, dressed in a funeral suit, his face as gray as the clouds. He gave me a steely look.

"Jose and Imelda," I said. "Where are they?"

Nobody answered. Nobody seemed to know.

I cursed.

"What's going on, Tres?" Lindy asked me. "Where is Alex Huff?"

If I had been thinking more clearly, I would've caught the deadly resolve in his voice, like a machine that had been set to automatic. But I had other concerns.

"Stay here," I told Maia. "Do *not* follow me."

I ran for the house.

Inside: first floor. No one in the dining room except the corpses. They looked wet and they smelled terrible—doused in tequila. I didn't have time to give their smell much thought. The kitchen was empty. The parlor and the office, nothing. I yelled for Jose and Imelda. No answer. I ran upstairs.

Third floor: Jose and Imelda's room. The little altar had been cleared away. Some clothes had been packed and removed. The bed hadn't been made.

The closet was open. One suitcase on the floor. Empty coat hangers. Their window had been un-barricaded. I looked outside; I wasn't sure why. At the back end of the house, a line of battered dunes led down to the old boathouse where I'd scuttled the fishing boat the night before. And there were Jose and Imelda, just going into the boathouse. Imelda turned. She looked at the house, as if saying goodbye. She found her own window and locked eyes with me. For a brief second, she wasn't sure who she was looking at—a ghost, perhaps. Then her eyes widened.

That's when I heard the first noise. From the opposite side of the hotel, a rumble, like an approaching earthquake. The floor trembled.

And then a strange clicking sound nearby, like a toy being wound up.

I focused on the suitcase in the closet. The noise was coming from inside it.

I hurled myself against the window and the room erupted in flames.

I imagined Mr. Eli looking down at me, his face illuminated by fireworks. Alex's father stood next to him. There were others there, too, but I couldn't make out their faces.

"Alex will make me proud someday," Mr. Eli said. "He has a good heart."

Mr. Huff grunted. "Nothing but trouble, if you ask me. Must've gotten that from his mother."

Mr. Eli didn't answer. In the next explosion, I saw Ralph Arguello's face illuminated. He smiled at me, like we were sharing a good joke. Peter Brazos stood next to him, his eyes red and his face haggard. He held a candy skull in his hands.

"*Vato*," Ralph greeted me. "It's *loco* who you choose to sacrifice yourself for, ain't it? Just gotta hope they make the best of it, eh?"

Red and orange starbursts lit up the sky, interlocking spheres of color.

I seemed to be moving, as if I were lying in a boat, slipping out to sea. Alex was taking me fishing again—back into the channel with the sharks.

He had a good heart, unless you asked him about his dead mother. He would hide me. He'd get me away from my father.

You can't hide on this island, runt.

I opened my eyes and saw nothing.

I was being dragged backward through the sand, Maia's voice saying: "He's bleeding. We need bandages."

I hurt in so many places I was pretty sure I was dead. My left leg felt like it was broken. Something smelled like smoke, and I was afraid it was me.

I saw Ty's face above me. I was being carried away from the hotel, or what was left of it. The windows were boiling with fire. Smoke billowed into the sky. The building had been gutted, at least three explosions, maybe more. Already I could see the walls thinning, gobbled up from the inside by heat.

I sat up and blacked out. Maia was making a fuss, but I managed to promise her I was okay. She didn't look reassured. There was a deep gash on my arm that Jose was wrapping in his own shirt. My leg . . . I didn't think it was broken anymore, but I wouldn't be doing tai chi exercises anytime soon.

I'd been very lucky, landing on the sand.

"Jesus," Garrett said. "The hotel—"

"Did everyone make it out?" Lane asked.

Markie said, "Where's Huff?"

"The lighthouse," Garrett said.

Chase paled. "Mr. Lindy."

"What?" I croaked. I looked around and realized the old man wasn't in the group. Surely he hadn't gone in after me?

"I saw him," Chase said. "He went up that way, toward the lighthouse. He had a gun."

38

Ty shivered on the beach. His eyes stung from the smoke, but he was glad to be outside. He couldn't imagine anything better than watching that horrible old building burn.

"Calavera will shoot us now." Chase paced a rut in the sand. "So what if we got out of the building?"

"Maybe not," Markie said halfheartedly. "He can't take us all." He had a smudge of ash on his jaw like war paint, but it made him look ridiculous. For the first time, Ty didn't feel afraid of him. After seeing the Mexicans in the boat, Ty found it hard to be scared of his companions. He'd seen the real threat, and it had calmed his nerves. If the Mexicans decided he needed to die, there wasn't much he could do about it.

"He'll fucking execute us," Chase insisted. "There's no help coming. Nothing."

Ty scanned the ocean. The rain had stopped. He still felt claustrophobic. The island was too small. His skin itched with the need to leave. But it was so much better than being inside that hotel.

Suddenly he knew what he would do. If he got off this island, he would quit school and head back to the ranch. The hell with what his father said. The hell with Chase and Markie. He would work cattle the way his family had done since his great-grandparents' time. He would live under the open skies again, and if the Mexicans ever came after him, he would see them coming. They would learn how well he could shoot.

A dark spot appeared on the horizon. Ty watched as it got bigger. Then he started to laugh, because he knew either death or rescue was coming, and he wouldn't have to wait much longer.

"What's your problem?" Markie growled.

"A boat." Ty pointed to the sleek black cruiser that was racing straight toward Rebel Island.

39

The first gunshot came as I reached the light-house doorway.

Normally, this would not have inclined me to rush inside, but things weren't normal. Benjamin Lindy was standing in the middle of the room, a .22 in his hand. I didn't know how he'd found a second gun. At the moment, it was not my first concern.

Alex Huff was still sitting at the table. He was hunched over, fingers laced together, like a man in casual prayer. There was a bullet hole in the floorboards between his feet.

"To answer your question," Lindy told him, "it *is* loaded."

Both men saw me at the same time.

Lindy turned the gun on me. "No offense, son. But I'd like you to step outside. You won't be taking my sidearm twice."

"Don't do this, Lindy."

"Mr. Huff is the only one who can dissuade me," Lindy said. "And I'm sorry to say he hasn't done much on that count."

Alex looked dazed. I doubted he could've mounted a rational defense even if he'd been so inclined. And he did not look inclined.

Black smoke drifted into the lighthouse from the burning hotel. The heat on my back was intense. I figured there was a good chance the building frame would collapse against the lighthouse and kill us all—or at least those of us Lindy didn't shoot first.

"It's all gone, isn't it?" Alex tried to focus on me. I wasn't sure if he realized who I was. "The hotel. Everything."

"You destroyed it," Lindy told him. "You killed my daughter. Her two little girls. You tried to kill everyone on this island. You will account for that, sir."

The smoke stung my eyes. The roar of the burning house was louder than the storm the night before.

Alex swallowed. He looked at Lindy with an expression of pain, maybe even regret. "It's not the way you think."

"You deny you killed them?"

Alex looked down.

Outside, a distant voice yelled, "Hey! Heeeeey!"

It sounded like Ty down by the beach, as if he were trying to get someone's attention. Almost as if he was hailing a boat.

Too optimistic, I thought. I couldn't be that lucky.

Garrett would be coming up behind me sooner or later. I didn't know how he would make it up the path, but I knew he would try. I wanted this resolved before he got here. Unfortunately, Lindy still had his gun pointed in my direction.

"Lindy," I said, "when your wife left you, you know where she went?"

His jaw clenched. "That is none of your business."

"She left you for another man. Alex's father. She came here, to Rebel Island."

Lindy's gun hand sagged. I thought about jumping him, but his expression made me hesitate. The old man looked like he was collapsing from the inside, like someone had set off a firebomb in his chest and any second it would burn through his skin.

I turned to Alex. "The statue you made. That was your mother."

"She died of cancer when I was young," Alex murmured. "My father never got over it."

"Rachel was your half sister," I said. "After the bombing, you saw her picture in the papers. You realized who she was."

Alex closed his eyes tight. Then he nodded.

"That's why you tried to turn yourself in," I said. "You realized you'd killed your own sister."

"No, it wasn't like that," Alex said. "I didn't—"

"Liar." Lindy turned the gun on Alex. I tackled the old man just as he fired.

Unfortunately, my balance was off. My leg was hurt and I was weak from the fall I'd taken. We both went down and I slammed my head on the table's edge.

Maybe Alex hadn't been as dazed as I thought, or maybe the adrenaline was just counteracting the booze. He bolted for the door but Lindy was already back on his feet, blocking the way. There was only one other way for Alex to go—up.

He took the stairs as Lindy fired again. And somewhere down at the beach, I heard Ty yelling.

I was staggering up the stairs as fast as I could. The eighty-year-old man beat me by a mile.

By the time I got to the little landing at the top of the tower, Alex Huff had realized the obvious—there was no way out—and had turned to face his accuser.

Benjamin Lindy didn't try to stop me from climbing into the room. His gun was an arm's length from Alex Huff's forehead. If I tried to tackle him, if I interfered . . . the gun would go off.

Both men were breathing hard, completely focused on one another.

Out the windows behind Alex, gray sea stretched to the horizon, but there was something startling nearby—a black boat slicing through the waves, headed for the shore. It seemed impossible—an intrusion from some other world. After twenty-four hours of isolation, I would've been less astonished to see angels streaming from the sky.

"The Coast Guard," I said.

Neither man moved.

"Lindy," I said. "The Coast Guard is here. They'll take Alex into custody."

"You tried to make a deal for your life," the old man told Alex. "After all you've done."

"You don't understand."

"You contacted the Marshal's Office."

"No."

"I won't let you go free," Lindy promised. "I won't let you just disappear."

"He won't go free," I told Lindy. "Not with Longoria dead. They won't make any deals with him now. Let the law handle this, Mr. Lindy. Put the gun down."

"I didn't kill Rachel," Alex said.

No statement could've infuriated Lindy more.

"Try an apology," the old man said. "Plead for your life."

Outside, the boat bobbed closer. Several men stood at the prow. Out the opposite window, a column of smoke billowed up from the hotel—wet wood and plaster and carpet going up in a blaze.

"We have to get out of here," Alex said. "The rest will go soon."

"He's right," I told Lindy. "There's enough explosive material in the bomb room to blow up ten hotels. It'll take out this tower."

"Don't change the subject," Lindy growled. "I

want to hear why you killed my Rachel. I want to hear you justify that."

"Lindy," I said. "He's all that's left of your wife. Let him stand trial, but don't kill him."

Lindy's finger tightened on the trigger. Alex locked eyes with me. He was trying to tell me something. Like a silent apology.

Too late, I realized what he was going to do. He made a desperate grab for Benjamin Lindy's hand, and the gun fired.

The shot pushed Alex against the window. The glass cracked under his weight but didn't break. He slumped to the floor, holding his chest, his shirt already soaked with blood.

"Go," Alex groaned. "Hurry."

I knelt at his side. His face was colorless. He clutched his shirt, struggling to breathe, just like Ralph Arguello had done the night he died.

"I'll help you," I told him.

Alex shook his head.

Then he closed his eyes and didn't move again.

The hotel rumbled behind us as another section collapsed into flames.

"Tres!" Garrett shouted from the bottom of the stairs.

I rose to face Benjamin Lindy. His face was blank, like a man who had decided his life was over.

"I'm done here," he said simply. And he dropped the gun.

●   ●   ●

Garrett and Lane were waiting at the bottom of the stairs. Both looked sweaty and out of breath. Garrett was in his chair. Apparently, Lane had helped him up the path.

"We heard the shots," Garrett said. "Where is Alex?"

"Upstairs," I said.

I guess my tone said the rest.

Garrett focused on Lindy. "You bastard."

Garrett took out the .357—Maia's gun. My luck keeping track of weapons had never been worse.

"Your friend murdered my daughter," Lindy said. "Do what you need to."

He did not look concerned. He looked strangely like Alex Huff—as if he were caught in a riptide he couldn't possibly control.

"He wasn't a murderer," Garrett said. "He couldn't have been."

"Garrett," I said. "There could be more explosions. We need to get out of here."

"This bastard killed Alex in cold blood." Garrett's voice trembled. "You didn't stop him? You let him?"

I wanted to protest, but he was right. After months of reliving Ralph Arguello's death, wishing I could've thrown myself in front of the gun that took my best friend's life—now another man had died the same way, right in front of me. And I hadn't been able to stop it.

Garrett nodded, like he was reading my thoughts. "Well, then, don't stop me now, little bro. You just keep on being a spectator."

He raised the gun.

"Garrett, no." Lane stepped between him and Benjamin Lindy. She knelt down in front of Garrett so they were eye to eye.

"Lane, get out of the way."

"I won't." She sounded more determined than I'd ever heard her. "You can't kill him. You're not like that."

"He shot my friend."

Lane cupped her hands on his knees. "Garrett, you promised to help me. Now let me help you. We're going to go down to that boat together. No one else is going to die."

"I don't need help."

"Yes, you do, love." She turned her palms up. "Give me the gun."

Garrett's face was gray with pain. He arched his back as if he were trying desperately to stand—to use the legs he'd lost twenty years ago. Then he slumped back in his chair, defeated. He dropped the gun into Lane's hands.

The four of us were almost to the beach when the hotel disintegrated.

40

Calavera watched the smoke boil into the sky.
Windows melted. The southwest gable collapsed
with a sound like distant thunder.

He could not enjoy the explosion. Nothing had
gone right. Some had died, perhaps. He wasn't
sure. But too many had gotten free.

Your own fault, he chided himself. *You set the
explosion too late in the morning. Your will was
weak.*

The gun felt heavy in his pocket. The solution
would not be so clean now, but he would have to
act soon.

Across the island, someone was shouting. Another wall of the house collapsed in on itself. A
tongue of flame curled up the side of the roof.

Soon, the only place that had ever offered him sanctuary would be a pile of rubble and ash. Maybe that's really what he'd been after with the bombs—destroying this place. He had no heart for killing anymore. But this place had let him down. He'd let himself believe he could change his life here, find peace at last. And the island had deceived him.

Whether he wanted to kill or not, he had to protect his last secret. He had no choice.

And so he put his hand in his pocket, felt the rough cross-hatching of the gun handle, and waited.

41

I watched the remaining palmetto trees burn. Stripped to the trunks by the storm, they leaned sideways from the wreckage of the hotel and smoldered like birthday candles on a stomped cake.

The hotel had gone up in a second blast of glory, just as Alex predicted. Boards and plaster and ashes were sprayed across the dunes and against the lighthouse. The heat had cracked the tower's side. The glass top had melted and collapsed, and as we watched, the structure's cracks widened.

The poor captain of the Coast Guard boat wasn't quite sure what to do with us. He was a reservist, a former merchant marine, probably—the kind of guy who knew boats and storms and preferred both to humans. From the trapped look he gave us, I thought he probably would just as soon leave us stranded and sail away. He had a crew of two, both of whom looked pale and shaken from a night riding out the storm. They had sidearms, but I doubt they'd ever used them. The captain told one of the men to radio in our situation.

"Radio who, sir?" the guy wanted to know.

The captain frowned impatiently. "Everyone, I guess."

Maia and I sat on the beach watching the clouds break and the ruins burn. It seemed insulting that the sun should break through the clouds so brilliantly after the weekend we'd had. Gulls were starting to reappear. Sand crabs dug their way out of the surf, bubbling little geysers to clear their tunnels. The sea wind blew the smoke and ashes toward the mainland and fanned the flames.

The heat was finally too much for the lighthouse. The cracks deepened and the tower crumbled, imploding on itself in a pile of charred white blocks and burning boards.

"Nothing left," Maia said.

The way she said it, I got the feeling she was talking about more than the buildings.

I put my hand on her belly. Normally, this irritated her—another sign of my constant worry. But this time I think she realized that I was doing it for a different reason. I needed reassurance—not that the baby was all right, but that I was.

She put her hands over mine. "I felt him kick a minute ago."

"You didn't tell me that."

"You were busy almost getting killed."

"That's no excuse. I'm always busy almost getting killed."

She shrugged, conceding the point.

One of the Coast Guard guys came up and offered us granola bars and water, but neither of us was hungry.

"An EMT is en route, ma'am." He looked nervously at Maia's belly. I figured it would probably make his day if he had to assist in childbirth. We thanked him, and as soon as he was sure that Maia was not going to start labor immediately, he nodded and moved off with visible relief.

"The police won't have much of a crime scene," I said.

Maia nodded. "What will you tell them about Lindy?"

The old man was sitting at the top of a sand dune, staring out at the sea. His white hair was blown the wrong way, like a frosty wave. His expression was empty. I imagined he could turn to stone up there and no one would know the difference.

I wondered if Lindy might go free for killing Alex Huff. The crime scene, the body, the evidence would be hard to use. Not impossible, but it would take an act of will to bring charges against a well-known local attorney and make them stick. I wondered what the D.A., Peter Brazos, would think of all this.

"I'll tell the truth," I told Maia. "Not sure it will do any good."

"Lindy wants to be punished." Maia was sizing the old man up, the way I'd seen her do many times with clients. "It fits with his idea of right and wrong."

"Some system."

"Everybody needs closure," she replied. "This is his. He'll want people to know he took his revenge. He succeeded."

He succeeded.

I remembered Alex's attitude in the lighthouse—fatalistic, resigned. But also denying that he was a killer. *I didn't kill Rachel.*

It may have been his shot nerves, the cumulative effect of years of a double life that made him sound so convincing. But his denial bothered me.

I looked down the beach where Markie was talking with the boat captain. Telling survivor stories. Ty stood to one side, calmly eating a granola bar. Chase was sitting in the boat like a kid ready to go home. He had an orange blanket around his shoulders, though the sun was rapidly warming things up. When he met my eyes, he asked me a silent, anxious question—*Will you tell the police about the drug running?* His weekend of panic behind him, reality was starting to sink in. He was beginning to realize that he might go to jail, or worse.

Garrett and Lane were talking nearby in the

shade of the washed-up oil tank. Lane was sitting on her suitcase, Garrett in his chair. They were holding hands.

The waves washed the beach. The fires seemed to be burning out. Soon, Rebel Island would be just another sandy dot along the Gulf Coast. No distinguishing features. Its stubborn landmarks finally scoured off the map.

Something was wrong. It took me a minute to think what.

"Where are Jose and Imelda?" I asked.

I stood.

Maia's face turned pale. "You don't think they were inside?"

I looked at the burning wreckage of the hotel and the crumbled tower. "I'll be back."

Maia asked where I was going. There was, she reminded me, no place left to go.

"Almost no place," I agreed. And I headed toward the ruins.

The Coast Guard guys paid me no attention. They were making no effort to contain people, or keep us separated the way any cop would know to do in a crime scene. These guys were first responders. Their job was to rescue us, feed us. Not interrogate us. That was just as well. At this point, no amount of investigation was going to bring justice.

I imagined Benjamin Lindy would say the same thing.

I walked around the side of the hotel. The path

was still there in places—gravel and paving stones blown with wet sand in a tortoiseshell pattern. I made my way past a burning tree trunk, a broken rowboat oar, a spray of sodden clothing half buried in the sand. Gnats wove a hazy cloud above the sea grass. Sand fleas had survived, too. They were delighted to find my legs—fresh meat walking through their territory.

The heat of the building was not as intense now. I could walk next to it without feeling like my shirt would combust. My leg still felt like it would collapse on me any minute, but I managed to hobble over the rise and down the other side of the island.

The boathouse was the only structure still standing, though ashes had settled on its blue-shingled roof along with an odd assortment of other flotsam—a few dead fish, some seaweed and part of a shrimper's net. The door was open. Jose was standing in the doorway, watching me approach as if he'd been waiting.

He had changed clothes. He wore jeans and a red beach shirt and sandals that all reminded me uncomfortably of Alex Huff's wardrobe. As I got closer, I realized it *was* Alex Huff's wardrobe.

"Is Imelda all right?" I asked.

Jose considered for a moment, then gestured inside the boathouse.

"The Coast Guard is here," I said.

"Yes. I saw them." His eyes drifted up toward the hotel. "Did you find Mr. Huff?"

"We found him."

"Was he—"

He faltered as Imelda came up behind him. She, too, had changed clothes—a simple gray cotton dress. Her hair was pulled back and her face looked older in the sunlight—her wrinkles deeper, her eyes sunken and pale.

"Señor," she said. "Is—is your wife all right?"

"She got out before the explosion," I said. "Barely."

Imelda's shoulders relaxed a little. "I am glad."

"You two made it out as well," I noticed.

"We were lucky," Jose said. I noticed the *señor* was gone, no doubt burned up with the linens and the kitchenware and the dead bodies.

"The police will be here soon," I told him. "They'll hear the story of Calavera. I think we should talk before they get here."

I nodded toward the doorway. Jose regarded me, then said reluctantly, "Yes. Perhaps we should."

Inside the boathouse, Jose and Imelda's pos-sessions were stacked neatly against one wall. Two battered suitcases, a few cardboard moving boxes spotted from the rain, a garment bag full of clothes.

"Lucky," I said. "You just had time to pack everything you own and move it out here."

Imelda twisted the top button on her dress. She backed up, looking for a place to sit down, but there wasn't much—just the fishing boat, half submerged on its side in the slip, a few piles of ropes, a bait bucket. The water in the slip sloshed angrily. The doors had come loose. One banged back and forth against the other, showing snapshots of the gray sea outside.

Imelda said, "Señor, we didn't—"

"Imelda was upset," Jose interrupted. "I told her I would move our things."

"Makes sense," I said. "Since you knew the house would blow up."

Jose's expression was as calm as a career gambler's. "Señor?"

"You did have the key to the lighthouse. You just didn't want me getting in there and finding Alex."

He shook his head. "Why would I do that?"

"Maybe because Imelda *was* upset. Killing Jesse Longoria to protect your identity was one thing. Killing Chris Stowall, even. You never trusted him. But Alex was a friend. He helped you, gave you refuge. I don't think Imelda wanted him killed. So you stashed him away in the lighthouse instead, doped up and drunk, until you took care of the rest of us."

Imelda was watching her husband intently, as if she expected him to do something amazing—combust into flames or start speaking in tongues.

"Mr. Huff was kind to us," Jose said.

"Very kind," I agreed. "And trusting. He gave you freedom to do whatever you wanted. You set up shop right under his nose, in room 102. You were running the hotel, the two of you, until Chris

Stowall came on board. After the Brazos hit went wrong, Chris found that email and realized Calavera was at the hotel, but he thought it was Alex. He saw it as a moneymaking opportunity and got Longoria and Benjamin Lindy involved. You realized what Longoria was here for right away. You confronted him and killed him. Then you gave Chris Stowall the same treatment. Alex didn't know what was going on. He only began to suspect when he found the bomb room, but even then he wasn't sure who to blame. I imagine you directed his suspicions toward Chris Stowall."

"Mr. Huff told you all this?"

"No. He's dead."

Imelda cupped her hands to her face.

"He tried to take Benjamin Lindy's gun away rather than throw the blame on you," I said. "He died without giving you away. He was still willing to believe you were innocent."

"Don't say any more." Jose's voice was tight. "Don't stir up more trouble."

"You were an assassin in Mexico. You worked for the cartels down there. You knew explosives."

He didn't answer.

"Then your family became a target," I said. "Your children were killed, but it wasn't random violence. They died because someone was getting back at you. You left Nuevo Laredo and you found your way here. Maybe you tried to go straight, but you had lots of anger. You had skills that were going to waste. And you had Alex, who trusted you implicitly and had a background similar enough to yours—working with explosives. A perfect fall guy, should you need one. It wasn't long before you were rebuilding yourself a new career as Calavera."

Imelda started talking to him in rapid Spanish. I could hardly follow. She said she'd told him a thousand times. He had taken things too far. He should never have gone back to his old work.

He raised his hand and she fell silent instantly. I got the feeling she'd had a lot of practice at this over the years. She had learned to hold back, to fear her husband when he raised his hand like that.

Jose's face, which I'd thought of as made for smiling, now had the sharpness of a knife.

"I did what I needed to," he said. "For Imelda and for me."

"Because of money? You took the drug payoff away from the college kids—easy to do when you've got the keys to their rooms. I imagine you've got a lot more stashed away. Is Chris Stowall's twenty grand in one of those boxes?"

"Even before that, we had enough to go anywhere."

"Then why didn't you leave?"

He glanced at his wife. "Leaving anywhere...is difficult."

"Huff *was* your family. This place was all you had. You messed that up when you murdered Peter Brazos's family."

"An accident."

"But you didn't contact the Marshals Service yourself. You've got no remorse."

"No."

"Alex, then," I guessed. "The Brazos killings were more than he could take. He contacted the Marshals Service, pretending to be Calavera. He was going to turn you in. Or maybe you made him think Chris was the killer."

"No," Jose said. "You do not understand. It was not Mr. Huff. The person who wished to turn me in was my wife."

"You should have gone along," Imelda said softly.

"For what?" he asked. "You would lose me, too? Is that what you want?"

"No, *mi amor*. I do not want to lose you."

"You already have, Imelda," I told her. "Your husband kills people. It's how he deals with his anger, keeps it in check. That's why he chooses explosives instead of guns. The timer, the sense of control, the complete destruction of someone's household—that has a lot of appeal to you, doesn't it, Jose?"

His eyes were steely, but I doubted I could make him lose his cool. Jose was not the type. He wanted to be the master, the timer. He would kill in his own way.

"People die," Jose said. "My children died before my eyes. Why should other lives matter to me? Why should I not choose the time and the way? I'm good at it."

"But you made mistakes."

He shrugged. "That's over now. I will not make any deals. I will not apologize."

"Jose," Imelda said.

"You will stay with me," he told her, "as you promised. I will take care of you. It will be all right."

"No, it won't," I said. "This boathouse is a dead end, Jose."

Then he surprised me. He did another calculation, came to a decision I didn't anticipate.

He took out a gun—the same .38, I imagined, that had killed Jesse Longoria—and he aimed it at my chest.

42

Maia tried to stay put, but it wasn't something she did well.

She couldn't shake the feeling that Imelda had been trying to tell her something earlier. She told herself it didn't matter now. Help had arrived. They would head home and Maia would never see this place again. Tres would be right back, with good news or bad. The worst was over.

But it was hard to believe that. Maia had a tingling feeling between her shoulder blades that usually meant something was wrong. The far end of the island was hidden behind the rubble of the hotel and clouds of smoke. She knew Tres had gone to the boathouse, but she'd never seen it and didn't know exactly how far it was.

Damn him for running off. He was in worse shape than she was, for God's sake.

A shadow fell over her. "You sure I can't get you anything, ma'am?"

It was one of the coast guardsmen. He reminded her of Chris Stowall—young, blond, a little nervous. Then she remembered Chris Stowall was burned to ashes inside the hotel.

"Could you help me up?" she asked.

He looked a little flustered, but he took her hand and helped her to her feet. It was difficult to do this with dignity. She felt as if she was carrying a bowling ball around her middle, but she did her best.

"I'm going for a walk," she announced. "Over that way."

The guardsman frowned. "You sure that's a good idea?"

"No," Maia answered. "It's probably not."

And she began walking toward the boathouse.

43

"No," Imelda said.

Jose hesitated. I hoped he was having second thoughts. It's a different thing, killing a man while you're looking him in the eyes.

On the other hand, Jose had shot Jesse Longoria in the chest. He'd bludgeoned Chris Stowall to death and stuffed his body in a freezer. I doubted my boyish charm was going to keep him from pulling the trigger.

"They'll hear the shot," I said, trying to sound reasonable. "They'll find me dead and know you killed me. You can't cover that up."

I could tell his mind was chewing on that, coming up with solutions. I didn't want to give him time.

"Imelda," I said, "do you want to stay with him?"

"Of course." No hesitation, but her voice was full of despair, as if I were asking her whether she'd like to walk on the moon.

"Tell him," I said. "His only chance is surrender."

The doors of the boathouse slapped shut and creaked open with a gust of wind. A curl of seawater sloshed over the concrete and doused my shoes.

"You'll go in the water," Jose decided. "Get in."

"No, Jose," I said. "It's over. No more planning. No more hits."

"Your body will be underwater," he said. "Under the boat. They'll find it eventually, but not for a while. We'll be gone by then."

Imelda was shivering. I needed her help. She was the only possible leverage I could use to make Jose change his mind. But I also couldn't wait for her. I was out of options. I was weighing the odds of attacking when the worst possible variable got added to the equation.

The boathouse door opened and Maia walked in.

"Ah," she said. "I caught you at a bad time."

I locked eyes with her and I told her silently to go.

Not surprisingly, she did the exact opposite. She came to stand next to me and took my hand. "I got worried."

"Señora." Imelda's voice trembled. "You shouldn't be on your feet..."

Her voice trailed off. I suppose she realized the futility of what she was saying, given the fact that her husband was planning to put a bullet in me.

As for Jose, he looked like a juggler who'd been thrown too many plates. His forehead beaded with sweat.

"Hello, Jose," Maia said. "Do you mind if I sit down?"

She didn't wait for him to answer. She pulled up an empty ice chest and sat down as best she could, holding my hand for support.

I was beyond worried. I was ready to unzip my own skin and run screaming into the sand dunes. I wanted, by sheer force of will, to make Jose and his gun disappear off the face of the earth.

"You remember when Imelda was pregnant?" Maia asked him. We might've been at a dinner among friends. Her tone was maddeningly casual.

Jose stared at her. I was sure he was going to shoot us, but finally he said, "I remember."

Imelda closed her eyes. A tear traced its way down her cheek.

"Why did you come?" Jose murmured. "I'll have to kill you both now."

"The third trimester is brutal," Maia said. "But sometimes you feel the baby move, and there's nothing like that in the world. Did you put your hand on Imelda's belly and feel that? Did you speak to your babies before they were born?"

"We need time to get away." Jose's voice

sounded ragged, almost apologetic. "We can't have anyone tell."

"Let them go," Imelda begged.

Jose shook his head. He watched as Maia placed her hand on her belly.

"There it is," Maia said. "A kick."

Her smile was as astonishing as the storm, or the way the lighthouse had crumbled after one hundred and fifty years.

"The killings didn't stop the hurt, did they?" Maia asked.

Jose didn't answer.

Imelda knelt at his side. "Please, *mi amor*. Don't."

She tried to take his gun. He raised it so she couldn't, but he didn't push her away, either.

"Imelda knew what she was doing," Maia said. "After those girls and their mother died...there really wasn't anything for you to do except turn yourself in. You'd arrived right back where you started. Pain. Grief. The death of children."

"It wasn't my fault," Jose said.

"Perhaps the death of *your* children wasn't your fault," Maia said. "Everything you've done since then is."

A new sound cut through the surf. It sounded like a small engine, something fast. Too soon for civilian watercraft to be back on the waves. Police, perhaps. Or a water ambulance.

"We can't get away if you live," Jose said.

"You'd have to kill us," Maia agreed. "You were prepared to do that last night. You planned on destroying the entire hotel, hoping everyone would be in it. Was it hard, knowing that would include a family, an unborn child?"

"I told you to get out. I tried...It would have been all right if you hadn't come here. Alex Huff—"

"Alex would've taken the blame as Calavera," I said. "Even in the end, he didn't give you up. He would've let you go. Despite everything, he cared about you two. He believed everyone on this island deserved a chance."

Jose shook his head. His eyes were red now.

"You'd have to kill us," Maia said. "But that would be the wrong choice, Jose. It would be starting all over again."

She made it sound so sensible. All I could see was the gun and a distraught killer. I had been here before. The odds were terrible. I had seen too many people die. Everything I'd seen in my life told me that I had only one chance—to overpower Jose.

But Maia held my hand, gently restraining me. Maia's voice was calm, confident.

"*Mi amor,*" Imelda said. "You would have to kill me too. I can't go through this. Please. No more."

Jose focused on her, as if seeing her for the first time.

She held out her hand.

Jose's jaw tightened. His eyes were as turbulent as the water in the slip. He pointed the gun at his wife's chest. Then he crumpled, kneeling next to her while she held his head against her breast, and he let out a sob that had been trapped inside him since the death of his children.

For a long time, the four of us sat in the boat-house. The only sounds were the waves against the hull of the sunken boat and the crackle of the fires dying on the hill.

44

Imelda waited for someone to confront her, but no one did.

They treated her like a sick child—someone to be checked on occasionally, spoken to gently, sheltered from the others in case she was contagious.

Jose was taken from her. A last kiss, and he whispered in her ear, "Say nothing."

His only wish: to protect her from what she had done.

She sat on a tarp and wrapped herself in a shawl that smelled faintly of candles and altar incense. She thought about the day Peter Brazos had visited the island.

He had questioned Señor Huff, yes. But mostly he had questioned her.

The lawycr's cycs had been like a falcon's, dark and without mercy. *I know Jose was involved. Tell me how, and you could save him.*

She had no idea how Brazos found them: a confession from someone, a deal to betray Jose. They had been so careful, and yet someone knew who they were. After their children were murdered in Laredo, they had moved north, hoping to escape. Jose promised to stop working for the drug lords, but he still built his devices, still used the workroom Señor Huff had given him to plan occasional jobs. Bomb-making was in his blood like a drug. He could not leave it behind completely.

After Peter Brazos found them, she told Jose what they must do. She located his home in Corpus Christi, his other house in Port Aransas.

We should run, Jose told her. *We have enough money.*

But Imelda had run too many times. She loved Rebel Island. She wanted to grow old here with Jose, tending the hotel rooms, listening to the ocean. When she thought of Peter Brazos, threatening to take her husband away from her, her hands trembled. She lit a candle at the altar of her dead children, and made a promise.

If you will not, she told Jose, *I will.*

In the end, he had relented. But it had been her idea—her murder. The wife and children—if Imelda had not pushed Jose, if she'd given him time to plan...

Imelda had been coming out of the grocery store in Port Aransas when she heard two men talking about the explosion—the mother and the two little girls. Imelda's knees turned to water. She collapsed in front of the IGA and her grocery bag split, oranges and soup cans rolling through the parking lot. The men had tried to help her, but she ran. She didn't stop until she found a pay phone and called Jose.

They waited for Peter Brazos to revisit the island with an army of police. But nothing happened. At first Imelda did not understand why. Then she realized she had misjudged. Brazos knew less than he let on. He had no idea Jose was Calavera. He had simply been pushing on them as one of many leads to get at his targets in court. Brazos's wife and children had died for nothing.

Something had broken inside Jose when he learned about the little girls. He wandered the hotel at night, muttering the names of his victims, the dates of his kills. His believed the police would come for them eventually. Or worse, the drug lords. They would resent Calavera's botched, unauthorized assassination. It had caused them too much grief.

Jose made a plan. He would negotiate with the American Marshals Service, exchange information for immunity. Imelda pleaded with him not to, but Jose would not listen.

It is the only way to save ourselves, he told her. *They will find us otherwise, wherever we run.*

The marshal Jesse Longoria had arrived, but he did not want to negotiate. And everything had spiraled out of control.

• • •

Imelda watched another boatful of police come ashore. They brought black plastic cases, yellow tarps and cameras. They joked easily with one another, offering drinks from coolers as if they had come for a day on the beach.

Señora Navarre was talking to one of them. Her hands were cupped around a coffee mug. The señora's eyes caught hers, and an electric charge passed through Imelda.

The señora paused in her conversation. She fixed Imelda with a strange look—almost like pity. Then she turned her attention back to the policeman. She did not look at Imelda again.

She knows, Imelda realized.

And yet...Señora Navarre would not tell the police. Imelda wasn't sure how she knew this, or why the señora would keep silent, but she sensed it was true.

Imelda clenched a handful of sand. She was free, but she would never see Jose again. She had the blood of children on her hands.

I will pay the price, Jose had told her. *You must not. Please, you are all I have. Please, my love, let me do this.*

She wrapped her shawl around her. She would pay a price—only a different price than Jose. The world would be her prison until she answered before God.

She would go back to her cousin's in Corpus Christi. From there...she didn't know. She would find a new job, something to help people. She would add three candles to her altar and pray for the family she had destroyed.

Suddenly she understood Señora Navarre's look of pity. Imelda needed no more punishment. She would live alone with her ghosts and her altar, struggling to make amends, knowing it would never be enough. The police could do nothing worse to her than that. Señora Navarre understood, as only a mother could.

A pilot fish jumped from the water—a silver spark like a camera flash. Imelda watched for it again, but the waves churned gray and empty. She would have to settle for that single splash—a tiny sign that the sea might come back to life.

45

I had some idea how the Taino Indians must've felt when Columbus and his men rowed ashore.

The three Coast Guard guys were only the beginning. An ambulance boat arrived next, followed by the Aransas Sheriff's Department, followed by the ferry filled with FBI agents and marshals and FEMA personnel. By the afternoon, the island was overrun by strangers. White tents were set up on the beach. Forensics teams combed the wreckage of the hotel. Three bodies were found, photographed, bagged and removed.

Jose and Imelda were separated from the rest of us, led away somewhere. I never saw them leave the island.

I had a series of interviews, most of which I

would not remember later. Maia was checked out by a doctor. Some interviews we had to do separately. Some we got to do together. I ate a doughnut and drank a cup of tepid orange juice. Later on, a homicide detective from Corpus Christi gave me a chicken sandwich. He told me something that had happened to him once at a barbecue for Peter Brazos. I don't remember the story, or why he felt he needed to confide in me.

It's strange how that happens. Being a witness, a victim, a participant in some terrible event seems to give you some of the qualities of a priest confessor. Instead of people comforting you, people look to you for comfort and understanding, as if you, by virtue of your trials, have gained some insight the rest of the world sorely needs. A capacity to endure.

Or maybe the guy just had a poor sense of social etiquette. I wasn't in much frame of mind to judge.

A medic who didn't know better told me all the gossip.

Jose had given a full confession to the police. He'd claimed responsibility for the murders of Jesse Longoria and Chris Stowall. He had cleared his wife of any knowledge or guilt. Imelda, I suspected, would go free. That was the only condition Jose demanded in exchange for telling the FBI all about his employers during the time he worked assassinations. Strangely, Imelda's dream of relocation under a new name would most likely become a reality. She and Jose would disappear. But they would not be together. Jose would be in prison somewhere. And Imelda...I didn't know where she would go. She would be swept out of our lives and gone.

Benjamin Lindy had collapsed shortly after hearing about Jose's confession. The medic told me Lindy was suffering from exhaustion, emotional fatigue. The smallest shock can be a big thing when you're eighty years old, and the past twenty-four hours on Rebel Island had been more than a small shock.

I'd given a statement about Lindy shooting Alex Huff, but I doubted it would make much difference. The crisis had already broken Lindy. He'd killed the wrong man. Now he would have to watch as the right man slipped out of his grasp, the very thing he'd tried so desperately to avoid. God had done a much better job punishing Benjamin Lindy for his deeds than the courts could ever do.

As for the UT boys, Ty, Chase and Markie had been questioned and released. Ty was given a sedative. The other two had been given Sprites and chicken sandwiches and told to please go away. They were the first to leave the island. I watched them go, and they stared at me nervously from the back of the police boat.

I had no desire to tell on their little drug smuggling problem. They would have enough to deal with when they got back. I would neither help them nor bust them. They weren't kids after all, I decided. They would figure out a solution, or go to the police, or face some gruesome consequences. It was their problem, not mine.

That left Lane and Garrett—a situation which was not so easy to put on a boat and forget about.

They were sitting in front of the police tent after their interviews. Garrett's chair had been cleaned up. He had, too. He'd managed to wash the soot off his face and pull a fresh Hawaiian shirt out of his luggage. Lane was sipping coffee, watching the sun go down. The sunset made her face look healthier, her eyes brighter.

Garrett acknowledged me with a brief nod as I sat on the canvas tarp next to him.

"It's just now sinking in, little bro. I can't believe Alex is gone."

"He was something."

Garrett drank his beer. The smell of Lane's coffee drifted by and was blown away by the sea breeze.

"We can leave soon," I said. "The ferry should be here in half an hour."

Garrett shook his head. "I'm not going just yet. I need some time to think about the island."

"What do you mean?" I asked.

He locked eyes with me. "Alex left it to me."

I stared at him. I tried to wrap my mind around what he was saying. "You mean . . . Rebel Island?"

"The papers he gave me last night," Garrett said. "That was his will. He said if anything happened to him, he wanted me to know. He was leaving the place to me. He named you executor."

"*Me?*"

Garrett looked back at the smoldering wreckage. "Congratulations."

Part of me wondered why Alex would do such a thing. It would make Garrett a suspect. He'd have a strong motive for threatening Alex's life. But Alex had never thought that way. He hadn't been a killer, just a lonely man who'd tried to live up to Mr. Eli's trust.

After all this, coming here to say goodbye to Rebel Island, my brother had ended up owning it. There was a lesson there somewhere—one of life's little ironies. But I wasn't sure how to take it.

"What'll you do with the place?" My tone probably said what I was thinking: *Why would you want it?*

"Do with it?" Garrett looked out at the sea and breathed in, as if clearing the smoke of the ruins out of his lungs. "Don't know. Maybe a smaller house. Maybe nothing at all. But I like being here."

"And you?" I asked Lane.

"I'll stay the night with Garrett," she answered. "They're leaving the tents set up until morning. Then I'm going back to the mainland."

"What about your ex-husband?"

"I'll confront him," she said. "And bring charges."

"If you want help—"

She shook her head. "I appreciate it. But I'll tell you the same thing I told Garrett. I have to do this myself."

She looked nothing like the crying lady she'd been at the start of the weekend. I wondered if she was just putting on a brave face, if she would crumble again in the presence of danger, but something told me she would not. She'd left her fear behind in the burning hotel along with most of her luggage—the last reminders of her failed marriage.

"You'll bring the police," I said.

She smiled ruefully. "I'm not stupid."

"And when she's done," Garrett said, "whenever that is, she might come back here."

"I might," she agreed.

It was tenuous. As tenuous as the idea that my brother could ever live on this island. Or ever have a relationship, for that matter. But at the moment, Lane and he were holding hands. They seemed at peace. And they really didn't need my presence.

"Good luck," I said.

I shook my brother's hand, told Lane goodbye, and walked away toward the ruins of the ferry dock.

"You weren't even arrested," Maia observed, "much less killed."

"Yeah," I agreed. "Kind of disappointing."

We watched from the ferry's stern as Rebel Island receded into the distance.

The sunset made a blood-red sky and a copper bay. Without its hotel or lighthouse or palmetto trees, Rebel Island looked like nothing much—a sandbar, a trick of the light. A shallow break where

Jean Laffitte might run a Spanish ship aground. The kind of island that vanished in the space of a breath.

And yet ... It was still there. It probably looked more now like it did three hundred years ago, when Cabeza de Vaca was shipwrecked nearby and hunted for lizards with the locals.

The ferry rose and fell on the waves.

"According to the EMT," Maia said, "I'm due any minute. He was amazed the baby held out through the weekend."

"Tough kid," I said.

She kissed me. "Tough parents."

We watched the island disappear. It didn't feel like the final goodbye I'd imagined. If the island really was Garrett's now, I might be forced to come back someday, but that didn't bother me. I wasn't so much worried about the things I was leaving behind. I was more interested in what I was going back to.

"I might take a PI case once in a while," I said. "If the right one came."

Maia raised an eyebrow. "If it didn't interfere."

"It would depend on the case," I said.

"Oh. Naturally."

She tried to hold a poker face as long as possible, but finally a smile made its way to the surface. "You almost made it seven months. Not bad."

"Oh, be quiet."

"Hey, when we broke up, you stayed away from me a whole year. Should I be insulted?"

"I shouldn't have brought this up until we were

closer to the shore. Twenty minutes trapped on this ferry with you. Gonna be a long ride."

She kissed me again. Between us, the baby kicked. It felt like a tiny reminder, the kid telling me, *Get a grip, Dad.*

"Not such a long trip," Maia promised. "Tell me what you want to do first when we get home."

And so we sat together in the stern of the ferry, and we talked about the future.

About the Author

RICK RIORDAN is the author of six previous Tres Navarre novels—*Big Red Tequila*, winner of the Shamus and Anthony Awards; *The Widower's Two-Step*, winner of the Edgar Award; *The Last King of Texas; The Devil Went Down to Austin; Southtown;* and *Mission Road.* He is also the author of the acclaimed thriller *Cold Springs* and the young adult novels *The Lightning Thief, The Sea of Monsters,* and *The Titan's Curse.* Rick Riordan lives with his family in San Antonio, Texas.

A revised and enlarged edition of The Art of Landscape Painting

Landscape Painting Step-by-Step

BY LEONARD RICHMOND

WATSON-GUPTILL PUBLICATIONS · NEW YORK
PITMAN PUBLISHING · LONDON

Paperback Edition
First Printing, 1978

First published 1969 in the United States by Watson-Guptill Publications,
a division of Billboard Publications, Inc.,
1515 Broadway, New York, N.Y. 10036

Published in Great Britain and by special arrangement with Pitman Publishing Ltd.,
39 Parker Street, Kingsway, London WC2B 5PB,
whose *The Art of Landscape Painting,* © Executors of the late
Leonard Richmond, 1958, furnished the basic text for this volume.
ISBN 0-273-01230-4 Pbk.

Library of Congress Catalog Card Number: 77-82747
ISBN 0-8230-2616-7 Pbk.

Manufactured in U.S.A.

Introduction

This book is intended to be a guide for students who are desirous of taking up landscape painting. The average art student, fresh from the schools, is oftentimes concerned at the difficulties connected with the manifold aspects of nature. This book, then, is primarily intended to be a solid help, so that the student can tackle anything and everything without any fear of wasting time unnecessarily. The author has suffered personally by having his thoughts turned in many directions and trying all sorts of experiments, the majority of which were quite unnecessary, and he feels that the whole of this book, if carefully read, will save thousands of pitfalls for the beginner. There is only one thing which is really of every importance for the would-be landscape painter, and that is to cast away all feeling of timidity. Nature is so overwhelming, and she has so much to say, that to the beginner she seems to be chattering incessantly. It is up to the student, when making a sketch, to ignore everything except one motive. The great charm of landscape painting consists in the fact that it is full of possibilities for self-expression. The portrait painter, to a certain extent, has a more limited field.

Art is changing today. Gone forever are those days when merely a copy of nature was sufficient for the artist. There is no earthly reason why an art student should not have a black sky and vermilion trees in a landscape if he or she feels so inclined. Yet I would advise a student, in the initial stages of sketching out of doors, to stick to actual facts, until his mind becomes an encyclopedia of knowledge, based on natural form, color, and tone. Invention follows when knowledge leads the way.

My experience in the past, as a teacher of landscape painting, has been that quite ninety percent of students, in their earlier days of sketching out of doors, invariably try to put in all they see. They are too conscientious. This endeavor to portray everything they see out of doors defeats its own purpose.

What is to be done? Simplification is the only thing that matters for the beginner, and sometimes simplification is the only thing that matters for the advanced painter. Avoid hero worship of other people's paintings. A cool appreciation of Turner is better than a fevered adulation. Remember your own individuality is just as important to you as their's was to the great men and women of the past. Elimination of detail in sketches and finished pictures explains their meaning in a much clearer manner than overstatement. To make a sketch in color of a tree, paint the tree, not the leaves, except the few that may be noticeable on the edges of the general silhouette form. Later on, experience gives suggestions of detail without breaking up the unity of tone.

To attain to the status of a practical workman is essential to the landscape painter. The brush, when charged with color, must obey the mind. Always use a paintbrush with a clear understanding of its flexibility. It is ludicrous to see a painter use a paintbrush like a lead pencil, thus missing the chance of letting the brush function naturally. Whatever medium the student happens to use for sketching, it is a good thing to bear in mind that strength in his painting, for the first few years at all events, is more desirable than delicacy. Delicacy rarely leads to strength, and is often effeminate; but a painter who is successful in strong handling, rich coloring, and striking pattern, is generally very interesting when tackling subjects of delicate tints.

L. R.

Contents

Page 5   INTRODUCTION

Page 11   CHAPTER 1: A FRESH LOOK AT LANDSCAPE

Architecture, 11
Ships, Trains, Automobiles, Industry, 11
Painting Unpromising Subjects, 12

Page 15   CHAPTER 2: THE PLAN OF A PICTURE

Importance of Planning, 15
Dominant Subject, 15
Making Subordinate Elements Interesting, 16
Making Small Experimental Compositions, 16

Page 19   CHAPTER 3: ELEMENTARY COMPOSITIONAL EXERCISES

Placing Horizon Line, 19
Introducing Curves, 19
Composing with Straight Lines, 19
Monotony, Contrast, and Asymmetry, 21
A Note on Perspective, 21

Page 23   CHAPTER 4: ADVANCED COMPOSITIONAL EXERCISES

Inventing Compositions, 23
Designing with Straight Lines, 25
Designing with Curves, 27
Experimenting with Tree Forms, 29

Page 31   CHAPTER 5: VALUES

Comparing Values, 31
Learning About Values, 32
A Difficult Tonal Subject, 33
A Simpler Tonal Subject, 33
Precision of Tone, 33

Page 37   CHAPTER 6:   OUTDOOR SKETCHING

Color Sketches and Pencil Drawings, 37
Media for Color Sketches, 38
Be Decisive, 38

Page 41   CHAPTER 7:   MORE ABOUT OUTDOOR SKETCHING

Direct Watercolor Sketch, 41
Tinted Pencil Drawing, 41
Oil Painting Based on a Sketch, 41
Watercolor Sketch in Two Stages, 42
Pastel Sketch for a Watercolor, 42
Pastel and Watercolor Compared, 43

Page 45   CHAPTER 8:   DETAILED STUDIES IN PENCIL

Tree Study, 45
Two Landscape Studies, 45
Hold the Pencil Naturally, 49
Pencil Notes, 49

Page 51   CHAPTER 9:   STUDIES OF CLOUDS

Memory and Invention, 51
Sky and Cloud Colors, 51
Catching Fleeting Effects, 52
Gradated Color, 52
Types of Clouds, 53

Page 55   CHAPTER 10:   STUDIES OF HILLS AND MOUNTAINS

Avoid False Charm, 55
Emphasize Ruggedness, 55
Mountains in Watercolor, 56
Mountains in Oils, 57

Page 59   CHAPTER 11:   STUDIES OF TREES

Importance of Silhouette, 59
Eliminate Detail, 59
Studies of Mass Foliage, 60
Wooded Landscape, 61
Studies of Foliage Details, 61

Page 63   CHAPTER 12:   STUDIES OF WATER

Water Without Reflections, 63
Reflections in Light and Shadow, 63
Shallow Water, 64
Make Lights Darker and Darks Lighter, 65
Reflections Analyzed, 66

Page 69   CHAPTER 13:   STUDIES OF BUILDINGS

Painting in the City, 69
Observation Can Lead You Astray, 69
Architectural Painting in Oils, 70
Avoid Cold, Chalky Color, 70
Architectural Painting in Watercolor, 71

Page 73   CHAPTER 14:   STUDIES OF BOATS AND SHIPPING

Studying Boats, 73
Barges, 73
Fishing Boats, 74
Gondolas, 74
Combining Ink and Watercolor, 75

Page 77   CHAPTER 15:   UNDULATING LANDSCAPES

Undulating Hills, 77
Undulating Foreground, Middle Distance, and Distance, 77
Color and Design, 78
Clouds in Undulating Landscapes, 78

Page 129   CHAPTER 16:   MOODS OF NATURE

Expressing Mood, 129
Tranquility, 130
Storm, 130
Moonlight and Evening, 130
Violence in Nature, 130
Majesty in Nature, 131
A Melancholy Mood, 131

Page 135   CHAPTER 17:   THE USE OF OUTDOOR SKETCHES

Working in the Studio, 135
Avoiding Mannerisms, 136
Sketch and Finished Picture in Oils, 136
Sketch and Finished Picture in Pastel, 136
What Matters is Decisive Statement, 137

Page 139   CHAPTER 18:   VARIOUS MATERIALS

Pastel Materials, 139
Watercolor Materials, 139
Oil Painting Equipment, 140
Suggestions About Color, 140
Colors for Oil Painting, 140
Colors for Watercolor Painting, 140
Selecting Pastel Colors, 141

Page 142   INDEX

Color Plates

PLATE I. Four basic tones for foreground, middle distance, distance, sky 81
PLATE II. Same landscape in washes of full color 81
PLATE III. *A Gray Day at Bruges*, pastel 82
PLATE IV. *The River Doubs Besançon, France*, watercolor 83
PLATE V. Rapid watercolor note 85
PLATE VI. Pencil sketch on ordinary writing paper, with watercolor tints 85
PLATE VII. *Tor Steps, Exmoor, Somerset*, oil painting 86
PLATE VIII. *A Minehead Cottage, Somerset*, first stage of watercolor 87
PLATE IX. *A Minehead Cottage, Somerset*, final stage of watercolor 87
PLATE X. Pastel sketch, preliminary study for watercolor in Plate XVI. 88
PLATE XI. Watercolor sketch emphasizes design 88
PLATE XII. *Study of Moving Clouds*, watercolor 89
PLATE XIII. Gradated watercolor wash 90
PLATE XIV. Watercolor sky 91
PLATE XV. *Cathedral Mountains, Canadian Rockies*, oil painting 92
PLATE XVI. *A Decoration*, watercolor based on pastel sketch in Plate X 95
PLATE XVII. *Emerald Lake, Canadian Rockies*, first stage of oil painting 97
PLATE XVIII. *Emerald Lake, Canadian Rockies*, final stage of oil painting 98
PLATE XIX. Watercolor study of mass foliage, first stage 99
PLATE XX. Watercolor study of mass foliage, final stage 99
PLATE XXI. *Elm Trees at Windsor*, watercolor 100
PLATE XXII. *Fir Trees, Pas-de-Calais, France*, watercolor 101
PLATE XXIII. Watercolor study of foliage detail, first stage 103
PLATE XXIV. Watercolor study of foliage detail, final study 103
PLATE XXV. Watercolor study of fir 103
PLATE XXVI. Watercolor study of chestnut leaves 103
PLATE XXVII. *A Venetian Canal*, oil painting 104
PLATE XXVIII. *Bolton Abbey, Yorkshire*, first stage of pastel 106
PLATE XXIX. *Bolton Abbey, Yorkshire*, final stage of pastel 108
PLATE XXX. *The River Thames, Marlow*, watercolor 109
PLATE XXXI. *The Bridge over Bruges Canal*, oil painting 111
PLATE XXXII. *The Fountain, Besançon, France*, watercolor 113
PLATE XXXIII. *Boats at Gravesend*, first stage of watercolor 114
PLATE XXXIV. *Boats at Gravesend*, final stage of watercolor 115
PLATE XXXV. *Chateau de Polignac, France*, pastel 116
PLATE XXXVI. *Tranquility*, watercolor 118
PLATE XXXVII. *Storm*, watercolor 118
PLATE XXXVIII. *Moonlight*, watercolor 118
PLATE XXXIX. *Evening*, watercolor 118
PLATE XL. *A Canadian Waterfall*, oil painting 119
PLATE XLI. *Bow Falls, Banff, Canadian Rockies*, first stage of watercolor 120
PLATE XLII. *Bow Falls, Banff, Canadian Rockies*, final stage of watercolor 122
PLATE XLIII. *The Estuary, Barmouth, North Wales*, first stage of oil painting 123
PLATE XLIV. *The Estuary, Barmouth, North Wales*, final stage of oil painting 125
PLATE XLV. *The Watchet Coast, Somerset*, oil sketch 126
PLATE XLVI. *The Watchet Coast, Somerset*, finished oil painting 126
PLATE XLVII. *The Brendon Hills from Williton, Somerset*, pastel sketch 127
PLATE XLVIII. *The Brendon Hills from Williton, Somerset*, finished pastel painting 127
PLATE XLIX. *Old Net Houses, Hastings*, oil sketch 128
PLATE L. *Old Net Houses, Hastings*, finished oil painting 128

TOWER BRIDGE by Donald Teague, watercolor, 18¾" x 27¾".

Painting cityscapes often becomes difficult because of the extreme clutter of architectural elements. Here the artist has organized his composition into three distinct planes to minimize this kind of confusion. The foreground is an extreme, detailed close up of a ruined wall, with careful rendering of the broken surface. Looming above this, in the middle ground, is a dark central cluster of buildings, in contrast to the lighted ruin in the foreground. And in the distance, the viewer sees the bridge silhouetted against the sky and the strip of buildings on the far shore, in shadow. The secret of the painting's success is really the decision to devote half the picture to the extreme closeup of the wrecked wall, with its intricate textural detail. (Courtesy Virginia Museum of Fine Arts, Richmond, Virginia)

A Fresh Look at Landscape

Speaking of a landscape picture, one presupposes that the picture contains within its boundaries a foreground, middle distance, distance, and sky; but landscape art includes more than this in its outlook towards nature.

ARCHITECTURE

Although buildings may not be described as nature's children, yet architectural subjects, whether fine buildings or cottages, form a very important branch of landscape painting. It matters little how modern buildings may be. As soon as they are erected and stand in company with nature's moods, they become part of the general effect. The glow of light from the sky will cast its mantle of beauty over the crudest structures that have been built. Nature has a good way of balancing things up by leaving the impress of herself on surrounding objects. An iron bridge of hideous design is capable of reflecting beautiful color from the river below. Likewise, a similar bridge, if entirely neglected by man, will show bronze and orange tints and other colors caused through rust, etc.

It is a mistake to imagine that modern architecture is of no landscape value. Those who have been privileged to see the skyscrapers of New York, and particularly the view from the district of Brooklyn Bridge, know otherwise. Such massive dignity of ever-rising heights, connecting up to the sky from the earth below, gives fine opportunities to the landscape artist. The wonderful illumination at night on the buildings in New York, the source of which is mostly disguised, is a revelation to the artistic mind. At the close of day, when the sun has set, and with still a glow left in the sky caused by the afterglow of the sun, these skyscrapers have shown marvelous color, and, nearly all detail being eliminated, their massive proportions looked even greater than when exposed to sunlight.

SHIPS, TRAINS, AUTOMOBILES, INDUSTRY

When one speaks of landscape, the sea is invariably included, paradoxical though it may sound. Travel posters today take artistic advantage of those magnificent liners crossing the Atlantic and Pacific Oceans. Watching one of these large, but beautifully designed boats coming slowly into harbor, with such unconscious grace and charm, awakes an esthetic thrill in the soul of an artist. Then there is the modern locomotive plying on the railways. Thanks partly to the great boilers needed to cope with the necessary speed on the express routes, the design of the engine today is genuinely beautiful and good to look upon. Then there are automobiles. Certain types of automobiles may be described as first cousins to the locomotive for artistic form.

There have been pictures painted with a weird and beautiful light thrown by the headlights of a car on the roads and adjoining trees. The results have been fantastical and quite original. Modern invention is always capable of giving fresh ideas to a landscape artist.

One has only to think again of the great steel yards, dock yards, shipping yards, etc., to realize what a success certain artists have made of these subjects. Some of the finest lithographs ever executed were done by Joseph Pennell of the huge works and cranes, engineers and men, who were engaged during the construction of the Panama Canal.

There is a good deal of ugly beauty in industrial subjects. With blast furnaces working, the glare is easily seen at night, and the adjoining slag heaps often taking on sinister forms. Then we have canals, with the attendant low-lying barges; cathedrals, churches, public buildings, mountains, lakes, famous cliffs and caves, barns and farmhouses, villages, inns, rivers, quick-running streams, many types of trees, cattle, and other items.

It should be understood that the outlook for the landscape painter is very big and comprehensive. The elements of a landscape being of so wide a range, the student will do well to remember that the years fly along so quickly for the serious landscape artist that there is an urgent necessity for continuous work, both in and out of doors, not neglecting to sketch out of doors in the winter sometimes, if the weather is suitable.

PAINTING
UNPROMISING
SUBJECTS

Some modern artists have successfully translated the most unpromising subjects. This requires intelligence of no mean order. It is not easy to select a subject of a hard iron railing, one or two flower pots, a trash can, and stray articles, and create something fine and big in pictorial language. It is comparatively easy to create charm and delicacy by painting a picture of honeysuckle, violets, or any other flowers in a garden. The mentality of people today is on a more interesting plane, certainly on a much higher plane, where pictorial art is concerned. Triviality is not asked for—nor necessary. There is as much difference between a picture of intelligence and thought and a picture of a little robin redbreast on the snow, as there is between a good book and the sweet, nauseous short story in the cheap magazine.

Many artists apparently must go to well known places, where they are sure there is something charming and something—we might almost say pretty. Wherever an artist happens to be, whether on the top of a mountain, in the courtyard of slum tenements, or any other place on this earth where there is light and air, that artist should be capable of finding something of interest to paint. Many painters have felt insulted when visitors to their studios have quite innocently said of a picture, "Oh, how pretty!" That is severe condemnation for the unfortunate painter—not praise.

It is difficult to imagine Shakespeare, with his mentality, if he had been a pictorial landscape painter, producing pretty, meaningless pictures. Certainly it would be very difficult to imagine Ibsen producing sweetly dull landscapes.

The problem of color in pictures is difficult. Certain subjects demand a quiet, restrained color scheme, while other subjects insist on a sumptuous color effect. Glowing colors sometimes explain too much in a landscape, whereas restrained colors do not always tell their message at one glance, and, indeed, suggest sometimes mysterious reserve, which helps to arouse one's curiosity. All these and other problems are for each person to settle individually. Bright colors in most media can unquestionably become dull when the hand of time takes a part in their destiny.

THROUGHWAY by Hardie Gramatky, watercolor.

Industrial subjects are not normally thought of as landscapes, but they often make striking landscape subjects. This study of the construction of a highway makes particularly interesting use of light and atmosphere. The viewer's eye follows the lighted roadway back into the distance and the intensity of the light is strengthened by the splash of dark shadow that cuts across the foreground. Beyond the focal point of the painting, where the actual construction work is going on, the landscape melts into a grayish haze, with few contrasts of light and shadow—no strong darks and no distinct lights, except for the buildings on the extreme right, across the river, which catch a flash of sunlight and thereby balance the action in the center of the picture. (Photograph courtesy American Artist)

HILLSIDE HOUSES by Antonio P. Martino, oil.

The surfaces of old buildings give the painter an interesting opportunity to experiment with the textures of paint. This artist has rendered the crusty surface of the snow and the weathered walls of the buildings as patches of broken color. Broken color effects, as distinct from flat color, are achieved by painting one tone into another, using either a brush or a knife, and carefully avoiding the temptation to blend the wet paint. The strokes are simply put down and allowed to stand, thus retaining the vitality of the artist's touch. (Photograph courtesy American Artist)

14

2

The Plan of a Picture

A picture which was not planned originally by the painter might be compared with a house that was built without any previous consideration being given to its style of architecture, or without any consideration as to whether it is suitable for utilitarian purposes. Such a house, through the want of definite thought on the part of the builder, might prove interesting as a freak dwelling, but the chances are very remote that it would be suitable to live in, and the lack of cohesion in design would give no rest to the mind of its tenants.

IMPORTANCE OF PLANNING

It is obvious that every picture, whether good or bad, has some sort of arrangement or design behind it, which was originally planned by the artist. The plan of a picture can make or mar the final result of the painting. Therefore, too much stress cannot be laid on the supreme importance of this branch of landscape art. It is of genuine advantage to the student to take the subject up in the early stages of training for landscape art. Development in painting follows naturally, and in some instances quite quickly, if the student facilitates his future progress by acquiring the habit of good picture designing.

The pictures of old masters of landscape art are living examples of fine compositions, displaying adroit skill in the spacing of their pictures. Students should become so soaked in the science of picture planning that eventually they will subconsciously do the right thing for each sketch or picture, in much the same way that we are rarely conscious of breathing for the purpose of keeping the body alive.

DOMINANT SUBJECT

The subject of a picture must be master of the whole scheme of design. If the main subject happens to be a bridge over a stream, everything in that picture, whether in color, tone, or drawing, must result in making the bridge pre-eminent in the final result.

There are many interesting tidbits of nature, and it is quite easy to wander away from the main theme when sketching the landscape, so it becomes a matter of self-control or self-discipline when one is tackling a complicated subject.

A picture must have something to say. It can speak more eloquently when planned with judicious spacing. Too many elements in one landscape cause confusion in the mind of the spectator. It is like several people all speaking together, such a lot of noise that nothing can be clearly heard or understood. Many good pictures do not need a catalogue to give you the title. It is already self-evident in the clever manner in which they have been treated by the artist.

MAKING
SUBORDINATE
ELEMENTS
INTERESTING

After the student has acquired the necessary skill in placing the primary interest of the picture right across the mind of the spectator, the next thing to learn will be to make all the subordinate portions of the painting really interesting, each in its own compartment, yet without interfering with the unity of the whole picture.

To attain this purpose, it is admirable practice to design little drawings and color sketches indoors. The result is sometimes amusing, but it is always interesting to try some creative work, and, moreover, the winter evenings can be profitably used for this type of drawing and painting, as daylight is not necessary for invention experiments. To make designs away from nature leaves the mind in peace to function naturally, so that designs invented at home can at least display more intelligent spacing than is generally possible when the artist has to overcome several difficulties out of doors.

MAKING SMALL
EXPERIMENTAL
COMPOSITIONS

It is a good plan to have definite titles to work from, such as: The Storm, Tranquillity, The Bridge, Sunrise, Moonlight, Evening, etc. There are scores of subjects for the artist, waiting to be selected, and which are appropriate for landscape art. Miniature sketches about 2″ x 3″ are quite large enough for experimental compositions. It is far easier to see the effect and design of a little sketch than it is to grasp the meaning of a larger painting or drawing. That is why so many artists rule squares all over the face of a sketch, with a corresponding number of squares ruled on the larger picture, so that they can faithfully copy the original subject from the sketch by using the exact proportions seen in the smaller picture.

The more indoor creative sketches the student makes, the more fit that student will be to select proper subjects from nature. The eye becomes trained to see good pictorial subjects, and to select that point of view out of doors which is all-important for the correct spacing of the subject on canvas or paper.

Pastel is a splendid medium for indoor inventive sketches, if used on a fairly dark paper, warm gray or brown for preference. Soft pastel is best for this purpose, and the tinted paper should have a fairly smooth surface, so that the pastel can glide quickly and easily over the paper. Mistakes are easily altered by rubbing the pastel off with a wad of cotton or a bristle brush. When using pastel for little landscape designs, it is better for this medium not to work on a scale smaller than 4″ x 3″.

Apart from pastel, it is also good practice, in doing these small sketches, to suggest the subject rapidly with a lead pencil; then, with a small watercolor paint brush, say No. 3, use brown, green, or black ink and indicate by line, or mass, or both, the subject that you wish to portray. Pencil is sometimes insufficient to suggest the weight and bigness of a design, even though that design may be only 1″ square. As soon as the brush is used in addition to the pencil, the design becomes manifest and explains the intention of the one who designed it. It is also good practice, in making small, inventive sketches, to draw your sketch lightly in pencil, outline it in brown or some other colored ink with a brush, and then tint it with ordinary watercolors. (See Plates XXXIII and XXIV.) The charm of adding color to a design fascinates the would-be artist, and usually results in an increase of work.

The student must work, if possible, at least six days a week. Yet work is of no value if the student is tired. Good physical health is an asset for good results. No landscape painter of normal health should ever suffer. Two thirds, or even six months, of the year spent out of doors usually provides the necessary store of health required for the remaining portion of the year spent indoors.

MARKET STREET WEST by Philip Jamison, watercolor.

Rain is a particularly difficult subject to paint because a gray, rainy day tends to minimize contrasts of light and shade, and form tends to disappear. In this cityscape, painted on a rainy day, the artist has not made any attempt to paint the falling rain itself, but has simply painted the reflections on the wet street and buildings. The wetness lends a fascinating luminosity to the street, wihch breaks up into interesting patterns of dark and light, with reflections from the buildings above. The wet walls and windows of the buildings, too, pick up touches of reflected light. (Photograph courtesy American Artist)

FACTEUR by Stuart Garrett, watercolor.

A symmetrical subject always runs the risk of being monotonous. The artist has avoided this problem by shifting his subject slightly off center to the viewer's right, so that a glimpse of townscape appears to the left. Thus, the center of interest appears not in the middle of the picture, but one third in from the right hand side. This landscape is a particularly strong use of perspective, with all elements leading the viewer's eye to the vanishing point at the head of the stairs. Yet any effect of rigidity is avoided by the sinuous shapes of the trees, which lend a delicate rhythm to a composition which would otherwise seem barren. (Photograph courtesy American Artist)

18

Elementary Compositional Exercises

In Chapters 3 and 4 on compositional exercises, the whole secret of landscape designing from a pictorial standpoint is fully explained. Students who wish to be proficient in composition should start straight away. Knowledge gained indoors is vastly useful for outdoor painting.

PLACING
HORIZON LINE

To start, then, from the very beginning, one of the first things to avoid in a landscape is the unfortunate effect of making the sky occupy half the area space of the picture. Fig. 1 shows the monotony of such spacing. In Fig. 2, the horizon is placed about one quarter of the distance up from the bottom line of the picture, with the sky occupying the remaining three quarters of the area space. This creates a more interesting ratio between the earth and sky. It is also possible to raise the horizon about two thirds or three quarters of the distance up from the lower line of the picture, with the sky occupying the remaining area space. This lends itself to an agreeable foundation for picture planning.

INTRODUCING CURVES

The next step in composition is the introduction of curves instead of horizontal lines. Under all circumstances and conditions, nature will insist on balance. For instance, in Fig. 3, the larger curve extending across the picture is balanced by the smaller curve on the right. Two similar curves are repeated above the two lower curves so as to create the illusion of distant hills, as demonstrated in Fig. 4; the only difference is that the smaller curve resting above is placed on the left instead of the right side. Simple as these curves are in this sketch, they already suggest a landscape in which the balance is evenly distributed. Students are advised to make several designs of swinging intersecting curves, keeping the less circular curves in the higher portions of the picture. There is a good deal of room for invention, even in the restricted area of curves, without the assistance of straight lines.

COMPOSING WITH
STRAIGHT LINES

In Fig. 5, instead of having curves with which to plan the pattern, straight lines only were used. As in Fig. 2, the horizon is placed somewhat low down in the picture. The larger triangular hill spreading across the picture, which is balanced by the smaller hill, is similar in direction to the two intersecting curves in Fig. 3.

In Fig. 6, the same procedure is adopted as in Fig. 4, with the added advantage of a foreground. This little picture has quite a pictorial value. The converging lines in the foreground, spreading towards the hills, create a sense of distance, and the dark tone of the nearest hills helps to give a feeling of solidity, and almost a sensation as though they were covered with nature's own shadow. The two farther hills suggest the illusion of being in sunlight, since they are opposed to the solid and dark hills in front.

The student who is keen on invention could, by using Fig. 6 as a starting point for further progress, introduce groups of trees or intersecting fields on the side of the hills; or minute cottages, to accentuate the scale of the hills; or cloudlets in the sky; and might indeed continue for hours developing ideas, none of which is wasted when it comes to the actual sketching out of doors.

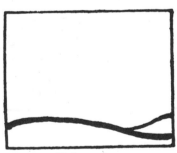

Fig. 1. Monotonous spacing.

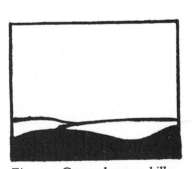

Fig. 2. More interesting spacing.

Fig. 3. Balanced curves.

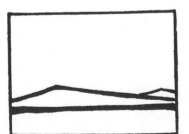

Fig. 4. Curves become hills.

Fig. 5. Pattern of straight lines.

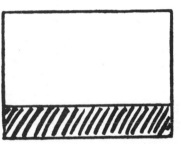

Fig. 6. Straight lines become landscape.

MONOTONY, CONTRAST, AND ASYMMETRY

The next group of sketches, Figs. 7-10, consist of various arrangements of trees. In Fig. 7, two trees are placed on either side of the picture. This does not make a pleasant design, the chief fault being lack of contrast; but by taking one tree out of the picture, say from the right, the contrast now gained by two versus one, adds a little more sparkle to an otherwise monotoous effect. The result is shown in Fig. 8. An even better contrast is gained by placing another tree in the group on the left, thus giving additional strength to this group when compared with the one tree, as seen in Fig. 9.

Still further interesting results can be obtained by arranging what might aptly be described as the "inward composition." To do this in Fig. 10, for example, the nearest tree is left in the foreground, while the other trees are placed at various intervals, each one receding farther from the foreground tree. In this sketch not only do we get the contrast as demonstrated in the previous sketch, but there is an additional interest caused by the fact that no two trees are of the same height or the same distance from the spectator.

Fig. 7. *Symmetrical design lacks contrast.*

Fig. 8. *Asymmetry adds contrast.*

Fig. 9. *Greater contrast adds strength.*

Fig. 10. *Recession adds interest.*

A NOTE ON PERSPECTIVE

It is taken for granted that the student of landscape art has some knowledge of elementary perspective. If not, some lessons in perspective are advisable, particularly that section relating to buildings and reflections on water. There is no need to go through an advanced course in this subject. Personally, I think observation, backed by a few lessons, is quite sufficient. My own experience has been that observation is far more important than any scientific or academic training in perspective, though this may not apply to every individual. A picture can be spoiled by too close an adherence to the rigid laws of perspective. Some modern painters almost ignore its existence.

Córdoba by Donald Teague, watercolor.

The beginning painter should remember that buildings are simply geometric forms and must be visualized as one visualizes blocks and cylinders. Because the light enters this painting at a low angle from the left, the artist is able to model his forms quite simply: all the planes that face left receive the light, while the forms that face the viewer are in shadow. Having established this simple division of light and shadow, the artist is then free to render the intricate textures that appear within the shadows. Observe how the forms at the base of the bridge are rendered as cylinders, with the light and shadow subtly gradated around them. The artist has reduced the possible confusion of the architectural detail by placing most of the cityscape in shadow and highlighting only the critical architectural elements. (Photograph courtesy American Artist)

4

Advanced Compositional Exercises

In this chapter are some advanced exercises which owe their origin entirely to invention.

Figs. 11 and 12 show a skeleton groundwork of straight lines. Figs. 13-16 below explain their origin by the skeleton plans above. When drawing the original straight lines, I had no preconceived ideas as to what the ultimate result might be. First of all, it was exceedingly interesting to design three solid roofs in the Fig. 13. After completing this with colored ink, I drew parallel vertical lines to make the building solid in tone. When these vertical lines were completed, giving a halftone value, I added windows and doors. The next idea was to have an entrance into the picture, so a pathway was drawn leading towards the building. For the sake of pictorial contrast, I then drew horizontal parallel lines or curves to suggest the flatness of the ground, with two curves on each side and behind the building so as to suggest distance. The clouds are very simple—merely a direct outline.

Fig. 15 is precisely the same subject as the one above, but instead of a solid roof, the solidity of the colored ink was used entirely for the sky, leaving the cloud white. The experiment of adding a shadow partly on the face of the building, instead of on the whole frontage, and also leaving some of the foreground in sunlight, made the subject far more interesting. There is a certain feeling of pictorial comfort in Fig. 15. This is partly accounted for since light always looks well on a dark surface, instead of a dark surface being silhouetted on a light background. The darkness of the sky instinctively supports the cottage. In Fig. 13 above, the cottage appears to a certain extent to be isolated from the distance. In Fig. 15, by judicious arrangement of shadows, the cottage belongs more to the surroundings in which it is placed.

Fig. 14, based on Fig. 12 suggests a ruined castle or some building of antiquity which has long been in disuse. Here, again, the sky is dark and solid. The feeling of light on the building is due to the fact that there is no shading whatsoever on its surface. There is a certain amount of movement in the foreground, caused by curved lines and unintentional or accidental handling, which helps to make the subject more interesting. The Fig. 16 sketch is also based on the top skeleton plan in Fig. 12 above. In Fig. 16, instead of buildings, the idea of trees is suggested, still keeping the geometric form of the original straight line drawing in Fig. 12.

It is not for one moment suggested that this a high form of art, but what it does do, in ninety-nine cases out of a hundred, is to stimulate interest in invention.

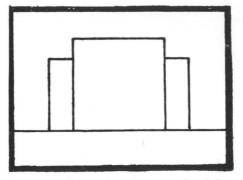

Fig. 11. Symmetrical geometric skeleton.

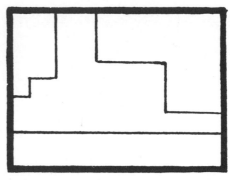

Fig. 12. Asymmetrical geometric skeleton.

Fig. 13. Architectural scheme based on Fig. 11.

Fig. 14. Architectural scheme based on Fig. 12.

Fig. 15. Another variation based on Fig. 11.

Fig. 16. Landscape based on Fig. 12.

It is really astonishing what an extraordinary number of variations can be based on one simple geometric plan. There does not appear to be any limit to invention, If a student designs a thousand geometric plans by merely using straight lines enclosed in a rectangular framework, that student would have no difficulty in getting three designs on each of those thousand geometric bases. Obviously, this would give three thousand inventions based on geometric form. There is no reason why half a million could not be designed, if such a thing were physically possible, and still fresh thoughts would arise in a never-ending procession.

DESIGNING WITH STRAIGHT LINES
Figs. 17 and 18 are designs based on straight lines. The motif of these two pictures was the Canadian Rocky Mountains. It was difficult to resist the feeling of curvature in addition to straight lines. Any curvature which may be discovered in these two sketches is caused by the inability of the artist to draw straight lines without a ruling pen; but, fundamentally speaking, it is all based on rigid lines. It is quite entertaining to design pictures with this limitation. The student who may be rather weak in composition would find invention on straight lines not only a good tonic, but a good stimulant towards creating more powerful results.

Fig. 17. Straight line design based on mountain subject.

Fig. 18. Another mountainous straight line design.

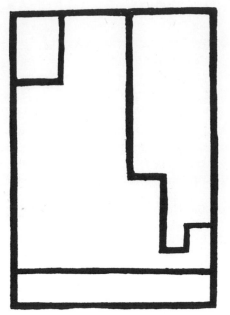

Fig. 19. *Geometric skeleton for vertical composition.*

Fig. 20. *Landscape design based on Fig. 19.*

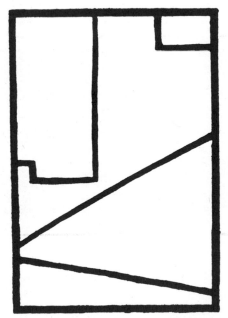

Fig. 21. *Skeleton of verticals, horizontals, diagonals.*

Fig. 22. *Composition based on Fig. 21.*

Figs. 19-22 are based on straight lines, but instead of having horizontal pictures, we now have the upright or vertical design. Again there was no premeditation when these lines were drawn as to what the result might be. It is not necessary to explain Figs. 19-22. They should now explain themselves quite clearly to the intelligent student.

Figs. 23 and 24, representing circular construction, give the plans of the pictures below, and the lower drawings (Figs. 25-28) demonstrate the vagaries of an artist. There is a feeling of excitement in drawing designs where practically every portion of the composition is based on curves. Here, again, there is no limit to invention. As in the previous examples, the artist had no advance knowledge as to what the results of the formal planning of these drawings would lead to. Had space permitted, at least fifty different results could have been shown from each of the two skeleton plans, but it is obvious that the four examples given are quite sufficient to encourage others to make their own experiments, and to do something where their own mentality is more important than any outside influence or environment.

Fig. 23. Compositional skeleton based on curves.

Fig. 24. Another compositional skeleton based on curves.

Fig. 25. Landscape design based on Fig. 23.

Fig. 26. Landscape design based on Fig. 24.

Fig. 27. Another landscape design based on Fig. 23.

Fig. 28. Another landscape design based on Fig. 24.

Fig. 29.   *Compositional skeleton with circular movement.*

Fig. 30.   *Landscape design based on Fig. 29.*

Figs. 29 and 30 are two more examples of circular movement in design. These also are self-explanatory. The suggestion of trees in Fig. 30 counteracts, by reason of their vertical shapes, the otherwise overwhelming number of curves. In Fig. 31, there is a circular formation, inside of which is spaced a whole group of trees. As the trees recede farther away towards the right, they are, according to the arbitration of this design, much smaller in height.

The last drawing in this chapter (Fig. 32) consists of a rectangular form in which trees are placed, showing the pattern caused by the interstices of light between the branches and foliage. Quite a number of designs of this sort can be made by students without ever worrying as to the nature, origin, or species of the trees that they may invent for their own pleasure. A separate sketchbook can be used for making serious studies of the many varied types of trees in nature, irrespective of pattern planning.

Fig. 31. Circular form suggests recession.

Fig. 32. Composition of tree forms.

MOGADORE by Roy M. Mason, watercolor.

In a complex landscape like this one, it is helpful to visualize the various forms as flat shapes. In this painting, four masses of rocky land jut upward, and each has a distinct silhouette which was considered before any detail was painted in. Within the silhouettes, the artist then added as much detail as he thought necessary: the nearest land mass, on the viewer's right, has the greatest amount of foliage detail; the next nearest, above the figures, has somewhat less detail and less contrast; and the two distant masses are virtually devoid of detail, except for a faint indication of shadow. The area of highest contrast (in the lower left hand quarter of the picture) is the focal point and the artist has relied upon crisp light and dark accents to draw attention here. (Photograph courtesy American Artist)

5

Values

Some professors of art have talked in a learned way of values or tone. What is value? It is nothing more than the depth or density of one color and its correct relation to the surrounding colors.

COMPARING VALUES

To be as simple as possible, I would refer the student to Plates I and II. These are two examples of values. For the sake of making the definition clear, these two landscapes have four tones—foreground, middle distance, distance, and sky. In either example, every detail of color or form in the foreground must be of the right density or the right depth of color. The paintings would be failures in this respect if any portion of the landscape, say in each foreground, appeared to belong to the middle distance or the distance. These remarks are equally true when applied to the middle distance, distance, and sky.

The student who goes out sketching will have some difficulty, in the first year's work, in ascertaining the best way in which to manage these four tones. As a general rule, the foreground is darker in color, the middle distance is a little lighter, the distance is lighter still, and the sky the lightest of all. Do not, however, be misled by this statement, because it is possible—but not usual—to have the sky darker even than the foreground. Experience should teach the student the best way of obtaining the desired results of tone. Intelligent thought soon clears away all difficulties. The mind has to assert its control over the student's actions in painting tone.

I do not advise any student in the early days of sketching to try the type of landscape where there is a great variety of tone. As the majority of people know, Turner was a master of values. He was not satisfied in the average landscape pictures to express four tones; most of his pictures show quite a large number of varying tones. But even so, it is possible for the average student to paint a fair number of tones in one picture, provided that he makes a start in the manner suggested on Plate I, and gradually feels his way as experience ripens.

A lead pencil, as well as color, can suggest tone. Some artists use several lead pencils of varying density with which to draw landscape subjects out of doors—a 6B pencil for the foreground, 5B, 4B, and 3B pencils for the varying lighter tones receding in the picture, and sometimes finishing with a harder pencil, such as an HB, for the distant mountains or clouds floating over the sky. If a pencil can suggest tone accurately, it should not be a very difficult matter for a painter to express tone in color.

The two landscapes already mentioned, although of the same subject, show different colors, the idea of the artist being that each color in the corresponding place of each picture should be of exactly the same density or tone. The foreground of the top landscape is as dark as the foreground in the lower landscape. The middle distance in the top landscape is just as dark in tone as the middle distance in the lower landscape. The same remarks apply to the distance and the sky. Allowing for reproduction, which is nearly perfect in these days, the author of this book claims that these two landscapes are a very fair representation of similar values.

LEARNING ABOUT VALUES It is instructive to try several watercolor tints of different colors on one sheet of paper and see if each tint can be made of the same depth or density as the adjoining tint.

A wash of yellow ochre could be washed side by side with a wash of pearly gray; burnt umber may be washed by the side of dark gray, or a tone of light red could be washed by the side of purple. Students should keep on practicing in this way, trying to get the same depth of tone, although a fresh color is used in each wash. Eventually, when the student goes out of doors to sketch, the mind is under control as regards the possibilities of tone in nature.

There may be a rare subject in which value is of less importance; that is a matter for the student to decide. Even so, there is a certain tonality in an apparently chaotic picture, which may not represent the orthodox feeling of tone as seen in nature.

A small white cardboard mat (the width of the mat, say, 2", and the opening about 8" x 10"), if held up to nature out of doors, will help the student to see the tonality of the subject. This will also help the student to compare the tone of the sky with that of the distant hills, fields, houses, foreground, or whatever is contained in the subject which has been selected for sketching.

It is impossible for the student to show decisive values in any landscape if he will insist on paying a lot of attention to unimportant detail. The tone of a tree is quickly seen if painted in the first instance in a flat mass; the tone of a distant mountain is at once evident in its relation to the sky if painted perfectly flat in the first stage of the painting. The same with the foreground, or any other important features in a landscape. It nearly always pays students to paint in all the tones as if they were doing a design for a flat poster. When that is accomplished, step away from the sketch some two or three yards, and compare all the flat tones with the tones of nature itself. If these tones are found to be accurate, then the student can put in a certain amount of detail; but whatever detail is used, it must not, on any account, break up the unity of the picture. That is the whole problem that confronts the student, and it is a big problem.

A DIFFICULT TONAL SUBJECT Of three examples given of values, the first, entitled *A Gray Day at Bruges* (Plate III), is far more difficult to represent from a natural standpoint than the second, *The Bridge over Bruges Canal* (Plate XXXI). This first picture has nothing definite for the artist to work from as regards light and shadow. It is true that there is a shadow under the bridge, and that there is some design in the picture, but as there is no positive light, a great deal of observation was needed to convey the correct values. To take a small point, such as the figure on the bridge with the reddish-purple cloak—if that figure had been much lighter in color, it would have come away from the bridge and been quite out of tone. Or if the boat beneath the bridge had been twice as light in color, then the boat would not have been resting on the water. It would have appeared as if it were in the air above the water. The lightest portion in the immediate foreground on the water, namely, the reflections of subdued light, had to be very carefully rendered as regards density. Every color relating to the surface of this water must be exactly right in light or depth, so as to keep the water one flat surface.

Unity is achieved in this pastel painting through the restraint shown over the whole of the picture. A certain amount of daring was used in the lighter touches of the pastel by suggesting the drawing of the stonework around the arch of the bridge. These few light touches would have lost their purpose if many more light touches had been added in the same neighborhood. The student, then, has to learn the adroit use of light, whether it be brilliant or subdued. It is nearly always safe to do too little than too much.

A SIMPLER TONAL SUBJECT To take the second subject demonstrating values, the picture entitled *The Bridge over Bruges Canal* (Plate XXXI,), this is a vastly different proposition, and ever so much easier. The brilliant light on the house immediately behind the bridge, in the center portion of the picture, made it comparatively easy for the artist to determine the tone of the bridge, the tone of the shadow below the bridge, the warm grays and yellows in the water, and the colors of the right hand building. The positive depth of color used in the foliage of the tree, and the trunk, with the two figures below, rendered everything quite a simple problem. It is possible that the depth of the sky has been slightly exaggerated, but as the light is so brilliant on the house immediately behind the bridge, the feeling of the painter, when sketching this picture out of doors, was helped by this possibly exaggerated tone of the sky in order to enhance the strength of sunlight on the building.

PRECISION OF TONE The third example of values, *The River Doubs, Besançon, France,* (Plate IV), is a sensitive subject as regards the general distribution of light colors.

The tonality of the road in the lower foreground, which is light in tint, retains its place (although quite as light as the distant hills) through the warmth of its color. The darker bushes adjoining the road, being low in tone, are invaluable because, through tone contrast, they cause the river, hills, etc., to take their correct places in the picture. Had these bushes been painted a little lighter or a shade darker, the picture would have been a failure if judged from the standpoint of values.

A very light groundwork was used for the first stage of this watercolor painting, consisting of a mixture of yellow ochre, white tempera, and cerulean blue. The tint of the sky was painted from the top of the picture down to the water's edge. While this color was still wet, the hills extending right across the picture were painted in with a flat watercolor brush. Detail, painted on wet color, was added to the hills towards the left. With the exception of the river, the foreground consists of pure transparent washes, the drawing of the bushes towards the right being strengthened with sharp touches of dark violet.

In the analytical diagram of this picture (adjacent to Plate IV), the chief point of interest is the way in which the lines of the river connect the foreground with the middle distance and extend to the foot of the distant hills. The dotted curves explain the composition of this picture. Notice how the dotted curve which sweeps across the river carries the rhythm of the middle distance into the foreground.

There are altogether twelve different analytical diagrams of this sort in this book, showing clearly the construction or composition relating to the corresponding twelve color plates. This number should be quite sufficient to make it easy for students to understand the underlying principles of construction that may be seen in other pictures.

It is a good plan, when visiting art galleries and museums, to make pencil notes of well known landscape pictures, indicating the main features of compositional lines and other items of general interest.

WINTER LANDSCAPE by Tom Nicholas, oil.

Because nearly all of this dramatic landscape is in shadow, the viewer's eye is drawn immediately to the snowy area which catches a flash of light from a break in the overcast sky. The snow is not merely a flat area of white, but is carefully modeled in planes of light and shadow. Note the extremely selective use of detail and finish. The trees in the foreground are scrubbed in very roughly. Much of the landscape is simply blocked in and left in a semi-finished state. And the forms on the horizon are merely blurs of tone. Only the central rocks and snow are painted with real precision. Thus, the viewer's attention is directed not only by selective lighting but by selective finish. (Photograph courtesy American Artist)

THE SUGAR MILL by W. Emerton Heitland, watercolor.

The central element of the picture, the mill, is essentially geometric and the painter has contrasted the rectilinear lines of the mill with the free, washy forms of the sky. In painting landscapes with architectural elements, it is often wise to emphasize this contrast of free forms and rigid forms. The artist has also paid careful attention to the direction of the strong tropical sun, which throws a dark shadow around the cylindrical form of the mill. This strong directional light also enables him to render the distant trees as dark silhouettes emerging from a strip of shadow. (Photograph courtesy American Artist)

6

Outdoor Sketching

For outdoor sketching, the simplest and lightest outfit, whatever the medium used, is the best for all intents and purposes. In mountainous districts, anything in the form of weight becomes so physically distressing after traveling for some distance that there is not much energy left to make any sort of sketch from nature. It is almost equally true that when traveling, even in normal districts, with a heavy sketching outfit, the weight thereof is inclined to destroy all feeling of response for anything that nature may have to say to the artist. From an economic standpoint, the lighter the weight the cheaper the outfit.

As hinted elsewhere in this book, the student who wishes to express individuality cannot get too much knowledge of natural form, color, and detail. Outdoor sketching means something more than passing a few pleasant hours a week copying nature. The subject is too big for feeble application. In good weather, go out sketching not less than twice a day. Utilize the whole morning, when the light is good; slack off work for a couple of hours, perhaps, at midday; and then fit in the remainder of the day, doing at least another two sketches. A good average for three months' work, if the climate be suitable, is three sketches a day. To achieve that, one sometimes has to make five sketches in one day so as to allow for bad weather. There is every prospect, if the student has artistic leanings, that by adhering to the average output of three sketches a day, he will become a good landscape artist.

COLOR SKETCHES AND PENCIL DRAWINGS

Chapter 5 on values gives practically the keynote to outdoor sketching. The placing of correct tone against tone is invaluable when reference is made later in the studio to the sketch. Little more can be desired than good tone in a sketch, combined with very careful pencil studies so as to back up the outdoor color work. In fact, every sketch should have its corresponding pencil drawing. Personally, I find the pencil drawing sometimes more useful than the colored sketch, but that is only because of the knowledge gained after having painted some thousand odd sketches out of doors. It is much better for the student to show boldness with the paintbrush than it is to paint in a timid style. Concise work, or clear statement, achieves far more than in-efficient earnestness in rendering natural effects.

MEDIA FOR
COLOR SKETCHES

To sketch in oils, little time is required for any sort of preliminary drawing. An oil paintbrush, provided that the first coat of paint is thin, is quite capable of building up a practical sketch, suggesting proper draughtsmanship. To sketch in watercolor, it generally pays to draw carefully all the main outlines of mass formation and a good proportion of the detail before coloring.

It is also a very good thing for the student to sketch in pastel. Many students commence their sketching career in watercolor, which is probably the most difficult medium of the three. Certainly, it does not help to accelerate the speed of the student along the path of art.

One advantage of sketching in pastel is that mistakes are very quickly remedied. If the whole sketch is wrong, a rag or bristle brush will flick out most of the offending colors, and the ground-work caused by that brushing off of color is sometimes perfectly delightful to work on. It is also very suggestive. Indeed, it is inclined to make the work too artistic, if such a thing be possible.

BE DECISIVE

When strolling around, looking for an appropriate subject to sketch, one is often mentally excited by some passing effect which has a strong artistic appeal. I have nearly always found it a fatal error not to commence work at once while that effect still held good. It is a mistake to walk forward or backward, or to stroll around seeking a fresh subject, when one has already been discovered, thinking perhaps the next will be better. The next never seems to come. Therefore, when searching for a subject, as soon as something thrilling happens to you, sketch right away without a moment's hesitation. This not only saves time, but it makes for inspirational art.

The second difficulty which arises is that, having found the subject, and completed a portion of the sketch, the student is often, through technical difficulties, inclined to wander away from the first mental impression. There is nothing worse than a sketch which shows two or three thoughts of a contradictory nature. A sketch should have one definite message which rings throughout the whole of the painting.

The third mistake that misapplied sincerity makes is to sketch on the same subject so long that the sun has moved its position; shadows are in a totally different place, and the whole thing has become messed up from a logical standpoint. Too much speed in sketching is desirable rather than a slow and laborious effort.

Weather conditions have always to be taken into account. Yet, although sunlight is usually much to be desired for outdoor sketching, a resourceful artist can overcome nearly every obstruction that may occur.

One of my sunniest pastel paintings was made when sheltering from the rain, by sketching under a doorway leading into a shop. The subject was a market scene with various groups of figures and local buildings. The absence of definite light and shadow created the necessity for invention and design. So well balanced did this sketch become, with an arrangement of imaginary light and shadow, that it quickly found its way to a patron of the fine arts.

On Mount Mansfield, Vermont by Ted Kautzky, watercolor.

The vitality of this wooded landscape stems from the fact that the artist has caught the subject at a time of day when the light is coming from the extreme right. The trunks and branches of the trees, as well as the weeds in the foreground, are edged with bright, crisp notes of light, which give the painting unusual sparkle. Most landscape painters prefer to work early in the day or late in the day, when the light is coming from the sides or from behind the subject. The most difficult light to paint is at mid-day, when the sun is pouring straight down and filling the entire landscape, destroying form and creating pools of shadow directly under each shape. Side or back light creates roundness of form, divides shapes into distinct areas of light and shade, and produces strong horizontal shadows that indicate the shape and direction of the terrain, as one sees here. (Photograph courtesy American Artist)

HUDSON OVERLOOK by Ranulph Bye, watercolor.

The winding course of a body of water can be a convenient compositional element to lead the eye of the viewer through the picture. In this winter landscape, the near shore of the river carries the eye back along a winding course from the foliage in the immediate foreground out into the distance. In painting water, it is important to remember that the surface is not a uniform tone, but is enlivened by reflections. Observe how the land mass on the horizon appears as a dark reflection in the upper reaches of the river. At the same time, the mound of snow at the turning point of the river appears as a lighter reflection within the darkness. (Photograph courtesy American Artist)

7

More about Outdoor Sketching

In Plates V and VI are two watercolor sketches; Plate V was done at express speed in about thirteen minutes. There was no striving for actual facts of nature. It was painted in an utter sense of irresponsibility, with no thought of careful handling or technique. Any artistic virtue it may show is the result of years of practice in outdoor sketching. There is no reason why an artist should not have as easy a command in using brushes, paints, etc., as the well equipped musician—whose technique is only the unseen foundation on which is built the personal interpretation of music—has over his instrument.

DIRECT WATERCOLOR SKETCH

It is possible that this sketch is more artistic than many a studio picture that has taken a month to complete. There is a certain feeling of friendliness between the two trees in the sketch—the one on the left bending towards the one on the right. The latter tree is slightly inclined, with a certain amount of reserve, to respond. The simplicity of coloring is caused through the lack of time to try any other way—just flat, running washes, partly mingling with each other, with the paper showing here and there, which gives a feeling of sparkle that is so difficult to obtain in a picture which has been painted over with two or three washes.

TINTED PENCIL DRAWING

The sketch immediately below (Plate VI) represents a tinted pencil drawing on a piece of ordinary notepaper, torn from a writing pad. The pencil outline is still noticeable in the sketch, and the watercolors were used merely to tint and suggest the tonality of the picture, without resorting to strong highlights or deep shadows.

OIL PAINTING BASED ON A SKETCH

In Plate VII is seen the possibility of a serious oil painting from this little colored pencil sketch (Plate VI). Here we get the tonality of nature, the deep greens of the trees, the dark color of the water, and the deep colors of the roofs of the cottages. By comparing this picture with the sketch, one can see at a glance that the sketch has artistic virtues of its own, being quite luminous and easily rendered, but it lacks the tone of the oil painting. The oil picture shows a rich, sombre effect of heavy foliage, as opposed to the sun-lit background. It has lost the luminous transparency of the little watercolor.

The following colors were used for the groundwork of this picture, later modified by overpainting and blending.

Sky: yellow ochre, cerulean blue, light purple.

Trees, and roofs of cottages: burnt umber, burnt sienna, viridian, and deep purple.

Water: burnt sienna, purple, burnt umber, raw sienna, yellow ochre.

Hill and stone bridge: Warm gray and grayish purple. A little zinc white was mixed with some of the groundwork colors.

Note that in this and all other examples referring to the colors used for the first stage or groundwork, it must be clearly understood that the colors—whether oil or pastel—are, as far as possible, kept flat in tone, with no blending of one tint with an adjoining tint. For this purpose, the above colors can be kept separate one from the other, allowing the canvas or paper to show through in places if necessary. It is only in the later stages that the blending or dragging of one color over the other is advisable, but even this needs caution. These remarks apply chiefly to studio pictures painted from outdoor sketches.

WATERCOLOR SKETCH IN TWO STAGES
Plates VIII and IX are two sketches of the same subject, painted in watercolor, the top one being the first stage and the lower the finished stage. The artist here purposely drew with some care, and all the border lines of the cottage and the contours of the tree were kept scrupulously in their place. The sketch is a cool calculation of a design seen out of doors. Notice how pleasing the color of the paper is in the first stage, particularly the sky, before the final colors were washed in. The same cottage and trees could, of course, have been sketched with less precise drawing, more vigorous color, and deeper tones, particularly as regards the tree on the left.

PASTEL SKETCH FOR A WATERCOLOR
An outdoor pastel sketch (Plate X) I found very useful for reference when painting the watercolor in Plate XVI. This watercolor is designed entirely from the information gained in the pastel sketch. Notice in the original sketch that the outlines of the water meet in a point on the left side. In the watercolor, the water extends horizontally across the whole picture, causing a more agreeable pattern. In the pastel sketch, the color of the foreground is rather heavy, and lacking in delicacy. The watercolor shows improved color and form in this respect. The lighter foreground in the watercolor gives emphasis, through tone contrast, to the rising hill occupying the left half of the picture; also the water, being deeper in color, assists the design, while arbitrary lines were used in other portions of the painting to emphasize the rhythm of the picture. The pastel sketch was made very quickly—just an idea—hoping to create another idea, with no intention whatever of trying to show careful drawing. Any good draughtsmanship which may appear is accidental or innocently obtained—without conscious effort.

The difference between the strength of a pastel and the suggestiveness of a watercolor sketch should be quite obvious to the student when examining the two reproductions in Plates X and XI. They both show their own peculiar virtues. It would be less difficult to make a finished oil painting from the pastel than from the watercolor sketch. The general tone of the pastel sketch is somewhat similar to the tonality of the average oil painting.

Plate XI has one merit—design. The horizontal feeling of the upper and lower clouds harmonizes, and carries on the horizontal spacing of the landscape below. To make a picture from this sketch, I would suggest that the whole of the sky, including clouds, be a little darker in tone, that some of the blue tints should be turned into grayish blue, and that the green fields in the higher portion of the landscape on the left be made more restrained in color. The sky, being darker, would then, through tone contrast, emphasize the light on the sand dunes spreading horizontally across the picture.

RABBIT RUN by John Folinsbee, oil, 32″ x 40″.

Snow is one of the most difficult of all subjects to paint because the beginning landscape painter tends to forget that his subject is not mere white paint, but contains shadows, textures, and forms. In this painting, the artist has carefully observed that the snow has distributed itself over the landscape in a series of swelling shapes; he has placed trees, rocks, and patches of shadow at strategic points to separate these shapes. Thus, the nearest trees and a single rock indicate where the foreground ends and the middle distance appears. The brushwork is particularly interesting: the broad, sweeping strokes follow the curves of the forms and reveal their roundness. Observe how little of the snow is actually white and how much of it is subtle, constantly shifting tone. The dark, moody sky emphasizes the whiteness of the landscape below. (Photograph courtesy American Artist)

PASSING SHADOWS by Tom Nicholas, watercolor.

The artist has plunged his entire landscape into shadow—as the title of the painting suggests—in order to focus the viewer's attention on a few foreground trees and a rock formation, which receive virtually the only touches of light in the painting, except for the break of light in the sky. The lighted tree trunks are placed before a mass of dark foliage. This is the only point in the picture where the artist has introduced precise detail. The more distant trees and the shape of the cliff melt into the atmosphere and are put out of focus, like the background of a photograph often appears to be. The outer edges of the composition, and particularly the corners, contain no detail at all and are nothing more than patches of tone. (Photograph courtesy American Artist)

8

Detailed Studies
in Pencil

In this chapter, I will discuss four studies in pencil made out of doors—the first an elm tree, the second the Château de Polignac, the third the Château de St. Voute, and the fourth several pencil studies of incidental outdoor subjects. These are included in this book merely to show students that careful pencil drawings are part of the art student's outfit if he wishes to achieve good landscape painting. It is best to use at least three different pencils, varying in degree of hardness or softness. A 5B, a 3B, and 1B make a good repertoire for the pencil artist. Sometimes, for hard outlines, an HB, which is not liable to smudge under normal conditions, although less artistic, is useful for giving a truthful account of material facts.

TREE STUDY In making the study of an elm tree (Fig. 33) in pencil, the artist left out quite a lot of detail, yet on the other hand, there is enough information in relation to the shape of the branches, the general growth of the tree, and the massing of the whole, to make this drawing far more valuable than any photograph of the same subject could possibly be.

Apropos photography, it is a curious thing that the lenses seem to take in everything that is not wanted and obscure the main issue. A pencil draughtsman instinctively gets just what is required for the subject of the future picture. Pencil drawing is an art unto itself.

TWO LANDSCAPE STUDIES The drawing of the Château de Polignac (Fig. 34) was made principally not only for the contours of the château, but for the various groups of trees and cottages and other buildings grouped around the château above.

The drawing of the Château de St. Voute (Fig. 34) has a certain amount of sparkle in the little trees in the foreground. The illusion of light on the roofs of the lower houses at the foot of the château was obtained by shading the walls and leaving the roofs free of pencil lines, while the lighter tone of the distant drawing, with the delicately suggested clouds, has all the accessories necessary for an experienced artist when working in the winter months.

Fig. 33. *Study of elm tree leaves out detail, emphasizes mass.*

Fig. 34. Pencil study of Chateau de Polignac.

Fig. 35. Pencil study of Chateau de St. Voute.

Fig. 36. *Page of pencil studies of incidental details.*

48

HOLD THE PENCIL NATURALLY Pencil drawing is liable to create difficulties for the average student unless the pencil is held in an easy manner. The least attempt at gripping a pencil tightly, or at holding it like a pickaxe, is fatal for natural draughtsmanship, or easily rendered drawings. I have seen students, not knowing that the pencil they were drawing with was held in a clumsy manner, looking quite depressed in trying to copy a maze of detail out of doors. It is a peculiar fact that as soon as a pencil is held somewhat loosely, and the hopeless attempt abandoned of trying to rival the camera in the matter of detail, the result is far more faithful to nature because of the more fluent linework, which is only possible when the pencil is used naturally.

PENCIL NOTES The nine pencil reproductions in Fig. 36 are invaluable for the information they contain. Students would do well to have their notebooks full of all sorts of outdoor subjects. Apart from their use for picture painting in the studio, notes of this character should have an art merit of their own.

Pencil drawings which are to be used as aids to picture making in the studio need only be done in outline, with a few simple shadows. This, as a rule, gives a more truthful or more reliable help to the painter than any highly finished drawing, as it shows the intricacies of tone, light, and shadow.

At the same time, pencil is sometimes used entirely as a medium for pictorial renderings from nature, and beautiful, too, are the results at the hands of a capable artist who understands the possibilities of pencil art.

BOMB CRATERS COLLEVILLE SUR MER by Ogden M. Pleissner, watercolor.

Because of their romantic appeal and jagged forms, ruined buildings often make more interesting subjects than buildings which are intact. The power of this landscape stems, in part, from the artist's choice of a strong light that enters the picture from a low angle at the extreme left. The light strikes the left hand planes of the buildings and leaves the right hand sides in pools of deep shadow. In the same way, the light creates strips of brightness on the landscape and leaves touches of light on the wreckage in the foreground; but most of the landscape consists of great pools of shadow. By contrast, the sky is extremely pale, with only a touch of cloud. (Photograph courtesy American Artist)

VIEW OF VERONA by Burton Silverman, oil, 23" x 31".

A panoramic view of a landscape with architecture can be difficult to compose because of the multiplicity of detail. Here the artist has solved the problem in several ways. First, he has kept detail to a minimum in most of the landscape: look closely and you will see that nearly everything is rendered in patches of broken color, with very little attention to specific rock formations, masses of trees, or shapes of buildings. Second, he has thrown most of the landscape into shadow, with just a few touches of light to illuminate the group of buildings at the center of interest, and to swing the viewer's eye along the river bank to the central dome that breaks against the sky. Third, he has decided on a low horizon, so that more than half of the picture is actually sky, with the cloud formations organized to draw attention to the cluster of buildings beneath. (Photograph courtesy American Artist)

9

Studies of Clouds

So many students, when sketching cloud effects in watercolor, handle their medium with greater success than they paint the landscape below. The lower portion of the sketch is often overlabored and not always clean in color, whereas the sky has escaped such a calamity. They probably feel a sense of irresponsibility when tackling clouds and ordinary sky subjects. If they had this sense of irresponsibility sometimes when sketching trees, fields, buildings, and so on, their technique would not bother them quite so much. All the same, the study of clouds needs definite concentration. There is nothing more satisfactory than a picture of clouds in a landscape where the subject has not been under the technical control of the student who painted them. Clouds need as much designing as a good carpet pattern.

MEMORY AND INVENTION

The picture in Plate XII shows a study of clouds. The preliminary study was done out of doors direct from nature, but the wind was so great that the effect seen in this picture lasted only a few minutes. It is here that a scheme for design, as well as a trained memory for natural effects, comes to the rescue of the artist. Without the facility for some invention, it is almost hopeless to get a satisfactory study of clouds when the wind is blowing at the rate of some forty or fifty miles an hour.

The design of this picture helps the illusion of movement. The larger cloud on the top left side swings in a downward direction towards the right, so as to connect up the clouds near the horizon and the dark hills with the adjoining landscape below.

SKY AND CLOUD COLORS

This watercolor study was painted with a good deal of body color (opaque white). The following colors were used.

Sky: Grayish blue, yellow ochre, and a little crimson. Each of these two colors was mixed with a small quantity of white tempera.

Hills: Permanent blue and warm gray. Blue was mixed with a little permanent crimson.

Trees: Hooker's green (middle tint). Deep Hooker's green was mixed with burnt umber. Deep Hooker's green was also mixed with burnt sienna.

Foreground: Mostly yellow ochre mixed with a little raw sienna and laid on with transparent washes.

The cloud tints immediately above the hills were carried over the surface of the hills in places, while the colors were still wet and amenable to treatment.

Body color (white tempera, gouache, designers' colors, Chinese white) is an excellent medium for blending one color into an adjoining tint without leaving a scratchy surface.

In the final stage, permanent blue was added to the contours of the trees, towards the left, with yellowish or russet green in portions of the foreground.

CATCHING
FLEETING
EFFECTS

The first impression out of doors was made with considerable rapidity in pastel, on tinted paper. How important it is for the one who works at great speed to have a constructive sense! As suggested in Chapter 2, the pursuit on winter evenings of creative designs, whether of sky or any other form of landscape, is of real use when working under some form of emotional excitement.

A successful cloud study on a windy day asserts its success in the fact that, when one looks at the sketch, the clouds still appear to be moving. The artist does not claim such a high standard in this picture, but he does claim that the design itself suggests that nature was not in a state of placid tranquillity.

GRADATED COLOR

Plate XIII shows a gradated color scheme, starting at the top with rather deepish blue, gradually becoming lighter, and changing its color, until it reaches the lower portion of the sketch.

The watercolors used for this prepared groundwork were mixed in saucers, preparatory to painting, and the paper was well damped in advance. While the colors were being washed on, the paper was tilted at a slight angle to allow the colors to blend naturally. Not only is this good practice in watercolor, but it is also very useful in preparing a ground for painting a cloud study in this medium.

Plate XIV is precisely the same sky, done in the same gradated manner, but the lighter clouds were washed out with a little sponge. The intention here is to show that there is a certain amount of aerial perspective in the size of normal clouds. The clouds at the top of this picture are larger in dimension than the clouds in the central portion of the picture, and they become smaller and smaller until they reach the horizon. The landscape in the foreground was painted on purpose to prove that the tone of the darker clouds was not too strong for the earth below.

It is admirable practice to paint quite a number of imaginary cloud studies indoors. This will give control of any medium that the student is interested in, and it will also help the mind to receive some advance information as to what nature may be up to when sketching out of doors.

It is not advisable to paint a naturalistic picture of clouds on a sky where the tone is the same all over, rather than gradated. Sometimes, in posters, the whole sky is painted in one flat tone, which serves another purpose.

TYPES OF CLOUDS The student will discover, in looking carefully at nature, many different tone qualities in the sky. The early morning sky is different from the midday sky, and so on. According to scientists, there are three primary types of clouds, which are easily recognizable.

(1) *Cirrus:* showing parallel, flexuous or diverging fibers, extensible in any or all directions.

(2) *Cumulus:* representing convex or conical heaps, increasing upward from a horizontal base.

(3) *Stratus:* a widely extended and continuous horizontal sheet, increasing from below.

There are four derivative or compound forms.

(1) Cirro-cumulus.

(2) Cirro-stratus.

(3) Cumulo-stratus.

(4) Cumulo-cirro-stratus, or nimbus.

Clouds, despite their classification in science, are nevertheless capable of an extraordinary number of variations in their forms, to which there seems to be no limit. If there were only some five or six definite shapes in clouds, then it would be interesting for the student to invent others; but as an experienced landscape artist I know that almost any form is possible in nature.

A sky painted without any clouds and with a lowlying horizon makes an impressive landscape. It is fairly obvious to most students that horizontal clouds create a feeling of tranquillity. Some of the best pictures of the more sumptuous type of clouds have been painted when the artist has worked at high pressure.

Over-modeling of a cloud is not at all pleasant in a picture. The student is advised to keep dark clouds fairly flat in tone. The same remark applies to the sky and to the lighter clouds. The darkest cloud is usually considerably lighter than various features seen in the landscape. A dark reddish-brown rock, say in the foreground, which has escaped the rays of sunlight, is much darker in tone than the darkest rain cloud that nature has ever shown. I have, however, seen a yellow cornfield in the foreground much lighter in tone than a distant cloud, caused through the rays of brilliant sunlight; but without the aid of sunlight, the tone of foreground objects, and even sometimes of the distant objects, is invariably darker than anything that the sky or cloud has to show.

EARLY SUMMER by Emil J. Kosa, Jr., oil.

Here is a particularly clear example of atmospheric perspective, in which the picture is carefully divided into foreground, middle distance, and distance. The growth in the immediate foreground is rendered in sharp detail with precise contrast of dark and light. Beyond this is the plane of the trees, which are the darkest notes in the painting. And beyond the trees are three mountainous forms, each a separate and distinct shade of gray to indicate its placement in space. The farthest is the lightest. The most distant is also entirely lacking in detail. (Photograph courtesy American Artist)

54

10

Studies of Hills and Mountains

In dealing with this chapter on hills and mountains, particularly mountains, the student should avoid the ideas demonstrated in Chapter 15 on "Undulating Landscapes." Mountains are so important in themselves and appear to have a mental atmosphere which almost forbids any feeling of a rhythmic or lyrical nature. I trust that the student will realize that anything in the nature of ordinary charm—relating to mountain subjects—has no place in a good pictorial conception of mountainous material.

AVOID FALSE CHARM   In days gone by, quite a number of painters would ruin a most excellent mountain subject by showing, on the lower part of the mountain, a quantity of charming purple heather, with the top portion of the mountain sometimes lost in mist or fog, so that by the time the picture was finished, what with the heather and the mist, the original message of the grandeur of the mountain was entirely obscured. It is better to ignore all unnecessary clothing, if the student wishes to emphasize the structural formation of mountain subjects. A mountain in Switzerland or in Canada, of some ten or twelve thousand feet high, weighs, as the average student knows, millions or billions of tons. It is the painter's business, then, to convey that feeling of immensity of weight, as well as beauty of color. The picture of a mountain that shows a texture of a soft, fibrous surface, with part of its beauty lost in mist, and with so many charming surface accessories spread over its body, is almost incapable of showing the fundamental meaning of the subject, and rarely expresses the psychology of the mountain.

Some artists of today are successfully rendering mountain subjects. They are stripping the mountain bare of all superfluities and making manifest the spiritual essence. The old fashioned calendar picture has no place in the mentality of painters with modern tendencies.

EMPHASIZE RUGGEDNESS   The picture in Plate XV, entitled *Cathedral Mountains, Canadian Rockies,* is a fairly good example of aggressive rock-like formation. The sharp angularity of the top portion of Cathedral Mountain triumphs over the encroaching snow and ice. While it is true that these peaks are partly hidden by mist on some days, the character of the mountain should still be retained even so. In this picture, the sketch was done when every portion of the mountain was exposed to view.

The first stage of this picture was painted in the same manner as *Emerald Lake, Canadian Rockies* (Plate XVII). It is worth noting that the greenish tint of ice, visible in the snow immediately below the highest peak, was first painted with a coat of yellow ochre mixed with a little white paint.

The following groundwork colors (modified by later color applications) were used in this oil painting.

Sky: yellow ochre, warm gray, cobalt blue, zinc white and viridian mixed.

Distant mountains: raw umber, raw sienna, cobalt blue mixed with a little permanent crimson, burnt sienna, terra verte mixed with a little zinc white.

Snow: yellow ochre and zinc white.

Snow in shadow: Dark warm gray, purple.

Foreground mountains: Burnt umber, burnt sienna, deep purple, dark warm gray.

Another view of this mountain, which is not represented in this book, has on its upright surface a horizontal band of different colored rocks, about two thirds of the distance from the higher peak to the snow's edge below. This band suggests a geometric form such as might be seen in the design for the border of a carpet. As suggested before in another portion of this book, geometric shapes are very often beautiful and are always interesting.

The analytical lines of this picture (adjacent to the color plate) demonstrate unity of design, despite the number of angular forms which assert their existence in the top portion of the picture.

All the topmost peaks of Cathedral Mountain are bound together in the dotted marginal line, which extends in an outward, or convex direction. The opposite effect is gained below, as the lower masses of rock formation at the foot of the picture extend in an inward, or concave, direction.

MOUNTAINS IN WATERCOLOR

Plate XVI is a watercolor entitled A *Decoration* (designed from the pastel sketch in Plate X). The leading constructional lines in this picture are shown in the diagram adjacent to the color plate. They are of a harmonious character, supported by the horizontally straight line extending right across the lower portion.

The following groundwork colors were used in this picture.

Sky: ultramarine blue well diluted with water.

Dark hill: purple (made by mixing cobalt blue and permanent crimson), yellow ochre, burnt sienna.

Light hill and foreground: yellow ochre and warm gray (middle tint), painted strongly on damp paper.

Water: cobalt blue, viridian.

In the final painting, the highlights were painted with thick tempera white mixed with yellow ochre, etc. All the trees, whether light or dark in tone, were painted on top of the first stage. The darker toned trees were painted two or three times over, so as to get the rich tone effect as seen in the reproduction.

MOUNTAINS IN OILS The oil painting entitled *Emerald Lake, Canadian Rockies*, is shown in two stages. In the first stage (Plate XVII), the general design, strengthened by flat color tones, is painted in a decisive manner, practically all the colors being kept darker than those seen in the finished picture (Plate XVIII). It is most important to remember that snow subjects, whether in oil or in pastel, need a warm colored underpainting, consisting of yellow ochre and white, so that the final coat of lighter colored paint echoes some of the warm color below.

A large surface of pure white paint, representing snow, and painted direct on a raw canvas, looks more like a representation of dry white chalk.

The finished picture shows the addition of lighter tones, painted generally over the mountains and snow, while the trees received more detail, and the surface of the water is more broken and luminous.

The diagram relating to the oil painting of *Emerald Lake, Canadian Rockies* (Plate XVIII) illustrates precisely the same principle of convex and concave construction as shown in the Cathedral Mountain picture (Plate XV). The tops of the mountains demonstrate convexity, as seen in the dotted lines and the central portion concavity. The rigid horizontal lines, denoting the boundaries of Emerald Lake, support the great weight of mountainous material above.

When painting hills, which might be described as juvenile mountains, there is less cause to resort to drastic measures representing weight or volume. There are some types of mountains, particularly in the Canadian Rockies, where the student has only to sketch and faithfully copy the original mountain, with its formation and its detailed suggestions, and the resultant picture might be classified as "modern art." This is due to the fact that some mountains have such unusual formation, and appear "modern" in their suggestion of dynamic force, their cubistic angles, and their suggestion of geometric detail.

TREE RHYTHMS by John F. Carlson, oil.

Tree trunks (except in a pine forest) are unlikely to be parallel vertical forms, but tend to sway to right and left. In the same way, clusters of foliage tend to have a distinct direction. Here the artist has designed his picture to take advantage of the rhythmic tilt of tree runks to right and left; his strokes indicate the "gesture" of the foliage, which interweaves with the rhythm of the trunks. In painting a wooded landscape such as this, it is often good strategy to allow the viewer to look through the trees into a vista beyond; this creates a welcome break of light in the darkness of the forest. One should also be careful to allow frequent patches of sky to appear through the foliage itself. (Photograph courtesy American Artist)

11

Studies of Trees

Time and time again, when taking students out sketching, I have been told that they are unable to sketch trees in color from nature. They are quite sure it is a very difficult subject, and, being so sure, they really find it difficult. As soon as that idea is cut away from the mind, it becomes comparatively easy. The student is quite as important as the tree which he wishes to sketch—perhaps more so.

IMPORTANCE OF SILHOUETTE The reason why students have shown some timidity or modesty in painting trees is because they are clearly conscious that trees generally have a very lavish display of leaves, an intricate number of branches, and a trunk which is easier to draw than paint.

The character of a tree should be known, apart from any detail whatsoever, by its silhouette form when seen against the sky or some lighter background. The fir tree is easily discernible, even at a distance, from a weeping willow. This has nothing whatever to do with the detail of the trees just mentioned; it is simply the fact that the general mass determines the genus of the tree. As soon as the student understands this, and paints the *mass* of the tree rather than the leaves, then he has partly solved his problem, and the sketch can be made in a workmanlike manner.

ELIMINATE DETAIL It is distressing to see a sketch of a woodland scene where one is unable to see the trees for leaves. It is worse still to see a sketch of a tree where the main features of the tree are entirely lost through the sincere effort of the artist to paint its clothing in faithful language. How interesting a sketch of a tree can be when all detail is eliminated and only the salient points are exposed by the artist!

I have sometimes hurt the feelings of a student very much indeed by taking the paintbrush from his hand, and working all over a careful study of a tree which was quite wrong in tone value, and painting out nearly all the mis-applied detail. This feeling of the surgeon's knife is sometimes necessary if the operation is to have a successful result.

Painting trees, then, requires a certain amount of moral courage in the beginner. A photograph easily gives all the detail which it is possible for the lens to show. The roughest sketch of a tree sometimes conveys more of the psychology of that tree than the most careful rendering in pencil or color can give. Personally, I find it useful, after finishing the sketch of a tree, to make little drawings in my notebook of any important feature that I feel might be useful when painting the finished picture indoors. Chapter 8 shows, to a certain extent, what I mean. Here you see various studies in pencil from nature, including trees, made after I had completed the colored sketches.

There is something magnificent about the elm tree. It is dignified and restrained in color. Trees are analogous in their character to human beings. Often in nature one sees a group of stately elm trees, and sometimes, grouped in front, may be seen little delicate willow trees, lighter in tone, lighter in foliage, and physically more fragile, supported by the darker toned and friendly elms behind.

STUDIES OF MASS FOLIAGE

Plates XIX and XX are two stages of a study of mass foliage, showing quite clearly the first stage painted with flat tints. The final stage was gained by adding strongly defined shadows of deep color.

Students are advised to copy this example in watercolor, and then design some mass foliage of their own on which to practice painting.

Indecision of handling is fatal if the broad effect is sought, as seen in the reproduction.

Plate XXI, reproduces the watercolor entitled *Elm Trees at Windsor*. After mastering the mass foliage example, students should profit by copying the elm trees in this picture. The same principle of flat color painting as in the previous example can be applied here, the darker toned shadows in the foliage of the elms being added in the final stage.

This watercolor was painted on thick paper, and the following foundation colors were used in the preliminary stages.

Sky: light yellow ochre, light ultramarine blue.

Trees: deep Hooker's green mixed with a little yellow ochre, purple, permanent blue.

Distant buildings: yellow ochre mixed with light gray; light purple mixed with a small quantity of yellow ochre; vermilion mixed with light gray.

Foreground: Hooker's green (middle tint) mixed with burnt sienna.

The lower portion of the sky was finished with a small wet sponge for wiping out. The contours of the tall elm trees received the same treatment so as to prevent hard edges.

Blotting paper was used after wiping out, for quick drying and softening effects.

It is a revelation to the average individual who studies trees to know what an astonishing number of different varieties there are. To do justice to this chapter, it would need at least another volume. It is possible that the student who wishes to know a great deal on the subject of trees might suffer from mental indigestion before arriving at that happy stage. Time will bring experience. For the purpose of this book, then, let the student paint simply and easily, and concentrate solely on the big mass effects.

WOODED LANDSCAPE The watercolor painting in Plate XXII, entitled *Fir Trees, Pas-de-Calais*, is a careful rendering of the characteristic shapes peculiar to fir trees. In the first stage of this picture, the colors were laid on with pure washes, in the final stage, body color (opaque white) was used for the sky and certain portions of the foliage and foreground.

The diagram adjacent to Plate XXII shows the general construction of this picture, emphasizing the sky opening on the right, which is oval in formation and travels upwards to the higher left side of the picture.

The vertical direction of the trunks cuts sharply across the circular formation of the sky opening, affording a piquant contrast, while the winding pathway in the foreground is harmoniously related to the constructional lines above.

STUDIES OF Plates XXIII, XXIV, XXV, and XXVI are four watercolor studies of foli-
FOLIAGE DETAILS age. The first study (Plate XXIII) is just a flat wash indicating branches and foliage. The second drawing (Plate XXIV) shows the same study with the addition of darker tints both on the branches and on the leaves. These darker tints were added before the first wash of watercolor was quite dry. Here and there, the edges are partly lost, while elsewhere they are definite and strong. Notice how the branches are improved by adding deeper tints in places. This is quite a common feature in nature.

Plate XXV is a colored drawing of the top portion of a fir tree. The same method was used as seen in Plate XXIII and XXIV. The fir, excepting the trunk, is fairly deep in tone, so that the first wash was painted in with low toned colors. The second wash, as before, was added before the original wash was quite dry.

In watercolor painting, it is important to know the exact moment when to add your second tint. There may possibly be some subjects where it is necessary to wait until the first coat is quite dry; but in most studies in watercolor, it is advisable to paint the second wash before the first is dry, so as to create a softer surface, and lose that hard and unpleasant outline which can so easily be obtained if the first color is dry. These remarks apply only to watercolor painting in which no body color (opaque white) is used.

The study (Plate XXVI) was done just outside my studio. This is a study of chestnut leaves. So as to retain the characteristic feeling of the chestnut leaf, considerable time was spent in the preliminary pencil drawing. There may be a certain mannerism in this little study, where darker paint has been used to outline the characteristic shape of the chestnut leaf, but truth in detailed form was sought for, rather than artistic handling.

It is not a very difficult art to make small studies such as these, but, as stated before, care should always be taken so that the student is able to keep under control all knowledge of detail when painting the whole tree. The second or third year's apprenticeship to outdoor sketching should be about the period when the student might be advised to make detailed studies of leaves, branches, etc., from nature without fear of losing the knowledge gained by sketching the more important mass forms.

LAKE ERIE SHOREWAY by Carl Gaertner, gouache, 20½″ x 30½″.

A dark sky does not necessarily mean that the landscape below will be uniformly dark. The artist has introduced a break in the clouds, through which light flows downward to illuminate the roadway in the foreground. The light also breaks on a portion of the breakwater, which occurs just behind the single house. The water on the other hand, reflects the darkness of the sky, except for a few touches of reflected light. (Courtesy Metropolitan Museum of Art, New York)

12

Studies of Water

Clear reflections on still water, caused by objects resting on the landscape above, offer no difficulties to the painter, inasmuch as the artist has only to reverse the shape of the objects above onto the surface of the water below. This, combined with a few horizontal lines or streaks of color across the vertical reflections, creates a feeling of transparency in a picture. It is the easiest possible way of rendering water in a picture, but it is not so interesting as other problems in that direction. With all water studies, whether moving or tranquil, it is best to play for safety in the earlier stages of the sketch, keeping all the dark reflections fairly light and the light reflections fairly dark, thus helping to flatten the surface of the water, as well as create harmonious tones. Mature judgment is needed towards the completion of a sketch to decide how much or how little is required, to deepen or lighten the reflections in places.

WATER WITHOUT REFLECTIONS   Then, again, certain lakes and rivers reflect very little of their adjoining surroundings. In some American and Canadian lakes, the general color is oftentimes an opaque, greenish blue, probably caused by alkali in the substance of the water. In water hurtling down from precipitous waterfalls, it is almost impossible to get a suggestion of any reflection whatsoever. Plate XL is a picture of a Canadian waterfall, the spray of the water, particularly in the lower part, creating so much foam that it has lost all transparent qualities. Even the rocks themselves are affected by this continual spraying of water. The shadows on the rocks at the foot of the picture are quite light in tone, since the surrounding light is reflected on their wet surfaces.

REFLECTIONS IN LIGHT AND SHADOW   A very good example for demonstration purposes is the water study shown in Plate XXVII, entitled *A Venetian Canal*. This picture clearly displays the different effects of light and shadow on the same sheet of water. Water in shadow, if fairly transparent water, is capable of showing clear reflections. In this instance, the reflections are easily seen in the top portion of the canal, which is in deep shadow, while all the foreground water is exposed to the glare of the sun. The brilliancy of the sun neutralizes the normal tone of the canal water, causing it to be lighter in tint, and making it impossible to reflect the dark toned buildings. The left side of the gondola throws its shadow on the water and prevents the sun from shining on this restricted area, with the result that a clear reflection is made visible.

The general color of this water is of a greenish blue tint. This tint is, of course, more noticeable in the shadow. At the same time, although the sun has such a strong effect on the water which happens to be exposed to its glare, even there the local color of the water is not entirely lost.

The following colors were used in solid flat patches for the groundwork or foundation of this picture.

Water in shadow: raw sienna, viridian and permanent blue, both mixed with a little zinc white.

Water in light: viridian mixed with zinc white, yellow ochre, and raw sienna.

Walls in shadow and dark figures, etc.: burnt sienna, permanent blue mixed with a little zinc white and deep purple.

Walls in light, bridge, and steps: warm gray (middle tint), and yellow ochre mixed with a little raw sienna.

Sky: deep blue mixed with a little permanent crimson.

The reproduction clearly shows the final colors used in this oil painting. Various colors occupying a small space, such as the rectangular wall immediately above the right hand side of the bridge, must be painted with definite touches and allowed to remain unmolested. If wrongly painted, the only way to remedy the defects is to scrape the colors off with the palette knife, without, of course, disturbing the foundation paint below.

Note the adjacent skeleton plan of *A Venetian Canal*. The dotted curve on the right, commencing from the bridge downwards, includes the miniature figures and boat at the foot of the building, finishing up with the figure of the gondolier, which slopes towards the bridge. The sweeping lines of the gondola connect up, as shown by the dotted line, with the vertical line of the building on the right, which adjoins the bridge.

SHALLOW WATER   Plate XXIX is a pastel entitled *Bolton Abbey, Yorkshire*. Here we have quick running, shallow water, with the bed of the river showing in places through its surface. This is a very difficult problem for an artist. The tendency sometimes is to make the local color of the soil below the water too strong for practical purposes. That is to say, the reflecting glow from the bed of the river needs to be neutralized to a certain extent by an opaque suggestion of some grayish tint, whether warm or cold. In the first stage (Plate XXVIII), the local color of the soil was first laid on. The pastel was used sparingly so as to allow for the later tints. A positive color, such as pure red, is impossible in the finished picture, but pure red with a coat of gray over its surface gives that peculiar quality suggesting shallow water.

The student who has had no experience of pastel painting will find it useful to copy the first and finished stages of this picture. The warm colors —red, brown, yellow, etc.—seen over the whole of the first stage are invaluable as a groundwork for the final touches of colder colors, such as gray, green, blue, etc.

The adjacent line drawing of *Bolton Abbey, Yorkshire* shows the leading compositional lines that connect the trees, which spread across the whole landscape.

The solid masonry of the abbey, with its horizontal and vertical lines, acts as a foil to the restlessness of the running water below. The clouds are in harmony with the abbey since they extend in the same horizontal direction.

MAKE LIGHTS DARKER AND DARKS LIGHTER   The watercolor entitled *The River Thames, Marlow,* although perhaps not scientifically accurate as regards water reflections, very faithfully carries out the suggestion (made at the beginning of this chapter) that the lights should be darker and darks should be lighter (Plate XXX). The reflection of the mansion in the water on the left side of the picture is darker as regards the color of the walls, and the reflection of the roof of the same building is lighter. Then again, the reflection of the dark mass of trees in the water on the right is obviously lighter. This feeling of unity on the whole surface of the water helps to suggest the necessary flat, horizontal plane of the river. It is too simple, when sketching out of doors, to forget this important fact.

This picture was painted in transparent color washes. The following foundation colors were used.

Sky: yellow ochre, light warm purple.

Dark trees: Hooker's green (middle tint), mixed with yellow ochre and very little light red.

Poplar trees: chrome yellow mixed with Hooker's green (middle tint).

Roofs of building: light red mixed with chrome yellow.

Water (right): a small quantity of ivory black mixed with permanent blue, with a little crimson, yellow ochre, and deep Hooker's green added in places.

Water (left): yellow ochre, warm gray, yellowish gray-green, and light warm purple.

Deep Hooker's green, deep purple, viridian, and touches of burnt sienna, together with bluish purple, were invaluable for the final painting of the dark toned trees. The sky and the water were completed in one wash, the colors being carefully mixed in advance. The tone of the paper can be seen in the sky, the lighter portion of the water, and the pathway in the foreground.

In the adjacent line diagram the dotted lines, suggesting the position of the cloudlets in the sky, demonstrate their harmonious relations to the landscape below. The two thin and tall poplar trees (on the left) contrast sharply with the circular formation of the heavier group of trees on the right.

The little flagstaff on the tower behind the mansion echoes the vertical direction of the poplar trees.

Figs. 37-40 are four drawings of reflections on water. Fig. 37 represents three poles and a stump. The horizontal dotted line represents the exact place where the water, if continued, would meet the poles. The thick, slightly curved horizontal line marks the place where the water meets the bank. The height of each pole above the dotted horizontal line is exactly the same as the distance of each pole below this line.

The illustration in Fig. 38 is of a tree trunk and two outbuildings. The circular drawing in the foreground represents the shape of a pond. The principle of reflection is precisely the same as in the first mentioned illustration (Fig. 37). The lower horizontal dotted line shows the junction of the tree trunk with the water if the surface of the water had been continued as far as this horizontal line. The higher horizontal line (below the more distant outbuildings) gives the height of the outbuildings above the height of the water. Here again, we must imagine that the flat plane of the water has been continued until it meets the junction of the buildings, which penetrate through the earth until they meet on the water plane. The reversed height of the building, then, is exactly the same below the higher horizontal line as above.

In Fig. 39, the illustration shows the drawing of a building, mountains, and some trees, with their reflections in the water. As the mountains are farther away than the buildings, etc., a second horizontal line was required to measure the heights of the mountains so as to get the same distance immediately below the higher horizontal line. It is interesting to note that the buildings, being nearer the edge of the water, are larger proportionally in their reflections than the taller mountains in the background. The mountain on the left, rising up behind the nearer mountain, should of course have another horizontal line to obtain more exact measurements, but sufficient has been shown to demonstrate that the perspective of reflections on water is not an exact science, although it is approximately correct.

The drawing in Fig. 40 is a naturalistic sketch of the reflection of a bridge, etc., on moving water. The other three drawings represent reflections on water which is motionless. The water in Fig. 39 shows a slight but perceptible ripple.

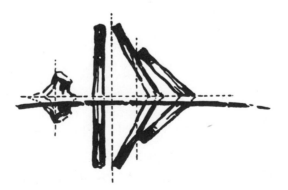

Fig. 37. Three poles, a stump, and their reflections.

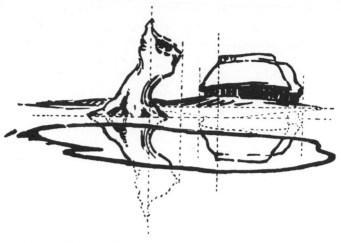

Fig. 38. Nearby tree trunk, two distant buildings, reflected in pond.

Fig. 39. Nearby buildings, distant mountains, and their reflections.

Fig. 40. Reflection of bridge in moving water.

67

INTERSECTION by Jeanne H. McLavy, oil.

The effectiveness of this cityscape is based, in part, on the unusual point of view taken by the painter. The street and nearby buildings are not seen from street level, but from above, as if the artist was looking from a second or third story window. This permits the painter to look down on the street and create an interesting pattern of the intersecting roadways, the curves of the trolley tracks, power lines, lamp posts, and other linear elements. Then, beyond this, the faces of the buildings create an interesting design of flat shapes in light and shadow. (Courtesy Pennsylvania Academy of Fine Arts, Philadelphia, Pennsylvania)

13

Studies of Buildings

The student who is able to paint still life objects should be well equipped for the study of buildings. They have the same thing in common in that they are stationary and least of all affected by passing events. On the other hand, a still life group in the studio, carefully arranged and left undisturbed, has the same effect each day under normal conditions, whereas buildings out of doors have a vastly different surrounding, and nature very rarely expresses the same color effect on two consecutive days.

PAINTING IN THE CITY Cities like London and New York offer fine opportunities for tone studies of buildings. These great cities suggest restrained color when compared with cities like Siena, Venice, Tunis, or Tangier. Moreover, at the approach of winter, when overcast weather and fogs have their own way, there are sometimes wonderful effects in tone, where positive color is almost eliminated, and the detailed sections of buildings are entirely lost. This provides excellent groundwork if the student already has the courage to paint out of doors.

Fortunate is the art student who has been through a course of practical architecture. Even a slight knowledge of architecture is of use to him when sketching palatial dwellings, particularly in Italy and in some parts of France and Spain. It is well known that many architects have successfully translated into terms of pictorial art buildings with which they are familiar as regards structure and detailed forms.

What might be described as artistic charm exists in old walls, with their various textures and colors. Too much attention to this sometimes is inclined to destroy the scale of a picture. On the other hand, the ability to express in a painting the texture as seen on old walls, etc., is not without its virtue. Oil and pastel are excellent materials for these textural surfaces.

OBSERVATION CAN LEAD YOU ASTRAY A general mistake some students make, in the early days of outdoor sketching of architectural subjects, is that sometimes their observation leads them astray. They notice that windows reflect light. This is perfectly true, yet the fact is generally forgotten that, when painting the main wall of a house, particularly if the wall is dark in tone, with several windows in it, the student must first represent the flat plane or surface of the whole wall, irrespective of any light and shadow on its surface. There is a tendency to make the light reflected from windows much stronger than the natural effect. In such a case, when the sketch is taken home and seen under normal conditions, it is found that the lights reflected from the windows, by being painted too high in key, cause the windows to appear as if they were in front of the house, instead of on the surface of the wall. The best plan then, when light is reflected from windows, is to keep the tonality of the light darker than it actually appears to be.

ARCHITECTURAL PAINTING IN OILS

The oil painting in Plate XXXI, *The Bridge Over Bruges Canal*, already described in Chapter 5, demonstrates the alternative possibility of showing brilliant lights reflecting from windows.

Here the face of the house immediately above the bridge, in the central portion of the picture, is in no way disturbed by light from the windows, because the whole of this building is almost as light in tone as the brightest light in the windows, thus giving the necessary flat surface.

In the first stage of this oil painting, the buildings, bridge, and water were well primed with touches of raw sienna, burnt sienna, deep chrome yellow, yellow ochre, and warm purple.

The tree, two figures, and the foreground on the left, received a preliminary coat of burnt umber, permanent blue, and a little permanent crimson mixed with burnt umber and burnt sienna.

For the sky, permanent blue, mixed with a little crimson and yellow ochre, was used. Notice how, in the final painting, the groundwork colors—particularly burnt sienna, deep chrome yellow, and yellow ochre—are allowed to show their existence in various parts of the picture.

The different brush marks of warm grays, etc., were mostly obtained accidentally through mixing odd colors left on the oil palette after a day's work. These color blends were then kept in a small zinc pan or dish filled with water to prevent the oil pigment from becoming hard, and held in readiness when required for this picture.

The green foliage of the tree and the circular reflection below the bridge and foreground, at the foot of the tree, were painted chiefly with viridian and a little terra verte, without losing sight of the rich toned groundwork below.

The principal interest in the adjacent diagram, apart from the general spacing of the tree and buildings, is the introduction of the two figures in the foreground, forming part of the general composition. They are enclosed in the curved dotted lines which extend upwards on either side and are continued along the contours of the tree until they reach the boundary lines enclosing the picture.

The general direction of the back and head of the seated figure, if continued as seen in the illustration, eventually touches the outer part of the lower building, finishing with the line of the roof above.

AVOID COLD CHALKY COLOR

When making sketches of white structures or other buildings of light tones, especially in pastel or oil, there is nothing worse than a sketch where the white walls look chalky and cold. (Notice also the remarks about snow painting in Chapter 10.) There is no definitely cold color in nature. A tinge of warmth is everywhere, since all light in daylight subjects comes from the sun. Shadows which reflect light therefore reflect warmth, and it is safer, when possible, to paint shadows with a slight suggestion of some warm pigment in their depths.

The easiest way to make a sketch of a white building in oil colors is to lay a foundation of small touches of yellow ochre, yellowish red, and gray. This must be done with thin pigment, leaving bare patches of the canvas in places so as to allow for the paint which follows. The next and final coat of paint must be pure white, mixed with a very little yellow ochre, and painted boldly over the wet surface below. The result should look almost like white paint, but not quite. It has just that subtle difference which makes the white part of the building rich with color, and yet consistent with natural effects.

The same remarks apply to pastel, and also to opaque watercolor.

ARCHITECTURAL PAINTING IN WATERCOLOR

For transparent watercolor, where no opaque color is used, the best plan (after dampening the paper) is to tint the white paper slightly with delicate yellow ochre and little touches of warm gray, slightly mingling one with the other. That should be sufficient to suggest a white wall bathed in sunlight.

Another way in which to paint the same wall in watercolor is to wash in equally distributed patches of yellow ochre, light crimson, viridian, and gray, the colors more or less touching one another on the surface of the white paper. While the surface is still somewhat wet, use a small sponge with pure water, and wash most of this color out with vigorous movements of the sponge. This will also suggest the effect of light on a white wall. Moreover, it is a very artistic way of expressing soft edges, and unexpected detail often appears, which in no way disturbs the serenity of a wall.

The watercolor entitled *The Fountain, Besançon, France* (Plate XXXII) is painted with the sky and the greater portion of the buildings in direct transparent washes. Practically the whole of the fountain in shadow is painted in thin running body color—transparent watercolor mixed with opaque white—allowing the natural color of the paper in places to give the correct value.

An undercoat of liquid yellow ochre was first painted, before there was added the slightly yellow tinted body color for the highlights extending downwards, on the left side of the fountain, onto the road and distant figures.

It is interesting to observe that not only do the three figures in the foreground give a sense of scale to the size of the fountain, but they also help, through their dark colors, to accentuate the tonality of the whole picture.

There is just enough dark blue sky in the top of the picture to help, through contrast of color, the atmosphere of warm and cool grays of the fountain, and also of the darker toned buildings behind. Only a small area is occupied by sunlight. Consequently, it was of importance, when spacing the position of the sunlight, to see that it made a good pattern.

Besançon, in France, has a good many subjects of buildings without too much detail. It also has excellent country of a distinctive character in the neighborhood. Some of the nearer villages have buildings showing the influence of Spanish architecture.

Adak Harbor by William F. Draper, oil.

Ships and harbors lend themselves to coastal lendscapes with a lot of lively detail. In this panoramic view of a harbor with mountains, the light comes from above and slightly behind, illuminating the more distant mountains and throwing the nearer ones into shadow. The darkness of the sky heightens the effect of the snow on the mountains. On the water at the foot of the mountains, the artist has carefully observed the patterns of light and dark, which generally reflect channels, wind, and other natural phenomena which the beginning landscape painter should learn to recognize. Although the ship is the focal point of the painting, it is not allowed to dominate the surrounding landscape. Most of the ship is in shadow and it melts into the total atmosphere of the painting. It is interesting to watch how the painter adds a small touch like the flash of reflected light on the water at the stern of the ship, deftly separating the dark shape of the ship from the darkness of the water beyond. (Photograph courtesy American Artist)

14

Studies of Boats and Shipping

To draw boats, ordinary ships, and barges, is a genuine test of draughtsmanship. The foreshortening of a boat, when the front part is facing the spectator, necessitates obtaining exact proportion in a sketch. Before beginning a drawing of a barge seen in side view, the artist must also give very careful thought to the dimensions.

STUDYING BOATS The best way to acquire the necessary knowledge relating to boats is to draw those which are beached on the seashore, and likely to remain there for some considerable period. Then there is some opportunity of understanding the constructional meaning of a boat. It is advisable to draw boats in side view, three quarter view, end view, and in all the positions you can possibly conceive. After considerable practice of this type, one can tackle the same boats floating on the water. It is interesting to feel that a heavy piece of mechanism like a boat is floating easily on a soft, flexuous surface.

Sailing boats, when moving on the river or on the sea, require rapid observation on the part of the artist. Personally, I have often used a small brush, No. 3 or 4, with brown or greenish ink, and made rapid notes without any preliminary pencil drawing. If this is done on tinted paper, one not only gets a feeling of tone, but there is also a chance of getting a sensation of movement.

Some modern yachts are works of art apart from their sailing ability. It is marvelous to see them in a regatta, with their great sails spreading upwards, and displaying so much delicacy in color and swiftness in movement.

BARGES There is a curious solemnity about some of the barges on the canals near London, and the even larger barges on the river Seine in the neighborhood of Paris or on the Hudson River in New York. The fact that this type of barge has no tall, tapering masts to disturb the flat deck heightens the effect of solemnity. There is nothing to break up the noble formation of these low-lying river boats. At the close of day, when daylight is disappearing, the massive dignity of some of the Parisian barges becomes more noticeable through the elimination of detail lost in the evening shadows. An interesting aspect is created when the flexible and soft human figures of the barge's occupants are seen in contrast with the rigid structure of the woodwork, making fine pictorial matter for the landscape artist.

FISHING BOATS   Students who are able to travel are earnestly advised to go to Chioggia, near Venice. It is about two hours' trip down the lagoon. There are three or four boats plying daily from Venice. On arriving at Chioggia, you will see an amazing spectacle of old fishing boats similar to those used in mediaeval times. Some of these boats have brass headed, hand chased bulwarks, showing a fine sense of form.

The sails represent the chief feature as regards color. When the boats are returning in the evening, bathed in the strong sunlight which is so noticeable on the Adriatic Sea, its brilliancy is reflected on the sails of these boats, some of which are bright orange in tint, with patches of emerald green where the sail has been repaired. Other sails have warm browns, relieved with patches of bright yellow, or any colored bits of sailcloth which happen to be handy in the sail yard when repairing torn or worn out sails. There are oftentimes drawings on the sails themselves, such as an olive wreath, or some Latin inscription. In years to come, these boats will entirely disappear. It is important to keep a pictorial record of them, since a faithful copy will in future times have historical value.

Some of the Chioggia boats look somewhat like the conventional schoolboys' pirate ships of fiction, where the boats have a rakish mast and a big, devastating sail. They are not quite so large, perhaps, as the boats described in juvenile stories, but they certainly are noble and fine in appearance. Incidentally, Chioggia, apart from the boats, is worth a prolonged visit for the study of old buildings. There is street after street of ancient houses, with curious arches, and people may be seen sitting out of doors mending nets, or engaged in making lacework from their own designs, and in other decorative homecraft.

The modern liner is not to be despised as an object of pictorial beauty in form and color. A good oil painting of one of the Atlantic liners should give as much aesthetic pleasure as the oldest boat at Chioggia. It is all a matter of personal interpretation.

GONDOLAS   What can be more dainty or charming than the gondolas of Venice? They are so superbly constructed that they appear almost to be out of the water, so lightly do they touch the surface. The vitality of the gondola is almost uncanny. It springs and bobs and leaps at the least irritation caused in the water. Very few artists have been able to translate successfully the spirit of these boats in their sketches or pictures. Accurate drawing seems almost fatal in conveying the truth. The lively spirit of the subject does not seem compatible with sound drawing. Possibly the best way to tackle the movement of a gondola in a picture is not to draw it conventionally, but with a few rapid touches of a brush to suggest the general mass of the gondola.

Plate XXXIII is the first stage of a picture entitled *Boats at Gravesend*. This was done on tinted paper, the color of which is clearly noticeable, and drawn carefully as regards the nearer boats. The distant sailing boat was sketched in quickly at sight. After the pencil work was finished, all of the drawing was strengthened with a small brush and waterproof brown ink. This gave a feeling of security before any color washes were used.

The finished picture (Plate XXXIV) needs little description. It is merely transparent watercolor used to tint the previous ink drawing. Notice should be taken of the depth of the color in the farther sailing boat, since its richness of tone in the darker sails helps to suggest the feeling of a luminous background. This is a faithful representation of an actual scene off Gravesend. The patchwork on the smaller sail on the right of the picture prevents the sail from looking too opaque in color. Little touches of variety keep pictures from appearing commonplace.

The chief colors used for the sails were burnt sienna and light red—warm gray for the sky and water—vandyke brown, purple, and delicate green for the woodwork of the boats. It had to be borne in mind that the natural color of the paper had a neutralizing effect on *all* these colors.

It is interesting to note that Gravesend, which is so easily reached from London, is quite unspoilt so far by the effects of modern life like similar towns in Maine. The town has many old buildings, narrow streets, and alley ways. There are always varied types of craft on the water, while occasionally a big liner steams slowly down the middle of the Thames on its way to the sea, causing the everyday boats and ships to look very small in contrast.

The river Mersey at Liverpool has many sailing craft worth sketching. Cornwall is famous for its fishing boats, whilst Whitby, in Yorkshire, attracts numbers of artists. Similar subject matter can be found in America—on the New England coast or the San Francisco bay area, for example.

A Perthshire Moor by Ogden M. Pleissner, watercolor.

*Painted at a time of day when the light comes from behind, the rock forma-
tion is almost entirely in shadow, with just a few touches of light along the
upper edge. The same is true of the foreground rocks, which are simply
touched here and there with a fleck of light. This kind of lighting is particularly important when painting rock formations and mountains, which
need a clear definition of light and shadow planes. The figures not only
establish the focal point of the composition, but also lend scale; without
them, it would be impossible to determine the size of the rock formation.
(Photograph courtesy American Artist)*

15

Undulating Landscapes

Undulating landscapes suggest a certain amount of charm in landscape art. Such a subject dissipates the thought of anything relating to a powerful, or characteristic, mountain scene. It is the antithesis of everything which is not harmonious. What is usually meant by undulating landscape is subjects consisting of hills and valleys, with their flowing curves meeting each other at harmonious angles, thus suggesting the method of construction underlying this type of picture.

The Sussex Downs in England, the rolling green landscapes of Vermont and Pennsylvania afford good examples of undulating landscapes. The simple line work of curves in Figs. 3 and 4, Chapter 3, displays the elementary stage of flowing curves. In some places there are truly delightful pastoral scenes, where intersecting or tangential curves play an important part. Any monotony that might have been caused through an overdose of harmonious lines in these landscapes is avoided through the contrast of groups of trees, sharply intersecting fields, and sometimes even farmhouses and barns.

UNDULATING HILLS

Plate XLVIII, entitled *The Brendon Hills, from Williton, Somerset*, shows a good example of undulating hills clothed with intersecting lines of fields, groups of trees, etc. The distant hills in this picture have the same constructional basis as the middle exercises in Figs. 3 and 4. Notice how the fields take up less space as they recede towards the high horizon.

UNDULATING FOREGROUND, MIDDLE DISTANCE AND DISTANCE

Plate XXXV is a full page color illustration, entitled *Château de Polignac, France*. This picture displays undulation in the immediate foreground at the foot of the pastel painting, and the middle distance, as well as in the flowing distant hills. To help the composition, the ascending line of the fields, at the foot of the hill below the château, converges upwards from the right, center and left side respectively, thus leading the eye towards the château itself, and concentrating on the most important part of the picture: the Château de Polignac.

The upright trees in the foreground, spaced chiefly on the right, act as a contrasting factor to the fields spreading horizontally between the château hill and the foreground. The vertical tower of the château and the smaller spire (lower in the picture) on the left, echo the upright direction of the foreground trees.

The lower part of the picture is dark in tone, and as the château and adjoining buildings are also dark, it is important that the lower portion of the picture should be strong enough in tone to support the heavy portions above.

To give full value to the flowing, distant hills, the sky is painted very nearly flat, and any clouds that are introduced are on such a small scale that they do not interfere with (or render irritating) the general appearance of the picture. There is a good deal of chatter and detail shown in the little rectangular fields in the middle distance, hence the value of a comparatively flat sky, so that the spectator's attention shall be diverted to the points of interest shown in the middle distance.

COLOR AND DESIGN

The color of the paper—a warm gray—is more noticeable at the foot of the picture, particularly towards the right. The preliminary pastel colors were laid on in the same manner as in the first stage of the picture seen in Plate XXVIII.

It cannot be emphasized too often that all pastel pictures, irrespective of the subject matter, must first receive on the tinted paper a loosely handled groundwork of dark and warm colors, so as to give a solid foundation, on which can be placed touches of lighter and sometimes colder colors.

For this picture, the following pastel colors were used as the foundation.

Sky: yellow ochre, light warm gray.

Distant hills: yellow ochre; Prussian blue.

Château, dark hills, and foreground: burnt sienna, deep violet, and dark warm brown.

Patchwork fields, etc.: chiefly burnt sienna and yellow ochre..

Light Prussian blue was worked over and between the sky colors mentioned above, with cream white shade for the cloudlets, to complete the sky in the final stage.

All the above colors are much influenced and modified in strength through the tone of the paper on which they were used. In the diagram adjacent to Plate XXXV, a happy contrast is shown. The straight lines of the château produce a sensation of security when seen in company with so many undulating curves. The trees on the right also demonstrate the principle of contrast, which is so important in picture designing.

CLOUDS IN UNDULATING LANDSCAPES

Cumulus clouds can often be used to advantage in this type of landscape. The rolling forms of undulation can be echoed in the cloud shapes peculiar to the cumulus formation.

The dignity of shape generally associated with cumulus clouds is also in harmony with the movement of the landscape below. Long, thin clouds, horizontally inclined with a slight curvature, are quite adaptable to this style of landscape; while one or two cloudlets at the top of the picture, in a large, simple, and flatlooking sky, create a feeling of serenity.

Hills of Manayunk by Francis Speight, oil.

Here is an interesting use of perspective. The buildings are on two levels and those on the lower level recede to a vanishing point which indicates that the horizon is just one third of the way up from the bottom of the picture. However, above this horizon rises a hill which is crowned by another cluster of buildings, all of which are well above eye level. The effect is to give loftiness to the hill and to the buildings on it. Observe how the stormy sky swirls around the buildings on the top of the hill, with each patch of light and dark methodically placed to direct attention to the center of interest. Such casual brushwork is always more carefully planned than the viewer might suppose. (Photograph courtesy American Artist)

MERCER QUARRY by John Folinsbee, oil.

Free, spontaneous brushwork is not an end in itself, but must reflect the forms that the artist is painting. The bold, lively brushwork in this landscape is carefully planned to express the nature of the landscape itself. In the sky, for example, the broad, blurry strokes interpret the direction of the cloud. Along the sides of the quarry, the strokes follow the changes in direction of the light and dark planes. The trees are interpreted in jagged strokes that communicate the movement of the trunks and limbs. And even the distant house is painted in flat, geometric strokes. (Photograph courtesy American Artist)

Plate I. Four basic tones for foreground, middle distance, distance, sky. Every detail of this watercolor must be right density. Picture would fail if any portion of landscape appeared to be in wrong spatial plane because of incorrect value.

Plate II. Same landscape, in washes of full color, again places all elements in correct spatial plane by establishing four values for foreground, middle distance, distance, sky.

Plate III. A GRAY DAY AT BRUGES, *pastel. This was a difficult subject because artist had no definite lights or shadows to work from; without positive light, careful observation was needed to convey correct values. If small color notes, like figures on bridge or boat beneath, were too light, unity would be disrupted. Every color on water had to be just right to keep surface one continuous plane. Unity is maintained through restraint. It is nearly always safer to do too little than too much.*

Plate IV. THE RIVER DOUBS, BESANCON, FRANCE, *watercolor. Very light groundwork of sky was mixture of yellow ochre, cerulean blue, opaque white (body color). Sky tint was painted down to water's edge; while this color was still wet, hills were painted in with flat brush. Hill details were painted into wet color. River contains some opaque white, but rest of foreground is transparent. Bushes toward right are strengthened with sharp touches of dark violet.*

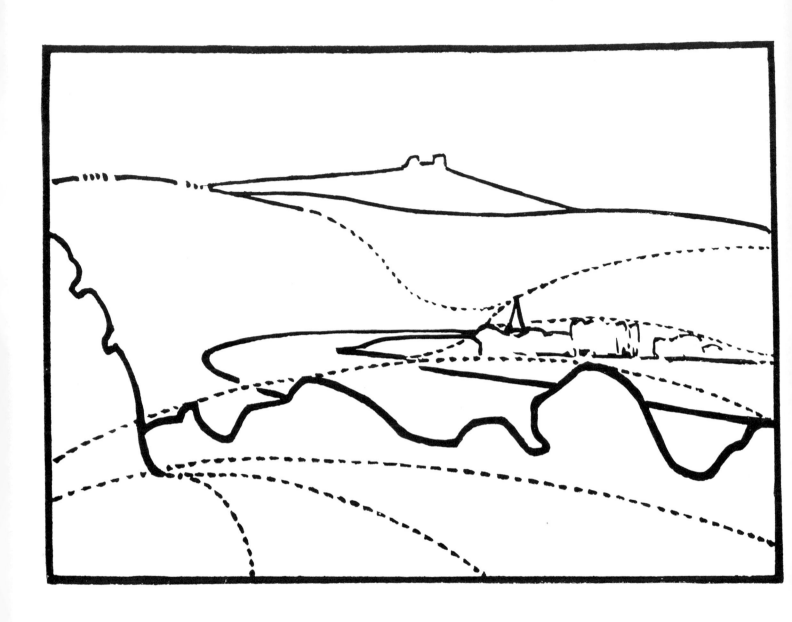

Analytical diagram of Plate IV shows lines of river connecting fore-
ground with middle distance and extending to foot of distant hills. Dotted
curves explain composition; notice how dotted curve, sweeping across river,
carries rhythm of middle distance into foreground.

Plate V. Rapid watercolor note was done in about thirteen minutes, without striving for actual facts of nature. Simplicity of coloring is result of lack of time—just flat, running washes, partly mingling, with paper sparkling through here and there. Such sparkle is difficult to obtain in more finished studio picture which has been painted over with two or three washes.

Plate VI. Pencil sketch on ordinary writing paper, with watercolor tints. Pencil lines are still noticeable. Colors were used merely to tint and suggest tonality without strong lights or deep shadows.

Plate VII. TOR STEPS, EXMOOR, SOMERSET, *oil painting, shows how full scale painting can evolve from simple sketch like Plate VI. Here we get tonalities of nature—deep greens, dark water, deep colors of rooftops, sombre effect of heavy foliage—in contrast to luminous transparency of little watercolor. Groundwork colors (later modified by overpainting) were yellow ochre, cerulean blue, light purple in sky; burnt umber, burnt sienna, viridian, deep purple in trees, rooftops; burnt sienna, purple, burnt umber, raw sienna, yellow ochre in water; warm gray and grayish purple in hill and stone bridge. All colors were applied flat in early stage and kept apart from one another; only in final stage were colors blended, dragged over one another to produce mixtures, broken color effects.*

Plate VIII.   A Minehead Cottage, Somerset, *first stage of watercolor. From the very beginning, all border lines of cottage and contours of tree were kept scrupulously in place.*

Plate IX.   A Minehead Cottage, Somerset, *final stage of watercolor. Final colors were carefully contained within precise preliminary design. Same subject could have been drawn more freely, with more vigorous color and deeper tones, for very different effect.*

Plate X. Pastel sketch, preliminary study for watercolor in Plate XVI. Compare strength of pastel with suggestiveness of watercolor sketch in Plate XI.

Plate XI. Watercolor sketch emphasizes design. Horizontal feeling of upper and lower clouds harmonizes with and reflects horizontal spacing of landscape below.

Plate XII. STUDY OF MOVING CLOUDS, *watercolor. Design helps illusion of movement: larger cloud on top left swings downward toward right to connect up clouds near horizon and dark hills with adjoining landscape below. Colors used included a good deal of body color (opaque white): gray-blue, yellow ochre, a little crimson mixed with some opaque white in sky; permanent blue (mixed with a little permanent crimson) and warm gray in hills; Hooker's green (middle tint and deep) mixed with burnt sienna in trees; yellow ochre and raw sienna in foreground, laid on in transparent washes. Cloud tints immediately above hills were carried over parts of hills while still wet.*

Plate XIII. Gradated watercolor wash is deepish blue at top, becoming lighter and changing color as it moves downward. Paper was tilted slightly to allow colors to blend naturally.

Plate XIV. Watercolor sky was done in same manner, but clouds were washed out with small sponge. Note that clouds become smaller as they near horizon, suggesting aerial perspective.

Plate XV. Cathedral Mountains, Canadian Rockies, *oil painting.*
Basic colors used in foundation stage were: yellow ochre, warm gray, cobalt
blue, zinc white, viridian in sky; raw umber, raw sienna, cobalt blue, per-
manent crimson, burnt sienna, terre verte, zinc white in distant mountains;
yellow ochre and zinc white in snow; dark warm gray and purple in snow
in shadow; burnt umber, burnt sienna, deep purple, dark warm gray in
foreground mountains. Greenish tint of ice was first painted with yellow
ochre and white.

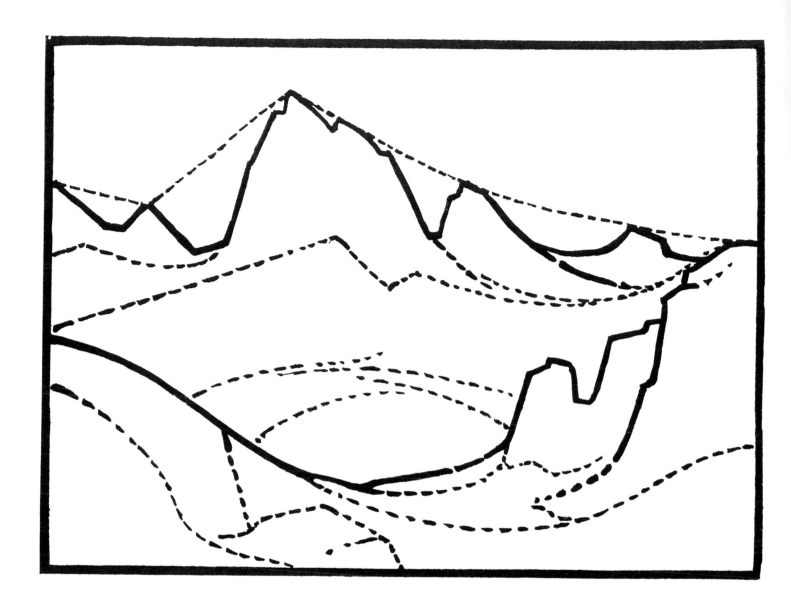

Analytical diagram of Plate XV shows unity of design despite angular forms. Topmost peaks are bound together in dotted marginal line which extends in outward (convex) direction. Lower masses of rock formation at foot of picture show opposite effect, extending in inward (concave) direction.

L.Richmond.

Plate XVI. A Decoration, *watercolor, based on pastel sketch in Plate X. Groundwork colors were: ultramarine blue, well diluted with water, for sky; purple (cobalt blue and permanent crimson), yellow ochre, burnt sienna in dark hill; yellow ochre and warm gray, painted on damp paper, in light hill and foreground; cobalt blue and viridian in water. In final stages, highlights were painted with thick opaque white, mixed with yellow ochre, etc. Darker toned trees were painted two or three times over to get rich tones.*

94

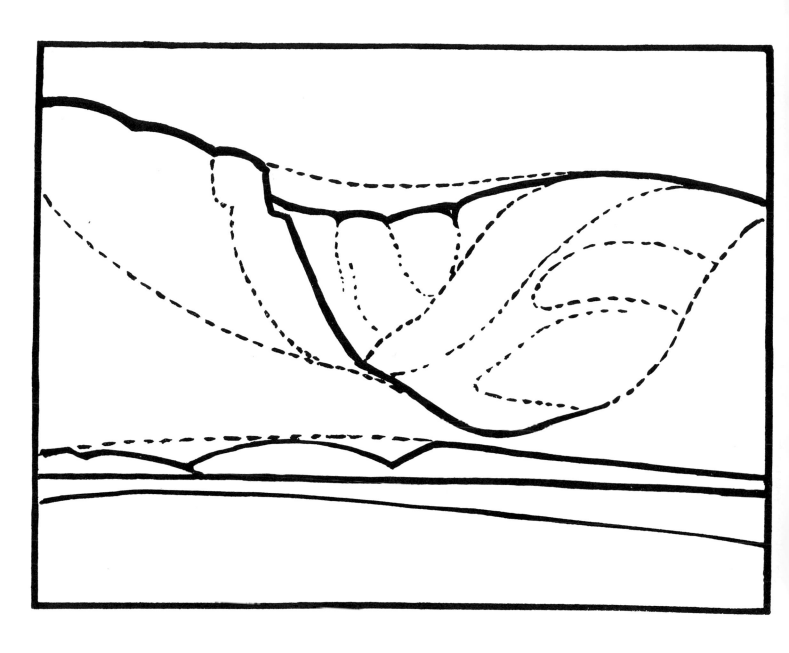

Analytical diagram of Plate XVI show harmonious curves supported by straight horizontal line extending across lower portion.

Plate XVII. Emerald Lake, Canadian Rockies, *first stage of oil painting. General design is first blocked in with decisive flat tones, with practically all colors kept darker than those in finished picture (Plate XVIII). Remember that snow colors need warm underpainting of yellow ochre and white so that final, lighter coat echoes some of warm color beneath. White snow, painted directly on raw canvas, looks dry and chalky.*

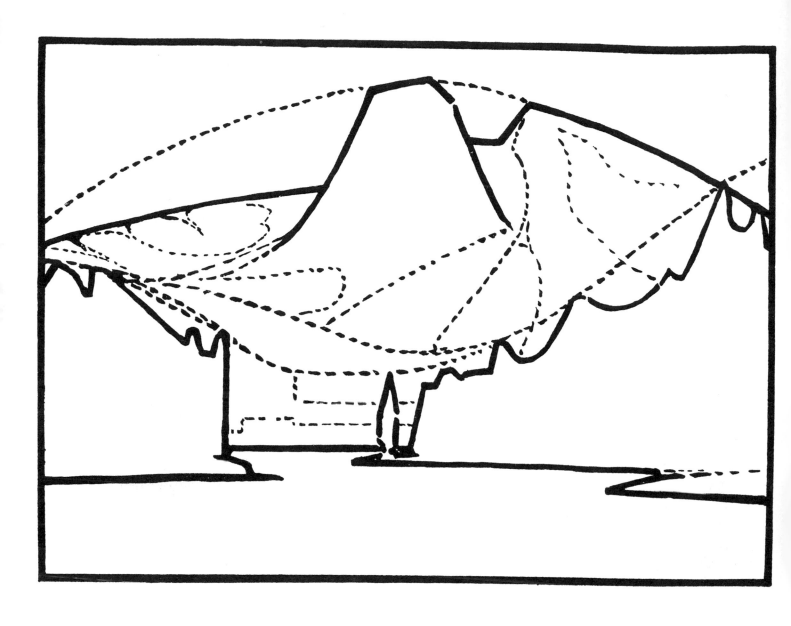

Analytical diagram of Plate XVII follows same convex-concave principle shown in Plate XV. Tops of mountains (dotted lines) demonstrate convexity; central portion demonstrates concavity. Rigid horizontal lines (below) support great weight of mountains.

Plate XVIII.   Emerald Lake, Canadian Rockies, *final stage of oil paint-*
ing. Finished picture shows addition of lighter tones, painted generally over
mountains and snow, while trees received more detail, and surface of water
is more luminous and broken. Flat tones of first stage are now animated
by rough brushwork.

Plate XIX. Watercolor study of mass foliage, first stage, is painted in flat tints, with minimum detail and only slight tonal variation.

Plate XX. Watercolor study of mass foliage, final stage, shows addition of strongly defined shadows of deep color. Some detail is suggested, but handling is still broad.

Plate XXI. ELM TREES AT WINDSOR, *watercolor. Try copying trees in this picture, following same principles of flat painting demonstrated in Plates XIX and XX, adding dark shadows and suggestions of detail in final stage. Foundation colors were: yellow ochre and ultramarine blue in sky; deep Hooker's green, yellow ochre, purple, permanent blue in trees; yellow ochre mixed with light gray, light purple mixed with yellow ochre, vermilion mixed with light gray in distant buildings; Hooker's green (medium) and burnt sienna in foreground. Lower portion of sky was wiped out with small sponge; contours of tall trees received same treatment to prevent hard edges.*

Plate XXII. Fir Trees, Pas-de-Calais, France, *watercolor, was begun with pure washes of transparent color. In the final stage, body color (opaque white) was used for the sky and for certain portions of the foliage and foreground.*

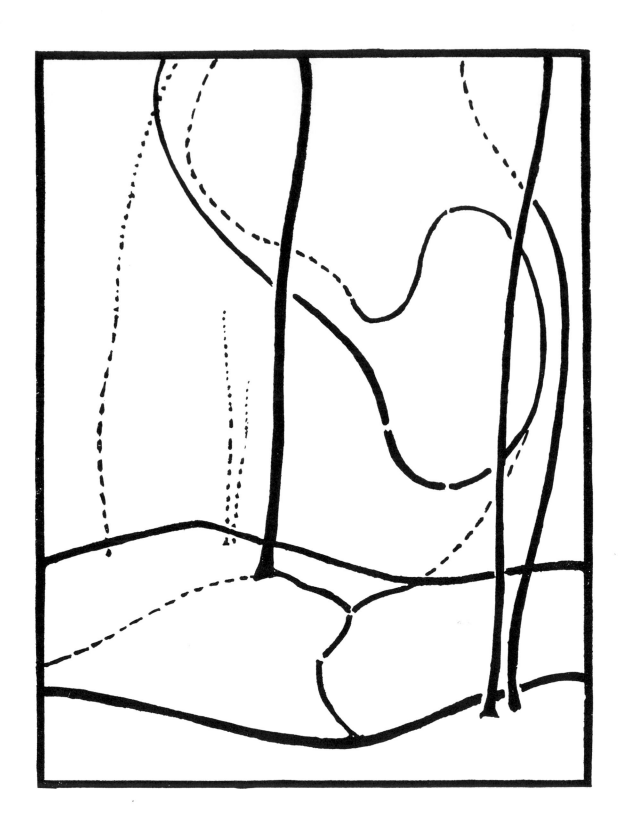

Analytical diagram of Plate XXII emphasizes sky opening on right, which is oval and travels upwards to higher left side. Vertical trunks cut sharply across sky opening. Winding pathway is harmoniously related to constructional lines above.

Plate XXIII (left). Watercolor study of foliage detail, first stage, is just flat wash indicating branches and mass of leaves.

Plate XXIV (right). Watercolor study of foliage detail, final stage, shows darker tints added before first wash was quite dry.

Plate XXV (left). Watercolor study of fir followed same method, beginning with flat tones, then adding shadows and detail.

Plate XXVI (right). Watercolor study of chestnut leaves follows careful pencil outline; detailed form was sought for, unlike preceding plates.

Plate XXVII. A VENETIAN CANAL, oil painting. This study clearly displays different effects of light and shadow on same sheet of water. Reflections appear in top portion of water, in shadow, while brilliant sun neutralizes normal tone of foreground water, making reflections of dark toned buildings impossible.

Analytical diagram of Plate XXVII. Dotted curve on right encompasses bridge, miniature figure and boat at foot of building, figure of gondolier. Sweeping lines of gondola connect with vertical line of building on right, which adjoins bridge.

Plate XXVIII. Bolton Abbey, Yorkshire, *first stage of pastel. Quick running, shallow water, with bed of river showing in places through surface, is very difficult problem. Warm glow from river bed needs to be neutralized to some extent by opaque suggestion of grayish tint. In first stage, warm local color of soil was first laid on; pastel was used sparingly to allow for later tints.*

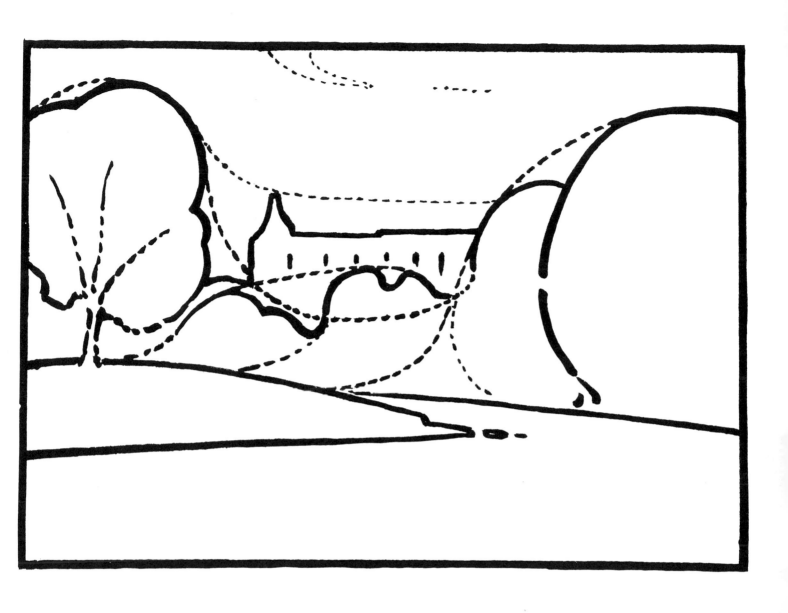

Analytical diagram of Plate XXVIII shows leading compositional lines that connect trees, which spread across whole landscape. Horizontal and vertical lines of abbey act as foil to restlessness of water below. Horizontal clouds harmonize with direction of abbey.

Plate XXIX. BOLTON ABBEY, YORKSHIRE, *final stage of pastel. Warm colors in first stage—red, brown, yellow, etc.—form invaluable groundwork for final touches of colder colors, such as gray, green, blue, through which warm colors are reflected. Student will find it useful to copy first and final stages of this pastel.*

Plate XXX. THE RIVER THAMES, MARLOW, *watercolor, follows recommendation, made in text, that lights should be kept darker than in nature, while darks should be kept lighter. Reflection of mansion (in water at left) is darker than color of walls, while reflection of roof is lighter. Reflection of dark mass of trees is lighter. Purpose of this subtle distortion is to maintain unity of flat, horizontal plane of water. Foundation colors were: yellow ochre, light warm purple in sky; Hooker's green medium, yellow ochre, light red in dark trees; chrome yellow and Hooker's green medium in poplar trees; light red and chrome yellow in roofs; ivory black, permanent blue, crimson, yellow ochre, deep Hooker's green in water at right; yellow ochre, warm gray, yellowish gray-green, light warm purple in water at left.*

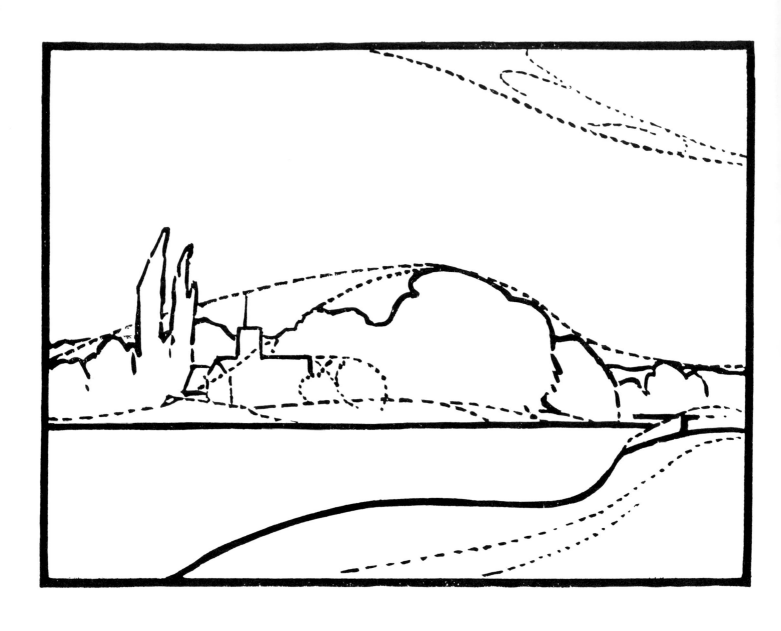

Analytical diagram of Plate XXX. Dotted lines, suggesting position of cloudlets in sky, demonstrate hormonious relations to landscape below. Thin, tall poplars (left) contrast sharply with circular formation of heavier group of trees on right. Little flagstaff on tower behind mansion echoes vertical direction of poplars.

Plate XXXI. THE BRIDGE OVER BRUGES CANAL, *oil painting. In first stage, buildings, bridge, and water were well primed with touches of raw sienna, burnt sienna, deep chrome yellow, yellow ochre, warm purple. Tree, two figures, foreground on left received perliminary coat of burnt umber, permanent blue, permanent crimson mixed with burnt umber and burnt sienna. For sky, permanent blue was mixed with a little crimson and yellow ochre. Various grays were obtained by mixing odd colors left on palette after day's work. Note how, in final stage, green foliage of tree and circular reflection below bridge (painted chiefly with viridian and a little terre verte) still show rich, warm undertones from first stage.*

Analytical diagram of Plate XXXI shows how two figures in left foreground form part of composition. They are enclosed in curved dotted lines which extend upwards on either side and interlock with other elements of design.

Plate XXXII. THE FOUNTAIN, BESANCON, FRANCE, *watercolor. Sky and greater portion of buildings were painted in direct, transparent washes. Practically whole fountain was painted in thin, running body color—transparent watercolor mixed with a little opaque white—allowing natural color of paper to come through in places. Undercoat of yellow ochre was painted before yellow tinted body color was added for highlights on left of fountain and road. Note that only small area is occupied by sunlight; remainder is in shadow. Three small, dark figures give sense of scale and accentuate tonality of whole picture.*

Plate XXXIII. Boats at Gravesend, first stage of watercolor. Painted on tinted paper, the color of which is clearly noticeable, this watercolor began with pencil sketch, which was then strengthened with waterproof brown ink, applied with small brush. This gave feeling of security before any color washes were added.

Plate XXXIV. Boats at Gravesend, *final stage of watercolor. Here transparent watercolor was used to tint ink drawing in Plate XXXIII. Note depth of color in farther sailing boat; richness of tone in darker sails helps to suggest feeling of luminous background. Patchwork on smaller sail to right prevents sail from looking too opaque in color. Little touches of variety keep pictures from appearing too commonplace.*

Plate XXXV. CHATEAU DE POLIGNAC, FRANCE, *pastel, displays undulation in immediate foreground, middle distance, as well as flowing distant hills. Lower part of picture is dark to support heavy portions above. Sky is painted nearly flat to give full value to hills and to detail in middle distance. Foundation pastel colors, underlying final colors, were: yellow ochre, light warm gray in sky; yellow ochre and Prussian blue in hills; burnt sienna, deep violet, dark warm brown in chateau, dark hills, foreground; chiefly burnt sienna, yellow ochre in patchwork fields. Light Prussian blue was worked over and between sky colors mentioned above, with creamy white for cloudlets. All colors are modified by warm gray tone of paper.*

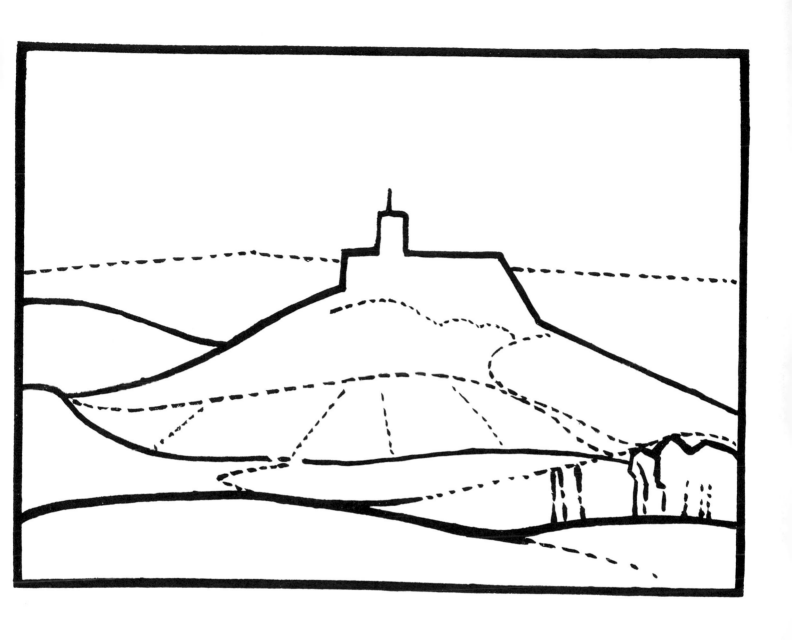

Analytical diagram of Plate XXXV. Ascending line of fields from right and left leads eye towards chateau. Upright trees in foreground act as contrasting factor to fields which spread horizontally. Vertical tower and spire echo upright direction of trees.

Plate XXXVI (left). Tranquility, *watercolor. Mood is obtained by severe upright parallel lines of trees, rising at right angles to flat ground; absence of flamboyant curves or tonal contrast.*

Plate XXXVII (right). Storm, *watercolor. Sketching storms must be done from memory, for obvious reasons. Note how direction of clouds and trees reflects violent mood.*

Plate XXXVIII (left). Moonlight, *watercolor. Luminous warm tones and sombre cool colors reflect glamor of night.*

Plate XXXIX (right). Evening, *watercolor, expresses calm of declining day in general horizontal design; large empty space of sky; rich, yet restrained color.*

Plate XL. A CANADIAN WATERFALL, *oil painting, reflects violent mood of nature. Foundation colors, later modified by succeeding colors and brush-work, were: warm gray interspaced with patches of yellow ochre, bluish purple in sky; dark warm gray, bluish purple, terre verte mixed with yellow ochre in mountains; permanent blue mixed with purplish gray in distant trees; burnt umber, ivory black, raw umber, permanent blue in nearer trees; burnt sienna, yellow ochre, purple, silver gray in rocks; yellow ochre, warm gray mixed with viridian, light reddish purple in water.*

Plate XLI. Bow Falls, Baniff, Canadian Rockies, *first stage of water-color. Trees were so dark and sinister that artist had to exaggerate tones to convey powerful effect of lowering clouds, dark trees, light foam of falls. First stage shows some of preliminary pencil drawing, particularly in light area at center. Picture was painted entirely in transparent watercolor, without aid of opaque color (body color), on canvas grained paper.*

Analytical diagram of Plate XLI. Strength of horizontal lines in lower portion of picture contrasts with jagged contours above. Apex of each mountain touches dotted curve.

Plate XLII. Bow Falls, Banff, Canadian Rockies, *final stage of water-color. Compare with Plate XLI. In final stage, deep shadows were added, trees were darkened, and detail shown where needed. Whole sky and distant mountains were united by one flat wash of light yellowish gray. In water-color, it is nearly always essential—when no body color is used—to wash transparent light tint over portions of colored groundwork to unite and solidify whole scheme.*

Plate XLIII. The Estuary, Barmouth, North Wales, *first stage of oil painting. Drab, quiet, melancholy day is difficult subject for artist to paint. Contrast is low, strong sunlight is absent, and sky is nearly as dark as distant hills. In first stage, colors were painted in fairly bright tints, somewhat flat, to enliven overlying colors.*

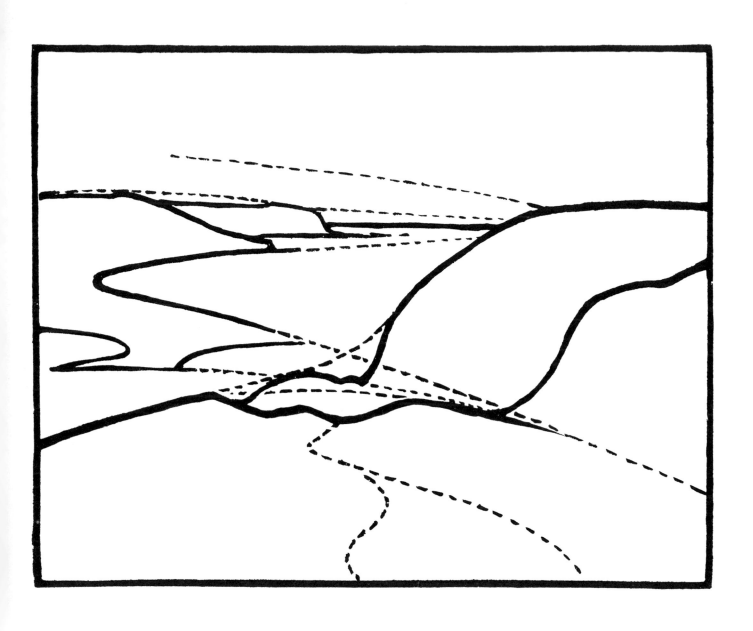

Analytical diagram of Plate XLIII. Horizontal line of sea is placed two thirds of distance up from bottom line. Coast lines (see dotted lines) connect with foreground construction.

Plate XLIV. THE ESTUARY, BARMOUTH, NORTH WALES, *final stage of oil painting. Completed picture retains subdued quality of nature's mood. Colors are far less intense, more muted, but more varied than groundwork colors in first stage. Yet underlying colors lend vitality.*

Plate XLV. THE WATCHET COAST, SOMERSET, *oil sketch. When sketching in oils, paint vigorously with strong brushstrokes. Do not hesitate to make mistakes—they may suggest something—but paint decisively, get strong sense of tone and color.*

Plate XLVI. THE WATCHET COAST, SOMERSET, *finished oil painting. In final picture, sky has lost cold, grayish blue; rocks show more form and better drawing; slight color changes establish better tone relationships.*

Plate XLVII. The Brendon Hills from Williton, Somerset, *pastel sketch. First sketch shows strength without delicacy. Tones are incorrect, but subject is clearly stated.*

Plate XLVIII. The Brendon Hills from Williton, Somerset, *finished pastel painting. Clouds no longer assert themselves at expense of foreground; delicate color of hills places them at proper distance; trees and shadows show more interesting pattern.*

Plate XLIX. OLD NET HOUSES, HASTINGS, *oil sketch, was done with real excitement, no attempt to show rock strata. Colors are too strong, but sketch conveys power of subject.*

Plate L. OLD NET HOUSES, HASTINGS, *finished oil painting. Strong colors are painted out on cliffs behind houses; structural formation is more clearly expressed by warm grays, bluish shadows, obvious brush handling.*

16

Moods of Nature

Nature has many moods, some of which are of very short duration. It is difficult to respond to these moods unless the artist is quite alone and in a state of receptivity to outside influences. To be alone in a woodland area, where little sunlight can get through the dense foliage, suggests a totally different feeling from that produced if the same wood is occupied by a party of holiday trippers.

EXPRESSING MOOD   Another curious feature as regards moods is that no two artists ever appear to receive the same message from nature, even if they are painting precisely the same subject. On this principle, supposing a thousand or so artists painted the same subject, and nature had a different message for each, no two pictures would be the same. Does not this open up boundless possibilities for landscape pictures displaying varying moods? It is noticeable that the majority of easily rendered sketches, if done with some measure of vitality and painted without any technical difficulties, convey the message nature had intended to transmit to the artist.

Presuming this to be true, how is it that in so many exhibitions and art galleries there is a similarity of expression in landscape pictures? It is possible that material environment and studio life have something to do with the loss of the real message. Selecting art committees, too, often play havoc by taking in only those pictures that show fine technique in the conventional sense of the word. Men in high positions in art have been known to exclaim, on viewing a picture, "What a splendidly painted picture that is!" Where, then, does the art come in? Where is nature's message as interpreted by the artist? Have landscape painters no power to arouse aesthetic feeling or some emotional sense in the mind of the spectator? Most decidedly they should have.

The moods of nature are without end, and should the student not find the mood of the moment, then he can superimpose his own mood in a landscape. It is comparatively easy for an artist to suggest sentiment in a picture, provided that he has a wide knowledge of nature's forms and colors. Without this wide knowledge, it is not easy for any student to express a mood when using nature as the medium for expression.

TRANQUILITY Plates XXXVI, XXXVII, XXXVIII, and XXXIX are four pictures painted in watercolor on canvas-grained paper, with a little body color (opaque white) in places; considerable wiping out was done to obtain a luminous and liquid effect. Each of these pictures represents an obvious mood. There are far more subtle moods than these in nature, but for the sake of a clear understanding, the four illustrations are given as a beginning point for the greater moods to follow.

Plate XXXVI is entitled *Tranquility*. Tranquility in this illustration is obtained by the severe upright parallel lines of the vertical trees, rising at right angles to the flat ground below. The absence of flamboyant curves, or dark shadows opposed to brilliant highlights, supports the title of the picture. The horizon leaves plenty of room for the comparatively flat sky above. This is seen in Fig. 2, Chapter 3.

STORM The next example, Plate XXXVII is entitled *Storm*. This is always an interesting subject for artists. It is obvious, when sketching storm subjects, that the painter is rarely able to sit out of doors for any length of time without the chance of being deluged at any moment. All that the artist can do is to visualize the scene, and, while the excitement still lasts, to go back to the studio and render the impression of what was seen out of doors. This sort of impression of a scene is sometimes much more faithful than an attempt to imitate the impossible.

Notice in the colored illustration, how the taller trees on the left slant towards the right, and how the smaller trees bend in the same direction. The whole landscape is under the influence of a violent gale, moving from the left towards the right, and the illusion of wind is created by the more or less parallel direction of the trees and clouds.

MOONLIGHT
AND EVENING
Plate XXXVIII, entitled *Moonlight*, possesses the glamor of the night. It needs little explanation. So many moonlights have been painted before. Plate XXXIX is entitled *Evening*.

VIOLENCE IN NATURE Plate XL is a full page illustration of a Canadian waterfall. This represents another mood. As regards the design of the picture, the sky and distant mountains are kept low in tone so that the attention of the spectator can be focused on the subject—the waterfall. There is a certain amount of velocity in the movement of this water. The foam is too great to allow for any positive reflections.

The dark pine trees, particularly towards the central portion of the picture, through which the water is flowing, give an admirable illustration of contrast because of their vertical lines, suggesting rigid form when seen against the flexibility and softness of swiftly running water. The same idea applies also to the solid rocks. The lower rocks, being well splashed with spray from the waterfall, are light in tone, both in the highlights and in the shadows. The sunlight on the foreground reflects its brilliancy in the wet shadows.

The foundation colors in this picture are as follows.

Sky: warm gray interspaced with patches of yellow ochre and bluish purple.

Mountains: dark warm gray, bluish purple, terra verte mixed with a little yellow ochre.

Distant trees: permanent blue mixed with purplish gray.

Nearer trees: burnt umber mixed with a little ivory black, raw umber, permanent blue.

Rocks: burnt sienna, yellow ochre, purple (middle tint), silver gray (fairly dark in shade).

Water: yellow ochre, warm gray mixed with a little viridian, light reddish purple.

The mixing of any stated color with another must be done on the palette so that, when painted on canvas, the two colors will make one tint. These remarks apply to all the pictorial subjects in this book.

MAJESTY IN NATURE

Plate XLII is a picture entitled *Bow Falls, Banff, Canadian Rockies.* This picture represents a mood of its own. The trees were so dark and sinister in nature that the artist had, to a certain extent, to exaggerate the tones in the painting to convey the powerful effect felt in the lowering clouds, dark trees, and the light colored foam of the falls.

There are two stages shown in this picture. The first stage, Plate XLI, explains itself to a great extent. There is still some of the drawing left, as can be seen under the first wash of watercolor paint. This picture was painted in transparent watercolor on canvas grained paper, without any assistance from opaque color. In the final stage (Plate XLII) deep shadows were added, the trees darkened, and detail shown where necessary, while the whole of the sky and distant mountains were united through one flat wash of light yellowish gray.

In watercolor painting it is very important sometimes—in fact, nearly always so when there is no body color used—to wash a transparent light tint over portions of the colored ground work so as to unite and solidify the whole scheme involved in the painting.

The chief item of interest in the adjacent line composition is shown in the strength of several horizontal lines in the lower portion of the picture, contrasting with the jagged contours above.

The apex of each mountain touches the dotted curve from left to right. The line of the group of trees above the falls on the left, by being extended, continues upwards at a tangent to the group of trees on the right.

A MELANCHOLY MOOD

Plate XLIV is entitled *Barmouth Estuary.* This is a very difficult subject for an artist to paint. There is nothing in the natural subject to create a feeling of exhilaration. There is no strong sunlight, and the sky is nearly as dark as the distant hills.

In the first stage (Plate XLIII) the colors were painted in with fairly bright tints, and somewhat flat. Had the groundwork been a little darker in color, it would have made an easier surface on which to paint the final colors. This subject has no sparkle and very little vitality, yet it is one of nature's own moods. Pictorially, it possesses little to attract the average spectator, merely depicting one of those drab, quiet, melancholy days which is usually followed by rain.

Its construction is explained in the adjacent diagram. Notice that the horizontal line of the sea is placed two-thirds of the distance up from the bottom line of the picture.

The coast lines on the left, in the middle and farther distance, connect (as shown by dotted lines) with the foreground construction.

Enough has been said in this chapter to suggest the possibility of obtaining plenty of variety in landscape pictures, should the artist be blessed with the gift of interpretation.

DEMOLITION by Harry Leith-Ross, oil.

When clouds move across the sky, partly obscuring the sun, partly allowing light to go through to the earth below, so-called cloud shadows are produced. Such shadows are often a convenient way for enlivening a landscape. In this painting, a cloud shadow falls partly across the face of the building which looms against the sky. Thus, part of the building is in shadow and part is illuminated. The sky, itself, is a lively pattern of dark clouds, with light breaking through, and the areas of dark and light are carefully placed to dramatize the building. As the receding boards in the foreground indicate, the horizon line is low; thus, the main elements of the picture are above eye level, which makes them even more imposing. (Courtesy Pennsylvania Academy of the Fine Arts, Philadelphia, Pennsylvania)

MAPLE SUGARING IN VERMOUNT by Paul Sample, oil.

The artist has used the whiteness of the snow very much as he might use the whiteness of the paper in a watercolor. The snow shapes are kept flat and un-modeled, but are divided with great care into a variety of interesting flat shapes by patches of foliage and the bare trunks of the trees. It is particularly interesting to see how the upright trees bend in slightly toward the center of the picture and frame the central action; most important of all is the fallen tree which cuts diagonally across the composition to center the viewer's attention on the house and figures. Despite the strong, clear light, there are few tree shadows; however, a single tree shadow points diagonally inward from the foreground, leading to the center of interest. (Photograph courtesy American Artist)

BREATHING SPACE by Joshua Meador, oil.

The artist's vigorous brushwork and the dynamic texture of the paint exude vitality. The paint is applied in a direct, spontaneous way, with very little attempt to blend tones or produce smooth textures. The roughness of the paint in the forest, for example, is calculated to express the tangle of trunks and foliage. In a different way, the direction and texture of the strokes express the quality of the wood of the buildings in the foreground. Notice, in particular, how thickly the paint is applied in the areas struck by sunlight; this is an old master rule of thumb—"paint thinly in the shadows and thickly in the light." (Photograph courtesy American Artist)

17

The Use of
Outdoor Sketches

S ome people suffer from the idea that artists, if they cared to do so, could
give away the secret as to how they manage to turn their sketches to good
account when making indoor pictures. There is no secret; neither is there
any recipe for this achievement. It is merely a matter of common sense and
constructional ability in the studio.

WORKING IN THE STUDIO The feeling of liberty which naturally arises in the mind of the artist when
all the creature comforts of studio life are available, and all the trials and
tribulations of outdoor sketching are done away with, for the moment, is a
good augury for a successful and well balanced painting. Generally, one is
more courageous when away from nature than when facing all that she has
to say. Some of the finest things have been painted indoors as the result of
knowledge accumulated through outdoor sketching. It is possible to evolve a
passable looking picture indoors *without* a great deal of knowledge, but this
is a poor comfort for the earnest student. If your sketches have good values
and each sketch is backed up with pencil studies, there is every prospect of
achieving something really worthwhile. The lack of logical tones in a sketch
is a greater disaster than the lack of detail.

The artist, when painting the final picture in the studio from outdoor
studies, has the privilege of leaving out noticeable mistakes as seen in the
outdoor sketch or sketches. For instance, a sketch of quickly moving clouds,
which has failed to suggest the feeling of movement, can be remedied in the
studio partly through memory and partly through common sense based on
theoretical construction. Another sketch of a scene may be lacking in contrast. It is not a difficult matter, in the sanctuary of a studio, to brighten the
highlights and deepen the shadows without losing the general harmony of
the picture. There are no restrictions for the artist as regards any alterations
in the finished picture. I have not only altered a picture in the studio, but
have sometimes painted four of the same subject, and selected the best one
for exhibition.

AVOIDING MANNERISMS   Avoid mannerisms in painting. Mannerisms are usually caused through too much indoor painting: the artist adopts an arbitrary style of technique and uses it to express all moods of nature. The handling of pigment in a picture should help the subject. Every landscape demands just that style of technique which, without any ostentation, is best suited for the picture.

After some six months' outdoor sketching, one can become rather weary of the physical and mental work involved, and the reaction of going back to studio life arouses all the feelings of freshness and virility. Then, at the end of another six months or less in the studio, one becomes tired and jaded through lack of the fresh outdoor life, and it becomes advisable to go back to nature once more so as to regain the lost vitality.

SKETCH AND FINISHED PICTURE IN OILS   Plate XLV represents the sketch of a subject entitled *The Watchet Coast, Somerset*. Plate XLVI is the finished picture. The sky in the finished picture has lost that cold, grayish blue, which is seen in the sketch above. Dealing with the finished picture, notice that the rocks in the immediate foreground, resting on the shore, show more form and better drawing. The contour of the cliffs, commencing from the top left side and continuing downwards towards the central portion of the picture, displays fairly accurate drawing, while the slighter tinges of red on the edges send them back into proper tone relation. The strong light resting on the face of the cliff, coming more or less vertically downwards, has a suggestion of gray color which is missing in the sketch, thus helping to make the light appear to be in the surface of the cliff, instead of being in front of the cliff.

In an oil sketch of this sort, it is splendid practice and a tonic for the mind to paint vigorously with strong brushmarks. Mistakes are welcome—they suggest something. What does it matter if the paint is put on too thick or too thin, or if the rock is lacking in structural drawing in your sketch? It is, of course, preferable to achieve everything that is desirable right away, but that is almost impossible and the next best thing is to get as much workmanlike decision as time will allow, and a strong sense of tone, so that there is some chance of getting useful material that can be of help in the studio.

SKETCH AND FINISHED PICTURE IN PASTEL   Plate XLVII is another sketch, with the finished picture in Plate XLVIII, entitled *The Brendon Hills, from Williton, Somerset*. The sketch shows strength without delicacy. Tones are incorrect, but subject clearly stated.

The finished picture below—done in pastel also—is carried almost too far as regards finish. Here it is noticeable that the clouds are no longer trying to assert themselves at the expense of the foreground. Their lighter tints keep them in their proper tone relations to the distance, middle distance, and foreground. The drawing of the distant hills shows more scholarly knowledge. The hills that are farthest away in the distance (on the right) have light touches of bluish green and purple, and are so delicate in tone that they help to create a feeling of being a very long distance from the spectator. The drawing of the trees in the central portion of the picture shows a more interesting pattern of light and shadow. The rocky formation at the foot of the picture is constructed more logically. The heavy weight of the shadows thrown by the trees on the adjoining field is illuminated with reflected light, and the drawing is more carefully rendered.

Plate XLIX is another sketch, with the finished picture (Plate L), entitled *Old Net Houses, Hastings*. The sketch was done with real excitement, with no attempt at showing the strata on the rocks behind the old net houses. The blue is too strong and the purple is too strong, but what a feeling of consolation the artist had in knowing that here was something on which he could build the real thing!

In the finished picture (Plate L), it is noticeable that the strong reddish purple is painted out on the cliff behind, with the structural formation more clearly expressed by means of warm grays and bluish shadows with obvious brush handling. The drawing of the old net houses is more carefully handled, and the tonality of the foreground is more accurate with far less purple.

These pages, showing sketches and finished pictures, should convey to the student that the only thing that really matters is decisive statement in color and tone, whether it be oil, watercolor, or pastel.

The dark tones of the tall nethouses help, through contrast in the depth of color, to keep the cliffs well in the background. The figures in the foreground are mere color expressions, without positive drawing. For evening or night effects, suggestion of form is more important than definite statement.

CHANGING SEASON by Forrest Orr, watercolor.

The essence of this landscape is in the artist's control of values. The plant and cluster of trees in the foreground are rendered in strong darks which bring them close to the viewer. The buildings are painted in more subtle tones, which drop back into the distance. And beyond the buildings are a few patches of delicate tone that suggest remote forest and sky. The only really crisp detail is in the immediate foreground, where the branches and buds are painted with extreme clarity. The rest of the painting is surprisingly rough and lacking in detail. (Photograph courtesy American Artist)

VAL DE GRACE by Ogden M. Pleissner, oil 24″ x 36″.

In this cityscape, the horizon line is very low in the picture and the viewer feels that he is standing at street level with the figures in the foreground. Because of the low horizon line, the buildings loom high up in the sky and the street is seen in extreme perspective, with the buildings receding very rapidly into the distance toward a vanishing point which is somewhere at the very end of the street. This use of perspective lends great mass and strength to the forms of the buildings. It is also interesting to note that the strongest light in the picture is not on the buildings themselves, but beyond them in the sky, thus throwing their forms into silhouette. (Photograph courtesy American Artist)

18

Various Materials

In the last chapter of this book, it may appropriate to suggest a few practical things relating to materials.

PASTEL MATERIALS   In pastel sketching, it is not necessary to carry an easel or anything of a heavy nature. Take an ordinary sketching stool, a sturdy piece of hard board about 19" x 25", and half a dozen pieces of colored paper, about 18" x 24" so as to leave half an inch margin when clipped to the board.

The paper should be fairly smooth in texture and not too bright in color. Avoid rough paper, sandpaper, and felt surfaced paper. Gray, brown, and warm green are better than purple or bright yellow. The latter two are liable to fade quickly, whereas the former three papers have more permanent qualities. A box of handmade pastels, with some 70 to 100 varying tints— including a lavish number of sticks of yellow ochre, gray, deep brown, burnt sienna, black and blue, with a few sticks of red, deep violet, green, white, etc.—should also be included, as without some of the above there can be no foundation tints, which are so essential for laying in the initial stage of a sketch. Pastel boxes, as sold in art supply shops, have plenty of pleasing colors—sometimes too many for practical use.

Ordinary spring clips (to hold the paper to the board) should complete the outfit.

When the pastel sketch is finished, take the clips off, and (with care) place the sketch underneath the other pieces of paper, immediately clipping the papers once more along the edges of the board. When the pastel sketch is packed underneath the other papers, see that it has no chance of slipping. When traveling, the artist should see that all pastel sketches are bound securely together, either with tightly drawn string or with clips.

WATERCOLOR MATERIALS   In watercolor sketching, a small easel is sometimes used. Anything that is simple should lead to better work. Personally, I never use an easel for watercolor sketching, since I keep the paper almost horizontal, but I find it useful to have a miniature stool (in addition to the ordinary sketching stool) on which to place a large jar of water, together with the watercolor sketchbox. I hold the sketch (which rests on the knees) in the left hand, paint with the right hand, and any water that runs off the sketch falls on to an old cloth which is placed below the painting. I can think of nothing simpler than this method.

It is interesting, in watercolor sketching, to experiment with various papers. Well known papers include D'Arches, Whatman (now no longer made, but still sold here and there), Fabriano, Arnold, Crisbrook, R.W.S., and the popular Japanese papers. There are, of course, various lightly tinted papers with a fairly smooth surface, useful for both transparent washes or for body color.

OIL PAINTING EQUIPMENT For oil painting, it is necessary to have something sturdy and strong in the way of an easel, and to stand up to the work. An occasional step backwards will enable the artist to compare the tones. There are on the market simple easels for outdoor oil sketching, and any good artists' supply store invariably has several selections. An oil sketch box, fitted with brass telescopic legs, may appeal to some students. Its chief virtue is that the box can always be kept in a horizontal position, even on the sloping side of a hill, by adjusting the length of the telescopic legs. Also it is steady when opposed to powerful winds out of doors. The student will soon find out which appeals to him as regards an oil sketching outfit.

SUGGESTIONS ABOUT COLOR In oil sketching, it is nearly always best to paint low in tone with thin color, using plenty of oil medium, such as linseed oil and turpentine, with a little copal varnish, and finally place the solid lighter colors over the darker tints. It is very difficult to paint dark oil colors on top of light tints. Precisely the same remarks apply to pastel painting, and also to body color when used with watercolor.

In pure transparent watercolor painting, the opposite method is adopted to that employed in oil and pastel painting. The first stage should be lightly tinted, and in the final stage the deepest colors should be used.

The colors used for the paintings as seen in the various reproductions throughout this book were selected from the following list.

COLORS FOR OIL PAINTING

Zinc white
Lemon yellow (zinc yellow, cadmium yellow light)
Chrome yellow and orange
Yellow ochre
Vermilion
Light red
Permanent crimson (alizarin crimson)
Cobalt green
Viridian

COLORS FOR WATERCOLOR PAINTING

Tempera white (body color)
Chinese white (body color)
Lemon yellow (gamboge, cadmium yellow light)
Chrome yellow and orange
Yellow ochre
Vermilion
Light red
Permanent crimson (alizarin crimson)
Viridian
Deep Hooker's green

Terre verte
Permanent blue (phthalocyanine
    blue)
Cobalt blue
Cerulean blue
Raw sienna
Burnt sienna
Burnt umber
Ivory black

Permanent blue (phthalocyanine
    blue)
Deep ultramarine blue
Cerulean blue
Burnt sienna
Ivory black

SELECTING
PASTEL COLORS Pastels (and only soft handmade sticks are of any value) can be purchased in boxes ready for use, containing many colors of varying tints, nearly all of which are permanent. Carmine should be avoided, as it fades quite early.

The best way, when buying pastels, is to make a careful selection of some seventy tints, several of which, such as white, yellow ochre, gray, burnt sienna, and black, can be duplicated, since these colors are in constant use during the making of a sketch. Emerald green and the various shades of Hooker's green are invaluable, since they respond easily when in use. Certain other bright greens are known to be hard and gritty in quality. Good russet and olive greens are on the market, and there is an astonishing number of shades of red, orange, purple, brilliant yellow, etc.; but caution should be exercised when selecting the brighter tints, as they tend to cheapen the effect when used in a sketch.

It is excellent practice in this medium to try to get several tints with one color. Use light yellow ochre on dark gray paper. Break off a small piece of light yellow ochre, about an inch long, and use it by pressing lightly on the dark paper. The result will be fairly dark. Press again, only with more firmness, and the result will be a lighter tint. If heavier pressure be exercised, the result will be quite light, and about the same color as the original stick of pastel.

Architecture, 11; *see also* Buildings
Automobiles, 11-12

Boats and shipping, 72-75; barges, 73-74; beached, 73; colors of 75; of sails on, 74, 75; fishing, 74; foreshortening in, 73; gondolas, 75; in ink and watercolor combined, 75; moving, 73; ocean liners, 74; sail, 73; studying, 73; illus., 72, 114-115
Bridges, illus., 111-112; *see also* Rivers; Water
Brightwell, Walter, illus. by, 2
Brushes, 73
Brushstrokes, 5, 38
Buildings, 68-71; and danger of observation, 69-70; and study of architecture, 69; colors for, 70; compared with still lifes, 69; in cities, 69; in oil, 70; in watercolor, 71; white, 71; illus., 68, 87, 113, 128
Bye, Ranulph, illus. by., 40

Canals, illus., 104-105, 111-112; *see also* Water
Carlson, John F., illus. by, 58
Cities, 69
Clouds, 51-53; colors for, 51-52; fleeting effects in, 52; gradated colors in, 52; in undulating landscapes, 78; over-modeling of, 53; types of, 53; illus., 89, 91
Color, 42; and design, 78; and subjects, 13; blends of oil, 70; cold and chalky, 70-71; contrast in, 71; for pastel landscapes, 78; gradated, 52; mixing, 131; of boats, 75; of buildings, 70; of clouds and sky, 51-52; of hills and mountains, 51, 56-57; of mass foliage, 60; of rivers, 65; of sails, 74, 75; of sky, 64, 65, 75; of trees, 52, 60, 65; of walls, 64; of water, 64; of white buildings, 71; suggested for oil, pastel, and watercolor, 140-141; warm and cold in nature, 71
Color plates, 81-128
Composition, 18-29; asymmetry, contrast, monotony in, 21; curved and straight lines in, 19-20; diagonal, horizontal, vertical, 26; elementary, 19-21; geometric skeletons for, 23-24; horizontal line in, 19-20; inventive, 23-

29; "inward," 21; of trees, 29; small experimental, 16; spacing in, 19-20; use of curves in, 25-29; illus., 20-22, 24-29
Curves, 19

Design, 78; *see also* Composition; Planning
Draper, William F., illus. by, 72

Easels, 139
Edges, soft, 71
Estuaries, illus. 123-125; *see also* Rivers; Water
Evening, illus., 118

Figures, 70, 71
Foliage, illus., 99; *see also* Trees
Folinsbee, John, illus. by, 43
Foreshortening, 73

Gaetner, Carl, illus. by, 62
Garrett, Stuart, illus. by, 18
Gramatky, Hardie, illus. by, 13

Hard board, 139
Hills and mountains, 54-57; avoiding false charm in, 55; colors for, 51; emphasizing ruggedness of, 55-56; illus., 54, 92-98, 127
Heitland, W. Emerton, illus. by, 36
Horizon line, 19-20; illus., 20

Industry, 12
Ink, combined with watercolor, 75

Jamison, Philip, illus. by, 17

Kautzky, Ted, illus. by, 39
Kosa, Emil J. Jr., illus. by, 54

Lakes, illus., 96-98; *see also* Water
Landscapes, illus., 85, 86, 88, 116-118
Landscapes, undulating, 76-80; clouds in, 78; defined, 77; design and color in, 78; hills in, 77; pastel colors for, 78; planes in, 77-78; illus., 76, 80, 81
Leaves, 61

Leith-Ross, Harry, illus. by, 132
Light and shadow, 33, 69-70; on water, 63-64; reflected, 76

Mannerisms, 36
Martino, Antonio P., illus. by, 14
Mason, Roy, illus. by, 30
Materials, 139-141; for oil, 146; for pastel, 139; for watercolor, 139-140
McLavy, Jeanne H., illus. by, 68
Meader, Joshua, illus. by, 134
Modern art, 57
Mood, 129-133; expressing, 129-130; majestic, 131; melancholy, 131-132; moonlit, 130; stormy, 130; tranquil, 130, violent, 130-131
Moonlight, illus., 118
Mountains, see Hills and mountains

Nicholas, Tom, illus. by, 35

Observation, dangers of, 69-70
Oils, blending of, 70; for buildings, 70; for hills and mountains, 56-57; for sketching, 38; materials and equipment for, 140; suggestions about sketching in, 140; see also Color
Orr, Forrest, illus. by, 137

Paintboxes, 139, 140
Paper, 139; tinted, 73, 75, 78
Pastel, 33; and watercolor compared, 43; as indoor sketching medium, 16; for landscapes, 78; for sketching, 38; for water, 64-65; materials for, 139; paper for, 78
Pencil studies, 45-49; of landscapes, 45; of trees, 45; techniques for, 49; illus., 46-48
Pencils, and tone, 32; as sketching medium, 16-17; types of, 45
Perspective, 21
Planning, around main subject, 15-16; around titles, 16; importance of, 15; of subordinate elements, 16
Pleissner, Ogden M., illus. by, 49, 76, 138

Quarry, Mercer, illus. by, 80

Reflections, 63-64, 65; analyzed, 66; illus., 67; see also Water
Rivers, colors for, 65; illus., 106-110; see also Water

Sample, Paul, illus. by, 133
Scale, 71
Seacoast, illus., 126; see also Water

Shadows, warm, 71; see also Light and shadows
Ships, 11-12; see also Boats and shipping
Silvermann, Burton, illus. by, 50
Simplification, 5
Sketching, 37-39; 41-44; and final picture, 135-137; and technique, 41; colors for, 42; color sketches and pencil drawings as, 37-38; difficulties of, 38; equipment for, 37; for studio work, 135-137; from nature and indoors, 16-17; in pastel, 16-17, 42; in pencil, 16-17, 41; in watercolor, 16-17, 41, 42; media for, 38; miniatures, 16; oils based on, 41-42
Sky, 19; colors for, 51-52, 64, 65, 75; gradated, 62; illus., 91
Speight, Francis, illus. by, 79
Stools, 139, 140
Storms, illus., 118
Studio, working in, 135-137
Subordinate elements, 16; see also Composition; Design; Planning
Sunlight, 71; see also Light and shadows; Reflections

Teague, Donald, illus. by, 10, 22
Tones, 31, 32; complex, 33; flat, 42; in color sketches and pencil drawings, 37-38; of cities, 69; pencil, 32; precision of, 33-34; simple, 33; watercolor, 32
Trains, 11-12
Trees, 21, 29, 58-61; colors for, 52, 65; details in, 59-61; elm, 60; fir, 61; importance of silhouette in, 59; mass foliage in, 60; poplar, 65; willow, 60; illus., 21, 29, 58, 100-103
Turner, J. M. W., 31

Unity, 33; see also Composition; Planning

Values, 31-35; and detail, 32; defined, 31; of foreground, middle distance, and sky, 31-32

Walls, colors of, 64; white, 70-71
Water, 62-67; colors of, 63; in lakes, 63; in pastel, 64-65; light and shadows on, 63-64; reflections in, 63, 66; shallow, 64-65; illus., 62, 67, 82-86
Watercolor, as sketching medium, 16-17, 38, 42; combined with ink, 75; for buildings, 71; for clouds, 51-52; for hills and mountains, 56-57; for trees, 60; materials for, 139-140; pastel sketch for, 42; tints of, 32; washes, 34, 61, 71; illus., 90, 104-111
Waterfalls, 63; illus., 119-122
Windows, light from, 70